They moved out of the lights and there were no clouds and the stars were incredible in their brightness with the mountains rising up toward them.

They walked side by side, just barely not touching, and suddenly it seemed to her that whether or not their gloved fingers casually met or her coat touched his was terribly important.

In the hotel there was music and light again and voices. "What a mob," Abe said. One hand on her elbow, he led her through the people toward the elevator. Emily felt as though she were moving through a dream.

He turned to her and took her in his arms and kissed her.

She forced herself to move away from him, saying, "No, Abe, this isn't a good idea."

"Why not?" he asked. "Why didn't we have it a long time ago?"

"We did," she said softly.

A WINTER'S LOVE

MADELEINE L'ENGLE

BALLANTINE BOOKS • NEW YORK

Library of Congress Catalog Card Number: 57-6832

ISBN 0-345-30644-9

Manufactured in the United States of America

First Ballantine Books/Epiphany Edition: February 1984

For

LIZ AND ARTHUR

A WINTER'S LOVE

✧ *One* ✧

Abe Fielding
Abraham Fielding
Abraham K. Fielding
What is the K for?
Why?

There he was; she could see him from where she stood at the window of the sleeping house, see him walking quickly up the icy alley that climbed from the straggling outskirts of the village past the villa, past the big winter sports hotel, past the sanatorium, up to the scattering of chalets beyond. Where was he going?

Why?

He turned once and looked back towards the small villa where she stood at the window, an eiderdown clutched about her nightgown and bathrobe. She moved quickly aside as though he could see her through the dark cold pane of glass, then looked out again as he turned from the villa and continued up the path. Once she could see him slip and almost fall as his hobnailed boots failed to catch on the icy surface. Beside him on the snow moved his shadow, long and wavering, cast by the waning moon. Then he disappeared around the corner but still she stood there at the window. The moon was small and its light seemed old and feeble, paler than the luminous snow on the peaks of the mountains, more muted than the points of stars piercing through the cold sky. She could not see a cloud, only black sky and moon and stars and snow and shadows.

"Emily."

She turned sharply from the window.

"What are you doing?"

Somewhere outdoors an invisible dog bayed, the angry, lonely sound echoing against the mountains, breaking into pieces and repeating, repeating, repeating. . . .

"I couldn't sleep," she said. "Sorry, Court, I didn't mean to wake you."

His voice was muffled by sleep and blankets. "Get back into bed. You'll get pneumonia."

"I'm sorry, darling," she said. She unwrapped the eiderdown from her body and very carefully covered the small washbasin in the corner.

"I hope the pipes won't be frozen in the morning," Courtney said.

She climbed into bed beside him, still in her bathrobe, because she was shivering now, and her feet in spite of the woolly slippers she had worn felt like lumps of ice. She rubbed one cold foot against the calf of her leg. "I wasn't up long enough. Nothing'll be frozen in the morning except the ink. And that thaws."

"What time is it?" Courtney asked, his head still burrowed under the covers.

She raised up to look at the traveling clock with the luminous dial on the bureau. "Two o'clock."

Courtney made a muffled, sleepy noise, half grunt, half groan.

She rolled over so that she lay closer to him and put her arm about him. "I'm terribly sorry I disturbed you. Go back to sleep."

"Um." Then, a moment later, "Why were you up? Anything wrong?"

"No," she denied quickly. "Just wakeful."

They were silent again and after a moment she could hear the deep, regular breathing that meant he was sleeping. Then she raised herself and leaned, shivering, on her elbow, staring down at him, trying to see his face, but it was only a darker shadow on the shadow of the pillow. But she continued to stare down as though she could see, staring and wondering, wondering what it was she felt about the man who lay there, what beyond the habit of love. It was a deeply ingrained habit and there was nothing to have changed it, but she stared with a sort of horror as though daylight would reveal a stranger. It was not the first time that this had happened, but almost always at night, almost always when he was asleep and she, in the early morning hours, was awake; and she would look down at the vulnerable sleeping face, wondering if what she felt was love or hate, or worst of all, indifference.

She lay down again, shivering, and put her arm tentatively about him, waiting to see what she would feel, and the hard warmth of him was reassuring.—You're part of my life, she told him silently. Everything about us is too intricately entwined for me to be completely a separate person any longer.

Courtney shifted slightly under the weight of her arm, and she moved, reaching out with her toes for the copper hot-water bottle filled with boiling water each night. When she found it the protective towelling had come off, but the bottle was only faintly warm.

—I will make everything be all right, she said silently. *I will make it.*

In the cold night air the house creaked. The wind slapped against the windows, subsided. Across the hall her four-year-old daughter, her baby, cried out in her sleep. Emily raised her head, listening, suddenly tense, but the sound was not repeated and she lay down again.

—Oh, Connie. Oh, Connie, be all right.

She lay there listening. In the other bedroom no sound from Virginia, home from school for the Christmas holidays and worn out from a long day's skiing, or from Mimi Oppenheimer, spending the holidays with her. Sometimes Mimi snored but tonight there was just the creaking of the house in the frozen air and the wild cold baying of the dogs as they roamed the sleeping streets. And the clocks ticking, Virginia's battered alarm clock louder than the travelling clock just across the room. As she lay there listening, Emily thought she could hear strains of music drifting down from the big hotel. Perhaps they were still dancing there, and had Abe gone for a moment into the ballroom or stopped in the steamy warmth of the lounge to talk, or had he gone straight to his room? And where had he been in the village? At the casino, perhaps, losing a few francs at rouge et noir, or perhaps he had simply gone into the Splendide for a drink. . . .

Now Mimi began to snore, gently, contentedly, funny clumsy Mimi Opp who was both so good and so bad for Virginia. . . . And then voices, voices on the icy path, a happy, slightly drunken group returning to the hotel from the village. They were singing. *Chevaliers de la table ronde, goûtons voir*

si le vin est bon. American accents, though. She remembered
learning that song in college, brought back to the dormitory by
two girls who'd spent their junior year in France. A gay, foolish
song, wonderful after a couple of drinks or a few rounds of
beer. She felt faintly envious of the group singing it now, accents faulty, words not quite right, but completely uninhibited
and happy.

"Please be quiet," Courtney murmured in his sleep, not
even half-awakened by the song but nevertheless reacting to it.

The song began to fade as the revellers climbed upwards, and
in a moment was lost in the faint strains of music from the
hotel. Emily lay there under the covers and gradually warmth
began to return to her feet and her fingers. And as warmth came
back to her body her mind slipped imperceptibly from its cold
wakefulness into the comfort of sleep.

When she wakened she was cold again; the covers were half
off and the cold air lay heavier than blankets against her flesh. It
was dark in the room, not even moonlight now coming in the
window, only a pale glimmer from stars and snow. She had to
look at the clock to see that it was morning, almost six. She
slipped out of bed and, shivering violently, dressed, quickly
pulling on black ski trousers and a heavy red sweater. Over her
wool ski socks she put on an incongruous pair of battered ballet
slippers.

She ran downstairs, turned on the light in the hall, and went
down to the cellar to shake up the furnace and put on more coal.
Up in the hall again she turned off the light and padded softly
towards the front door, stepping over scarves that had slithered
from hooks, brushing against the sheepskin lining of Mimi's
jacket, tripping over Virginia's ski boots.

—Damn, she thought, I'll wake the whole house.

She stood still to listen, but there was no sound from upstairs,
and she bent down to pick up Connie's soiled pink teddy bear,
left overnight in the hall, reached for Mimi's ski jacket, the first
one her hand touched, and pulled it about her. She opened the
front door, still clutching the teddy bear, and stepped out; in the
sky the stars were still piercingly bright. She looked across the
small white patch that might in spring be a garden, through the
iron fence and up a white slope to Pedroti's Grand Hôtel Des
Alpes crouched at the foot of the mountain, the hotel grounds
separated from the villa's small garden only by the iron fence.
At the hotel at least there was some indication that morning was

approaching; in the servants' quarters high up under the eaves lights were burning, and again in the kitchen and in the proprietress' apartments on the first floor. Several of the guests' windows were lighted, too, vacationers rising early for skiing expeditions or perhaps a little climbing. Was Abe going skiing?

Up above the hotel there were lights on in the tuberculosis sanatorium, too; behind the sanatorium the mountains heaved up into the sky; there was still no faint line of light to outline the irregular peaks. The cold pressed against her chest in spite of the warmth of Mimi's jacket, the kind of cold one might feel on the outer planets, far from the sustaining warmth of the parent sun; she retreated into the house and went into the kitchen to make coffee.

On the back of the old coal stove was a kettle she had filled the night before, and the water in it was piping hot. She put the pink teddy bear on a chair (how had Connie gone to bed without it?), shook up the coals and held her hands over their living warmth. While she was measuring the coffee she heard footsteps, and there was Mimi standing in the doorway, wearing a heavy scarlet robe and enormous fuzzy red slippers. Her face was still rosy with sleep and there was a crease across one cheek where the pillow had pressed into it.

"Hello, Mrs. Bowen," Mimi said, "shall I go down and jiggle the furnace or anything?"

"No, thanks, Mimi, I've done it," Emily answered, thinking that if Mimi tried to tend to the furnace she would probably set fire to the house, if she didn't blow it up entirely. In spite of the grace with which the child moved her body she was singularly helpless when it came to any kind of household task.

"Well, may I have some coffee with you then?"

"Of course. Do you want to get the cups?"

Mimi opened the cupboard over the sink and took two saucers down from the top shelf. At sixteen she was almost six feet tall and she barely had to stretch. "These are the prettiest cups and saucers—" she said, "these up here. Is it all right if we use them?"

"Why not?" Emily asked. "As long as Connie doesn't get hold of them. She still breaks things very easily, and these are some Gertrude de Croisenois let me take from her chalet." She filled a saucepan with milk and put it on the back of the stove.

"And Virginia, too," Mimi said. "I don't think Virginia should consider making a profession of dishwashing. Though I suppose I shouldn't talk."

The smell of coffee began to pervade the kitchen, warm and comforting. "Do you know, Mrs. Bowen," Mimi said, looking earnestly at the cup she was holding, "I admire Gertrude—Madame de Croisenois—quite passionately."

Emily turned away so as not to smile at Mimi's childish intensity, very unlike the Mimi who seemed so sophisticated to Virginia. Emily liked this early-morning Mimi; there was about her a wistful quality that had not been apparent before.

"You're very good friends, you and Madame de Croisenois, aren't you?"

"Yes, Mimi. I guess we are."

"Mrs. Bowen," Mimi said, still studying the empty cup, "it means a great deal for me to be here with you this Christmas."

"We're happy to have you with us, Mimi," Emily said automatically, sorry that her own shyness kept her from saying any but the conventional words.

"I've never been in a real family before. I mean, I adore my mother and father absolutely passionately, but you can hardly call it a normal family life. I mean Jake's always off on tour and when Clare comes back from the lab sometimes she positively *stinks* of chemicals."

Emily gently took away the cup Mimi was turning between her large, strong, and well-cared for fingers, half-filled it with coffee, then poured in hot milk.

"There's sugar on the table by you, Mimi," she said.

—Is Abe up yet? she wondered—drinking coffee in his hotel room? Or is he in the enormous hotel dining room with his son, Sam?

Mimi helped herself liberally to sugar, then pushed her fingers through her mop of rather violently blond hair that was now in an early morning mass of untidy curls about her face. "It's really a very pleasant smell to me," she said, "the stink of chemicals. Virginia and I were listing once the things that reminded us of our parents, and when she was doing you the most important thing was your smell, Yardley's lavender soap and Coty's Chypre. Isn't that a lovely thing to be remembered by, Mrs. Bowen?"

"Horrors, Mimi, you make me sound as though I were dead and gone," Emily said lightly.

"As for *my* mother's smell," Mimi said, drinking down her coffee, "she uses perfume, of course, Gênet Fleuri, as a matter of fact, which is really quite divine, but when I think of her smell it's much more apt to be the rotten-egg smell of hydrogen sulphide and a sort of pervasive odor of Bunsen burner. Oh, and garlic. Clare and Jake both eat an inordinate amount of garlic.''

Emily laughed. ''How about your father?'' she asked. ''What's his distinctive odor?''

''Shaving soap and scotch whiskey. And the resin he uses on the bow of his violin. May I have some more coffee, please?''

''One more cup,'' Emily said, ''but that's all, because even though this is a big pot it has to do the rest of the family for breakfast and even Connie likes a little coffee in her warm milk.'' She put rolls in the oven to warm and brought out the oatmeal she had started the night before and left in the double boiler on the back of the stove.

After a moment Mimi asked, ''Can I help? I'm sorry. I should have asked before.''

''You can set the table if you like.''

''I'd rather sit here and talk to you,'' Mimi said, ''but I feel I should make myself useful.'' Emily smiled but said nothing as Mimi stood up and went into the dining room. She had been gone only a moment, when, holding a fistful of knives and spoons, she reappeared and stood in front of Emily. ''You know, Mrs. Bowen, it's a funny thing: this is only a rented house and, let's face it, quite an ugly one, but somehow you've made it like a home. I've only been here three days but somehow I feel completely at home. And Virginia! What a change there has been in Virginia!''

''What do you mean?'' Emily asked quickly.

At once Mimi's candid eyes became guarded. ''Oh, Virginia can be a bit tense sometimes.'' And she went back to the dining room.

Virginia at this point came bounding in and flung her arms around Emily—Virginia over a year younger than Mimi, and paper-thin. ''Good morning! Good morning, darling mother! Oh, it's so wonderful to be home! The stars are out so it'll be a nice day. May we go skating?''

''I don't see why not,'' Emily said, laughing and kissing her. ''Good morning, darling. Go on in the dining room and help Mimi set the table.''

''Mimi's been having coffee with you!'' Virginia cried. ''Miriam Oppenheimer, and you didn't even get dressed! No fair!''

''I'll go get dressed now,'' Mimi said from the doorway. ''Table's all set.''

Emily straightened the neck of Virginia's sweater. "Connie awake yet?"

"Yes. She's in bed with daddy."

"All right, I'll go rout them both out. Give the oatmeal a stir for me please."

Virginia gave her mother another hug. "Were you out watching the stars this morning?"

"For a few minutes."

"Oh, mother, what a one you are for looking at stars! Remember how you always used to fuss in New York because the city lights almost blanked them out? Mother, what's daddy writing?"

"At the moment? He's writing a paper."

"What on?"

"Anaximander."

"Who was he? Another early Greek philosopher?"

"Yes. An astronomer and geometrician. The first evolutionist, your father says."

"Then what?"

"He taught that there was one universal substance, I believe, and opposing stresses of unity and opposites."

"No, I mean about daddy. Is he going to stop teaching and be a writer? After this winter what are we going to do?"

"I don't know, darling. Let's just worry about this winter and not go any further."

"But I can't help wondering."

"Well, as long as daddy's happy here with his writing, we'll probably stay. After that I don't know. Maybe the college in Indiana. Now stir that porridge for me, you little fiend. I've got to go get daddy and Connie up." She put the back of her hand for a moment against Virginia's thin, freckled cheek. "You'd better have two helpings of porridge," she said. "You're much too thin." She turned and went upstairs.

In the bedroom Courtney lay on his back with Connie curled sleepily beside him in the half-circle of his arm. Emily saw that he was staring at the light fixture on the ceiling.

"The spider motif in this house is ubiquitous," he said as she came in. "This chandelier is definitely spider. So are the ones downstairs. The dado in the living room is composed of spiders with a scorpion or two for added interest. Now look at this wallpaper. Mixed skunk cabbages with a scampering of insects. I'm sure old lady Pedroti chose everything herself. Doesn't she remind you of a great enormous fat spider with little hairy legs?"

Emily laughed at this description of their landlady, and bent over the bed to kiss him.

Courtney received her kiss, then sat up in bed, dislodging Connie. "I think I shall write a short article proving Philopoemen was not a coward."

Emily picked Connie up, her cuddly little blond beauty, and the child twined herself about her mother like a little octopus. "Come on, sleepy head. Virginia and Mimi are downstairs. I'll give you your clothes and you can go down and dress in the kitchen where it's warmer." She stood Connie on the foot of the bed and took clean warm underclothes out of a drawer, a blue turtle-neck sweater like Virginia's, and ski trousers. "What brought Philopoemen up?" she asked Courtney.

"You forgot my socks," Connie said, yawning, her mouth opening pink and wide like a kitten's.

"Oh, so I did. Here, baby." Emily ran her fingers through Connie's fair curls, thinking idly that she looked more like Mimi's sister than Virginia's. "Now run on downstairs."

"You fixed the furnace, didn't you?" Courtney demanded of his wife as Connie scampered out.

"I was downstairs. And it's really no job."

"We should have someone come in to do it."

"But why, Court? It's money we don't need to spend and one of us is always up early."

"I don't like your doing it," Courtney said.

"That's nonsense. I'm strong as a horse and still young. Or can you call thirty-eight still young?"

Courtney looked at her, his eyes moving over her fair hair, her face, the red sweater, the dark ski trousers. Emily stood still under his gaze, looking back at him with her steady gray eyes under well-defined dark brows, much darker than the short fair hair. "You're extremely well preserved," he said.

"Oh, don't, Court!" she cried. "You make me sound pickled in formaldehyde. Everybody seems determined to make me feel ancient this morning. Mimi was telling me about the nice things Virginia's thought up to remember me by."

Courtney laughed. "That shouldn't be too difficult. And I think you'd make a very nice pickle. It was fun having Abe for dinner last night, wasn't it?"

"Yes," Emily said. She turned away from him and began straightening the top of her dressing table, putting the lid back on her powder box, lining up her small bottles of perfume, dropping her brush into a drawer.

Courtney sniffed. "I smell coffee," he said. "I dreamed about him last night."

"About Abe?"

"About Philopoemen," Courtney said in surprise. "You asked me what brought him up."

As Emily was in the midst of the breakfast dishes, the dishpan in the sink full of hot suds, the kettle on the stove heating for rinse water, Courtney stuck his head in the kitchen:

"I've lost all the notes I made yesterday on Anaximander."

"Oh, darling, how awful, I'm sorry," she said automatically, taking her hands out of the soapy water and wringing off the suds, trying to switch her attention to Courtney's problem and not quite succeeding.

"The point is," Courtney said, "where did they get to? They're rather important." His voice was low and calm, but she could tell from the pinched look about his mouth and nose, as though he were very cold, that he was upset.

"I don't know." She turned away from the sink and the half-washed dishes towards him. "Did you take them out of your office?"

"No."

She wiped her hands on her apron. "Then they must be there."

"The point is they aren't. Could Connie have been at them?"

"She knows she's not allowed in your office."

"I can't find them," Courtney said, his voice quiet, even. "It was a whole day's work. More than that, really."

"I'll come look," she said, and followed him down the dark passage to his office. In the small room books were piled on the floor and papers were scattered over the desk and falling out of the scrap basket.

"How can you expect to find anything in this mess?" she asked. Her voice had an edge of sharpness to it.

"The reason it's in a mess is that I've been looking for the things," he said. "Did you empty my wastepaper basket this morning?"

"Yes."

"Did you burn it all up?"

"Yes. I always do." She looked around the room helplessly. "Just an ordinary piece of paper like all the other pieces of paper in here?"

"Two or three ordinary pieces of paper."

"Did you shut them up in the book you were using?"

"I've looked in all the books. Held them up by the spines and shaken them. I wish you hadn't burned the trash."

"I'm sorry, darling. I just always do it early. You mean you think you may have thrown them away by mistake?"

"I can't think of anything else. Well, you certainly can't be expected to tell notes I mean to keep from those I'm through with. I'll just have to do the whole thing over again. But in the future I'd appreciate it if you wouldn't burn my papers." His voice was still flat, controlled.

"I didn't burn anything that wasn't in the wastepaper basket."

"You didn't pick anything up off the floor?"

"No. Anything on the floor I always put on your desk."

He shrugged. "Well, it can't be helped." He turned away from her and sat down at his desk. She stood there by him, but he didn't speak or turn towards her or in any way acknowledge her presence.

After a moment she said wonderingly, "You're angry with me, aren't you?"

"No. Why?"

"Because you think I burned your papers."

"If you did it, you didn't do it on purpose. I should empty my own basket instead of leaving it to you."

"Why don't you swear?" she asked. "It'd make you feel better."

He shook his head. "No."

"You used to swear on occasion in New York."

"I don't feel like swearing here." Again he turned from her, withdrew.

Like a child pressing a bruise, wondering if it will still hurt, she persisted. "If you're mad at me why don't you *be* mad at me, Court? I don't mind, I'd much rather have you angry with me than—than—" He did not respond and for a moment her voice soared. "For heaven's sake lose your temper with me! Because I'm in this house with you! I'm in this room! I've been here all winter!"

"In this room?" he asked mildly.

She moved to the door, teetering on the seesaw she had been riding with Courtney, hate and love, never knowing which was which, as she had ridden the seesaws of her childhood and had never known when her companions (always, it seemed, heavier, bigger, crouching close to earth, sneakered feet on the brown patch of ground where they had worn off the grass, leaving spindly Emily dangling high up, her skinny legs waving frantically, her stomach pounding with fear at being so high off the ground) would suddenly slide off the end of the seesaw, letting Emily crash to earth, her legs, her spine, her head jarred almost unendurably by the unexpected impact, so that she would stagger off, acutely sick at her stomach, to recuperate alone in the orchard.

"I'm sorry about your notes," she said at last. "I'm terribly sorry you have to do them all over again."

He nodded, not looking up, and she slipped out, shutting the door quietly behind her, feeling the familiar sickness as though the seesaw had been dropped. And she felt again, as she had felt so often that winter, agonizingly in the wrong, and lost, as though her identity had been jarred out of her by the crash, and until she found it again she would say and do all the wrong things.

After the dishes were done she went to the piano in the living room. It was not a good piano, an upright that had once been a player piano; and like all the furniture in the small room it was outsize, so that when she was in the room for any length of time Emily had a sensation of everything closing in on her, the mountains outside, the walls of the villa, and in the living room the four enormous over-stuffed chairs covered in puce plush, and the dark scratched wood of the piano. Several of the ivories on the piano keys were missing, and the others were yellow and stained, but it kept passably in tune except for the bass G which she pulled up every morning with a tuning hammer. She did this now, then sat down on the rickety piano bench. She played a few chords, then went into scales. After a moment Virginia looked in from the dining room where she and Mimi were keeping a promise to play a game of Go Fish with Connie.

"Oh, not *exercises,* mother!" she cried. "We can't hear ourselves think!"

"I like them," Mimi called. "I even like it when Jake plays exercises on the violin."

"Yes, but mother's not a famous musician," Virginia said.

"Jake's not terrifically famous. He's—I believe you'd call it distinguished, wouldn't you, Mrs. Bowen?"

"Very distinguished, Mimi," Emily said.

Connie's voice, still high in register, and not long out of baby talk, came rather petulantly. "It's my *turn*, Virginia. Come *on*."

Emily turned back to the piano again, but she did not play exercises. She opened a battered Beethoven and started the Appasionata. She had played two pages when Courtney stuck his head in the door. "You don't mind if I close the door, do you, Em? I'm trying to concentrate."

Emily sighed and laughed. "No. I think I'll spare you all and go for a walk." She went into the dining room. "Will you two girls take care of Connie for me this morning?"

"Where are you going?" Virginia asked.

"Just for a walk, I'll be back in plenty of time to get lunch." She left quickly, eager as always to get away from the confining walls of the villa.

On clear days Emily enjoyed the steep climb up the mountain (for always her desire was to climb, rather than to take the path down to the village), moving along slowly on her skis, letting the clear dry air slap at her face, push against her chest so that it was an effort to expand her lungs, and the cold cut like steel against her throat. When she was out of doors the mountains did not seem to press in and down upon her as they did in the house. Out in the open snow she could fling her head back and look up to the mountains and beyond them to the sky, in the daytime an incredible blue, at night a sparkling black as clear and hard as stone with the stars spearing through as though they would hurl themselves down into the valley. But it had seemed, that winter, as though clouds constantly blotted out sky and stars, dropped by day upon the mountains, letting the sharp peaks press into but not pierce their amorphous grayness. Even when it was not actually snowing the clouds leaned down into the valley so that it was as though the village and the outlying hotels and the tuberculosis sanatorium, crouched against the paws of the mountain, were completely enclosed by mountain and cloud, as though there were no escape from this one small thumbprint in the shape of the earth.

She herringboned up the steep slope to the hotel, grateful for the day's clarity, and stopped to rest for a moment and look down at their rented villa pressed against the iron fence of the hotel property, with the houses and shops of the village straggling downhill behind it. A group of skiers came out of the hotel, skis over their shoulders, laughing and shouting, and she moved on up the slope. Abe was probably already off skiing,

Abe and his son, Sam. How old was Sam? Virginia's age? Or a year or so older? She didn't remember. She had never seen a great deal of Sam, who was usually off at school.

For some place to go, to give direction to the morning, she started on up the path that led past the sanatorium to the chalet where Gertrude de Croisenois lived. The wind hurled itself down from the mountain, seeming to aim directly for her, to be directing its attack particularly against her, and she turned up the collar of her ski jacket and pushed on uphill, her head down against the wind, panting a little with cold and exertion, and saying softly under her breath, "Damn. Oh, damn, damn, damn, oh damn."

"And who are you damning?" a voice behind her said, and she turned swiftly, almost falling, forgetting her skis, and there coming up the path was Abe Fielding. He was not on skis but was tramping briskly up the icy path with hobnailed ski boots and a stout stick. He came hurrying towards her, holding out his leather-gloved hands, and she skied down to him, stopping in a swirl of snow, gasping and laughing.

"Oh, Abe, hello! Was I saying it that loud?"

"The wind blew it right to me. Who *were* you damning so fervently?"

She laughed. "Oh, myself. For letting the wind make me so out of breath and such an icicle. I felt ten thousand years old. I suppose I would have been just as cold and just as breathless ten years ago, but I wouldn't have put it down to old age then."

"My ancient Emily," he said, still holding her hands, "all rosy cheeks and shining eyes like some college kid on vacation. Where were you off to?"

"No place. Just escaping."

"Escaping what?"

"Oh—my own evil nature. There's nothing like the mountains for—for purification."

"Do you need purification?"

She threw back her head and laughed. "Do I!"

"You're quaking like an aspen," Abe said. "Come on down to the hotel and have a cup of coffee with me to warm you up."

She looked quickly at her watch. "I'd love to."

She skied slowly along beside him, holding herself back on the hard-packed snow of the path. For a moment they did not speak. Then Abe said, "It's good to see you again, Emily. You and Court. Thanks for having had Sam and me for dinner last night."

"You didn't think I wouldn't, did you?"

"It made a lot of difference, our first night here, to both of us. It made us feel warm and welcome, and that's rather an essential feeling at Christmas-time. Nothing's going to prevent you and Court from coming to the casino with me tonight, is it?"

"Nothing could," Emily said. "I'm anticipating like a kid. Now I really feel like Christmas. Vee and Mimi home and overflowing the house, and now you and Sam here. . . . Virginia and Mimi are thrilled to the marrow at the thought of having dinner at the hotel with Sam. At least Virginia is. Mimi's so blasé that her enthusiasm is perhaps a touch milder."

"Okay if Sam takes them to the movies afterwards?"

"I don't see why not. It doesn't hurt them to stay up late once in a while during the holidays."

"What do you do about Connie?"

"Françoise Berigot, the tobacconist's daughter, is coming to babysit. She does, occasionally, when Court and I go out. Though we sometimes takes Connie along when we go up to Kaarlo's and Gert's. She's very good about going to sleep there, no matter how loud we talk or how many records we play."

They had reached the hotel now, and Emily took off her skis; they went in through the lower level where Abe put them in one of the ski racks which lined the walls. Then he took Emily's arm and they went through the big, draughty room, cold and rather dark in spite of the naked light bulbs hanging from the ceiling. At one end a group of young men was busy waxing skis, and the room was permeated with the pleasant odors of hot wax and damp wool and melting snow and steam heat. Abe turned round so that he was facing Emily and put his hands on her shoulders and stood looking down into her face. But when he spoke his words were incongruous.

"This Gertrude de Croisenois. Is she good enough for Kaarlo?"

"Gert? . . . They adore each other," Emily started with caution, then: "Oh, I don't know, Abe. Who's to say who's good for someone and who isn't? It's a tough situation for them both."

"You mean Gertrude's health?"

"Yes, that. The whole thing."

"She's not French, is she?"

"No, American. She married a Frenchman, Henri de Croisenois, and she's more at home here now than she is at home."

"Why don't she and Kaarlo get married?"

"I don't know," Emily said. "I think Kaarlo would like to."

His hands tightened on her shoulders. "How terribly serious your face can get," he said. "Your eyes get grayer and grayer and deeper and deeper. . . . Come on, we're forgetting that coffee and you're still shivering."

In one of the lounges coffee was being served. Abe led the way through potted palms in enormous Italian pots, blue and yellow and green lions twined about with ivy leaves, to one of the small white-covered tables near the windows, and summoned a waiter. Emily looked up and she could see the enormous hulk of Madame Pedroti, proprietress of the hotel and the Bowens' landlady, bearing down on them.

"Ah, Madame Bowen! Monsieur Fielding! You have already become acquainted, I see!"

"We're old friends from New York," Emily said.

"Ah, but how charming! How delightful! Is everything to your satisfaction, monsieur? Any small way we may be of further service to you?" She clasped her pudgy hands together over her black satin bosom, but moved her fingers slightly so that the diamonds, half hidden in the flesh, glinted in the light.

"Just see that we have plenty of coffee and cakes."

"This instant, monsieur!" She moved slowly away among the tables, swaying a little like a top-heavy ship.

"Gertrude says she was a collaborationist," Emily said.

"Undoubtedly. Things like that aren't forgotten here, even after all this time, are they?"

"No. We rent our house from her. She does quite a thriving business in real estate, too. Some of the collabos met with strange and unexplained accidents after the war, but she managed to survive."

He smiled across the table at her. "Well, girl, how goes it?"

"It goes, Abe."

"Happy?"

"Reasonably."

"Not more than that?"

"Ought one to ask for more in this day and age?"

He mimicked her, but gently. "One ought not to, perhaps, but one does."

She looked down at the table. "Don't laugh at me. A couple of times this winter I've felt horribly sorry for myself. I've crept off into a hole and wept. And then I think of what other people are going through. In India. And China. And all over. Children with their little bellies bloated with hunger and their legs so weak they can't stand. People starving and being killed for no reason. And I am ashamed. So I don't think one should ask for more, Abe. Don't laugh.''

"I'm not laughing," Abe said.

From the long French windows the cold clear sunshine came into the room and fell in rectangles across the tables and floor. Abe's head was in a shaft of sunlight and Emily, looking up, saw that his nondescript brown hair was thinning and had perceptibly receded. But his brown eyes were as alert and lively as ever and she thought that his was one of the nicest faces she had ever seen. He took a bright blue pack of Gauloises out of his pocket and held it out to her. "Are you still a non-smoker?"

"More or less. I do like to smoke occasionally. But I don't think I've had a cigarette this winter. As a matter of fact, I think the last cigarette I smoked was with you."

"Have one with me now, then."

She smiled as she took one. "Thanks. Court smokes Gauloises, too."

"Court and I have good taste."

A waiter put cups in front of them, a pot of coffee, a bowl of cream, and a plate of cakes.

"I shall eat enormously," Emily said, "and not feel in the least like fixing lunch for the family."

"Emily," Abe said as she poured the coffee, "are you doing all the work yourself, cooking and cleaning and everything?"

She laughed. "Yes, I'm doing all the cooking and cleaning and everything. There isn't very much, Abe."

"Oughtn't you to have someone to help you?"

"I don't see why. I didn't have anything more than a cleaning woman once a week in New York."

"It's not quite the same thing." He pushed the plate of cakes across to her. "You've lost weight."

"I'll gain it all back during the holidays, and more. I certainly will if I go on eating like this."

"I shall stuff you tonight at the casino."

"That sounds like an entrancing way of spending an evening." They both laughed, and Emily suddenly realized that this was one of those rare, inexplicable moments when she was perfectly happy; there, for no reason, sitting opposite Abe with the winter sun falling across their table, laughing at banalities, she was suddenly awake and alive. These moments had been rare that winter and she opened herself to this one as sometimes in the summer she spread herself out to the sun.

"Emily," Abe said suddenly, "we've never seen a great deal of each other but we've always somehow been very frank when we have, haven't we?"

"Yes, Abe."

"May I ask you a question?"

"Shoot."

"This business of having no maid while Court's on his sabbatical—"

"It isn't a sabbatical, Abe," Emily said quietly. "He's lost his job."

"Damn it," Abe said. "I'm sorry, Emily."

"I know. It's not nice for him."

"But wasn't he due a sabbatical?"

"Yes. We'd been planning to spend the year here anyhow. So we came ahead."

"But why on earth, Emily? Court's a damn fine teacher."

Emily shook her head angrily. "Nothing exciting or dramatic. That's the worst of it. No loyalty oaths or Fifth Amendments or enormous blowups. Just one of those insidious, stupid, brutal things." She paused. "Part of it's Court being Court—" she continued, "what makes him what he is as a person, what makes him the fine classical scholar he is. The individual, stubborn personality that the kids worshipped. They did, Abe." She realized that she was defending him too vehemently, and stopped abruptly.

"Yes," Abe said. "That's easy to understand."

"They got a new head to the department," Emily said, her eyes darkening with grief and anger. "Tommy O'Hara. You know. He wrote a best seller on Herodotus. It wasn't a best seller because of Herodotus but because it was all Freudian and full of descriptions of sex. It wasn't as bad a book as I think it is. Let's be fair. But I don't feel fair about Tommy O'Hara."

"Court should have been head of the department, shouldn't he?" Abe asked.

"Yes. He should. I cared. I was angry. Court wasn't. It honestly didn't matter to him. He was happy the way things were and he didn't want to be bothered with departmental administrative problems and all he wanted was to have things go on the way they'd been going. But not with Tommy O'Hara. Tommy'd been brought in because he was modern and he'd written

a best seller and because of publicity. Oh, and sort of as a
trouble-shooter, too, I suppose. He was determined he was
going to change everything, and that included Court. He has
red hair and a boyish grin. Well, Court has red hair, too.
Tommy was too smart to try to get rid of Court overtly, but he
did it subtly. A sort of careful edging Court out. And sometimes it wasn't so subtle. Like taking away a couple of Court's
special courses and giving them to green instructors. And there
wasn't a thing I could do to stop it, Abe. Just sit and watch.
There was a bit of jealousy in it, too. Court was a Rhodes
Scholar and I gathered from a friend of mine in the sociology
department that Tommy had wanted to be one and hadn't quite
made it. And the students gave Court a reverence Tommy and
his ultramodernity could never get. So when it became evident
that the two of them couldn't work together Court finally eased
things for them by handing in his resignation.''

"Did he have to?"

"Yes, I rather think he did, Abe."

"How long had this been going on?"

"Let me see. About three years."

"Why didn't I know anything about it?"

"It wasn't—it wasn't anything we talked about, or anything
talking about could have helped."

"It's a rotten shame, Emily."

"Yes. It is. I sometimes get quite white with anger when I
think of that turned-up-from-under-a-stone bastard Tommy
O'Hara still sitting there, while Court—excuse my language,
Abe, but I feel rather hot about it still."

"Of course you do."

"Here we were living a reasonably valuable and contented
life in New York and all of a sudden for no valid reason it's shot
to hell." She stabbed out the butt of her cigarette. "Court
won't let on that it hurts him, he's stubborn and noble and we
don't talk about it any more, but I know it does hurt."

"So what's going to happen with you, Emily?"

"I don't know. Court's trying to write. Essays and papers.
He's sold a couple of them to obscure periodicals that don't pay
much except prestige, and he has an idea of gathering a group
of them into a book. They're terribly brilliant, Abe, too brilliant, and though they have a lot of charm, too, I can see that
they demand too much of the average reader to be readily mar-
ketable. I don't think he'll be able to make a reasonable living
out of writing, but he's taking this year to try."

"And then what?"

"I don't know. Tom Russell, an old friend of Court's, is president of Richwood College in Indiana. He wants Court to go there."

"What do you think?"

"I think we probably will."

"How do you feel about it?"

"Not too happy. But that's stupid and insular of me."

"There's more choice than that one college, certainly, isn't there?"

She shook her head. "Not really. Court's forty-nine, you know, and it's a lot easier to get a job teaching physics than classics. And he's made rather a reputation for himself of being pig-headed. And Richwood's a very good college, as colleges go. I just wish Tom Russell's first name weren't Tom. After Mr. O'Hara I have rather a Thing about the name Thomas. At least he doesn't call himself Tommy."

"It's a horrible thought," Abe said, "you and Court in Indiana. It's much too far away."

"Yes. I'm sorry, Abe, I didn't mean to burden you with all our problems."

"You haven't burdened me, girl," Abe said. "I had to drag it out of you."

"If you don't mind—don't tell Court I told you. If he wants to, all right, but I think maybe he wouldn't like my doing it. I shouldn't have. But there hasn't been—there hasn't been anybody all winter I could talk to." Her voice broke and she reached quickly for her cup of coffee and drank slowly, pressing the rim of the cup against her lip to stop its trembling. In a moment she was under control again, saying, "It's stupid of me to spoil our nice time like this. I'd better get on home now."

"Let's have another cup of coffee first."

She smiled, then laughed. "I'll probably float away. I've been drinking it all morning." Neither of them wanted the coffee, she knew. It was simply an excuse to stay there a little longer. "And let's talk about you," she added. "We've done more than enough talking about me for one day."

"I talked about myself last night all through your wonderful rabbit ragout."

"Business. Not really about yourself."

"You're a wonderful cook, Emily."

"I like cooking. I even like eating what I've cooked. But tell me about you, Abe, please."

"What the devil is there to tell?" he said, almost violently. "Abe, the hail-fellow-well-met, Abe, the happy, the successful, the carefree. That's the face I put up. That's the Abe people see. Nobody wants to see Abe abysmally lonely and depressed right down to hell."

Emily reached across the table and touched his fingers briefly. "I know. I wish you'd find someone. I'm sure you will someday, Abe. There must be the right person somewhere for someone like you."

"Time's running out, Emily." His voice was withdrawn and bitter. "And having made one mistake I don't want to make another. But after Kris died I thought I had to have a mother for Sam. I thought I had to have a wife. Any wife. I was so wrong. Damn it, Emily. No more about me. This is a holiday and I'm not going to spoil it. Tonight we'll be madly merry and forget all our troubles. I hate to let you go now." He smiled across the table at her, across the coffee and the plate of cakes and the napkin she had laid beside her plate. "But I suppose you do have other things to do besides sitting here with me. So I'll see you tonight. You and Court."

"Yes. Seven-thirty, you said?"

"If that's a good time for you."

"Perfect. I'll have Connie in bed and asleep by then. We'll be there."

"Good. I'll be waiting."

She left the hotel and stood on the front steps shading her eyes against the light. After a moment she was able to look up at the mountains without squinting, at the shadows from the billowing white clouds racing across, deep purple and startlingly concise in outline. It seemed strange that anything so white as those clouds could cast such darkness.

Carrying her skis she started walking, humming to herself, on past the villa and into the village to pick up Courtney's copies of *L'Aurore* and *Figaro* at the tobacconist's. In front of the window, their noses pressed in classic position against the pane, were two small children, admiring the gifts displayed within. *"Dis, dis, le beau chemin de fer!"* exclaimed one, while the other, smaller, thinner, not listening, lost in her own world of longing, whispered, *"Ah, ah, la belle petite poupée, qu'elle est mignonne!"* Smiling at them, Emily opened the door and went into the stuffy, cluttered little shop, where the patronne in a heavy gray man's sweater sat behind the counter, knitting as usual, her hands red and chapped from the cold; she reached for the papers as she saw Emily come in. They smiled and greeted each other, and Emily's hand as she took the papers bore the same winter marks of work and cold as did the older woman's.

"Madame looks so well and happy," Madame Berigot said. "Your big girl is with you now, is she not?"

"Yes," Emily said, looking around at the familiar shelves of the little shop, wondering if there were some small, inexpensive things she might pick up for Mimi's stocking presents. "For the holidays. She came with a friend from school."

"Madame has only the two children?"

"Yes," Emily said after a moment. "Only the two."

Noting the shadow that crossed Emily's face, darker in its essence than the black fuzz of her own not-inconsiderable moustache, Madame Berigot changed the subject. "Madame has a look of happiness behind the eyes this morning. It is good to see. Sometimes madam's eyes are sad. It is the loneliness here. But now with the holidays—and madame wishes Thérèse to come stay with the little one tonight?"

"Yes, if you please, Madame Berigot. I hope it doesn't snow again tonight."

Madame Berigot laughed. "Ah, snow doesn't bother us. Madame is from the city and is not used to the rigors of our mountain winters."

Emily laughed, too, and when she left she had the feeling of warmth that Madame Berigot always gave her. She enjoyed going to the small shop to get the papers; their conversations were always similar, always banal, but they had become, in a strange way, friends.

She prepared lunch and the day started suddenly to drag, stretching on and on like a tunnel and yet with a tingle of excitement to it because always at the end of a tunnel there is light. It was only after they had eaten and she had done the dishes that she realized that the light at the end of this particular tunnel was the gaiety of an evening at the casino, that the length of the day and the shiver of anticipation were because she was waiting for this party with all the eagerness with which she had waited for Christmas when she was a child.

She hung the dripping dish towel on the rack by the stove to dry, and turned around slowly in the kitchen. Everything was tidied and cleaned up and ready for the mess of the next meal when the whole thing would have to be done all over again. She turned her back on the cracked sink and walked out. She wanted to go to the piano and work, but she knew that her practising, the exercises, the repetition of phrases, disturbed Courtney when he was trying to work in this small house where every sound was intimately shared; and today he would be working especially hard redoing those lost notes. She had a shuddering feeling of claustrophobia, and when the antique phone on the wall in the dark hall outside Courtney's office began to ring and she ran pelting towards it, it was only partly so that the ringing should not disturb him.

"I'm lonely. Come see me. Come right now," said Gertrude de Croisenois' voice without preamble.

"Connie's having a nap."

"Well, aren't Virginia and her pal there?"

"Yes, but—"

"Tell them to listen for her, then. *They've* been to see me. Twice. Where've you been?"

Emily chuckled. "They think you're a heroine."

"And so I am—to them. You have a different opinion, eh?"

"Not at all. I've just grown used to it."

Now on the other end of the line Gertrude laughed. "Oh, damn you, Emily, do come on up, just for a few minutes." Without giving Emily a chance to answer she hung up.

It was a place to go; it was an excuse to leave the confining walls of the house, and, asking Virginia and Mimi to listen for Connie, she set off.

She leaned her skis against the shed that jutted against the chalet where Gertrude lived with one of the guides, Kaarlo Balbec, and knocked at the side door, loudly, because indoors the phonograph was going full volume, the summer music of the Pastoral Symphony superimposed on the snowy landscape.

The music was not lowered but Gertrude called out, "Come in, come in if you feel you must," and Emily opened the door and went into the kitchen and through into the big living room where Gertrude, in red velvet slacks, lay on the couch, a steamer rug over her feet.

"Oh, it's you," she said, as though she had not just so summarily summoned Emily.

Emily took off her outdoor things. "At your bidding, Madame de Croisenois. How are you this afternoon?"

Gertrude sat up on the couch, crossing her legs under her like a Turk. "How am I ever? I get so damned impatient, Emily, but our pal Dr. Clément rules me with a rod of iron."

"If he ruled you with a rod of iron you'd be in the sanatorium, not here."

"I'd die there," Gertrude said. "Water's on the stove for the tea. Do you want to fix it?"

"Sure."

"And turn off the phonograph, would you please, so we can hear ourselves think." Gertrude reached up with an impatient hand and pushed her heavy, dark hair back from her face.

In the kitchen getting cups, sugar, a lemon, Emily could continue to talk through the passway to Gertrude lying on the couch that had been pushed close to the windows. Beyond this chalet was another, and then a great stretch of snow fields leading upwards into the winter-dark of evergreens. When Emily brought in the tea tray and put it by the fireplace Gertrude had turned away and was looking out the window towards the higher chalet.

Emily followed her glance. "Homesick?" she asked.

Gertrude shrugged. "Nothing as active as that. Just thinking for some reason or other that when Henri and I bought the chalet we never expected to spend so many years in it. A week-end place in the Haute Savoie that's what we thought we were getting. Nor did I ever expect Kaarlo to find me lying there in a pool of blood. Good guy, my Kaarlo, isn't he?"

Emily poured the tea. "A prince. It *is* lemon you like, not milk, isn't it?"

"If I must drink the filthy stuff at all. Clément seems to think it's better for me than coffee. Don't know why. Another good guy in his own uniquely nasty way, that Clément. Hey, Em, I met a friend of yours yesterday."

Emily put another log on the fire, stirred her tea, sitting in the one comfortable chair in the chalet. It had been brought down from Gertrude's chalet and was of nubbly, zebra-striped material, and did not look anywhere nearly so comfortable as it was; and it always seemed out of place to Emily in this room that was otherwise completely Kaarlo's. "Who?" she asked.

"Abe Fielding."

"Oh, did Kaarlo bring him around?"

"Yes. I kind of liked him. Full of sweetness and light today, aren't I? Three passable people in a row. Old Gert de C. must be slipping. I much prefer being sour and vindictive. Fielding'll never win a beauty contest, anyhow. Ugly as a mud fence, isn't he?"

"I've never thought of him as being particularly ugly," Emily said.

"Nobody with a bobbing Adam's apple is handsome. And a big beak of a nose. Virile ugly in a funny sort of way. Good body. Good eyes. Tall and rangy. You and Courtney known him long?"

"Since the war."

"What's he doing over here? I thought he was some kind of big insurance muggy mug in New York."

"He is. His firm sent him over for a year."

"Nice kid he's got, that Sam."

"Yes."

"Maybe he'll be a beau for your Virginia."

"That would be nice," Emily said. "Virginia hasn't had many beaux."

"Did you before you were married?"

"Nope."

"And how's my pal Courtney? Coming to play chess with me one of these evenings?"

"Sure, Gert, I know he'd love to."

"Now what I'd really like," Gertrude said with a malicious grin, "would be to say to hell with chess and spend an evening getting drunk with my pal Courtney. Courtney looks so pretty with vine leaves in his pretty red hair. Pretty like a fox. Long skinny face like a fox and pretty chinky blue eyes too close together. He'd look pretty with a pink coat riding to hounds, with a hey and a ho and a hey nonny no and a mixed metaphor in the springtime, the only pretty ringtime. . . .Or in bed with me under the gay plaid of this charming steamer rug designed to cheer the low spirits of poor dear Gert de C. By all means let's pretend we aren't sick unto death or we wouldn't be here and resort towns are made for romantic rendezvous so why shouldn't I think of it? . . . I love to tease you, little vulnerable Emily. I don't want your darling Courtney, little stupid monogamous Emily."

"You're feverish this afternoon, aren't you?" Emily asked.

"I have to be feverish, because on occasion I talk the way I feel instead of playing my pretty little part? I only do it around you, my pet. When Courtney comes I let my hand hang limply over the side of the couch and sigh until he holds it, but that's all, and a slight unnecessary cough to incite his pity; Courtney wears compassion well. And when Virginia and Mimi come I'm all brave and noble and full of wise philosophy, the wounded heroine, oh, so brave, stricken by her noble deeds instead of by her riotous living. A pardonable deception, don't you think?''

"And more than half the truth," Emily said, more gently.

"Let's have some music," Gertrude said. "I'm doing my damndest to like it for Kaarlo's sake. What'll it be?"

"Why not finish the Pastoral? It's still going around in my head where we left off. And I have to go in a minute."

"What's your rush? Stay and keep me company. I've been sitting here brooding all day long." The fire blazed up and she put her hands to her cheeks. "God, it's hot in here. Don't keep building up the fire." She kicked at the steamer rug, pushed up the sleeves of her black sweater. For a moment Emily's glance fell on the numbers branded on her arm. "Nice to see you without Connie for a change," Gertrude said. "Not that she's a bad brat as brats go. But it's good for you to be able to get away from her for five minutes. . . . Em, I've been a lovely good girl all day. Would you feel like going to the Splendide for a drink before dinner? Just us—or if Kaarlo's home early Court might like to come, too."

"We can't this evening, Gert," Emily said.

"Why not?"

"Abe's asked us to the casino for dinner."

"Oh, hell and damn. I'm bored with behaving. I've a good mind to ski down alone."

Emily said nothing. Gertrude did not take kindly to warnings.

"I'm bored, bored, bored," Gertrude said. "That makes two of us, doesn't it? Well, doesn't it? Why don't you say something?"

"If I say I'm not bored you'll tell me I'm being a sanctimonious prude," Emily said, "and if I agree with you, you'll ask me what the devil I've got to be bored about."

"That's right, spoil my fun. Half the time I envy you and the other half I'm sorry as hell for you." She pulled the blanket up about her again. "Do you know, Em, I never really ever had a woman friend before you."

"Should I be flattered or insulted?" Emily put the tray on the counter into the kitchen. "I'll wash up the tea things and then I have to go. Anything I can do to start dinner for you?"

"Oh, Kaarlo'll open a couple of cans or make us an omelette or something. He's a good cook. Much better than I am. Can Courtney cook?"

Emily laughed. "No."

"Turn down the phonograph while you're doing the dishes, so I can hear you."

"I wasn't planning on saying anything worth listening to." Emily turned on the light over the sink. Darkness had fallen while they were talking and in the big main room of the chalet light from the fire flickered against the dark beams, and only a faint reflected light was thrown in the windows from the snow. Emily put the tea things away and put on her outdoor things. "I'll probably see you tomorrow, Gert. I'm sorry about the last couple of days."

Gertrude shrugged again, pulled down her sweater sleeves, shivered, and huddled under the blanket. Emily put another log on the fire. "I would like a nice plain white-plastered New York apartment ceiling," Gertrude said. "I keep seeing faces in this ceiling. See that knothole up there? Doesn't it look just like a disapproving spinster? You know, Em, I think Kaarlo got a real bang out of seeing Abe Fielding again. They just had that one mission together during the war, but I guess things sort of clicked with them. They both like the same kind of things—skiing and climbing and this sort of music. I guess we'll have to submit to some more evenings of listening to records. Turn the phonograph off, Em. I can't stand any more of that stuff."

Emily silenced the music, put the record carefully away. "Anything else I can do for you before I go, Gert?"

"Not unless you can dig up some excitement."

"Wish I could," Emily said lightly. "See you tomorrow," and stepped out through the shed into the cold.

Back at the villa she got the hip bath out from under the kitchen table and filled it with hot water for Connie. There was a tub in the bathroom upstairs, but even when it was filled with hot water from the ancient geyser and the window blanked out by steam the room remained so cold that all baths were taken in the kitchen near the comforting heat of the coal stove.

"Where's daddy?" Connie asked, pulling off her shoes and socks.

"He went into the village to get rolls for breakfast. I forgot them this morning."

"With Mimi and Vee?"

"Yes, Con. They ought to be back any minute now."

"Where's my fish? I want my fish in the bath. Where's my fish, mama?"

"Here on the window sill where you left it last night."

"Why can't I go have dinner at the hotel with Vee and Mimi Opp?"

"Because you weren't invited."

"Why weren't I vited?"

"Because you aren't old enough."

"Mimi says I speak better French than Vee does."

Emily laughed. "You do, but that still doesn't get you an invitation to dinner."

"When can I go to a movie?"

"I don't know, Con. Sometime. Not tonight."

"But when?"

"If a good movie comes later on in the winter maybe I'll take you."

"Daddy, too?"

"If he wants to. Hop in the tub, now, Connie."

As Connie climbed in they heard the front door slam. "That's Virginia and Mimi! I want to see them!"

"Emily Conrad Bowen, stay in the tub," Emily said sternly. "You'll see them soon enough. They'll probably come in here looking for us."

And in a moment Virginia's voice came, "Mother!"

"In the kitchen," Emily called.

Virginia came in and stood in the doorway. "Oh, there you are. May Mimi and I have a bath?"

"I don't think you'd better, darling, and then go out in the cold. Just wash up a bit when you change."

"Mother, it's going to be fun!" Virginia cried, her green eyes suddenly shining out like a kitten's in her little pointed face. "I'd be petrified if I had to go alone but with Mimi Opp it'll be fun. We'll wear our black velvet school dinner dresses and be like sisters. Like twins."

"Like before and after twins, then."

"Before and after what?"

"Oh, you know the ads, Vee. Before eating Dr. Podder's Porridge. After eating Dr. Podder's Porridge."

"Oh. I get it. I'm Before. You do like Mimi, don't you, mother?"

"Very much."

"Have you ever heard her father play the violin?"

"Not at a concert. He hasn't played often in America. But Kaarlo has some of his records. He's very good."

"Mama, scrub my back," Connie demanded, and then

added as Emily looked at her: "Please." Emily took the soapy cloth and rubbed it up and down the small soft pink back. "More. More. It feels so good."

"My lascivious little daughter," Emily said, rubbing. "Now scrub your knees and wash your feet."

"Mrs. Bowen!"

"We're in the kitchen," Virginia called.

"Oh. Hi." Mimi came hurrying in, her red robe pulled about her, her feet stuck in the outrageous, fuzzy slippers. "Mrs. Bowen, have you got something Virginia could wear tonight?"

"I rather doubt it, Mimi. Why?"

"All we've got is our bloody school dinner uniform. Can you imagine, Mrs. Bowen, going out to dinner at the Grand Hôtel dressed exactly alike?"

"I thought it would be sort of fun," Virginia said faintly.

"Why not?" Emily said quickly. "You can make a game of it. And those dresses aren't bad at all."

"For uniforms I suppose they're all right," Mimi conceded grudgingly. "You can't go too wrong with black velvet. But I could do with a nice décolletage instead of those cosy little white-lace collars. And honestly, Virginia, we're too old for this twin business." Then, seeing the quickly hurt look in Virginia's eyes, she flung an affectionate arm about her. "Oh, okay, idiot, we'll play twins like mad and make Sam do everything as though we were Siamese. Do you think he could manage to dance with both of us at once? That *would* cause a sensation, wouldn't it? Though I suppose if we're going to the flicks we won't be dancing tonight. Thank goodness I managed to sneak in a little scent in spite of matron's doing the packing, and you can use some of your mother's—can't she, Mrs. Bowen?"

"Certainly. Now look, you two young ladies, run along and get dressed and then sit quietly in the living room till Sam comes for you. Where's daddy, Vee?"

"He stayed in the village to get a paper or something."

"I got his papers this morning. Bother. I wanted him to go get Thérèse. Oh, well. Go on, you two. Get dressed."

"I want to go up and watch them get dressed," Connie said.

"No, darling. You stay here where it's warm." Emily held out the big towel she had put to heat on a chair by the stove. "Come on, Con. Out you get."

Connie stood up and let Emily wrap the towel around her. "I'm still hungry."

"You can't be. You had two poached eggs and three pieces of toast and two dishes of compote for dinner."

"But I am."

"You may have some bread and butter, then."

"With sugar on it?"

"All right. With sugar."

Connie thought this over for a moment. Then her lower lip began to quiver and her big blue eyes filled with deliberate tears. "Mama, I don't want you and daddy to go out tonight!"

Emily knelt down by the child and put her arms around her, but her voice was firm. "Now, Connie, don't start that. Please. Daddy and I are going, and we're looking forward to having a pleasant evening with Mr. Fielding."

"Who's Mr. Fielding?"

"Abe Fielding. Sam's father."

The lip quivered more noticeably. "I don't want you to go. And I don't want Vee or Mimi to go."

"We're all going, Connie, but not until you're sound asleep in bed. And Thérèse will be here if you want anything and you love Thérèse. Now. Here are your pajamas, all nice and warm. Hop in. I mended the hole in the toe."

"Will you take me to bed and sing to me?"

"Yes."

"How many songs?"

"Oh—six."

"Six long ones?"

"Six medium-sized ones."

Connie thought this over. Her lip started to quiver again, then she thought better of it, and said, "I think I'd go to sleep even more faster if I had two pieces of bread and sugar."

Connie was settled for the night when the front door slammed. Emily got up and tiptoed out of the room, softly drawing the door to behind her. Courtney stood in the front hall, his muffler pulled halfway up over his face, his hat down over his ears. He took off the hat and hung it on one of the pegs.

"It's colder tonight," he said.

"I know. You can hear the house creak and crack the way it always does when the thermometer plummets. Darling, it's time to change. It'll be time to meet Abe in half an hour and I wanted you to go get Thérèse first."

"I'm not going," Courtney said casually. And as Emily looked at him in astonishment: "I mean I'm not going to the ca-

sino. So there's no need for Thérèse. You can telephone her."
He began to sing a rather bawdy sixteenth-century round.

"Said Sir John to his Lady, as kissing, as kissing they sat,
'Shall we now go to dinner or to you know, to you know
what?'

"Come on, Emily. Sing it with me."
Emily stood very still. At last she said, "But, Court, why?"
"Because I feel like singing rounds."
"No. Why aren't we going to the casino?"
"I've been fighting a scratchy throat all day and if I go to that crowded, over-heated place it's bound to turn into a bad cold. If I behave sensibly and sit at home with a book I can in all probability lick it. I stopped at the Splendide and had a couple of brandies and I'm feeling very warm and comfortable and not in the least like going out again. So I'm not going." He started to sing again, another round.

"Banbury ale! Where, where, where!
At the blacksmith's house! I would I were there!"

—More than a couple of brandies, Emily thought. Oh Court,
I wish you wouldn't. . . .
But then she thought quickly, defending him in her own mind as though from an attack from the outside—He's disappointed and unhappy! No wonder he wants to forget it once in a while.
—But I want to go tonight!
Aloud she said, "I know Abe has made reservations ahead.
He'll be—he'll be awfully disappointed."
"I don't think it'll make that much difference to him.
There'll be other nights—what's wrong with next week?—and I'm damned if I want to come down with a cold right now. You know I always have the devil of a time shaking one. You must admit going out at this point doesn't make sense. Abe's a good fellow. He'll understand that."
"All right," Emily said, her voice flat with disappointment.
"I'll call him and say we can't go."
"There's no need for you to stay home," Courtney said. "I know how you love a party and there haven't been very many this winter."
"Don't be silly," Emily said, her voice a little sulky. "You know perfectly well I'm going to stay home with you."

Courtney picked up his muffler where it had slithered off the hook. "Come on out of the hall. It's dark as a dungeon and cold as an icebox here. Let's go in the kitchen. No, I don't want you to stay home with me. You know I detest being fussed over. Go along and have a good time. Was Abe going to pick us up?"

"No. I think we were to meet him at the casino."

"I don't like your walking there alone at night. Are Gert and Kaarlo going?" Courtney led the way into the kitchen, pulled up a chair and sat down.

"No," Emily said. "I was with Gert this afternoon so I'm sure they're not going. And I've walked to the village plenty of times alone in the evening. And Abe will see that I get home safely. But I don't think I should go without you."

"Oh, come off it, Emily! I don't want you hanging around wishing to hell you were at the casino. As for me, nothing could please me better than having an evening completely alone. One of my chief pleasures this winter is that there's no Tommy O'Hara to tell me which social functions he expects me to attend and I get a positive satisfaction out of turning them down." He hitched another chair closer and put his feet on it. "I don't envy you. It's bitter cold out tonight. I shall wrap myself up in a blanket and read. Connie asleep?"

"I hope so, by now."

"Virginia and Mimi?"

"Upstairs changing for their big date with Sam. I'll make you an omelette and some toast and coffee before I go."

"I'm not particularly hungry."

Emily put her arm about his shoulders. "You don't think I'd go off to feast at the casino and leave you unfed, do you? It won't take me a minute." She took eggs from a bowl on the shelf, then said, "Court, I'm not a bit happy about leaving you. Are you sure you don't want me to stay?"

"Damn it, Emily, I told you I didn't, didn't I?" He pulled a paper out of his pocket and began to read as she prepared his meal. "I am hungry after all," he said, smiling up at her suddenly with the singularly sweet smile that had become very rare that winter; she smiled back and put his plate and a steaming cup of coffee on the kitchen table.

"There's some good compote in the icebox for dessert," she told him. "I'm going up to change now, darling. There's lots more coffee in the pot if you want it. I've just shoved it to the back of the stove." At the door she turned. "What do you suppose the K in Abe's name stands for?"

Courtney paused with his fork halfway up to his mouth. "I don't know. Kevin? Kabalevsky? Kuala-Lumpur? Kouangtong? Kilkenny? Konstantin? Konstantinople?"

Emily laughed, a happy laugh, now that, like a child, she had her way, now that she was going. "Why do lots of modern Greek names begin with K and no ancient ones? Or at least none that I can think of? I'm off, darling, or I shall be late." She ran upstairs.

—He should be teaching, she thought, standing for a moment in the dark, cold bedroom without turning on the light. We shouldn't be here. Not this way. For a sabbatical, yes, with out lives stretching out in an orderly pattern behind us and ahead of us. But not this way with all of it behind and nothing ahead.

She turned on the light, shivering, and changed to her only warm evening dress, a very old one, but one which she felt would never lose its style, a sea-green brocade, cut very simply with a full skirt, a tight bodice, and long sleeves (which were what, she supposed, made her feel that it was warm), and a décolletage that would have pleased even Mimi. She sat at her dressing table, shivering a little because the upstairs was always cold, and began to make up very carefully, rubbing a little rouge gently into her cheeks, blending it up towards her eyes and into her hair line. Then she fished around in the drawer of her dressing table until she found a small pot of eye shadow. She looked at her face in the mirror as though seeing it for the first time in months, and this was in a sense true, she thought; she had not wanted to look at herself. Not that it was an extraordinary face in any way, neither particularly beautiful nor ugly, the only unusual thing about it being that her eyebrows were dark and definite and her eyelashes long, an unexpected brunette accent against her fair complexion and light hair. As she finished her make-up she thought—Oh, lord, I haven't phoned Thérèse, and flew downstairs to the phone on the wall in the small, dark back hall that led to the cubbyhole Courtney used as his office. As she explained to Madame Berigot that Monsieur Bowen had a sore throat and they would not be needing Thérèse that evening, she heard the girls come downstairs, and their laughter was in her ears as she called Abe, but he had already left the hotel. She went into the living room where Virginia and Mimi sat, each in one of the hideous plush chairs, looking utterly different in their identical black velvet dresses with the small lace collars.

"You both look charming," Emily said.

They stared at her. Mimi cried, "Mrs. Bowen, you look absolutely beautiful!"

"Why, thank you, Mimi."

"It's like Clare in her lab coat and when she dresses for evening. A complete transformation. What a gorgeous dress, Mrs. Bowen! And I never noticed your eyes were green like Vee's before."

"They aren't, really," Emily said. "They're gray. They just pick up the color of the dress."

"And your hair," Mimi said. "The dress goes so beautifully with your hair. Now what color would you call your hair?"

"Mouse," Emily said.

Mimi shook her head impatiently. "No. Beige. And not a scrap of gray in it. You don't have it touched up or anything, do you?"

Emily laughed. "No, Mimi."

"Clare does. But she started to go gray awfully early and Jake didn't like it. He pretended to, but she could see that he hated it. You can't tell, of course. She has an awfully good job done on it. My hair being blond like Jake's I don't suppose I'll go gray as early as she did."

"Where's daddy?" Virginia asked suddenly. "Isn't he ready?"

"He's not going, Vee. He has a scratchy throat so he's going to stay home and take care of it."

"You're going alone?"

"Yes, Vee."

"Oh, too bad, mother."

"Yes, it would be more fun with daddy. But I expect I shall enjoy myself anyhow. It's quite a treat, dinner at the casino. Now. I have to leave in a few minutes. Virginia, daddy's in the kitchen if you should want anything before Sam comes. But I think he's working so don't disturb him if it isn't necessary."

From upstairs Connie's voice came loud and clear and demanding. "Vee! Vee—ee! You didn't say good night to me!"

"For heaven's sake run up and say good night to her, Virginia," Emily begged. "I'll feel a lot happier if she's asleep before we leave, so daddy won't have to be disturbed."

"I want Vee to tell me a story!" Connie called.

"A short one," Virginia called back, and started up.

"Virginia'd rather make up stories than eat," Mimi said.

"Mrs. Bowen, I didn't want to ask this around Virginia, in case you—is Madame de Croisenois going to get well?"

One couldn't fob Mimi off with pretty answers and Emily didn't try. "I don't know, Mimi. At least there's a good deal of hope now, and Kaarlo said that a couple of years ago there wasn't any."

Mimi nodded. "I've noticed when we're there that she gets very tired if we stay more than a few minutes. Are she and Kaarlo in love?"

Emily leaned back on the piano bench where she always sat, as though the mere physical contact with the piano gave her some kind of assurance, and pressed her elbows gently against the keys so that they made a soft discord. "They're very good friends," she said carefully.

"Why don't they get married?"

"It's hardly any of my business, is it, Mimi? But I imagine that Gertrude feels it wouldn't be fair to Kaarlo to marry him while she's ill."

"But don't people talk, I mean about their living together and not being married?"

"You're old enough to know that people always talk, whether or not there's anything to talk about," Emily said rather sharply. "In any case people would do well to remember that Gertrude is far too ill either to be alone or to provide them with much material for gossip. And, please, my dear Mimi, just because you admire Gertrude so much, don't try to glamorize her situation. Illicit love affairs aren't glamorous. Usually they're sordid. But certainly I'm no one to judge or criticize."

"But why not, Mrs. Bowen, when you're happily married?"

"That's exactly why. Now let us change the subject."

"Okay," Mimi said agreeably, unrebuffed. "Anyhow, she's still alive. That's something. I don't often feel this way about an adult, like a schoolgirl—which technically I suppose I am—with a crush. So I'm very glad she's managed to stay alive."

"Yes."

"And that's been a fight, too."

"Yes, Mimi."

Virginia came in, then, saying. "Well, she's asleep. She fell asleep in the middle of my story. Imagine that!"

Mimi, with a quick change of mood, twirled around. "Do you suppose I could make anything out of this dress if I took the scissors and cut the neck out?"

"I think you'd make a mess of it," Virginia said, "and you'd get into terrible trouble at school."

"Who cares about that? I'm thinking about Sam. I have a feeling he's quite a boy, that Sam."

—Oh, no, Mimi, Emily protested silently. Let Virginia have Sam. I know it would be so easy for you to take him, but please don't.

"I'd probably make it look worse," Mimi said, "if I started cutting at it. I'll just have to reconcile myself to looking like you. I could do worse, of course. You're really not unpleasant to look at. I like red hair. And you'll probably outgrow the freckles. And you have *very* good eyes. I'd give anything to have green eyes. And a sensuous mouth. Did you know you have a sensuous mouth, Vee?"

Virginia peered at herself in the faulty mirror over the fake mantelpiece, embarrassed and pleased.

On the piano Emily played a quick and determined G major chord. "You're both of you quite fascinating, but it's time for me to go. Bless you for putting Connie to sleep, Vee. Have a wonderful evening, both of you."

"Same to you, Mrs. Bowen."

"Will you be home before we are, mother?"

"I imagine so."

"We're going to be out terribly late!" Virginia cried. "What fun! Good-bye, mother. You have fun, too. Too bad daddy has a sore throat."

Emily put on her old fur coat and ski boots, put her evening slippers in a bag. She stopped in the kitchen to say good-bye to Courtney. He was sitting tipped back in the chair, his feet up on the table, reading the newspaper. "I'm off, darling," she said.

He looked up. "Oh. Have fun."

"I will. How's the throat?"

"Not bad. It'll be all right in the morning."

"I don't think Connie'll wake up," Emily said. "She never does. . . ."

"And if she does I know where her room is, and I've tucked her in and given her drinks of water and picked up fallen pink teddy bears before. Stop worrying and go on and have a good time. I'll undoubtedly be sound asleep when you come in. You can tell me about it at breakfast."

She kissed the top of his head. "Good night, darling. I do feel funny going without you. Terribly mean."

"Nonsense. I shall be snoring happily when you get home."

* * *

"Let's go say good-bye to daddy," Virginia said after Emily had left.

"If he's working, won't we disturb him? Jake'd murder me if I disturbed him while he was practising."

"Oh, daddy'll expect me at least to say good night," Virginia said.

They went into the kitchen. Courtney had dropped the newspaper to the floor, poured himself a fresh drink, and had a book and some papers on the table in front of him. He looked up with an inquiring smile as the girls came in.

"Are we bothering you, daddy?" Virginia asked. "We just came to say good-bye."

Courtney pushed his papers to one side and put his glass down in front of him. "Connie asleep?"

"Yes."

"What are you writing, Mr. Bowen?" Mimi asked, lounging in the doorway.

He looked over at her. "Tonight? A paper on a Greek warrior who had a reputation for being a coward. Matter of fact, I don't think he was. To be a warrior and a coward—the abysm of failure, isn't it?" He stared down into his glass. "The taste of failure is bitter in the mouth. It is not a sour taste, like lemon, but dull, like ashes. It has the sick finality of poor funerals in second-rate funeral parlors. It is a depressant like the sulfas or penicillin but it has no healing qualities. It is as difficult to realize as the loss of a limb and it often comes with as little justification as the maiming accident. And when failure is finally accepted it is as difficult to continue life with the knowledge of it as it is with no right arm." He put his drink down and stood up. "But was Philopoemen a failure? Was he a coward? Things are not always what they seem, and certainly not in history." He looked at Virginia, looked at Mimi, as though seeing them for the first time, and sat down again.

"I'm going up to check on Connie," Virginia said, in a voice as strained and as different from her own as Courtney's.

"Why?" Mimi asked. "She was asleep, wasn't she?"

"She might have kicked the covers off. It's fearfully cold upstairs." Virginia wheeled and went out of the kitchen and marched upstairs to Connie's room. Connie stirred slightly in her sleep and the eiderdown slithered off the side of her bed onto the floor. "There," Virginia said out loud in justification, and put it back on, tucking it clumsily around Connie's shoulders. Then she stood very still as she heard footsteps mounting the stairs, Courtney's tread, not Mimi's. She turned slowly and he stood there in the doorway, supporting himself by holding on to the frame, and swaying slightly.

"I'm so tired, Virginia," he said, his voice suddenly thick. "Daddy's so tired. So terribly tired."

She said nothing, but stood by Connie's bed, staring at him silhouetted against the hall light, his features not visible, his whole body sagging.

"Connie's eiderdown was off. It was on the floor," she said. She could not move until he moved, and he did not move.

"I should have gone," he said. "Or I should have made her stay home. And all I can do is . . . Oh, hell, Virginia, oh hell and damn. It's too unbalanced, it doesn't make sense—Does it make sense to you, Virginia?"

"I'd better not go with Sam and Mimi tonight," she said.

"Oh, Christ! Not you, too!" he cried as though in sudden pain. "Go on. Go downstairs."

"But, daddy, suppose—"

"Suppose what?"

"I don't want to leave Connie," she said bleakly.

Suddenly his voice was cold, authoritative. "Go downstairs and wait for your date. I am perfectly capable of coping with Connie and I do not care in the least for your attitude. Go on. Get out."

She wilted, dwindled, all in a moment younger than Connie, her voice a childish bleat. "Oh, daddy, please—"

And then at last he came into the room, leaving the support of the doorframe, and put his arm around her. "Run along, dear. Have a wonderful time. And tell me all about it in the morning."

With her evening shoes swinging in their bag by her side Emily left the house and walked down through the village to the casino to meet Abe. The feeling of heaviness (as though a greater gravity were pulling at her limbs) that had come upon her when Courtney came into the house announcing that he was not going to the casino, left her, and she felt almost light-headed walking down the icy path in the sharp, stinging air. When she reached the village, though there could be no change there in temperature, the holiday colors and sounds and laughter seemed to dissipate the cold. A group of guides pushed out of the Splendide, letting out a rush of warmth and noise, roaring at some private joke, the clouds of their breath white against the black air. Three young men came marching arm in arm down the middle of the street, just drunk enough to be uninhibited and happy, and one of them whistled at Emily and she felt absurdly gratified.—As long as I'm whistled at I'm not in that bottle of formaldehyde yet, she thought.

Abe was waiting just inside the lobby of the casino. He held out both hands to Emily and for a moment they did not speak. Then she pulled her hands hastily out of his, saying, "Abe, I did try to call you, but you'd left the hotel."

"Why? There isn't anything wrong, is there? Where's Courtney?" His face furrowed into an absurdly worried look.

"He's home with a sore throat. It isn't bad, but his colds are miserable when he gets them so he thought it would be foolish to come out tonight. I hope it hasn't upset your plans."

"I'm sorry Court's not well," he said, and then: "No, girl, it hasn't upset my plans." He stood looking at her for a moment as though he were going to say something else. Finally he said, "You look quite beautiful."

She was pleased and oddly embarrassed; she spoke quickly to cover her embarrassment, looking down at her feet in the heavy ski boots and laughing. "How do you like my delicate evening slippers? I'll just change my shoes, Abe. I have them with me, see? In this little bag. Satin slippers aren't much good for walking around here in winter."

When she had changed her shoes he looked at her again, his eyes travelling appreciatively over her hair, her face, down to the satin slippers. "I haven't felt as festive as this in a long time," he said; he also, it seemed, talking a little too rapidly. "I'd forgotten just how nice you are to look at. That's a lovely dress. Come, girl. Let's wine and dine and dance."

They sat side by side in the enormous, well-filled dining salon at one of the small white-covered tables, each with a single rose in a small vase.

"Listen," Emily said.

The orchestra was playing a Strauss waltz and light was reflected a thousand times over from the prisms of the chandelier. She heard the sound of a champagne cork being drawn carefully from the bottle and she turned to Abe, laughing with pleased excitement. "We've gone back a hundred years," she said softly. "Neither of the wars has happened. We're not living in a world of fear and consternation." And then in a different voice, happy and excited, "Oh, look, Abe, holly, and mistletoe, oh, and over there, the Christmas tree! Oh, how beautiful!"

"And we will have champagne, too," Abe said, smiling down at her, and Emily was suddenly terribly conscious of the physical person of Abe sitting there beside her, of the casual touch of his leg against hers as he held out the familiar blue package of Gauloises.

She laughed. "Why not? I feel like everything tonight! It *is* Christmassy, isn't it? I hope the children are having a good time." But she thought only fleetingly of the children. She allowed the music and the gentle lights and the luxury to take her completely away from the villa, and the coal furnace, and the washbasins that had to be draped in bedclothes each night to keep them from freezing.

"Shall I order for you?" Abe asked.

"Yes, please."

She sat beside him, relaxed, at the same time that her heart was beating quite rapidly. She held Abe's cigarette and sipped her drink and she was terribly, inordinately happy as Abe conferred with the maître d'hôtel and she watched the funny, absorbed look on his face as he ordered the wine to go with their dinner. Then suddenly it seemed desperately important to her that they talk, that they talk about nothing, that they put a barricade of words between them.

Abe, perhaps, felt this also, because he lit another cigarette and handed it to her, asking abruptly, "Tell me, how did Gertrude get TB?"

Relieved, Emily plunged in. "I suppose the foundations for it were laid during the war. She didn't have much chance to look out for her health while she was working in the maquis. And then, Henri, her husband, died just at the end of the war, too. After having gone all that time he died of pneumonia just a month before VE Day."

"And I complain," Abe said. "So what happened after the war? How did she get ill?"

"After the war she sort of went to pieces," Emily said. "Henri was gone, and danger was gone, too. That had a lot to do with it, of course, the sudden lack of danger." She continued to talk, to talk safely about Gertrude, the words in her relief tumbling over each other like water over stones (and what was she afraid of? Why was she relieved?). "Everybody here," she said, "the whole countryside itself—you never knew when a tree or what seemed like a tree might turn out to be a human being, or who might betray you, having seemed to be on your side, or who, playing along with the Gestapo, might have been working with the resistance all along. And then it was all over, everything she'd worked for, and Henri was dead, and trees were only trees, and for a while you could spit at people like Madame Pedroti, but it didn't help much. . . ." She paused.

"Go on," Abe said.

"She told me she went to New York for a while and then she tried going home to her family in Illinois, but it wasn't a success. Her experiences during the war had put her in a world completely different from the one she'd left to marry Henri, and she and her old friends didn't speak the same language any more. So she went back to Paris; she didn't take any care of herself, and it was there she became really ill. So then she came here and stayed alone in the chalet she and Henri had above Kaarlo's. She knew Kaarlo well, of course, from the resistance, and he used to check on her every day. One day when he went in she didn't answer when he called, and he found she'd had a hemorrhage and had been alone there, half-unconscious, for several hours. She was in the sanatorium for quite a while after that, and when Clément—her doctor—let her out, there was no question of her going back alone to the chalet, so she went to live with Kaarlo."

"She's had a rough time—" Abe started and then he broke off and half-laughed and said, "We're talking so nicely and politely about Gertrude and really I don't give a damn about Gertrude." She looked up at him, startled, and he said, "But Gertrude's a safe topic for us, isn't she? And we have to keep to safe topics of conversation, don't we, Emily?"

She looked down, away from him, at the white cloth of the table, at the crumbs of bread that had scattered, a small gravy stain, the fresh rolls and butter, the budding rose, and picked up her wine glass and sipped from it. She had finished the wine and she was sipping from an empty glass and when she put it down a waiter picked up the napkined bottle and filled her glass. "Thank you," she said. "It's—it's an excellent wine."

"You know, I've always considered Courtney one of my closest friends," Abe said. "Great admiration for the guy. One of the few human beings I really care about. Sorry things are so rough for him right now."

"Yes," she said.

"But they'll even out," he said. "They do in the long run for

people of Courtney's caliber. Can't stand the thought of your
going all the way to Indiana, though. Much too far away. . . .
How about a dance? I always liked that tune.''

They danced and, in spite of the crowded floor and other dan-
cers brushing constantly against them, they moved fluidly together, her body following easily his as it pressed strongly,
warmly, against her. They did not talk, now, they simply
moved together in rhythm over the dance floor until the music
stopped. When they sat down at the table again Abe turned to
her, saying, ''Why am I always so happy when I'm with you,
Emily? Relaxed and at ease and perfectly content to be myself.
But *happy*, that's the main thing. Actively and positively happy
instead of managing to cope, rather grimly, though perfectly
successfully, with life.''

''I'm happy when I'm with you, too,'' she said, and added
lamely: ''I suppose it's because we're such good friends.''

He looked at her and raised his eyebrows quizzically and then
his face hardened and he said, ''Yes, let's keep it safe.'' And
then he said under his breath, so low she scarcely heard,
''Damn it. Damn it to hell.''

She said, again lamely, apologetically, ''It's a wonderful
dinner, Abe. I'd always heard the chef here was terrific.''

''You haven't been here before?''

''No. Only in the bar for an occasional drink.'' She laughed.
''It's our frugal winter, remember. Someday we'll come back
and stay at Pedroti's palace and really have ourselves a time.
I'm sorry Courtney had to miss this evening. He'd have enjoyed it as much as I.''

''Would he?'' Abe asked.

''This is a beautiful room,'' she said, ''without being osten-
tatious. Much better taste than Pedroti's dining room.''

''Do you have to go straight home?'' Abe asked. ''Or could
you come back to the hotel with me for a few minutes? We
could have coffee in the lounge or play a game of ping-pong or
something wildly exciting like that.''

''I'd love to,'' she said. ''It's been such a beautiful evening
I hate to end it.''

''How about another dance before we go?''

They made their way to the dance floor and she moved into
his arms and Abe said gently, ''We fit together, Emily, you and
I.''

They left the big beautiful room with the crystal chandelier
and the Christmas tree, and Abe held out her old fur coat and

she put on her spiked boots and Abe carried the satin slippers and they went out into the night. In the lights of the crowded street he looked at her and she felt beautiful and this had become an unfamiliar feeling and an exciting one and her pulses and her pace quickened as she walked beside him. They moved out of the lighted streets and there were no clouds and the stars were incredible in their brightness with the mountains rising up towards them, their buttresses and pinnacles gleaming in the starlight.

They walked side by side, just barely not touching, and suddenly it seemed to her that whether or not their gloved fingers casually met or her coat touched his was terribly important. They moved along as slowly as the cold would permit, not talking, except for Abe to say once in a low voice, "How different this is from the way you and I used to walk together in New York. You're a good person to walk with, Emily." Then the village was behind them and they turned up the path by the villa; Courtney had left on a light downstairs and the window of the front bedroom was lit and Emily knew that he was lying there in the cold bed, reading.

"Court's still awake," she said, and Abe made no response but led her on up the path towards the hotel and she was not sure whether or not he had heard. Then he looked down at her with a quiet and reassuring smile.

In the hotel there was music and light again and voices and the smell of steam heat and cooking and wine and hot house flowers and cigarette smoke. Groups of people were drinking after-dinner coffee in the lounge, and others in evening clothes were moving to and from the ballroom. A group of students in ski clothes streamed out of the elevator and pushed their way, laughing, towards the gamerooms.

"What a mob," Abe said. "Let's go upstairs and talk." One hand on her elbow he led her through the people towards the elevator. They went upstairs and as each moment flowed into the next Emily felt as though she were moving through a dream, so that the grillwork of the elevator, a woman in bright pink satin, a white-bearded old gentleman, the elevator boy with the sad puckered face of a monkey, all were printed indelibly on the retina of her mind. The climate of her consciousness was not a waking one; this seemed to be a moment completely isolated in time, bearing no relationship to the days that had come before it or would come after.

"Would you like a drink?" Abe asked her as they stood for a moment in the center of the living room of his suite.

"Just water, please."

She stood watching him as he went into the bedroom and poured a glass of water from the carafe on his bed table. She noticed on the chiffonier the double frame containing pictures of Sam and Kristina, his first wife. She felt suddenly terribly sad.

He gave her the water and she stood there drinking it and he laughed and said, "Aren't you going to sit down and stay for a few minutes?"

She laughed, too, and handed him the glass. He put it down and then he turned to her and took her in his arms and kissed her.

"Abe—" she started, but he kissed her again, a long kiss, a passionate kiss, a returned kiss.

Then there was a moment of standing apart, of staring at each other rather incredulously, and then Abe pushed her gently towards the sofa. She forced herself to move away from him, saying, "No, Abe, this isn't a good idea."

"Why not?" he asked. "Why isn't it the best idea we've ever had? Why didn't we have it a long time ago?"

"We did," she said softly.

After a moment he took one of her hands and gently held it. "Yes. Why were we good about it till now?"

"We shouldn't have stopped being good," Emily said.

"We should have stopped long ago," Abe said, and drew her to him again.

She pressed her face into the darkness of his shoulder. "Oh, Abe, everything is so horribly complicated!" He didn't answer and after a while she said, "I love Courtney, you know."

"Yes, my darling, I know."

"I love him quite terribly."

"Yes, Emily. Kiss me."

And it was true that at that moment all that mattered was their arms about each other and their lips searching and this was still a moment outside time and as long as they could keep it outside time everything was possible.

And he was saying, "Emily, dear love, I've fought this subconsciously for years and I've fought it consciously all evening and I can't fight it any more. How could it possibly hurt anybody? Come."

She rose and stood for a moment swaying in an agony of indecision like a stick tossed into the ocean and flung towards the shore by the waves and sucked seawards again by the tide. But because there *was* the moment of indecision she was thrust over the edge of time again and she whispered, "I can't. I can't."

"Darling," he whispered. "Oh, darling, darling." His hand slipped gently inside her dress and rested, tender and strong, against her breast.

She spoke in a low, almost inaudible voice. "It isn't because I don't want to. I want to. Quite terribly. It's because of Courtney. If he were happy and secure it wouldn't matter so much. But he isn't. He's unhappy. Everything's gone wrong for him. I told you. And trying to write in that cold little box of a room. And worrying about money all the time. Oh, Abe, it's the wrong time for us to have stopped being good. Right now it would be—it would be a betrayal. And I can't, Abe. I can't."

She stood there in the middle of the room and at last he held his arms out to her, smiling at her with great tenderness as though she were a child. "Come and sit by me. That can't do any harm, can it? Just come and sit by me and let me hold you for a few minutes and then I'll take you home."

She ran quickly to him and sat enfolded in his arms, her eyes closed, suddenly completely relaxed and happy. She opened her eyes and looked at his face close up, seeing and loving with a great rush of tenderness the tired lines beneath the eyes, and the delicate, high-bridged nose, and the mouth, the mouth she had been kissing with such abandon; and she had never noticed before that the teeth were just slightly protruding, like a rabbit's, and in her mind she said—My bunny, oh, my darling bunny, and then half laughed as he touched his nose gently against hers and then kissed her again, pushing back passion with playfulness. The dark stuff of his suit felt warm and comforting against her cheek, and they sat there on the lumpy seat of the hotel sofa, kissing and laughing, and over and over Abe said, "Why am I so happy? Why am I so happy when I can't have you the way I want to?" and suddenly for Emily the effort to hold back, the wild struggle of body towards body, the need to crash through the barriers of individual flesh and blend together in one moment of ecstasy, ceased, and she was able to relax in his arms, for somehow at this moment she was spiritually fulfilled; a longing as strong as the physical one had been satisfied.

Finally she said, "Abe, the children will be out of the movies soon and Sam will be coming back and I must go."

With his cheek close against hers he murmured, "All right,

my darling, darling, my sweetheart, oh, my darling!'' (and it was as though having started calling her the words of love he could not stop and as though she were hearing the familiar words for the first time, as though they had never been said before).

They stood in front of the elevator and always she would remember the sound of the elevator and the green walls of the hall because she was standing there with him; and forever the trees in the gaudy urns in the lobby would be engraved on her mind and the fluted columns of the lounge and the concierge at the desk, because she was leaving the hotel with his hand against her arm. Everything they had touched that evening, everything they had seen, would forever be different, as though the lens of the camera had changed, as though Abe's presence had suddenly clarified the focus so that now she was seeing easily what had been blurred only a few hours before.

They left the hotel and walked down the driveway and at the great iron gates he stopped, saying, ''The trouble is that this isn't the end of this.'' He took her hand in his, then, and carefully drew the glove off and twined her fingers in his and then both their hands were plunged into the deep warmth of his pocket and they walked together that way down the steep path. Just as they reached the sharp turn before the villa he bent down and they kissed once more and then she went the last few yards alone.

✧ *Two* ✧

Virginia sat across from Mimi in the small dark dining room of the villa, dunking the heavy local bread into her café au lait. Everyone else had finished breakfast; Emily was in the village with Connie, doing the day's marketing; from Courtney's study they could hear the sound of the typewriter. Virginia put her elbows on the table and stared out the window, not seeing the iron fence that ran round the garden, nor the two dark pines, nor the white slope leading up to the hotel.

"Virginia, Virginia, strong and able,
Get your elbows off the table.
This is not a horse's stable,
This is a decent breakfast table,"

Mimi intoned.

"But we're not at school," Virginia said, "and I don't feel like minding my manners."

"What's the matter this morning? Got a new poem on your mind?"

Virginia shook her head. "I apologize for my father," she said shortly.

"For your father? For what?"

"The way he behaved last night."

Mimi reached for the bread, for the dish of apricot jam. "Virginia petunia, what on earth are you talking about?"

"His being drunk," Virginia said impatiently. "I apologize."

There was a moment of silence, during which Mimi finished her bread and jam, poured herself more coffee and milk. Then she said, "Virginia, are you absolutely mad?"

"No! What do you mean?"

"Your father wasn't drunk last night. He'd had maybe a drink too many. And he wasn't feeling very well. But he wasn't drunk."

"You don't have to see pink elephants to be drunk." Virginia stood up, collected her breakfast dishes and took them out to the kitchen. Then she came back in, picked up the coffee pot, said, "Want any more?" and without waiting for an answer started back to the kitchen.

"Look, Vee," Mimi said, pushing back her chair and following Virginia out to the sink, "you mean when we said good night to your father?"

"Naturally."

"You're cock-eyed. So he had a drink in his hand. He wasn't drunk!"

"For daddy he was. You don't know daddy very well. It was horrible and I said I apologized. Now let's talk about something else!" Virginia took the kettle from the back of the stove and sloshed water in the dishpan.

"Vee, you wrung-out tea bag," Mimi said, "what's there to get so excited about if your father gets a little tight? You act as though some terrible tragedy were taking place."

"You don't understand," Virginia said flatly.

"Well, I've seen *my* father drunk, and really drunk, plenty of times, if that's what you mean. Put him to bed plenty of times, too. It's nothing so frightful. He goes to a party and he has a good time and his glass gets filled a little too often and he has an even better time. It's not as though either of them was an alcoholic, our fathers, I· mean. They're just ordinary human beings."

"But daddy wasn't at a party," Virginia said. "Would you bring me the rest of the dishes from the dining room, please?" She leaned against the sink and said, softly, "Daddy's always been, as far as I'm concerned, perfect."

"Then you'd better grow up." Mimi plunked the sugar bowl down on the shelf.

"I don't mean I thought he *was* perfect," Virginia said slowly. "I mean just as far as I was concerned. But he's been different this winter."

"Or maybe you're the one who's different," Mimi suggested. "You've been away at school. You've grown and developed. That always makes you see things—and people—differently."

"No, it's daddy," Virginia said. "He's changed. Not just the way he talked last night. Or shutting himself up in his office; he always did that anyhow. But he doesn't laugh the way he used to. At table, I mean, he used to make jokes, and he used to play with Connie before she went up to bed—she used to ride on his shoulders and sometimes he used to dance with me. And he and mother laughed at things. And Christmas—we just seem to be forgetting Christmas this year." She glared at Mimi. "You're different here, Mimi. Not a bit the way you are at school."

"Oh, school," Mimi said. "At school I'm like a chameleon. I take on the protective coloring of the other kids. I forget I'm a potential human being and act like everybody else."

"But you're happy at school, aren't you?"

"Me? Oh, sure, I'm highly adaptable. I fought like a steer about going, but once I was there the only thing to do was enjoy it. As Confucius says, when rape is inevitable, relax and enjoy it."

"But you didn't seem to have any trouble at school," Virginia said wistfully, "right from the beginning. It was easy for you, wasn't it?"

"Easier than for you, I suppose, you mad, introverted poet. At school you're just like a porcupine, do you know that? Your quills are always out, preparing for the attack. But since you've been home you've kind of relaxed. One could almost stroke you without getting a palm full of spines. Up to this nonsense about your father. You're all bristly again. Come on, let's go for a walk. We can finish up these dishes later. Your mother put lots of holly around yesterday and she said we'd all fix the créche soon. She's not forgetting Christmas. And your father has a sore throat. No one feels like cracking jokes with a sore throat. As for his being perfect, how deadly dull to have a perfect father. I'd loathe Jake if he were perfect. But he isn't. Gad no. Come on, old thing, cheer up. I think your father's quite a boy. I should imagine he'd make a terrific teacher. Do his students adore him?"

"I don't know. I guess so. I mean, yes, of course."

"Sometimes," Mimi said in exasperation, "I wonder why I ever took you up. You're incredible, you're so backward. If I didn't think there was somebody in there, behind that blank, I'd drop you like a hot cake. And your mother, too. She's never grown up either, has she?''

''What do you mean?''

''Oh, she has an aura of innocence about her, just like you. Almost as though she were asleep and waiting to be wakened, like Sleeping Beauty. I like her, you understand. I like her very much. But she's nothing like Clare.''

''I don't imagine many mothers are,'' Virginia said a little tartly.

''Your mother likes Mr. Fielding a lot, doesn't she?'' Mimi asked, not accepting the reproof.

''Sure, I guess so,'' Virginia said. ''Mother and daddy knew him in New York. Pretty well, I guess. But they had lots of friends there. Not like here. We used to have sort of open house every Sunday night for faculty and students and anybody else who wanted to come. They were fun. Lots of times mother would play the piano for them to sing—all kinds of songs, even opera. But especially at Christmas, and then it was carols. She hasn't played any carols this year.''

''Did Mr. Fielding come to the open houses?''

''Oh, sure.''

''And Sam?''

''Oh, Sam was usually away at school.''

''Well, thank God for the thé dansant at the hotel this afternoon,'' Mimi said. ''That'll take your mind off your woes. A triangular date, wouldn't you call it? Except Sam promised he'd try to fix us up with someone else. There're quite a few kids at the hotel—notice them at dinner last night, and coming out of the cinema? So he ought to be able to grab someone halfway decent. I suppose he's off skiing with his father this morning. Come on, Virginia, let's go!''

Emily returned from the village with Connie, the child tired and dragging on her arm; and surely the weight of a roly-poly four year old could not be that great? With Connie following her with a dustcloth, she swept all the rooms, violently. She prepared a vegetable soup for lunch, went to the piano and started the Bach Prelude and Fugue in E^b minor.

''I want to play,'' Connie said. ''May I play, too, mama?'' She clambered up into Emily's lap.

Emily took the child's fingers and picked out ''Away in a Manger.''

"Now let's sing it," Connie said. " 'Away in a manger, no crib for a bed . . .' You sing, too, mama."

"I don't think I can sing this morning, Connie," Emily said.

"Why not?"

"You color mama a nice picture with your crayons," Emily suggested. "Sit at the table in the dining room and make mother a picture while she plays the piano for a little while."

"Sing me a song first. Sing 'I Met Her in Venezuela.' "

Emily got halfway through the song. She got to "When the moon was out to sea and she was taking leave of me . . ." and then suddenly she knew that she must cry. It had nothing to do with her mind or her emotions; it was a purely physical sensation, like being sick, and that would have been preferable, because if she had rushed to the bathroom and heaved it would have been a natural thing, blamable on an upset stomach, on the rich food at the casino the night before; but if she burst suddenly into tears it would throw Connie into consternation and distress Courtney. . . .

She walked quickly down the cold back hall to Courtney's office and knocked on the door. His room itself was warm from a small portable stove, and he was busy at his desk. "Court, I'm sorry to bother you," she said. "I forgot some things I need in the village and it's too cold to take Connie out again."

"Can't you put it off?" Courtney asked.

"No. I don't ask you to keep an eye out for her very often and she won't bother you. She'll be at the dining-room table with her crayons. I won't be any longer than necessary." She could not help the sharpness of her voice. If she did not speak with this jerky definiteness she could not control the tears. She settled Connie at the table, then pulled on her coat and cap and went out, wearing spiked boots, not stopping for skis, and for a moment the cold brilliant air slapped the tears back, but she knew the lull was only temporary. She looked up at the mountains, blindingly pure in the morning sunlight, and remembered, as though it had been aeons ago, looking with Abe at the mountains the night before. And then the tears rushed on her once more and where could she go? Where could she go to get rid of this elemental weeping?

Between the sanatorium and the outlying chalets was a small Catholic church, and she pushed blindly towards it. For a moment she thought the heavy doors were locked, but then she managed to push one open, and she penetrated into the darkness that smelled faintly of incense and damp wool. A few of the candles in front of the Virgin were lit, but there was no one in the church, and she fell into one of the small back chairs and put her hands over her face and the sobs tore out of her. She tried to keep them quiet while all she wanted was to be able to howl out loud as custom permits only small children to do; but she was afraid that the curé might be somewhere about or that someone else would come in, so she tried to push the weeping back into her throat till it threatened to choke her. Once for an uncontrollable moment she heard with surprise a burst of noisy sobs, but her very astonishment at the sound helped her to control it. If a voice had come out of the dimness in the back of the church asking her why she was crying she would not have known. Her only thought was the fear of being discovered; the tears were still entirely a physical thing.

At last the sobs wore themselves out and she leaned her head on her hands in exhaustion.

Courtney.

Courtney. When she thought about Courtney she came to a terrifying mental block. It was Courtney she loved, Courtney who was part of her life as the children were part of her life. . . .

But what had happened the night before she would not give up in her mind any more than a wanderer lost in the desert could turn away from an oasis.

She left the church and climbed, on up past the chalets, past Kaarlo's chalet, past the chalet that had been Gertrude's and Henri's, on up the whiteness beyond, through the dark shadows of the pines where for a moment the wind ceased to batter her, up into the naked snow fields above; for this swift climbing, pushing into the wind up the mountain, was the only possible solution to the sobs which threatened to rack her, rising like blood into her throat. If she exhausted her body by climbing, perhaps she would also exhaust this unbidden, incomprehensible need to cry; perhaps then she would be able to think only of Abe's lips against hers, his hands against her body, be able to think of it only as an isolated moment, a single event in time, an island quite different from and unaffected by the waters of daily living which surrounded it.

A few sharp, icy flakes of snow fell, but it was too cold for snow; the sky seemed frozen lead above her with a faint sickly splotch of yellow where the sun skulked. At the foot of a high rock formation she passed a small, cold-looking figure of a saint, barely sheltered from wind and weather, with snow piled about her feet and touching the faded-rose hem of her robe. She passed a few solitary skiers, several groups of advanced students with their ski instructors; she did not see Abe and Sam.

Above her, like a charcoal drawing on the snow, were the dark outlines of the first hut; she paused a moment, her heart thumping heavily against her ribs from exertion, and saw a single skier coming towards her; it was Kaarlo. He hailed her and came skiing down to her, sweeping to a stop at her feet with a great spume of snow. "Emily," he said, flashing her his quick shining smile. "How nice to see you! What are you doing all alone up here?"

"Just climbing," she said vaguely, smiling at him.

"How long have you got?" (How quickly they learned about each other there in the small village—who was tied down by children or ancient furnaces or jobs or invalid husbands; who was free to come and go as he chose.)

"Till lunchtime."

"Well, then, let us keep each other company for a while," he suggested. "Or would you prefer to be alone?"

She knew that with Kaarlo it would have been perfectly all right and understood if she said that she did not feel like talking and had come up to be solitary, but suddenly she was glad of his presence. She seemed to dwindle in size while the mountains grew enormous and the expanse of snow stretched out to infinity on all sides, snow and snow-filled sky moving one into the other. She shivered in her warm ski clothes, asking Kaarlo, "How do you happen to be free?"

"I've been off with Abe and Sam since six, but the kid's got a game leg and it started to bother him, so Abe took him back to the hotel. Abe and I are going off again this afternoon." He sounded and looked completely happy and free, his eyes against the deep tan of his skin shining like two chinks of sky; then suddenly his face clouded. "I suppose I should go right down to Gertrude, but she's in one of her moods and I think I'll give myself a few more minutes of relaxation first. Let's go up to the hut and I'll light a fire and you can stretch out on one of the bunks and rest—you do look tired, Emily—and we'll talk. Isn't that an excellent idea?"

"A noble idea," she agreed.

At the hut Kaarlo took off his skis and leaned them against the sheltered side where the roof extended deeply beyond the wall and long blue icicles hung, frozen hard as steel. Inside

Emily sat on one of the bunks while Kaarlo took some of the kindling that was always ready and laid a fire in the stone fireplace.

"Put one of the blankets over you until the place warms up," he said. "They're in the lockers under the bunks."

She leaned over and pulled out one of the blankets and wrapped herself up in it; it was rough and heavy and comforting and when it touched her cheek it reminded her flesh of the feel of Abe's suit the night before. Kaarlo sat on an upturned bucket and fed the fire till he had a high, hot blaze.

"I find," he said, speaking into the fire, away from Emily, "that when I'm looking into a fire or when I'm alone on the mountains, I do a good deal more thinking than I'd like to do."

"I know, Kaarlo," she murmured drowsily, exhausted by weeping and climbing, lulled by the warmth of the blanket and the fire and the lights and shadows of the flames shooting up over the ceiling.

If only she could talk to Kaarlo.

If she could say to him—Look, Kaarlo, I need help desperately. Something has happened that I didn't want to have happen—no, that's not right; I did want it to happen, but I should never have let it happen. Anyhow it *did* happen, and here I am with it, and I don't know what to do. Oh, Kaarlo, I don't know what to do. Help me, help me!

But none of this could she say to Kaarlo; they had already talked together too much; they knew too much about each other to let it be possible. In the first days of the winter when Emily had brushed up on her skiing by taking a few lessons with Kaarlo they had discovered immediately that they could talk; in the evenings, listening to records with Gertrude dozing on the couch, or, if Courtney were there, with Gertrude and Courtney playing chess, they had talked. So she could not talk to him now.

"Emily," he said, breaking into her thoughts, "what am I to do with my Gertrude?" He pronounced Gertrude the French way, with the G softened and the whole rather harsh name suddenly become melodic and beautiful.

She did not answer, but lay there on the bunk, watching him, waiting for him to continue.

"I don't know how to make her happy," he said somberly.

"I think you do make her happy, Kaarlo," Emily said gently. "As happy as Gert can be made."

"If she is to get well," Kaarlo said, "she should go back into the sanatorium. Clément has told her that again and again. But he cannot force her to go in against her will and she refuses. He has told me that several times he has almost given up her case. It isn't money that makes her so stubborn about it. She isn't wealthy, but I know there's some that comes from America and there's what Henri left her and whatever I have saved she could have, she knows that. But Clément told her she should have two years in the sanatorium and she cannot face it. She who faced so much cannot face that.''

''You can't persuade her?''

''All she says is that I am trying to get rid of her. You see how hopeless it is. And this drinking of hers—she is so clever about it. I try to watch her but it's far too often that she manages to get more than she should have. She is not a drunk, Emily, but she could be.''

''I imagine most of us could,'' Emily said, ''given the right circumstances.''

''We should not be living in the chalet together,'' Kaarlo said. ''She has strict orders from Clément, but I am a man and she is a woman and it is not always possible to obey.''

''I know,'' Emily said softly, and shivered.

''We do not come from the same world, Gertrude and I,'' Kaarlo said. ''My mother was a Finn and my father a mountain guide before me. Gertrude and I have the resistance common to both of us but that is all. I don't understand my Gertrude, Emily. I don't understand her at all. All I can do is love, and love isn't enough.''

''Of course it is.'' Emily swung round on the bunk, keeping her legs still wrapped in the blanket, her feet on the floor, her elbows on her knees. ''Do you think any human being ever understands another human being? I don't know Courtney and I've found this winter that I know him even less than I thought I did. I don't know what makes him tick and I never have. Even the people we love most we can't know, Kaarlo, nor they us, and it seems to me that the better we know someone, the longer we've loved him, the less we're able to understand him.''

Kaarlo nodded in assent. The big log on the fire had caught now, and he turned round on the bucket and faced Emily. ''You will forgive me,'' he said, ''but Courtney doesn't seem happy.''

''He's not,'' Emily agreed readily. ''He's quite desperately unhappy in a quiet sort of way. You say you can't help Gert and love isn't enough, and I though I think love *ought* to be enough, I know what you mean. I can't help Courtney, either.''

Kaarlo looked at her thoughtfully for a moment; then he stood up. ''I'm going to make us some coffee.''

Emily laughed. ''When I think of this winter I'll always think of coffee. It seems to me we do nothing but drink it.''

''It's a companionable thing, to talk over a cup of coffee,'' Kaarlo said.

Emily watched him hang the blackened pot over the fire, get the can of coffee from the shelf. ''I wish you could know Courtney the way he really is,'' she said. ''He used to be a person of—of action. That's hard to believe, seeing him just this winter, isn't it, when we can't even get him to put on skis except to go to Madame Berigot's for a paper. And he had a—a tremendous strength.'' They were silent, as Kaarlo dropped the coffee in the pot, then set it down on the great stone slab of hearth to brew. Emily said, ''We lost a little girl, you know, two years younger than Virginia. Pneumonia after an appendectomy, and none of the drugs helped her. While she was so ill it was Courtney who kept me going, who made it possible for me to be brave. He was magnificent, Kaarlo. He was—he was completely *Courtney*. But after it was all over he wouldn't let down for even a moment. He was *too* strong. And after a while it was as though he'd simply gone away. As though his body were there, doing the necessary things, but Courtney wasn't there. It was a long time before he began to come back, to be himself again. After Connie was born—when she began to laugh and play, and she was an adorable baby, Kaarlo—he began to take an interest in her. And then he began reading the little verses Virginia was writing, and gradually he was all right. But now he seems to be withdrawing. He seems to be going away again. And I don't know how to stop him.''

Kaarlo filled a mug with the steaming, fragrant coffee, and handed it to her, his blue eyes kind, concerned; but he did not speak. Emily got up and went to the window, carrying the hot, thick white cup, and stood looking out.

''It's like a kind of death,'' she said, and shivered. ''No. I don't really mean that. I don't want to mean it. . . . I suppose death will always be for me the white corridors of a hospital and the lights beginning to grow dim with dawn. I wasn't even with her when she died. I'd gone out in the corridor to have a cigarette. I smoked, then. I suppose that's why I don't, now. It means death to me. And when I take a cigarette I'm somehow defying death, stamping on his toes, spitting in his face. But I have to be feeling very full of life to accept a cigarette. . . . I stood there at the end of the corridor smoking and trying to pray and watching the dawn come. One of the doctors had told us that if she could get through another night she might have a chance. I was trying so hard to pray that my body, the whole of me, was nothing but part of a prayer. Then Courtney came out of Alice's room and came down the corridor to me and put his arm about me, and I looked round and saw his face. . . . We had to go home and tell Virginia. . . . We'd just abandoned Virginia in a panic, alone in a strange city—it was while we were in Washington—with no real friends to turn to, left her with a neighbor, a perfectly kind woman, too kind, and stupid, and unimaginative. And a smeller for death, a nose for death like a rat's for garbage or a vulture's for carrion. She knew before we'd come up in the elevator, before we'd opened the door. She flung her arms up and cried, 'God's will be done!' and burst into tears. Virginia as a child used to have quite frightening tantrums and she flew into one then, hitting the woman, and screaming, 'It was not God's will! How dare you say God would kill Alice!' And I remember the woman saying, 'God calls His own unto Him,' and a cup of coffee got spilled— thrown—all over the rug and I remember trying to clean it up, and Virginia screaming and screaming. . . . So we didn't have to tell her after all, and perhaps rage was the best thing that could have happened to her. . . ." She shook her head, turned away from the window. "I'm sorry. Death isn't unique with me. There's not a single person in the world who hasn't had some kind of contact with it. I know you've had your share. I'm upset this morning. You know I don't—I don't like to talk about things. I'm sorry—"

He cut her off. "It's important that we understand these things, that we face them, see what they've done to us. Just as it's important for me to understand what our situation has done to Gertrude and me if we are to work out any solution at all. It isn't difficult for me to see why Courtney would withdraw. That's what I do sometimes, too, when I go running to the mountains. I'm lucky. I have a place to withdraw to."

"But you come back."

"Courtney came back."

"But he has gone again."

"He will come back again," Kaarlo said. "With you to help him he will come back again."

"But I can't help him, Kaarlo," Emily said in a low voice. "I'm absolutely useless to him. About the only good I am to him is to feed him—and a competent servant could undoubtedly do it better—only I don't cost as much." She laughed a harsh, unnatural laugh.

"You know that's not so, Emily," Kaarlo said.

"But it is. I've never had any illusions about my—my importance. But he doesn't need me, Kaarlo; he doesn't need me at all. It's as though I were in a different town, a different country, much less the same house with him."

"Isn't it perhaps because he's trying to protect you?" Kaarlo asked.

"Being completely shut out isn't being protected. If a marriage is worth anything, things have to be shared, the bad things as well as the good. Sometimes with Virginia and Connie he shares himself. I mean he lets himself relax with them, he gives something of himself to them, but never to . . . He's always wanted me to be self-sufficient. And I've tried to be. But the more self-sufficient I become the more separate I become. And that isn't good for a marriage."

"Each branch of a tree is separate," Kaarlo said, "but they belong to the same tree."

"I seem to have become separated from my tree, then." She stopped, listening as the church clock struck, the sound barely rising to them, the notes dim against the snow. "I didn't realize it was so late," she said. "Please forgive me, Kaarlo." Tears rushed again, against her bidding, to her eyes. "I'm not a strong person, Kaarlo! I'm so terribly, terribly weak! And I have such terrible, terrible need of strength."

"Why do you say that, Emily?" Kaarlo asked gently. "I've always thought of you as a quiet little rock."

"And rocks have no need of forbidden fruit, have they? That's what I must be, Kaarlo, a rock."

"Emily, has something happened to upset you? Something particular?"

She stood up, not answering. "Kaarlo, we've got to hurry. At least I have. The family will be wondering where on earth I am."

"Take my skis, then," Kaarlo said, "and ski down as far as my chalet. Just lean them against the shed. I'll stay and put out the fire and come along in a few minutes."

She started to protest, but he cut her short, pushing her out of the hut and calling after her, "Why don't you come listen to records tonight? I have a new Mozart. Gertrude will call you."

But instead of going directly to the kitchen when she got home she went to Courtney's workroom, knocked and entered, shutting the door behind her. He finished writing something, then looked up.

"I'm back," she said. "Are you in the middle of a train of thought? Could I talk to you for a few minutes?"

"Is it important?" he asked.

"Yes. Desperately."

"Okay, let's have it," he said. "You look like a solemn little kid in college on the mat for not having a term paper in on time."

There was only the one chair to Courtney's desk in the room, but she needed the effort of standing to give her the strength to speak. "Court, I'm frightened," she said.

"Frightened? Why?"

Behind her back she twisted her hands together. "About us."

He leaned back in his chair. "What about us?"

"Court, you don't need me any more, and I need to be needed."

"Are you crazy?"

"Court," she said despairingly, "there has to be sharing and—and outgoing in a marriage, and you—"

"What?" he demanded, his voice growing hard.

"It isn't strength to be quite so strong, it's weakness. When you're unhappy you—you shouldn't keep it all to yourself—not if you love someone. You have to share the difficulties as well as the happiness."

He turned his eyes away. "Why should I be unhappy?"

"You know why! We both know why! It was hell for you to be forced out of a job you loved. You pretend it doesn't hurt and I know it does and until we both admit it it's as though there were a wall between us." He said nothing, but continued to stare away from her, rigid with resistance to her words, and she raised her voice as though he had retreated from her physically as well as mentally. "I know I'm being selfish to make this scene! I know you hate scenes and so do I, but I have to try this time. I have to! Don't you see that I want you to be selfish, too? It would be easier for me. For both of us. And if only your work can help you, if I can't help at all, then—"

At last he broke in on her, swinging round violently in his chair. "You think losing the job was my fault, don't you?" he shouted.

Suddenly weak, she leaned against the wall. "No," she said in a low voice. "But I don't think it was all Tommy O'Hara's, either."

"Did I ever say I did?"

"No. You didn't. You didn't say anything. That's just it. But lots of people said it for you."

"Oh, so you think I'm playing the martyr."

"No, Court, no! That's not what I mean. It's not what I wanted to talk about. It's us."

He stood up roughly, knocking over his chair. "For Christ's sake, Emily! Why do you have to do this!"

She whispered, "I had to try because . . ." and her whisper died out.

"I have to work it out in my own way," he said. "You have to leave me alone. I can't have anybody. I don't want anybody. Leave me alone, Emily."

"But I have been," she said, trying desperately to stop her lips from trembling. "That's what I've been trying to do all winter. And now I—now I think it was the wrong thing to do."

"You think what you're doing now is any better?"

"It—it—" she started, stumbling, and he broke in.

"It's my problem, Emily."

"But it isn't," she said. "It's my problem, too. You aren't living your life alone. It's my life, and the children's. What affects you affects all of us. If I feel I'm of no use to you, that I can't share, then—" She stopped because she knew that she could not go on without weeping.

"Then what?" he asked.

She shook her head, trying to force back the tears. "I don't know. I don't know."

He turned away from her again, saying finally, "If you haven't any more to say, I have some work to get through before lunch."

She whispered, "Do you love me, Court?"

But if he heard he gave no answer, sitting there, turned away from her, leafing through some papers, and at last she left him and went out to the kitchen.

After lunch Virginia went up early to dress for the thé dansant, running up the stairs silently in the old white moccasins she usually slipped into after she had pulled off her boots.

—Mother's amber beads, she thought. I bet she'd let me borrow them for this afternoon.

She stood for a moment at the top of the stairs, listening to the sounds of the house. Downstairs she could hear Mimi talking to Connie, could hear the sound of her father's typewriter; upstairs, nothing except the sound of her old alarm clock ticking loudly against the silence. She moved, quiet as an Indian in the soft-soled moccasins, to the door of her parents' room. It was pushed to, but not shut tightly, and as she leaned against it it swung open and there upon the bed she saw Emily, lying face downwards, her arms flung out, her body across the bed in an abandonment of despair, her eyes closed but with traces of tears still clinging to lashes and cheeks. Unseen, unheard, Virginia backed out, trembling, and went into her own room.

She stood at the window in the room already beginning to darken with the approach of evening. The garden lay still and white under the snow, only hummocks and ridges showing where there might be bushes and flowers. Stars were already beginning to flicker, disappear, then shine steadily as darkness seeped into the valley. Up the mountains the great hotel lay sprawled in indistinct shadows, above it the sanatorium, and lights were coming on in their windows; and a stranger would not know which was which, which the hotel where there was dancing and champagne and gaiety, and which the sanatorium where there was illness and pain. She stared at the two buildings, trying to blot out with their image that of her mother flung across the bed, staring until the outlines of the buildings blurred, merged into each other, separated, blurred again.

—I wish I were back at school, she thought.

And then—My stomach hurts (transferring the pain to something physical).

She took out of her bottom bureau drawer the small pile of Christmas presents she had bought or made, and put them on her bed and stood looking down at them for comfort, each one tied up carefully in a different kind of Christmas paper. She picked up the last present that remained unwrapped, a small bottle of "4711" eau de cologne for her mother, and turned it over and over in her hand, reading and rereading the inscription. *"No. 4711, Ferd. Müllens, Inc., always the first prize. Jedesmal den ersten preis. Toujours le premier prix."* Then she wrapped it up, slowly, and put all the presents away, shutting the drawer as Mimi came in.

While they were dressing, Emily knocked and there she stood with the amber beads, saying, "Vee, I thought these might help with the velvet dress," and her face was freshly powdered and you could not tell that so short a time ago there had been tears on her cheeks.

"I was going to ask you for them," Virginia said.

Emily laughed. "Two minds with but a single thought. Obviously they were meant for your dress, but mind you, I'm only lending them to you. I'm very fond of them myself."

"Put on Vee's lipstick for her, will you, Mrs. Bowen?" Mimi asked. "She never puts on enough."

Sam was waiting for them, looking about anxiously each time the great doors opened, his face breaking into a delighted grin as he saw them coming up the marble steps. Behind him was another boy, considerably taller and thinner than Sam, aggressively good-looking and expensively dressed, a studied look of boredom on his features and cream oil on his hair.

"Mimi, Virginia, I want you to meet Beanie. Snider Bean. They're staying here for the hols, too."

Beanie shook hands, his grip a little too forceful, his camaraderie a little too hearty. They went, the four of them, towards the sound of a small orchestra and cups clinking and voices speaking rather loudly, a conglomeration of languages, French, English, German, Italian. They sat down at one of the small tables. Beanie pulled out Virginia's chair politely, then turned his attention to Mimi. Sam's attention was already there, his gaze on Mimi's golden hair, always a little wild, on her gold-flecked eyes, her wide, smiling mouth: everything about Mimi was a little over-generous, a little out-size. Virginia drank two cups of tea and ate some of the petit fours and tried to smile and look as though she were happy. Sam turned to her suddenly, and she was grateful, at the same time that she resented the fact that he was talking to her mainly because he felt sorry for her.

"Hey, how about a dance, Virginia?" he said.

She dropped her eyes, started to say—I don't dance very well, then remembered Mimi saying to her, time and time again at school, *"Qui s'excuse, s'accuse,"* looked up, smiled despairingly, and said, "I'd love to."

It was Sam who said, "I don't dance very well," but so gaily it didn't seem to be an excuse at all. "I love barging about the floor, so I hope you don't mind if I stamp all over you. Just scream if I break your foot. One day I have hopes I'll catch on and make an elegant hoofer."

"I think you dance very well," Virginia said, tripping over his feet. Someone stuck an elbow into her neck, and Sam's heel came down on one of her toes and then she stumbled and he had to hold her to keep her from falling. "Maybe we could make a comedy routine out of this," she said desperately.

Sam chuckled. "You're quite a girl, Virginia. I like you. And you're good for Mimi. Mimi could go off the deep end without any trouble and that would be too bad. You're sort of ballast for her and that's a big help."

"Mimi's the one who's helped me," Virginia said. "I'd be miserable at school if it weren't for Mimi."

"How come?"

"Oh, I was completely Out. You know. And then Mimi took me up and now I'm In."

"Let's go back to the table," Sam said. "We seem to be a menace to everybody on the floor. We'll try again later."

They passed Mimi and Beanie, dancing tidily, not bumping into anybody, keeping their feet to themselves.

Sam pulled out Virginia's chair and the waiter brought them more tea. "How did Mimi come to take you up?" he asked.

"Oh, she discovered I write poetry. She likes people who're peculiar."

"Are you so peculiar?"

"The girls at school think I am. At least they used to. They don't so much any more."

"How did Mimi discover about this poetry business?" Sam asked.

—Golly, you're kind, Sam, Virginia thought. You could so easily sit and just drink tea and eat cakes and wait for Mimi and not sound interested a bit. "Well, I was going to give her a history assignment she didn't have straight. It was in study hall and I passed her the wrong notebook."

"You mean you gave her a notebook with your poems in?"

"Oh, no, I don't write them in any special notebook. This was in my geometry scratch book and it's the same color as my assignment book."

"What was this poem about?"

"Oh—the Earl of Northumberland. We'd been doing him in history. I like to write poems about people."

"Do you happen to know this poem by heart?"

"I—oh, no." Virginia blushed furiously.

Sam grinned at her. "You do, too. Come on, Vee. Out with it."

"I—it's—it's really kind of silly." *Qui s'excuse* . . .

"Don't be modest, Vee. If Mimi thought it was good it must be."

"I'm not sure she thought it was good. She just thought it was kind of peculiar. But I'll say it to you if you like."

"I do like."

Virginia stared down at the table:

"Northumberland robed in crimson, velvet, and gold,
Leans his head in its whiteness upon cold stone
And in the lingering silence frail and alone
Feels his bones stiffen and watches his mind grow old."

"Don't mumble," Sam said.

Virginia raised her head and her voice, though still a little shaky with embarrassment, came clearer:

"Tracing the lines on the walls so damp and cold
That the moisture trickles down, hearing the drone
Of the Thames ever flowing below, he drops a groan
For Northumberland young and aware, for North-
umberland bold."

"It's a sonnet," she interpolated. "There are six more lines."

"Go on," Sam said.

"Northumberland leaves without faith in himself,
or friends
To tell him good-bye. He hears the key in the rust
While somewhere Mary his wife in a velvet frock
Is pacing, tearless, alone. Northumberland bends,
Traces and kisses a cross in the blinded dust,
Then quietly kneels and puts his head on the block."

"Say, that's cool," Sam said, as her eyes dropped to the white tablecloth again. "When you said you wrote poetry I thought it was going to be soppy girl stuff, but that's okay."

Virginia's green eyes lit with pleasure; now her smile was

spontaneous and happy as she looked up and saw Mimi and Snider Bean coming back to the table.

"Hi, Mimi Opp," she called gaily.

"Mimi Opp?" Beanie asked as he seated Mimi. "Opp your last name?"

"No. Oppenheimer. Miriam Oppenheimer."

"Why does she call you Opp, then?"

Mimi's face became set. "It's simply a nickname," she said. "Like calling Virginia, Vee."

"Hey, let's dance, Mimi," Sam said.

Virginia watched them move onto the dance floor. Mimi's head rose above Sam's, the rather violent blond of her hair shining above his brown crew cut; but they did not seem clumsy, dancing together.

"You want to dance?" Beanie asked Virginia.

Virginia knew that dancing with Snider Bean would not be like dancing with Sam. "Not just now, thanks," she said. "I'm hungry," and reached for a tart she did not want. All around them in the salon were noise and laughter, and darkness gathering outside, pressing against the windows, trying to enter.

"Attractive, your friend, what's her name now?" Beanie asked.

"Mimi."

"No, her real name."

"Miriam Oppenheimer."

"That's why you call her Mimi Opp, isn't it?"

"What do you mean?"

"To help her get away with it."

"Get away with what?"

"Come on, stop kidding around."

"I'm not kidding. I don't know what you're talking about." Without quite knowing why, she began to get angry. She looked about the room as though for help and all around her she saw only laughing faces, except for one dark-haired woman who sat at a table alone, staring unseeing at her reflection in the black glass of window. Waiters moved about quickly with plates of pastry, pots of tea, coffee, whipped cream, their steps light, assured; and moving slowly among them was Madame Pedroti in her black dress and black shining hair, seeing everything, her little black eyes darting about, quick, quick, while her great body moved ponderously between the tables.

Beanie smiled at Virginia and it was the kind of smile, eager and cruel and also a little ashamed, that she had seen on the lips and in the eyes of some of the girls at school when they were about to tell a dirty story. "You know perfectly well what I mean," Beanie said. " 'How odd of God,' etc."

"How odd of God what?" Now she knew, but she had to make him say it before she would believe it.

"She's one of the Chosen, isn't she?" Beanie asked. He spoke quietly, pleasantly, but it seemed to Virginia that his voice was enormously loud, that everybody on the dance floor, everybody sitting at the tables, all the waiters, Madame Pedroti, everybody must hear the monstrous things he was saying.

Now her voice was cold. "I'm afraid I still don't understand." He would have to say it. He would have to say it out loud for them all to hear. She would not allow him to slide out of this with implications and innuendoes.—Oh, Mimi, I'm not saying the right things, what do I say to him?

"Oh, sure," Beanie said. "She's a friend of yours and I admire you for sticking up for her. But just between us I think it's a bit of a stinking trick to pretend you aren't."

Virginia stood up. "I don't think anybody around here's pretending anything. Except maybe you."—I'm handling this so badly, she thought. This is Mimi he's talking about—Mimi!

She grabbed her coat from the back of her chair.

"Hey, where are you going?"

Virginia was trembling. "I don't enjoy the company of slimy people."

She fled the room.

On the dance floor Sam and Mimi did not see her go. But Sam said, "Mimi, you're a gorgeous dancer, but I've got to stop in a minute. Leg's bothering me."

"What's the matter with your leg?" Mimi asked quickly.

"Polio when I was six. It's swell now, though. Just sometimes like in dancing or something I use different muscles and it gets tired."

"Let's go sit down, then. Come on."

At the table Snider Bean sat placidly eating.

"Where's Virginia?" Mimi demanded.

"Don't know. Walked out on me. Went home to mama, I guess."

"Why?"

"Got in a huff."

"You let her go alone?" Sam asked.

"Why not? Said she didn't care for my company."

Mimi sat down. "This is very unlike Virginia," she said. "What happened?"

"I told you. Got in a stuffy huff."

"I still think you ought to have walked her home," Sam said. Beanie helped himself to the last cake on the plate.

"What did she get upset about?" Mimi persisted.

"What's all the fuss? Can't a girl get upset without your acting like something world shattering's happened? Girls are always getting in huffs and pulling out."

"But not Virginia," Mimi said. "I happen to know Virginia rather well."

"Oh, sure. Your kind always think they know everything." Mimi looked at him sharply.

"Now what exactly did you mean by that?" Sam asked.

Beanie flung up his hands in mock dismay. "Everybody's picking on me!" he squeaked, falsetto. "Mummy! Mummy! The nasty childrens is being mean to poor l'il Beanie." He stood up, bowed politely to Mimi. "Uncle Beanie will go find your little red-headed vixen. Uncle Beanie always does the right thing. Farewell, *mes enfants.*"

They sat still a moment, watching him go. Then Sam asked, "What was that about?"

Mimi shrugged. "I can guess. I suppose it's occurred to you that I'm Jewish?"

For a moment Sam looked blank. "I hadn't thought about it. You mean you think Beanie—"

"Oh, sure," Mimi said, shrugging again, pushing it off.

Sam flushed with anger. "Golly, I'm sorry, Mimi. What a stinker. I picked a lemon."

"Oh, he's all right in his place," Mimi said, "only it isn't dug yet. Tell me about your leg, Sam."

"I told you I had polio. Now I'm okay. That's all there is to it."

"Look, tea bag," Mimi said, "I'm interested from a clinical point of view. How much paralysis did you have? What did they do for you? Etc. Now talk."

Sam looked angry again for a moment. Then he said, "Okay, then, you asked for it. But I don't generally go around talking about it. They said I'd never walk again without braces. But dad said to heck with that. I spent a year at Warm Springs. Then when I got back dad used to go swimming with me every day during his lunch hour. Then he got a fellow who used to be a circus performer to come work with me. Gus Swann. Greatest guy in the world. Everybody laughed at me, kidded me, nobody was sorry for anybody. What a guy my father is, Mimi. I could be a mess right now if it hadn't been for him. There was another kid at Warm Springs the same time I was, not as badly paralyzed. He still walks with a brace. While me, I'm so nearly normal I can say to heck with the one percent. Thanks to dad.''

Mimi looked down at her hands. She said, ''I expect your father's pretty proud of you.''

''Oh, go play in the traffic,'' Sam said. ''I told you it wasn't me. It was dad. And my grandmother. I lived with her while dad was overseas, and she kept me right at it.''

''All right,'' Mimi said. ''Don't take any of the credit. So you're just an old coward. How do you manage skiing? Don't your knees bother you?''

''Some. I tumble a lot. Kaarlo was showing me some good tricks this morning to help give me control. Swimming's my best thing, though. I feel as though I could swim the Atlantic if necessary.''

''Sincerely hope it won't be necessary. So go on, tell me more.''

''Why?'' Sam asked.

''I'm turning orthopedics over in my mind. I don't think research is my field. So what else?''

''When I was about ten,'' Sam said, ''they took a hunk of bone out of my good leg because the other one wasn't growing fast enough. That's why I'll never be as tall as dad.'' He looked down at the tablecloth, at a stained spot where Beanie had spilled cherry tart. ''Or as tall as you.''

''I'm much too big,'' Mimi said. ''I have all kinds of complexes about it. You're not short, Sam, only next to people like me, and when I'm with you I never think of you as being shorter than I am. Size is largely a—a quality of spirit rather than body, anyhow. So what are you going to do, after school and everything?''

Sam shook his head, then looked up and signalled a waiter to bring them another pot of tea. ''Don't know,'' he said. ''I have another year, though I really should be through by now. But I dropped back a couple of years what with being in the hospital and stuff. Anyhow I'll have to do a couple of years' hitch in the army, so maybe I'll enlist when I get through school instead of waiting to be drafted, and get it in before college. Good idea as anything. Nothing's struck me yet as being the Thing, the way you are about medicine, no questions, there it is. I don't see any point to living and doing something that you can't believe in as a way of life.''

"Lots of people do," Mimi said.

Across the table the solitary woman Virginia had noticed pushed back her chair and started out. She had been drinking and she moved a little unsteadily and as she passed their table they heard her murmur, *"Charmant, ses petites, touts à fait charmants."*

Sam, looking embarrassed, asked abruptly, "Hey, Mimi, this religion deal, how about it? I mean, what do you think?"

"I'm an atheist," Mimi said flatly. "With Clare a Catholic and Jake a Jew it's sort of the obvious conclusion for me."

"Why?" Sam asked. "Do Clare and Jake—that's your parents, isn't it?"

"Yes."

"Do they practise their religions?"

"Clare's religion is science and Jake's is music. So they practise them. How about you, Sam? What brought this up? Are you pious?"

"I'm not an atheist, if that's what you mean." Sam's voice was slightly defensive. "I believe in God, a sort of incomprehensible God, but still God with a captial G. At home dad and I go to the Episcopal church. St. Mary the Virgin. Or sometimes the Community Church, a Unitarian church. More often there. One extreme to the other. We don't make a big thing about it or anything. We just sort of go."

"Don't be so defensive, Sam," Mimi said. "If you want to drug yourself that's your affair."

"Yes," Sam said, snapping his jaws shut. "It is."

Mimi sighed and stretched her hand across the table towards him. "I'm doing it again," she said, "Being antagonistic. Clare says it's a sign of immaturity. I didn't mean to set up a mental block, just get into a nice semantic argument. Aping my elders as usual. I'm sorry."

Sam continued to glare for a moment; then he grinned. "I'm sorry, too. It was a dumb thing to get mad about." He looked around. The room was empty. "Hey, I'd better get you home. The Bowens will be wondering where you are."

Mimi looked up, startled, and remembered Virginia. "I forgot all about Vee!" she said. "I have an extremely disorganized mind. We'd better tear."

Virginia was almost home when Snider Bean caught up with

her, shouting down the alley, "Virginia! Say, Virginia Bowen, whoa up!"

She thought of making a wild dash into the villa, then imagined him coming in after her, shouting, disturbing her father at his desk, making a fuss so that all kinds of explanations would be necessary—She stopped abruptly, and waited, her back to him, until he came up to her.

"Listen, you haughty little pussycat," Beanie said, putting his hands on her shoulders and turning her around, completely sure of himself, "there isn't a thing in the world to be so upset about."

Now Virginia was facing him. "I'm not upset," she said. "Good-bye."

"Oh, no, you don't," Beanie said, "you don't get away that easily. I promise I won't rub your fur the wrong way about your precious friend any more. Now come on back up to the hotel with me. Sam's all upset about your leaving."

"Sam doesn't give a hoot whether I'm there or not. As a matter of fact, he's much happier being alone with Mimi."

"Okay, then let's you and I be alone together," Beanie said.

"Thank you, but I don't care to be alone with you, and I'm cold and I want to go into the house."

"Look, kiddo," Beanie said, "I'm not one to stay around where I'm not wanted, but you're old enough to grow up and face a few facts. Now your Mimi's probably a very nice girl, there are exceptions to every rule, and she's not right out of the grotto like some I've met, but why try to hide the fact that we'd all be lots better off if her race didn't always try to run everything?"

Virginia stared beyond Snider Bean, up the hill to the hotel, beyond that to the sanatorium. In the sanatorium the lights made neat stripes across the face of the building with blue-lit vertical ones crossing them and defining the stairways. It seemed neat and orderly and comprehensible. With an abrupt, awkward gesture she pointed to it. "My mother has a friend who was up there," she said, "in the sanatorium."

"Oh?" Beanie said. "I'm sorry."

"Do you know why she was there?"

"TB, I suppose."

"Yes, and do you know why?" She did not wait for him to answer. "Because all during the war which so many people seem to have forgotten, she fought Nazis and people who feel like you. Because she hated concentration camps and people burning books and—and—and *people*. Did you know that? Did you know people like you *burned* people like—like Mimi?" As she became more and more excited she could hardly get the words out.

"Oh, come off it, Virginia," Beanie said. "Don't you think you're exaggerating a little? Anyhow it's all over."

"Not when there are people like you," Virginia cried, her voice rising shrilly. "I *hate* you!" Now at last she managed to break from him and run into the villa.

In his workroom Courtney was not writing, though he sat at his desk, a piece of clean paper in his typewriter. The basket beside him was filled with crushed papers, and there were papers which had missed and lay on the floor. He looked at them and thought that he would get up and gather them together and ram them all down properly in the scrap basket, but he did not move from his desk. This afternoon with Mimi and Virginia out of the house he had hoped to accomplish a great deal. He had not been able to write since the two girls had come for the holidays. Their presence, youthful and vital, was a disturbing element in the house; it was as though an electric current had been turned on, and their high young voices disturbed him and made him restless, so that he could no longer sit in peace at his desk and let the precise, disciplined words fall with felicity from the keys of his typewriter. And this afternoon Connie had wakened early from her nap and now Emily was at the piano, playing Beethoven, and it was disturbing music, and he did not want to be disturbed. He started to call out, "Emily, please don't play for a few minutes," but it was too much effort, and he continued to sit there, his mouth opened to call, but no words coming out.

There should be no need, no desire, to ask Emily to stop playing. There should be more time, not less, for her to play, since music was so important a part of her life. If the words could fall from his typewriter keys as the notes were falling from the yellow keys of the piano! . . . If this year were the year it should have been, so that he could write with serenity surrounding him, instead of resentment and anxiety each leering over a shoulder. . . .

—Damn Tommy O'Hara, he thought. Damn his hide.

And then—No. Blaming Tommy O'Hara is nothing but an alibi. If I damn anybody's hide it's my own. Because I am the way I am.

He shook his head angrily, glaring at the typewriter in front of him, the pile of blank paper beside him, the carefully sharpened pencils, the filled fountain pen. He had always been able to write with complete concentration whenever he caught hold of a stray half-hour and a stub of pencil and scrap of paper. It was only now that he had all the time in the world and the accoutrements, that the paper remained blank for hours in front of him, the pencils unblunted, the pen never dry.

He pushed back his chair and went upstairs to get a book he had left on his bed table and in which he might want to look up something. As he started downstairs again he caught a glimpse of himself in a picture Emily kept on her chest of drawers, and he carried this glimpse with him back to his office. It was Courtney at fifteen, Virginia's age, Courtney on one and the same day having won a tennis match and a history prize, and he was grinning and his red hair was rumpled; for some reason, Emily loved the picture and carried it everywhere with her, Courtney, confident and victorious. That, probably, was why, the confidence that shone out of his eyes, the look of participating eagerly in life.

And was it that same spring, or the spring after (lilac in the garden, lily-of-the-valley under the big oak tree, old grads coming back), that he had almost got himself expelled from school?

He had written an essay, an essay on Thomas à Kempis for the Scripture master who was also the English master, a young man, small, and somewhat prissy. He had never won a tennis match, nor, in all probability, even watched one. He wore rimless glasses and his hair was stringy and his mind tight, and on occasion Courtney still dreamed about him and the dreams were bordering on nightmares.

So Ludkin had returned the Scripture papers that morning, making appropriately sarcastic remarks about most of them, but he failed to return Courtney's, saying, "Bowen, see me after class."

Courtney could think of only two reasons for Ludkin's withholding his composition: either the master thought it unusually good or he thought it unusually bad. In spite of his instinctive feeling of apprehension Courtney did not think his essay was bad.

He stood quietly by Ludkin's desk as the others filed out. When the classroom had emptied, leaving Ludkin sitting at the desk up on the platform and Courtney standing below, and the smell of chalk dust blinded the smell of lilac in the spring air,

Ludkin continued to study frowningly some papers on the desk in front of him.

Finally Courtney said, "You wished to see me, sir?"

"Bowen," Ludkin shot at him, "are you Roman Catholic?"

"No, sir."

"What do you call yourself, then?"

"Episcopalian, sir."

"Have you had extensive religious training?"

"Well, no, sir. I don't think you'd call it extensive. My mother goes to church a great deal."

The elastic band Ludkin was playing with snapped and stung his fingers and a look of temper flickered into his eyes. "Bowen, why did you pick *The Imitation of Christ* for your Scripture report?"

"Well, sir, I knew it was a book that had had an awful lot of influence on people, and I thought maybe it was something I ought to read. You told us just to choose anything off the Scripture shelf in the library, sir."

Ludkin had the report in his hand. Now he slammed it down on the desk in front of him. "All I can say of *this*, Bowen, is that if you *were* Roman Catholic you would certainly be up for excommunication. But since you claim to belong to the Episcopal Church, which is also my persuasion, and that of this school, all I can say is who the devil do you think you are?"

"Sir?"

"Don't stand there looking innocent. You know perfectly well what I mean. This paper is a disgrace, Bowen, a deliberate disgrace. Unless you are willing to rewrite it completely I shall be forced to show it to the headmaster as an example of wilful insubordination."

"Insubordination, sir?" Courtney was completely baffled.

"Yes, sir!" Ludkin shouted. "Insubordination, Mister Bowen!"

"I don't understand what you mean," Courtney said blankly, looking at his maligned paper lying on the master's raised desk.

"Bowen, are you or are you not willing to rewrite this paper?"

"Of course I'm willing to rewrite it, sir, if there's something wrong with it. But I don't understand exactly how you want it rewritten, sir. I did the best I could. I just wrote what I thought."

"*Think*, Bowen! You're not supposed to think! You're supposed to learn. A boy your age doesn't know how to think. That is why your parents send you to school. Remember that, Bowen. Your parents send you to school to learn what to think and I am here to teach you what to think. Do you hear me?''

"Yes, sir.''

"Did you read this entire book, Bowen?''

"Yes, sir.''

"Every page?''

"Yes, sir. We have two weeks between Scripture assignments and it isn't a very long book.''

Outside the windows he could hear shouts of laughter and the sound of a tennis ball hitting the racquet and someone giving a laugh of triumph, and he knew he would miss the game he had been supposed to play before lunch. He shifted his weight from one foot to the other, his hand closing convulsively as though around the handle of a racquet.

"Bowen!'' Ludkin shouted.

"Sir?''

"Pay attention.''

"Yes, sir.''

"I want you to drop that 'holier than thou' attitude, Bowen. I want you to rewrite your report, Mister Bowen, giving a résumé of the major points of the book, and then telling me why you agree with them.''

"I'm afraid I can't do that, sir.''

"Why not?''

"Because I don't agree with them, sir.''

"Bowen, who are you, if you please, to disagree with Thomas à Kempis?''

"Nobody, sir.''

"Then will you write the report?''

"Yes, sir. I'll be glad to do a résumé of the book, but I'm afraid I can't change my opinions, sir.''

"Opinions, Mister Bowen! This is only my second year at this particular school, Mister Bowen, but I have been teaching in various institutions for a number of years, and I have never seen a paper filled with such unpardonable arrogance as your paper, Mister Bowen.'' He read aloud from Courtney's paper in a high, nasal voice:

"'. . . although some of this is quite beautiful, much of its thought I disagree with violently. . . .

Violently, Bowen, violently! Who are you to use violence in connection with a religious book of which you obviously have no understanding? Hm:

> . . . I believe that since we are put in this world we are put in it to live in it, and to the full. . . .

If you have solved the problem of why we are put into the world, Mister Bowen, you have done more than most of us. I dare say Thomas à Kempis had given it more thought than you have.

> . . . Even if one believes unreservedly in immortality—

have you been reading Darwin, too, Mister Bowen?

> —there would be no point in being given life on this earth if our lives were to be spent in a rejection of life. . . .

I repeat, Bowen, what do you know about it?

> . . . We are advised by Thomas à Kempis to retire from the world largely because if we don't we are too apt to commit sins for which we will be punished. If we don't have anything to do with the world, then we won't commit the sins, and then we won't be punished. It seems to me—

You again, Bowen!

> —it seems to me that this is a very cowardly philosophy, and very unchristian in reality. I think that God put us into this world to live in it with courage, and to fulfill ourselves to the best of our ability, and to do as much as we can, even if we sometimes make mistakes. What about the parable of the three servants and the talents? If the servants had followed the advice in this book they would all have buried their talents. And if Christ had followed it He would never have argued with the sages in the Temple or dared raise people from the dead or knocked over the money-lenders' tables or asked his disciples to risk everything for him. He would have remained a carpenter and He would never have been crucified and we would have no Christian religion today. . . .

Bowen, this paper sickens me so that I cannot read any further. It nauseates me. This paper is sacrilegious to the nth degree. If I were Dr. Sterne I would not allow the boy who wrote this paper to remain in the school. But because your record has been excellent, Bowen, I am willing to give you another chance. I will be magnanimous. I will not show this paper to Dr. Sterne if you will rewrite it according to my specifications.''

Courtney said stubbornly, ''I'm afraid I can't do that, sir.''

''Then you leave me no alternative. I shall give your paper to Dr. Sterne to read and leave the matter entirely up to him, with my personal recommendation of expulsion.''

''Yes, sir.'' Courtney stared out the window into the clear spring air, bruised and baffled. Ping, came the sound of a tennis ball. He waited numbly to be dismissed.

''That is all,'' Ludkin said. Then, as Courtney turned blindly towards the door, he called him back. ''Just one minute, Bowen. What do you call this?''

''What do I call what, sir?''

''This—*thing*—you handed in for your English composition preparation?'' He held out a sheet of paper as though it had a nauseating smell.

Courtney's voice was flat. ''It's a poem, sir.''

''Yes, Bowen, I rather expected you to say that. It's exactly the sort of arrogant tripe I might expect from the boy who had the gall to hand in such a Scripture paper. Hm.'' The English master began to read aloud in a sarcastic, nasal voice; his voice seemed to be of the same sallow color as his complexion:

> *''I gaze upon the steady star*
> *That comes from where I cannot see,*
> *And something from that distant far*
>
> *Pierces the waiting core of me*
> *And fills me with an awful pain*
> *That I must count not loss but gain.*

Harrumph!' Ludkin cleared his throat loudly and continued:

> *''If something from infinity*
> *Can touch and strike my very soul,*
> *Does that which comes from out of me*
> *Reach and pierce its far off goal?''*

Courtney stared harder and harder out the window, although he no longer heard the sounds outdoors or saw the trees with their pale green young foliage, or smelled the fragrance from the lilac bush that was bursting with a fountain of blossoms he could easily have leaned out the window to pick.

"Are you listening, Bowen?" Ludkin asked.

"Yes, sir."

"I must say that I'm amazed you condescended to use rhyme and some sort of rhythm. But I wonder—can you tell me what it means?"

"Yes, sir."

"Well?"

"I'm sorry my meaning isn't apparent, sir."

"Apparent! I suppose you mean that you and the star were having some kind of communion. I can only say that you must have a very high opinion of yourself, Bowen."

"No, sir."

The bell for lunch rang, a strident clangor that silenced the English master as he opened his thin mouth for his next remark. Courtney sighed and squared his shoulders.

"Very well, Bowen," Ludkin said, "you may go now. I will take up the matter with Dr. Sterne."

"Yes, sir." Courtney wheeled and left the classroom, left the smell of ink and chalky blackboards and furniture polish and Ludkin's tobacco and the lilac, and rushed upstairs. The penalty for cutting a meal without permission was a heavy one, but he was too nearly weeping with the rage and fury of being so sorely misunderstood to be able to face going into the refectory. He rushed into the dormitory and into his cubicle, flinging himself down on his cot.

He had never been in the dormitory during a meal before. The curtains marking off each cubicle hung stiff and white. The beds were leeringly smooth under their white seersucker spreads, and the faces of various mothers and fathers and sisters seemed to look at him mockingly from their neat alignment on chests. From the refectory downstairs he could hear the muffled roar of conversation, like faraway breakers or distant thunder. Then, still like the sea, came the subdued murmur of grace followed by the great roaring of chairs being pushed back, the sound of laughter liberated.

It was evening before Dr. Sterne, the headmaster, sent for him. Something in Courtney made his footsteps slow and deliberate as he walked the length of the building, and through the green baize door that led to the headmaster's rooms. He knocked on the door of the study.

Dr. Sterne was sitting at his big desk reading what Courtney recognized as his Scripture paper. Ludkin was nowhere to be seen. The headmaster looked up and smiled.

"Sit down, Bowen, while I finish reading these literary efforts of yours. They seem rather to have upset Mr. Ludkin."

"Yes, sir." Courtney sat on the edge of a chair. Dr. Sterne read without hurrying. Once Courtney heard him make a sound that could have been a snort either of laughter or of disgust, but, looking at the headmaster's impassive, leonine face, he could not tell which.

As Dr. Sterne put the papers down on the desk in front of him, he said, "You know, Bowen, Mr. Ludkin is a deeply religious man. I'm afraid you've made him very unhappy with your unorthodoxy."

"I'm sorry, sir."

"Just what was your Scripture assignment?"

"We were to choose any book from the Scripture shelf and write a report on it. I thought that meant if we didn't agree with the book we were to say so, and why."

"A logical assumption." Dr. Sterne leaned back in his chair and lit his pipe; Courtney did not know why the smell of Dr. Sterne's tobacco was pleasant and that of Mr. Ludkin's somehow musty and full of decay. "Have a more comfortable chair, my boy. You aren't up for execution. Try that old red one. It's really very restful."

"Thank you, sir." Courtney moved to a huge leather chair into which his body sank, resistless. It was impossible to keep a stiff backbone in the chair; its sagging curves insidiously insisted on relaxation. But if one could not keep one's backbone stiff one at least had the upper lip.

"Tell me, Bowen," Dr. Sterne said. "Why did you pick on *The Imitation of Christ* by Thomas à Kempis?"

"Well, the title was familiar to me, sir; I think my mother reads it, she reads a lot of religious books, and I guess I didn't look at the name of the author very well, because I thought till I was about halfway through that it was St. Thomas Aquinas, and I've heard you talk a lot about St. Thomas Aquinas."

Dr. Sterne laughed. He was a massive man and his laughter shook all of him. "Well, I wouldn't confuse the two gentlemen again if I were you. They're really very different."

"Yes, sir. I hope so."

"Thomas à Kempis seems to have upset you almost as much as you upset Mr. Ludkin. Why?"

"Well, sir, I was rather shocked that a book I knew to be so influential should say some of the things it said. Like it's being better to be the servant than the master, it's better to be led than to lead—because it's safer. It seems so negative to me, sir."

"You know, Bowen," Dr. Sterne's voice was confidential, "I haven't read *The Imitation of Christ* since I was about your age and I'm afraid I don't remember much of it. I certainly don't remember being particularly upset by it. Are you sure you understood it?"

"Yes, sir, I think so. I mean, lots of it seemed to be not able to have two interpretations. I mean, when he said that we are held responsible for all knowledge, for everything we learn, so it's better not to learn anything, it's safer, because then we won't be held responsible—I think that's awfully bad, sir. It seems to me we ought to search for knowledge and truth, not run away from it."

"Well, I can't help agreeing with you, Bowen," Dr. Sterne said. "I think I'd better read the book again."

"And you see, sir, another thing that upset me until I found out it was Thomas à Kempis and not Thomas Aquinas, I thought it was a book you liked, and that bothered me, sir, because it seemed to me it was a book for weaklings, for people who were too cowardly to live life."

"I see. Of course you explained none of this to Mr. Ludkin?"

"Well, sir, the main thing was he didn't like what I thought of the book."

"He said you were stubbornly offensive about it." Dr. Sterne picked up the paper and looked at it again. Courtney could tell nothing from the expression in the headmaster's eyes, but he felt himself relaxing.

"I didn't mean to be offensive, sir, but I couldn't say I agreed with the book when I *didn't* agree with it so violently."

"A little less violence might have been easier on Mr. Ludkin, Bowen, and still expressed your opinion. However, I think we'll call it a misunderstanding all round and let it go at that. And suppose you read—let me see—fifty pages of Thomas Aquinas, and be sure you get the right Thomas this time, and you can write a quiet and unemotional report on him. Is that satisfactory to you?"

"Yes, sir. Thank you very much, Dr. Sterne."

"As for your poem." Dr. Sterne looked at Courtney, raised his strong gray eyebrows, and grinned. "Possibly it wouldn't have upset Mr. Ludkin at all if he hadn't read your Scripture paper first, though I can see it's not the kind of thing he's fond of, and I can see a little something of what he calls your 'arrogance' in it. However it's not a bad kind of arrogance. I really cannot see you as a subversive character, Bowen. Do you think of yourself as subversive?"

"No, sir."

"And in any event history is your subject, Bowen. Save your passion for history. As Thomas says—Thomas à Kempis—it's a lot safer."

Oh, clever, clever Courtney, appealing to Dr. Sterne's vanity by pretending he was upset to think the headmaster might have liked Thomas à Kempis. Only it was not cleverness, he had really meant it, and if Dr. Sterne were alive today he would seek him out and ask for a teaching post under him.

Only it was not Dr. Sterne he saw in his dreams; it was Mr. Ludkin.

And the Courtney here in this hollow of the Haute Savoie was as far from the Courtney of Thomas à Kempis as he was from the picture of the grinning Courtney with the tennis racquet and the book under his arm. Thomas à Kempis alas, was right, and Courtney wrong. It is not safe to make mistakes. It is not safe to search for knowledge and truth; it is much safer to run away. It is not safe to participate too violently in life: one participates and one marries and loves one's wife; one participates and one has children and a child dies. It is not safe to participate.

Oh, no, Courtney, let us withdraw. Let us follow Thomas' advice, Thomas à Kempis' advice, and withdraw. Let us not write anything new or exciting because it won't be exciting to Tommy O'Hara and it is the Thomas O'Haras who control the purse strings. Let's play it safe and if we're not quite truthful Tommy O'Hara won't care. And if we go to Indiana as we probably will, let's go for the wrong reasons, or Thomas would call them the right reasons, and let us not participate, let us not become involved in any issues, let us avoid the dangerous passions of the mind, far more dangerous than the passions of the body. And if we betray the young Courtney, he was a fool and didn't know what he was saying. Let us follow his much-scorned pattern of safety so there will be no more pain.

He looked at the blank sheet of paper in his typewriter, and

very carefully and with no emotion whatsoever he typed out,
PHILOPOEMEN . . .

Virginia stood a moment in the hall, breathing fast, listening
to the comforting sounds around her, the warm noise of the furnace purring like a great cat in the cellar, her mother playing
Beethoven on the piano, her father typing in his office. She
hung up her outdoor clothes and went into the living room.
Connie sat on the floor stringing a chain of silver beads made of
rolled-up tinfoil. At the piano Emily turned.

"Back, darling? How was it?"

"Oh, very nice, thank you," Virginia said. "I mean it stank.
I walked out."

"Walked out, Vee? Why?"

"Mimi says I don't stand up properly for my principles. So I
tried to stand up for them. Or for her, anyhow."

"What do you mean, darling?"

"Oh, Sam had arranged for a double date and the boy he
picked was a ghoul. I mean it wasn't Sam's fault or anything.
He didn't know what this creature was going to be like."

"What was he like?" Emily asked.

"Oh, quite a dream boat and tall and everything. But—
mother, what *is* this Jewish business anyhow?"

"What do you mean, Vee?"

"I called Mimi 'Mimi Opp' and Beanie—Snider Bean, that's
his name—made sort of a Thing out of it. And then when Mimi
and Sam were dancing he made cracks about Mimi being one of
the Chosen. Things like that. You know what I mean."

"Yes, Vee, I know."

Connie looked up from her beads. "Nobody's talking to
me."

"Suppose you listen to Virginia and me for a while," Emily
said.

"But I don't know what you're talking about."

"Maybe if you listen for a few minutes you will."

"Mother," Virginia said, "when you wrote Mrs. Oppenheimer and asked Mimi to come and everything, you knew
Mimi's father was Jewish, didn't you?"

"I don't suppose I thought about it, Vee."

"I mean, it didn't make any difference to you or anything,
did it?"

"No, Vee. Where's Mimi now?"

"Still with Sam, I guess. They were dancing when I walked

out on Beanie. This comes under the general heading of prejudice, doesn't it, mother? Like the Negroes in the South, and the Italians and Poles in New England?''

"Yes."

"Like daddy said about any minority group. Like sometimes even people who care about education and books and music and things being a minority group, too?"

"Yes, Vee."

"Well, I know what a Negro is, and Italians are born in Italy and Poles in Poland, but what exactly *is* a Jew?"

"That's the sixty-four dollar question, isn't it?" Emily swung around on the piano bench, facing her daughter. She sat and looked at her without speaking for a moment. "You've got me, Vee," she said at last. "I'm not exactly sure. I suppose it's something like being a Baptist or a Roman Catholic, or an Episcopalian, as we are. And even though most Jews aren't in Israel, it's sort of like being born in Italy or Poland, too. Doesn't make much sense, does it?"

"No," Virginia said. "And this is a thing that grownups—adults—people like you—can't explain?"

"It certainly is, Vee."

"It's not a separate race?"

"No. There are three races. Caucasian. Negro. Mongolian. We're Caucasian. So are Jews."

"So what's this all about?"

Emily held out her hands helplessly. "I don't know. I can't say it's not about anything because it is. But I don't know why, Vee. It just doesn't make sense to me. It never has. We judge people by what they're like as separate human beings. At least we should. Maybe daddy could explain it to you. He's much better at explaining things than I am. I don't know what makes it possible for people to meet Mimi and like her and then suddenly change entirely in their feelings towards her, feel that she's a completely different person when they find out that her father's a Jew. Prejudice is a funny thing, Vee. Funnier in Americans than anybody else."

"I'm kind of relieved you feel the way you do," Virginia said. "Some peoples' parents don't. Hate's such a peculiar thing, mother. I think Beanie honestly hates Jews without knowing what he's doing or why. And I hate Beanie. And it makes the inside of my stomach feel all quivering as though it were made of jelly. And it makes my mind blind so it can't see."

"Yes," Emily said. "Hate does that."

"Do you hate anybody, mother?"

"I don't know. Right at this moment I really don't know, Vee."

"Do you hate Mr. O'Hara?"

Emily looked at her sharply, wondering how much she had seen, how much she knew. "Yes. I'm afraid I do. But it's stupid of me. It does make your mind blind, Virginia. You're quite right."

"Daddy's students hated Mr. O'Hara."

Emily shook her head. "They were indignant, some of them, maybe, that he was—well, more or less taking daddy's place. But hate's rather too strong a word."

Connie dropped half her tinfoil beads on the floor and let out a shriek.

"Oh, do be quiet, Con," Virginia said. "I'll help you pick them up."

"I *have* been being quiet," Connie said. "Quiet as mices. You said if I listened I'd know what you were talking about and I did listen and I didn't. Was somebody mean to Mimi? Was somebody mean to daddy?"

"Just extremely discourteous," Virginia said loftily. "Come on, Emily Conrad, you're not picking up your share."

"But I've been making it," Connie said. "I've been making a beautiful silver chain for the Christmas tree and you and Mimi haven't helped at all."

"We'll help after dinner." Virginia reached under the chair for some beads. She dropped them into Connie's box, a small battered cardboard one inscribed, *OSWALD, Mme. Charles Andrieu, Dentelles, Blouses, Gants, Bas,* and rose up onto her knees. "Mother—"

"What, Vee?"

"Should I mention to Mimi what we've been discussing?"

"If she doesn't seem upset I wouldn't make more of it than it already is. It shouldn't be important, so maybe the best way not to let it be important is just not to do anything more about it. You'll know better when you see Mimi."

"Okay." Virginia put her arm around Emily and rubbed her cheek softly against her mother's.

Connie put her chain and her box of beads on the table and came over and climbed up onto Emily's lap. "Me, too. I want to be loved, too."

Emily gave her a little shake. "You are loved, you foolish

child. Virginia's been away at school all these months so don't you think she's due a few extra hugs and kisses?''

Connie did not answer, but nuzzled into her mother's neck.

"I'm sorry, Vee," Emily said. "I'm afraid I haven't been any help It's something you have to work out for yourself, like everything else, in the long run.''

"That's what Mimi says. She says there isn't anything important anybody can settle for you. You have to do it yourself. She says I'm backward that way. Would you like me to give Connie her bath?''

Emily looked at her in surprise. "I would adore it. I'll fill the tub for you.''

"No, I can do it. Come on, Con, let's go get your night-clothes and hang them in front of the stove to warm.''

When they had gone Emily sat for a moment with her head in her hands.—I sounded pompous and self-righteous, she thought. I didn't know how to help Vee because I'm almost as backward as she is. Courtney could have done it much better than I. Or Abe.

Abe.

She turned quickly around on the piano bench and held her fingers out over the keys. Then she started to play. Bach, this time. A fugue. A Bach fugue could keep one from thinking better than anything else.

After dinner Gertrude rang up. "Come along and have some coffee and cake with us and listen to some records. Kaarlo has a new Mozart quintet that he's mad about and he wants you to hear it.''

"Wait a minute," Emily said. "I'll ask Court.''

She let the earpiece to the phone dangle so that it knocked against the whitewashed wall by Courtney's study. She walked in time to the faint knocking, her heart beating quite rapidly, almost as though it had been Abe on the phone because Abe might be going to Kaarlo's and Gertrude's, too; it was perfectly logical that they would have asked him. . . .

"I don't want to go," Courtney said. "My throat's better, but I think I'll give it another evening of pampering. You go, Em, Kaarlo'll see you home, won't he?''

"He usually does, and I would rather like to hear his new Mozart.''

"Anybody else going to be there?''

"I don't know. I doubt it. I think Gertrude just called on the spur of the moment."—A lie in intention if not in actuality, Emily thought, and how easily I seem to be doing it. . . .

"As long as someone brings you home," Courtney said. "I don't like your going down the mountainside alone."

Emily kissed him. "I won't stay late. Connie's all settled for the night, and see that Vee and Mimi get to bed at a reasonable hour, will you?"

When she went into the chalet, through the kitchen, at first she did not see Abe; but he was there, sitting by the fire in his ski clothes, black pants and a yellow sweater, his body strong and younger-looking than his face, which was rough and windburned under his thinning brown hair. Gertrude was still in her bad mood and sat slouched in a chair, smoking and drinking cup after cup of coffee, but nothing else, thank God. Kaarlo crouched on the floor by the phonograph and turned the records and Emily and Abe sat on opposite sides of the fireplace, not speaking, but to Emily the feel of Abe was like a shout in the room and she could not hear the music above it. It was a piano quintet which she particularly loved but the music wove around and about her and she could not reach out with her listening and grasp it; it remained outside her. She wondered, too, if she had ever heard this music with Abe before, and she could not remember what they had listened to those half-dozen times they had gone together to Carnegie or Town Hall.

Kaarlo sat with a rigid, anticipatory look on his face as he changed the records, touching them with infinite care so that his finger marks should not mar the grooves; the records and the gramophone his most precious possessions, practically his only possessions. Emily watched Kaarlo but she could not look towards Abe until after the Mozart was over and they'd each had a couple of cups of coffee and Gertrude said to Abe, "Tell me, how do you and the Bowens happen to know each other? Did you live near each other in New York?"

"Far from it," Abe said. "The Bowens live up on Morningside Heights and I hang out down in the Village."

"Morningside Heights? The Village?" Kaarlo asked. "Are they what you would call suburbs?"

"No," Abe said, explaining quite seriously, ignoring Gertrude's laughter, "they're just affectionate names for two of the pleasantest parts of our island of Manhattan. Morningside Heights is famous for students, and professors, like our friend Courtney; and the Village is supposed to be the haunt of mad

Bohemians, full of dope fiends and *crimes passionnels* and no normal human beings within a mile of Washington Square. However, I live on a quiet street with trees and gentle houses and my only contact with Bohemianism came during the brief tenure of my second marriage.'' His face darkened and he paused.

"Abe has a beautiful house," Emily said quickly, "a whole house on Eleventh Street with a garden and a library that will be Court's eternal envy."

"Kris and I had a chance to pick it up for practically nothing when Sam was on the way. We planned on half a dozen children so a house seemed sensible, and we loved this one, though we'd never particularly thought of living in the Village. And Sam and I are very much at home in it, though when Sam's away I find I rattle about a bit.'' He held out his coffee cup for Gertrude to refill. "This seems to be a monologue on the life and times of Abraham K. Fielding. Wasn't the question how the Bowens and I met?"

"It was," Gertrude said, "though we drink up any further tidbits of information you have to drop for us."

"What does the K stand for?" Emily asked.

"How *did* you and Emily meet?" Kaarlo asked.

Abe hitched his chair a little further from the fire and the shadows moved grotesquely across his face, lengthening his nose, jutting out his forehead, hollowing his cheekbones. "We met in the lobby of Carnegie Hall. We were there to hear Serkin play the Appassionata—my God, how he can play it, Kaarlo—and during intermission we were all indulging the pernicious habit of a quick cigarette—we saw mutual friends, headed for them from different ends of the lobby, and got introduced. And after the concert we all went over to their apartment for a drink, bless their kind souls, and so a beautiful friendship was born.''

"Emily plays the Appassionata," Kaarlo said. "Maybe not like Serkin, but it's quite something, isn't it, Abe?"

"I've never heard Emily play," Abe said. He turned to her, demanding, "Why haven't I heard you, woman?"

Emily laughed. "I'm very well aware of my pianistic deficiencies. I love to play but I—I play mostly for myself."

"You've played for Gertrude and Kaarlo."

Emily held out her hands helplessly. "I'll play for you, Abe. Any time." She stood up. "Thanks for the Mozart and the coffee. I must be getting along home now."

"I'll walk you down," Abe said, and they bade good night to Gertrude and Kaarlo and went out together through the shed.

When they were out in the cold, Abe reached for Emily's hand and pushed it down into his pocket. "Why haven't you ever played for me?" he asked.

"As a matter of fact I think I have."

"When?"

"Those Sunday night parties of ours—you must have been there for some of the singing ones. I always played for those."

"I don't mean that way," Abe said, "with a lot of people happily drowning you out. I mean really play."

Inside his, her fingers moved a little nervously. She tried to laugh. "I don't go around giving concerts, Abe."

"But you do play for people."

"When the occasion arises. It just—it's just never seemed to arise with you."

"You didn't want it to, did you?"

"I guess not."

"Why not?"

"I haven't been able to practise much the past few years—since I've known you. You can't play if you don't practise. You know that. I've played for people anyhow when I—when I haven't cared terribly. I didn't want to do less than my best before you. You see I—I get terrible nervous and my hands tremble and I play abominably and I'm furious with myself afterwards."

There was a silence, only snow around them, and mountains, and stars. "As for Kaarlo, he's not you, and music's been a bond between us. We've both had our—our problems this winter. Music helps. And when I'm easy and comfortable with someone, the way I am with Kaarlo, I can sit down and play without breaking into a cold sweat."

"You're not comfortable with me, Emily?"

"No."

"Why?"

"You know why."

"Why?" he persisted gently.

"I care too much." She tried to make her voice casual to counteract the meaning of the words.

They walked along together, Emily's fingers still clasped in Abe's, deep in the warmth of his pocket. Every few steps they slid a little; the ice crackled beneath their hobnailed boots.

"What a hell of a way to make love to you," Abe said, "trying to tell you each time Kaarlo turned a record that what Mozart was saying was what I wanted to say to you."

"Yes," Emily said.

"It should be like Mozart," Abe said, "simple and pure and happy, instead of all tangled-up and complicated."

"Yes," Emily said.

"When you walked into the casino last night, and you were alone, and you told me Court had a sore throat and couldn't come, it seemed inevitable. It seemed that I had known all along that what happened was going to happen, though I managed to keep it out of my consciousness until it actually did happen."

"Yes," Emily said.

"You knew it would happen, too?"

"Yes," Emily said.

They stood then in silence, pressed against each other, against the cold darkness, and then they started walking again, moving together in silent rhythm almost as they had danced together at the casino the night before. When they came to the villa Abe turned around saying quickly, "Not quite yet," and they began walking uphill again, not particularly towards Kaarlo's and Gertrude's or the sanatorium or the hotel, not anywhere, just uphill for a few moments before turning around and walking back down to the villa again. Their silence as they walked was, Emily thought, almost worse than words because it said more than words, it seemed to cry aloud all the things that she would not and knew must not be acknowledged in words. And at the same time each step she took with his presence there by her side pushed her against her volition into happiness, into a soaring and incredible joy.

They turned around finally on the icy path and started back down towards the villa. They were almost there before Emily said at last, "I promised the children I'd go skating with them tomorrow. Will you come, too?" Because perhaps if they were not alone, perhaps if she were to see him with the children, with Courtney, back in a familiar pattern, perhaps then they could fall back into their old casual way. But it had never been really casual and that was why it was betraying them now.

"Of course," Abe said. "When?"

"I thought we'd start around four," Emily said. "It's more fun after dark. We can skate until the stars are all out and have tea there at the rink."

"Good," Abe said.

They were at the villa again.

"Until tomorrow, then," Abe said. "Good night, my sweetheart, my beloved." And then, "We'll work this out some way, Emily. There must be a way, a right way, and we'll find it."

"Yes," she said, still standing close to him so that his coat was touching hers.

"Good night, darling."

"Good night," Emily said, and broke away from him and ran into the darkened villa.

In pajamas and robe Courtney moved softly into Connie's room to make sure that she was covered. Clumsily he tucked the blankets in around her, picked up the eiderdown and the pink teddy bear where they had slithered onto the floor. He stood looking down at her, his baby, the light from the hall shining onto her sleeping face, the face of an angel as all children's are when they are asleep regardless of what little devils they may be when they are awake. She was breathing with her mouth slightly open, deeply, contentedly, and the sound was reassuring, although when you love there is no security, no safety, only a fleeting comfort from moment to moment; and the sleeping breath of a child is a brief assurance that all is well.

Was it a feather King Lear put against Cordelia's lips or a mirror to catch her breath? There had been no need to take a measure of Alice's breathing; her strangled gasps had seemed to be the only sound in the night. He had thought in one moment of fatigue when his mind had shifted a fraction from the child that it was like the big clock in his parents' brownstone house on Sunday morning when it needed winding. The ticking of the clock seemed to get slower and slower, and the bell as it struck the hours and the quarter hours seemed strangled with exhaustion until his father came in from his heavy Sunday morning breakfast in the dark, basement dining room and wound it with the big brass key. But his father was not in the hospital to wind Alice and set her chime to ringing clearly once more; and although Courtney had every once in a while to close his eyes to keep from looking at Alice running down and strangling to death with exhaustion like the clock, he could not keep his mind from looking at her, from examining each struggling breath, counting the intervals between each breath and feeling the way each gasp was a little fainter than the last.

He looked down at his sleeping child in the small room in the cold villa and love was a pain, sharp and demanding. He touched the back of his hand gently against her cheek, put the teddy bear close to her hand, and straightened up. In the next room he could hear Virginia and Mimi talking in low voices. As he crossed the hall he tapped gently on their door, calling out good night. Then he climbed back into bed, sliding down into the warm spot he had made as he lay there reading. He pulled his robe off, but left on his heavy sweater, turned off the light and lay down. He had formed the habit of reading until he was consumed with sleep, until his eyes would scarcely stay open, so that he would not have to lie awake and think. But checking on the children had chilled and disturbed him, and as he lay there he felt sleep ebbing from him. An odd thing, this sleep business lately. The need to fall asleep at once. A fear of lying awake with his thoughts. So he read in the cold bedroom until the book fell from his hands, trying to catch sleep as it were unawares.

He got out of bed again, unable to lie still, and went to the window. At the turn of the path he saw two figures standing together, then move apart, and one, a man, tramped briskly upwards while the other—yes, it was Emily—moved more slowly towards the villa. Kaarlo had probably walked her home, though it hadn't looked like Kaarlo. It might have been Michel Clément or Abe Fielding. He felt suddenly unutterably lonely and he turned from the window with violent revulsion and climbed back into bed. Had he heard Emily laughing out there in the snow or was it just in his imagination that she had turned from him towards a happiness in which he could have no share?

Oh, God, it would have to be Indiana. It didn't really matter where, as long as there were the students and a certain amount of latitude given him in his teaching. It was only that it *seemed* to matter.

Sam sat on his twin bed in the hotel bedroom, waiting for his father to come back before turning off the light. During the holidays, unless they were planning an excursion that meant particularly early rising, Abe put no restrictions on Sam's bedtime, and the boy had a feeling of freedom and pleasure as he sat there, his legs dangling over the side of the bed, writing a long letter to Mimi.

Abe had urged him to come to Kaarlo's and Maggie's with him, but Sam had said, "I don't think I feel much like listening to music tonight, dad. I think I'll take a long hot soak and write a letter."

"A love letter?" Abe had asked, grinning.

And Sam had answered, "Well, in a manner of speaking, yes."

He was putting the letter in the envelope when his father came in.

"Still at it?" Abe asked. "How many fortunate young ladies are going to be the recipients of your billets doux?"

"Just one," Sam said. "My mind's sort of been wandering most of the evening. Think I'll take my shower now before I turn in."

When he came out of the bathroom Abe was sitting on the edge of his bed in his blue-and-white striped pajamas staring at the picture of Kristina in the silver frame on the bureau. Sam climbed carefully into bed and lay there, his eyes wide open and awake, looking at his father. "Wish I could remember mother," he said at last.

"Yes," Abe said.

"I have an idea what she was like from talking to you, but it's not the same thing as knowing her myself."

"No," Abe said. "You're not unlike her. Both in looks and temperament. A masculine version."

"Not a bit like Betty, was she?"

"Kristina and Betty were diametric opposites. Betty was a mistake from all points of view."

Sam pulled the covers up under his chin and watched the hump his feet made under the blankets at the foot of the bed. "I know, dad. I'm sorry."

Abe sat there on the side of his bed, his thin ankles showing between the bottoms of his pajamas and his brown leather slippers so that he looked somehow vulnerable and Sam was fiercely angry at Betty, angrier than he had ever been while Betty was with them.

"I thought I had to—to have some sort of substitute mother for you," Abe said. "And I knew it would be impossible—wrong—to marry anyone because she reminded me of Kris. And I was hellishly lonely. So I blundered about as badly as anyone can blunder."

"I don't remember Betty too well," Sam said. "Just that you were always going out in the evenings. And she broke things a lot. Cups and glasses. I remember that. Not washing them, or anything. Just broke them. She didn't like to do things like washing dishes, did she? I can't imagine her doing cooking and stuff, and having fun at it the way Mrs. Bowen does, if you'd been poor. And parties. I remember parties with everybody making lots of noise and sometimes you'd leave everybody and come upstairs and sit with me. And then I had polio and I went to Warm Springs and when I got back she was gone and I was glad.''

Abe stood up and went over to the long windows that led out onto the balcony and pushed them ajar and cold air knifed into the room. He got into bed, lit a cigarette, and turned out the light. "It was a lousy deal for you, Sam," he said. "I should have put a stop to it sooner.''

"I used to lie awake at night worrying about whether or not you'd marry again,'' Sam said. "Do you have to pay her alimony or anything?''

"I did, and quite a sizable one, till she remarried.''

"Love's a funny thing,'' Sam said, watching his father's cigarette glow and fade in the rapidly chilling room. "But you never did love her like my own mother, did you?''

"No.'' Abe's voice was sharp.

"I suppose it was partly sex, wasn't it?'' Sam asked, able to put in the dark the questions that would have been impossible before the light was out. "I've come to the conclusion that sex is an even odder thing than love.''

"But take them together and they can light up half the planet. Don't minimize either of them, Sam, and certainly not in conjunction. It's a magic combination.''

"Was that the way it was with you and mother?'' Sam asked. "Yes.''

"Do you think it can happen more than once to the same person?''

There was a long pause before Abe answered. Then all he said was, "I don't know.''

"Do you think—you're not likely ever to marry again at this date, are you?''

Abe chuckled. "At this period of my senility? I don't know, Sam. I'm not entirely decrepit yet. Would you mind if I did?''

"Gosh, no,'' Sam said. "It would all depend on who she was. I just wondered.''

"Not without the magic combination, anyhow,'' Abe said. "Good night, son.''

'' 'Night, dad.''

Abe put out his cigarette, pulled the pillow half over his head as he always did for warmth in winter, and was almost asleep when Sam's voice came again.

"Hey, dad, are you asleep?''

"Well, not entirely, why?"

"Anti-Semitism reared its ugly head at the thé dansant this afternoon."

"Oh? How so?"

"This creep Snider Bean I picked up to be Virginia Bowen's date. He made snide remarks about Mimi."

"Snider made snide reamrks? So what did you do?"

"I didn't get a chance to do anything. He made them to Virginia while Mimi and I were dancing, and Virginia walked out on him and went home. So when we got back to the table Beanie went off after her and I said, what was that about? and Mimi said, I suppose it's occurred to you I'm a Jew, or words to that effect."

"Had it?"

"No. I don't go about wondering what people are. Just if I like them."

"That's okay, then," Abe said. "Don't change."

"Yeah, but what do you do about people like Beanie?"

"That's a tough one, Sam. Speak your piece, I guess. Stand up for what you believe in. Don't let cowardice or fear of not running with the herd make you slide into appearing to agree with anything you don't honestly agree with."

"Doesn't seem like enough," Sam said.

"It would be if everybody did it. If we all stood up for what we believed in."

"Do people ever?" Sam asked. "Look at the Bible. Peter three times before the cock crew. Hey, maybe I ought to be a minister."

"Worth thinking about."

"You wouldn't split a gasket or anything?"

In the darkness Abe smiled and lit another cigarette. The match flared and for a moment his face was illuminated in its tiny spotlight, the delicate arch of nose, the full, sensitive lips, the velvet brown of eyes that could turn cold as the frozen ground of February. "I'm with you a hundred percent in anything you believe in a hundred percent."

"Even with all the extra schooling and everything?"

"Yes, Sam. Fortunately we don't have to worry about that."

"Did mother? Stand up for what she believed in, I mean?"

"Yes, Sam."

"Anybody else you know?"

"Sure. Quite a lot of people."

"Who?"

"Kaarlo. Emily Bowen. And her husband. Courtney."

"That funny little Virginia did this afternoon," Sam said. "Walked out on Beanie. I guess that took courage for a kid like her."

"Quite a lot of courage, I should think," Abe said.

"I think Mimi would. She's quite a girl, dad."

"Yes," Abe said. "She'll be a beauty when she grows up to herself."

"Well, good night, dad."

"Good night, Sam."

Darkness and cold air slipping in through the crack in the French windows. Music from the ballroom. Voices and laughter in the halls. In the village a dog baying.

In the chalet in the small bedroom that had once been Kaarlo's Gertrude lay awake. The curtains were drawn at the window so that the moon, if it should break through the clouds, would not shine in on her, and the darkness was absolute, darkness so deep it had no edges, no thin line of light to mark a boundary of chest or bed or window's edge, no shape, no form. Kaarlo was on the couch in the big room and the door was closed between them and she could not see the door.

The sleeping pills were in the bathroom and if she got up, stumbling over things in the darkness, she would waken Kaarlo and it was not a sleeping pill she wanted. A sedative would quiet her for the moment but then there would be the headache in the morning, the hangover without any fun preceding it to compensate for it. Or was sleep compensation enough? Sleep had never seemed that important in the old days. Those were the old days and these were the now days (though they seemed all nights, just as fingers can seem all thumbs) and were there ever going to be any new days?

If she were still in the sanatorium she could ring for a nurse and she would have a glass of warm milk, which she loathed, but at least it would be a diversion. If she pressed the emergency button they would all come running. When she was first in the sanatorium Dr. Clément had promised her that if she ever rang the emergency bell that he would be there within sixty seconds. He did not lie. She knew that. She had found it out the night that she wakened for no apparent reason choking with blood gushing from her throat as it had done that day in her chalet, blood warm and crimson over the white sheets, the yellow blankets. In her horror she had still managed to press the emergency button and hardly had she taken her finger from it than they were all there and Sister Baldwin, the dour night sister from London, had been so suddenly kind that Gertrude had thought—I must be going to die or old Starchy would be furious over the mess on the bedclothes. But she had not died and the bedclothes were changed so swiftly and gently that she was hardly aware of any commotion and the blood was stopped and she lay flat on the bed holding a piece of ice in her mouth and Dr. Clément sat beside the bed holding her hand, not to take her pulse now, simply for the comfort of human contact. He had sat there holding her hand for a long time and his steady closeness had taken away her fear.

That, of course, was what she wanted.

The darkness seemed to deepen.—A coward, that's what I'm turning into. I was never afraid before, not of blood, nor of sleeplessness when I drank half the night or even all of it, nor of the dark when I spent night after night in deserted barns or alone in the chalet or in the huts up the mountain waiting, not knowing if the approaching footstep would be Henri or Kaarlo, one of our own people, or one of the Germans. I wasn't afraid then.

—It was because I had something to do, she thought. A tiger who's not afraid in the jungle is afraid in the safety of its cage. I am afraid to the point of screaming.

She put her hand over her mouth and pressed back the scream. When it was finally down, swallowed like the medicine Kaarlo had given her at bedtime (because neither he not Clément trusted her to do things properly herself) she sat up in bed.

—No, she thought. No, I promised Clément, and Kaarlo would be angry.

But she did not lie down. She sat there and she could hear the music from the hotel.—How long does it go on? What about people who want to sleep? And what about people who want to dance? What about little Emily dancing at the casino with Abe Fielding? I want a drink. A drink might put me to sleep. Damn it, why couldn't I have got this business during the war and then I could have died legitimately and without fear instead of in terror and boredom. . .

The music from the hotel seemed to get louder, the darkness deeper.

—I can't stand it.

She swung her feet out of bed, stood up, moved unsteadily towards where she knew the door must be.—The chair. Damn.

What a crash. Sure to waken Kaarlo. The door. Turn the handle. My God, it's frozen stiff.

She wrenched it free.

—Kaarlo!

She ran stumbling across the room to him crashing into the couch, pulling back the covers, crawling in beside him, pressing up against the steamy, sleepy warmth of his body, shivering violently.

He pulled himself up out of the deep pit of those first heavy hours of sleep.

"I couldn't stand it in there alone!" Her teeth were chattering.

He held her close to him, quieting her. She pressed her lips against his shoulder.

"You'd better stay till you're warm and then I'll carry you back and fix you a hot-water bottle and a warm drink and give you a pill," he said.

She shook her head against him, still shivering, pressing closer.

His hand had been rubbing firmly, soothingly, against the small of her back. Now he stopped. "No."

"Yes, Kaarlo!" She wriggled against him, higher, until she could reach his lips with hers. After a moment his hand started its rhythmic motion again.

Perhaps because of Courtney's restlessness, because of his cold feet drawing the warmth from her, Emily dreamed, dreamed that she was back in the small New England village where she had been born, where her father was the doctor. In her dream she had done something terrible. She did not know what it was, only that it had been a very great sin, and not knowing what it was that had been committed made it even more fearful. She knew that her only salvation lay in going to her father and confessing, and she moved on leaden feet towards the surgery. In the waiting room people sat in winter coats, collars turned up, hats pulled down towards ears. Gertrude was there in a sleek black low-cut evening dress. In the office her father sat at his big flat-top desk. Compassionate and brusque at the same time. No. It was not her father. It was not her father at the desk at all. It was Courtney. If she told Courtney he would assume responsibility for whatever it was that had been done and then everything would be all right.

She wakened. Across the hall she could hear Connie singing

softly to herself as she often did if she roused before the rest of the household.

" 'Away in a manger,' " Connie sang, " 'no crib for a bed. Silent night. Holy night.' "

Emily looked over at Courtney. He was still asleep.

For a long time she had thought that if you loved anyone you had to tell him everything; go to him and confess as in the dream; there could be no secrets. But now in the dark of early morning with the copper bottle cold against her feet she felt that this desire to tell all was simply an evasion of responsibility, a weakness in wanting to push on to the person you love something that is your own responsibility to solve. It would be easier for her to tell Courtney all about Abe, to come to him as he sat at his desk in the chill little workroom and confess, to hand the responsibility for her ambivalence to him, to let him settle the problem of her puny conscience for her.

—But I know, she thought, lying there beside him on Madame Pedroti's lumpy bed, that if I love Courtney that is the last thing I must do. If I love Courtney he must never know.

✧ *Three* ✧

Abe and Sam stopped at the villa to pick up Emily and Virginia and Mimi at four o'clock. Already it was night in the village. Light still lay on the upper slopes and the mountain peaks were brilliant, but in the village the shadows lurked around the corners and in the distance they could hear the night baying of the dogs. Sam and Virginia and Mimi hurried along ahead, their skates slung across their shoulders and thumping against their bodies as they moved.

"Look, Abe," Emily said. "The stars are beginning to come out and up on the mountains it's still sunlight."

"If you go down to the bottom of a well even on a very bright day you can see the stars," Abe said.

"Really, Abe?"

He laughed. "So I've been told. I've never had the opportunity to try it personally."

"I suppose it's logical," Emily said, "like living here in the village, only more so, but I don't really understand it. Vee came to me once with the fascinating information that if we could get beyond the atmosphere of our earth we could truly see the stars, but the sky would be black, absolutely black, with no atmosphere between us and the sun. Something about there being no light unless there are particles of atmosphere in the air to catch the light rays and refract them. Something like that. I don't really understand it. But it's sort of like is there a noise when a tree falls in the forest if nobody is there to hear it. . . ." She stopped. "I am babbling on."

Abe caught at her hand and pushed it into the depths of his pocket. For a moment she let it rest there; then she pulled it out. "No, Abe."

"Why not?"

"The children."

"They aren't looking."

"But if they turn around . . ."

"What if they do? We're friends, aren't we? Old friends. So what's more natural than for two old friends casually to hold hands?"

"It isn't casual."

"No," Abe said, "but to anybody but you and me it would seem as though it were."

Emily kept her hands deep in her own pockets and shook her head. "No. It wouldn't look casual with me. I don't hold hands with people. Virginia would—"

"All right, darling," Abe said. "We won't if it makes you uncomfortable."

She said, "Oh, Abe, I've never thought before that I was a bitch."

"You're not," he said.

"But I am. I must be. Courtney—"

"And what do you think this makes me?" he said. "Courtney's my friend. And here I am doing my utmost to make love to his wife without the slightest compunction." Then he said in an odd way, "I'm not jealous of Courtney. I wonder why? I'm just terribly happy."

"Yes—" she said.

"Emily, why couldn't this have happened years ago?" he asked. "Why didn't I meet you years ago?"

—Years ago there was Kristina, she thought, but she said nothing. In the New York days Abe had talked often to her of the bitterness of the years with Betty and the joy of those with Kristina; now he mentioned neither of them and she did not feel their presence; she was not jealous of Kristina as Abe was not jealous of Courtney; at this moment of falling night and blossoming stars she was simply happy; in spite of her words there was no feeling but joy in her heart.

Ahead of them Mimi lifted her voice in a Christmas carol, high and clear and triumphant.

"Ce matin
J'ai rencontré le train
De trois grands
Rois qui allaient en voyage."

* * *

Sam and Virginia joined in, Sam's voice still not entirely a steady baritone, Virginia's husky alto much less assured than Mimi's soprano.

"I was—I was going to ask you and Sam to have Christmas dinner with us," Emily said after a moment.

Abe nodded. "Yes, I thought you probably would."

Ahead of them the voices rang clear against the snow.

"Adeste fideles,
laeti triumphantes . . ."

"I don't think we'd better," Abe said. "Isn't that what you were thinking?"

"Venite, venite in Bethlehem. . . ."

"I don't know," Emily said. "I would like so terribly much to have you come." But she knew that Abe was right and that it would be better if they did not come.

"Sam's never been to the South of France," Abe said. "I think we'll leave a few days before Christmas and go to Bandol. We have some pretty good friends there."

"Are you sure it wouldn't work out for you to come?" Emily asked desperately, not willing to accept the fact of it. "Virginia and Mimi will be so disappointed."

"You know it wouldn't do, Emily," Abe said gently.

She wanted to be unhappy about it, she knew that she was going to be unhappy about it, but at this moment with the children singing ahead of them and Abe beside her, all she could feel was joy that she was alive once more; and even if what lay ahead was pain, pain was part of living.

Now the children, showing off their prowess with languages, were singing a German carol,

"Vom Himmel hoch, da komm ich her,
Ich bring' euch gute neue Mär . . ."

The snow around them and the crimson-stained peaks of the mountains, the dark pines holding the snow on their out-stretched arms, all these things communicated to Emily for the first time in weeks the strength of their beauty; and she felt a rush of physical well-being as the wind slapped against her cheeks and a few flakes of snow brushed her lips.

Ahead of them the children had reached the rink and Emily and Abe hurried to catch up with them, and now she let Abe hold her hand as they ran across the snow. The music from the amplifier blared loudly one moment, then lost itself in a gust of wind, then reverberated back like an echo as it hit the sides of the mountains. Emily and Abe followed the children to a bench near the long white-napkined table on which stood great aluminum urns of coffee and tea and hot chocolate, covered dishes of croissants, brioches, shortbreads, scones, all kinds of pastries. Several white-coated waiters stood behind the table, stamping their feet, beating their hands together against the cold.

Sam bowed deeply, almost losing his balance, and motioned the girls to a bench. *"Asseyez-vous, mesdemoiselles.* I brought a buttonhook. I'll put on your skates for you. Take off your shoes, Vee."

"You won't object if I offer to put on your skates for you?" Abe asked, smiling at Emily.

She shook her head and sat down and Abe went down on one knee on the ice before her and took off one of her ski boots. For a moment he held her foot in its heavy white woolen sock in the palm of his hand.

"I'd like to take that ungainly sock off," he said, and slipped his fingers for a moment down inside it, "but I suppose I'd better not."

She shook her head and he held out one of her skates and she pushed her foot down into it. "You have beautiful feet," he said softly, "and delicate, slender ankles."

At the far end of the enormous flooded field the hockey team was practising, and groups of skaters were standing around, watching. In the center of the rink, apparently oblivious of the admiring ring around him, a small, quite portly man with a silver goatee and a black beret, did figures with marvellous ease, his hands clasped behind his back, a look of serene concentration on his face, a monocle in one eye.

"Believe it or not," Emily said to Abe, "he's considered one of the best mountaineers in the Haute Savoie."

All around were skaters, a few learning, tumbling, shrieking upon the ice; others skating in pairs, intent on each other; a group of university students playing crack-the-whip; and above them all were the mountains rising, their peaks flooded with crimson in the last light of the sun so that Emily sitting on the bench, Abe kneeling at her feet, were bathed in flaming light.

Now Sam was putting on Mimi's shoes, leaving Virginia sitting on the bench, moving the blades of her skates back and forth on the criss-crossed surface of the ice there at the edge of the rink. "That's not tight enough, Sam," Mimi said, and Sam started tightening the laces of her skates all over again, pulling at the buttonhook until it started to slip out of his cold fingers. When he had done he offered the hook to Abe.

"Would you like this, dad? I should have asked you first."

"Thanks, I would, Sam," Abe said, and tightened the laces of Emily's skates. "Not too tight?" he asked her.

"No. Just perfect."

Sam had his skates on now and looked from Mimi to Virginia and back to Mimi again, holding out his hands to pull her up. "I'll be back for you in a moment, Vee," he said, "I'll just take Mimi Opp for a quick spin."

"Go on," Virginia said. "I like to skate by myself. Honestly."

The music was loud and gay, the old song that would always mean to them that winter and the skating rink:

Et—c'est le même songe
Qui—nous seduit jusqu' au jour
Oui.
C'est—l'eternel et doux songe
Qui—sonne aux heures d'amour.

"Hold everything," Abe said to Emily, and turned to Virginia. "Come along, Vee," he said, "how about taking the old man around the rink once?" He held out his hands and after a fraction of hesitation she took them. "You skate beautifully," Abe said after a moment. "How about trying a waltz?"

"Oh—I'll probably trip you up or something."

"I think we can manage."

She closed her eyes and her face stiffened into a grimace of concentration, but she managed the steps.

"Bravo," Abe said. "Now just relax. Enjoying the holidays?"

"Oh—yes, thanks."

"Have fun at school?"

"Yes, thank you."

"Sam tells me you write poetry."

"Oh—that. Yes."

"Want to be a poet?"

"Oh—yes. And stories, too. There's not much of a living in it, though. I guess I'd have to do something else, too. Teach, like daddy, maybe. Mimi says I should just marry money."

Abe laughed. "Mimi has the practical French way of looking at it."

"I wouldn't be surprised if I never married at all," Virginia said.

"What? Soured on marriage at this early age?" Abe asked.

"Oh, I'm not soured on it at all," Virginia explained earnestly. "It's just that I don't want to marry just anybody, and I'm afraid the right person might not ask me." Then she went rigid in his arms.

"What's the matter?" Abe asked, as someone touched his sleeve and a voice said:

"May I have the pleasure of this dance, Miss Bowen?" and there beside them was a thin, handsome lad, too handsome, grinning at them.

"No," Virginia said, "I'm sorry, I'm—I'm already dancing with someone." She looked pleadingly up at Abe.

"Still mad at me?" the boy asked.

"I'm just—I'm just already skating," Virginia stammered. "Please leave me alone, Beanie."

Beanie looked elaborately at his wrist watch. "I'll give you ten minutes, pussycat," he said. "Then I'm coming after you." And with complete assurance he skated away.

"So that's the famous Beanie," Abe said.

"Yes. I wish he—he does make it so difficult. He just—he just won't see he isn't wanted. I don't think I ought to dance with him if I—if I don't want to, do you?"

Before Abe could answer Sam and Mimi skated up to them. "Was that Beanie trying to make off with you?" Mimi demanded.

"Yes."

"What an impression you must have made on him!"

"Well, I'm not going to skate with him," Virginia said.

"Why not?"

"He can go sit on a tack and press down, as far as I'm concerned."

"Come on and skate with us," Sam said. "Mimi's trying to

teach me to waltz and not succeeding. Maybe you'll have better luck. I saw you just now with dad.''

Relinquishing Virginia to them, Abe turned to look for Emily. She was skating slowly around the edge of the rink, with long, dreamy strokes of her blades. Abe skated quickly over to her. "Come, darling," he said. "It's all right if we skate together, isn't it?''

She put her hands in his and they went the entire round of the huge flooded field together without saying anything. Then Abe smiled down at her. "Don't we do beautifully together, darling?'' he asked.

She nodded. Then she said, "Each time you call me darling I feel—I feel as though we were having an—an assignation.''

He laughed. "We are, aren't we?''

"Yes. But, Abe, please be careful. Don't let—don't let the children—''

His fingers tightened around hers. "Darling heart, please trust me.''

"But I do," she said. "I trust you implicitly. I always have.''

"This is a first time," Abe said. "When we're old something will remind us and one of us will say, 'Do you remember the first time we went skating together? The sky was full of stars and the Alps were beautiful about us. Do you remember how happy we were?' ''

"I'll never forget," Emily said softly.

"The first time we met," Abe said, "there in the crowded lobby of Carnegie Hall, full of cigarette smoke and people talking and coughing—and of them all it seemed to me that you were the only one who had listened to the music—Do you remember the night we went to the Lewisohn Stadium?''

"Yes," Emily said. "It was an all-Handel program.''

"Where was Court?" Abe asked. "Why wasn't he with us?''

"He was on a ten-week lecture tour for the university," Emily said, "speaking on the Homeric gods." She looked at Abe in his dark skating clothes, his blue knit cap pulled down over his ears, starlight on his face, his brown eyes, his thin, rather bumpy nose. "Do you remember how hot it was that night?" she asked, her woolen-mittened hand clasped in Abe's leather-gloved one, "at the Lewisohn Stadium?''

"You wore a thin dress," Abe said. "I don't remember what

it was like except that it was very pretty and your shoulders were bare.''

"The stars were blurry," Emily said, "the sky was so heavy and hot.''

"And right after the concert it began to pour. I remember the thunder rumbling all through it, but the rain held off till the music was over.''

"The people walking to the subway," Emily said, "holding newspapers over their heads. And running into drugstores to get a soda and wait till the rain had stopped.''

"And we walked," Abe said. "Why didn't we realize it then, Emily? People who aren't in love don't just walk for blocks and blocks in the rain the way we did. We didn't even look for a taxi. And your thin dress got soaking and clung to your body. Your beautiful woman's body. Why didn't we know it then? It would have been so much simpler.''

"Would it?''

"Wouldn't it?'' he demanded. "You've had that many more years tying you to Courtney and your children. And I've had that many more years searching desperately for someone when all along you were the one I needed.''

Across the rink Beanie was persistent. He skated to the end of the flooded field where Virginia, Mimi and Sam were practising figure threes, and bowed low before Virginia. "Come along, my haughty Virginia with the pretty cat's eyes. Don't be so mean to Beanie. Come skate with Beanie for five little old minutes.''

"Don't make an issue of it, Vee," Mimi said in a low voice. "He isn't worth it.''

Silently Virginia let Beanie take her hands.—Anyhow it gives Mimi and Sam a chance to be together, she thought.

"I saw you skating with Mr. Fielding," Beanie said, "and I wasn't deceived. You skate as well as I thought you did.''

Virginia said nothing.

They skated the entire length of the huge rink, and then Beanie swung around in front of Virginia, still holding her hands, and skated backwards. "Why so silent, pussycat?'' he asked.

"Because I haven't anything to say.''

"Did you know you have very pretty eyes? Pretty green kitten's eyes. I like girls with green eyes and red hair.''

"My hair's not so terribly red.''

"Come on, let's make up," he wheedled. "I said I was

sorry." She looked down at the ice helplessly. "Honest. And Parson Sam's doing his best to reform me. So please don't go on being mad at me. You can't stay mad at little old Beanie."

"No." Virginia smiled in spite of herself, pleased in spite of herself by Beanie's remarks about her eyes. "I suppose you wheedle everybody out of it."

"Usually." Beanie grinned at her. "Come on, let's skate fast. Hold my hands tight and we'll race."

They flew over the ice and now she could forget that it was Beanie with whom she was skating and simply enjoy the speed, cleaving through the cold dark air as a bird breaks through the sky.

Emily, still flushed from skating, was fixing dinner when Gertrude, in ski clothes, white parka and black trousers, stalked into the kitchen. "Where's everybody?" she demanded. "I knocked and I knocked and finally I just walked in." She sat down and tipped her chair back against the wall.

Emily looked up from the stove, a spoon in her hand, a smudge of flour on one cheek. "We're all right here. Court's in his office and Vee and Mimi are in the living room amusing Connie. Rather noisily, I admit. I guess they didn't hear you."

"What's that you're cooking?" Gertrude asked. "Smells good. Ragout?"

"Um."

"Got much more to do?"

"No. Just let it simmer for an hour."

"Come on down to the casino and have a drink. There's at least an iota of gaiety there at Christmas-time and I'm getting bored with the Splendide." Emily hesitated and Gertrude pushed her mahogony hair back from her white forehead with an impatient gesture. "Oh, come on. I had to get out or go nuts and if I go on down to the casino by myself I'll drink too much and get potted and Kaarlo won't like it. Bring the kids along if you want to. I'll treat them to lemonade. Or are Virginia and Mimi old enough for vermouth cassis?"

"They're all right here with Connie."

"Come on, then."

"All right, but I can't stay long."

"Who said anything about staying long?" Gertrude demanded. "I just want a drink. One lousy little drink. Even Clément wouldn't deny me one lousy little drink."

Emily put her outdoor things on again, told the girls where

she was going, and followed Gertrude. Outdoors the cold seemed as tangible as black marble, and Gertrude led the way, refusing Emily's arm, stepping quickly and nervously over the hard-packed snow. As they got into the village an urchin, far too scantily clothed, Emily thought, tagged along behind them, whistling through his teeth, one note, repeated and repeated, until he disappeared into an alley, yelling at some unseen antagonist, *"Hé, espèce de putain!"*

The hobnails of their boots scraped against the snow and Emily, slipping and almost falling, thought that the only reason she was tagging along with Gertrude like this was that she, too, found it impossible to stay alone with her thoughts. And then there was an only half-admitted desire to go back to the casino (like a criminal to the scene of his crime) so that she could live again that evening with Abe, knowing that his presence would be there, almost a visual impact against her retina, and that his words would echo against her ear, louder than when they had first been spoken. A strange thing, this desire to visit again the scene of that evening (though this time she would be going only into the bar, would indeed not even see the beautiful formal room in which they had dined) almost as though she had not skated with him that afternoon, as though she would not see him again.

But when? When? When Abe and Sam had left them at the villa nothing had been said about another meeting, and was it because this was understood, or because Abe felt that another meeting, like Christmas dinner, was something better avoided?

As they went into the casino Gertrude raised her head at the sound of music and laughter like a horse to the scent of danger. Through large open doors they could see the green baize of the roulette table, hear the sound of chips being raked across, and the voice of the croupier intoning, *"Faits vos jeux, messieurs, 'dames, faits vos jeux."*

"In the days when I had money to throw around I used to like rouge et noir," Gertrude said. "I'd probably go in now and then and lose my last sou trying to make a haul even now if Kaarlo weren't so dead against it."

They went into the bar and sat down at one of the small tables. "If I followed my inclination and there was no morning after I'd get drunk every night," Gertrude said. "What is it? A sort of death wish? An urge for oblivion? But I'm scared of death, Em, I get into a cold sweat when I think of it. And yet I can't wait to get to sleep at night. Half the time I take a pill so I'll go to sleep quickly, so I won't stay awake after Kaarlo. I can't wait to get out of myself into sleep—and that's after all a simulation of death. So why the hell am I so afraid to die? Are you afraid to die, Emily?''

"Yes," Emily said. "Of course I am."

"Is Courtney?"

Sitting at the small round table Emily shivered in the sudden uncontrollable way that the superstitious say means someone has walked over the place where your grave is to be. "I don't know."

"Kaarlo's not. He doesn't want to, but he's not afraid of it. And he doesn't like me to talk about it. I suppose it's the Finn in him, this reticence. He gets almost angry with me. Could be it is morbid. But after all dying's a part of living, isn't it, and it's something we all have to do sooner or later, so I don't see why we shouldn't have a certain interest in it.''

"I guess we all do. . . ." Emily said, but she was not listening. She was looking around the crowded, stuffy room, cold and damp under foot where snow and ice had melted off boots and the chill came up from the cellars and the frozen earth below; and yet the air was hot and dry from steam heat so that one felt almost feverish with icy feet and burning cheeks. She looked intently at the faces about her, some animated, some brooding, some drunken, looking for the face of happiness, the face that would be as a revelation so that she would know what to do. . . .

"I spoke passable Spanish for a while," Gertrude said, "and to me the most beautiful phrase in the whole language is *jornada de la muerte*. I suppose that's Freud's death wish speaking in me in spite of my fear of death. . . .*Why* are you afraid of death, Emily?"

"I'm not sure," Emily said. "I think if I could understand the meaning of life I wouldn't be afraid."

"That's it!" Gertrude exclaimed. "In the days when life had a point I wasn't afraid. . . .One day Kaarlo was three hours late coming down the mountain. I'd heard that horrible, low thunder sound of avalanches in the afternoon and I was sure he was dead. I worry about him now much more than I ever did during the war—or about Henri—or any of them. One had to learn to accept the fact of death, then, and I did, as I can't seem to now. I don't think you're really afraid of things, Emily. Not the way I am. Don't be. Don't ever let yourself be. Don't be afraid of life even when it knocks you down. Get me! You'd think I went in for Sunday School teaching and psychiatric interviews as a regular thing.'' She stopped, realizing that Emily's attention was no longer on her words.

She looked up and there was Abe walking towards them. He came casually into the bar of the casino, walking with an easy grace, walking as a mountaineer did, as Kaarlo did. Emily had never noticed before the extraordinary suppleness of Abe's movements, but now that she saw it consciously for the first time she realized in retrospect that all of his movements had the controlled and powerful rhythm of all people who move very close to nature: it had taken the eyes of love to make her see this.

Gertrude beckoned to him. ''Come and join us.''

He came over, smiling, quite casual, his greeting to both of them warm, Emily's not a shade warmer than Gertrude's.

''What'll it be?'' Gertrude asked him.

''Beer.''

''Nothing stronger?''

''Not now, thanks.''

''Going up the mountain tomorrow with Kaarlo?''

''Yes.''

—Gertrude knows what he's doing tomorrow and I don't, Emily thought. But of course he'd have to make plans with Kaarlo in advance and Gertrude'd know about them. . . .

''What the devil do you see in mountain climbing?'' Gertrude demanded.

Abe was silent for a moment. His beer was put in front of him and he picked it up and looked at it absently. ''I don't know,'' he said after a moment, and all of a sudden Emily felt that his words were for her and not for Gertrude at all, that he was trying to communicate to her something that was an integral part of his life. ''I've never been a particularly articulate person so I can't explain very well. . . .''

''But I want to know,'' Gertrude said. ''Kaarlo can't tell me. He says it's just part of him. But he can't tell me why. So please try.''

''I don't know,'' Abe said again. ''Just for the sake of the sport, to start out with. And then it becomes man against nature. The mountain is almost like a person. Tall and stern and adamant. But I am stronger. That's what I have to prove. And then something above and beyond all this. A sudden conception of size. A realization that size, like time, is only faintly grasped by our minds. The mountain is greater than I am, and I am greater than the mountain, and in the universe the mountain is smaller than a single flake of snow, and in that soft moist flake there is all infinity . . . I'm putting all this very badly.''

"No you're not," Emily said.

"Hey," Gertrude said, hardly listening, thinking of something else, "Kaarlo tells me you used to play football.''

For a moment Abe looked entirely blank, as though her words had no meaning. Then he said, "Only in college.''

"So you were a football hero.''

He seemed a little annoyed. "What brought that up?''

"Oh—curiosity," Gertrude said. "And you played some professional golf, too, didn't you?''

"Some," Abe said. "Would you like a complete biography?''

"I'd be charmed," Gertrude said, unrebuffed. She looked around as a gray-haired man stopped behind her chair, putting his hands on her shoulders. It was Michel Clément, her doctor.

"Oh, hello, Clément," Gertrude said. "Come join us.''

Clément sat down, speaking to Emily, and Gertrude introduced him to Abe. They talked for a while of mountain climbing, then Clément said to Gertrude, "When I said that it wouldn't hurt you to come in to the village occasionally for a drink I didn't mean every night. Did I, Gertrude?'' He, like Kaarlo, added music and gentleness to her name.

"Come now, Clément," Gertrude said. "This is the casino, not the hospital; you're not on duty here. It's Christmas vacation anyhow, isn't it?''

"Not for you, yet. Where's Kaarlo?''

"Hadn't got home when I left. He said he'd be late.''

"And when he gets home and finds you not there?''

"I left him a note, mother hen, saying I was going to stop for Emily and come to the casino. And I'm better, much better, so do stop nagging at me.''

"One of the reasons you're better," Clément said gently, "is exactly because I do keep nagging at you.''

"Okay, okay," Gertrude said. "Let's stop going on about it and have another drink." She turned to Abe who was talking to Emily about mountain climbing again. "So you were a football hero," she said, "and I was a fashion writer. Were you as serious when you played football as you are now?''

"Am I so terribly serious?" Abe asked, smiling.

"In a nice sort of way. I'd have died rather than be serious in the old days. A much more sensible way of life than the one

I've fallen into now. Start the day at three or four in the afternoon with cocktails and *never* to bed before three or four in the morning. Shopping for clothes, going to an opening, laughing at how stupid other people were—Clément, where's that drink you promised me?''

"I promised you no drink," Clément said, "but I'll get you one.''

"Oh, God, that was the life," Gertrude said. "Never having to think of anything more taxing than the latest shade of stockings or the length of a skirt. And could that ever be important!''

"If that is such an ideal life why don't you go back to it?'' Clément suggested.

"You know perfectly well that I did," Gertrude said. "And you know perfectly well that it was a fiasco.''

"Why was it a fiasco, Gert?" Abe asked gently.

A waiter put a fresh drink in front of Gertrude and she picked up her glass and downed half of it. "I tried New York first," she said. "I got my old job back, or at least a reasonable facsimile thereof. I bought clothes and went to parties." She looked angrily at Abe. "At one party I went to a woman came up to me and—I do not excuse her because she was high— looked at my concentration camp number branded on my arm and said, 'Oh, how cute, you have your telephone number on your arm.' " Gertrude hit her hand angrily against the veined marble top of the table. "I found myself hating my own countrymen. It had amused me before, people's stupidity; I made a damn good living out of it; but all of a sudden it seemed like treason. So I tried going home. To the dear darling family in Watson Falls. I was invited to speak at the Women's Club. Never never never accept an invitation to speak at a Women's Club. I tried to tell them about some of my experiences in Ravensbrück—because this, of course, was what they had come for, a vicarious thrill—and how when I was ready to escape I asked some of the other women to go with me, saying: it's either wait here and die slowly or take a chance of dying quickly and at once. Well. They're dead now. That's not the point. What I mean is all those flat, flabby women, those obese ghouls, sat there with their mouths hanging open and I thought that given the same situation they'd all be dead, too. Soft and stupid. All of them.''

"Is it that bad, Mrs. Bowen?'' Clément asked.

Emily shook her head. "Gertrude's been hurt and so she's generalizing. It's a pretty good country on the whole, and the people in it, too. We have our faults and they may be glaring, and we have individuals we may not be very proud of, but take us by and large we'll stick our necks out for something we believe in, and that in itself may be a fault, but it's one I like."

"Bravo," Abe said.

Gertrude finished her drink. "Emily's a bluestocking. She reads history for fun. I read *anything*—except maybe a fashion magazine—because I'm bored with doing nothing and Clément won't let me do anything that's fun. After I get well I'll never read another book."

"She underestimates herself," Clément said in a low voice to Abe as Gertrude began looking around for a waiter to bring her a fresh drink. "One of the greatest excitements of the war for her must have been discovering and utilizing for the first time a really good brain. . . ."

"Don't mumble, Clément," Gertrude said. "I can't hear a word you're saying."

"I didn't intend you to. Shall I walk you home now?"

"I think I'll have another drink first."

"But I must go now," Clément said. "I have to stop in at the hospital."

"I didn't think you were on call tonight."

"I'm not, technically, but there's a girl I'd like to look in on."

"A girl! Of course it would be a girl!" Gertrude jeered.

Ignoring her, Clément called for the bill. "Put your coat on," he said, and held out to Gertrude her white parka.

"And so I may take you home," Abe said to Emily.

She nodded, smiling. "If you would be so kind."

"A good doctor, this Clément?"

"He's supposed to be one of the best."

"I can imagine he might be. Have another drink, darling?"

"No, thanks. Clément had my glass filled the same time as Gert's."

"Sit with me while I have another beer?"

"I shouldn't. The family will be wondering where I am and getting hungrier and hungrier."

"Must you go?" Abe asked, only half joking. "Can't they get their own dinner?"

She shook her head, laughing. "They'd all starve. In fact they're probably starving right now. I really must go, Abe."

"Just say to hell with them," Abe suggested. "Say to hell

with them and come with me." She looked at him despairingly, and he said, "But you wouldn't be my Emily if you did, would you? All right, my darling, if I must wait I must—or lose you entirely, isn't that it? But not much longer. I can't stand it much longer." Still she said nothing, and at last he pushed back his chair. "I'll walk you home."

They left the casino and went out into the darkness. They walked without talking and the silence was too important and Emily felt that she must break it. She looked up at the sky and it seemed that Abe had cleared away the clouds because again it was an open night, the mountains like ivory, and the stars crusted thickly over the high black of sky. When she and Courtney had come to the village in the autumn the leaves were still on the trees and the grass was green but they didn't see the mountains for two weeks. When it wasn't actually raining the fog was thick about everything and the doors and windows stuck with the damp and the stove smoked and Emily was filled with a blind, frustrated hate for the house, the village, the situation that had plunged them into this place and this winter. And then one morning when she wakened, everything was shining and the mountains were so bright that she couldn't look at them for more than a second without black streaks dancing wildly against her eyeballs. The trees were still wet from the rain and all the small drops of water glistened. She walked out of the house with Courtney and they stood looking around them and it was as though they had been enclosed inside a shell and the shell had opened, and Courtney, suddenly quiet, had said, "See, this is where we live, the mountains, not the house," and she had been ashamed. But the shell had closed down about them again and it was only now, searching wildly for something to say to Abe to break the silence, that she remembered that morning and her exaltation and release at the beauty of it, and she tried clumsily to describe it to him.

But he took her hand and his grip was angry as he said, "Emily, Sam and I are going on Sunday."

She fell into silence as abruptly as though she had fallen off a precipice, and Abe went on, "But it's not the end of this, Emily. There isn't any point in either of us trying to run away from it. You must stop trying."

She could no longer look up at the mountains and the stars. She looked down at her feet as they moved blindly across the snow.

"I want you so terribly," Abe said.

"I want you, too," she said.

They kept on holding hands, tighter and tighter, and an American couple passed them, the woman in a mink coat and perfume, and both of them talking and laughing and happy and in a funny, overdone way quite beautiful.

"I want to be able to walk anywhere with you like that," Abe said. "I want to tell people that we're in love. I want to shout it out from the tops of the mountains. I don't want to have to be casual about you in front of Gertrude de Croisenois or Kaarlo or Michel Clément or anyone."

Emily walked along beside him and she could not speak for joy at his words. She forgot that she was walking home to her husband and her children; it was as though she were living a schizophrenic life, part of her completely for Courtney and the children, part of her never torn from them for a moment, part of her wife and mother as she had always been; and part of her with Abe, soaring wildly and ecstatically with Abe.

"I ought to feel guilty about you," she said at last. "I ought to feel that all this is wrong."

"It is not wrong," Abe said.

"No. I know." And then: "Oh, Abe, what we think we are and what we are are often two completely different people and it's impossible for us to see where one leaves off and the other begins. When I think about myself I don't feel as though I were a—a sinful woman. And yet I—if someone were telling me about me I wouldn't like me very much. I wouldn't be very tolerant. I've never thought much of wives who've played around with other men. Or even people who for one reason or another have simply flouted conventions. I haven't been—I haven't been very tolerant in my thoughts about Gertrude."

"But you are not Gertrude," Abe said. "You must never make the mistake of confusing yourself with Gertrude, Emily."

"I don't think it's a mistake," she said slowly. "It's just that we don't like to look in mirrors and see ourselves the way we really are. Have you ever been walking down a street and suddenly caught a glimpse of your reflection in a store window and not recognized yourself at first? And then you think, oh, no, that can't be me—that's sort of what happens when I'm talking or thinking about Gert and suddenly it's myself I'm catching a reflection of in the glass."

"No, Emily," Abe said sternly. "You and Gertrude might have come from two different planets; your codes of behavior bear no resemblance whatsoever to each other. Don't let your feelings about Gertrude's code confuse or influence you. You are making up your own mind about this, not Gertrude's.''

"If it were Gert's mind it would be a lot easier," Emily said.

"Yes, and not nearly as important. And it *is* important, darling, isn't it?''

She nodded mutely.

Now they had passed the lights of the village and the snow about them gleamed in the starlight. Up ahead of them the lights from the villa fell across the snow. Abe stopped and put his hands on Emily's shoulders and looked down at her and she knew that nobody had ever looked at her that way before and that there were no words to express it.

They stood there and then they started walking again, very slowly, and Abe said, "All I know is that this is good. It is the best thing that has ever happened to me. I have fallen in love with you and I am happy. At this moment that is all that matters.'' He drew her into the shelter of the shadows and kissed her.

Virginia walked through the lighted streets with Mimi and when Mimi spoke she did not hear. She clutched the bag of pistachio ice cream to her and stepped carefully into the warm splash of light spilled from the windows of the charcuterie, throwing comfort out against the cold dark of night. She was not with Mimi, she was not bringing ice cream home for dinner, she was not a schoolgirl. It was winter in another time and her coat and hat were of fur and her eyes dark ringed and shadowed and beside her walked someone: who? Not Mimi. Someone shadowy and strong. And they were together for the last night—for how long? They did not know. Perhaps forever. Tomorrow she would enter the sanatorium, but she would leave with him the manuscript of her latest book, her greatest book, and he would publish it, yes, that was it, he was her publisher—so that if she died young, if this was farewell forever, at least she would have left her mark, she would be in the company of how many others? Keats, of course, his splendor falling from castle walls. (But that was Tennyson, wasn't it?) And Chekhov. Chekhov drank champagne on his deathbed and they would drink champagne tonight, and she would remind him about Chekhov and they would laugh because never would she allow anything to destroy the gaiety of her beauty. And there was Katherine Mansfield coughing blood alone in small sad hotels and London flats. And Mozart with his music fluid and gay as lighted fountains.

And Gertrude.

Time slapped against her like a gust of wind and blew her back into the path by Mimi, leaving the lights of the village, turning now onto the darker, colder path leading to the villa. Gertrude could not die there in that firelit room in the chalet. Death in the present could not intrude like a discord into the harmonic pattern of death in the past and death in the future—

She clutched the ice cream bag to her and staggered slightly and put her hand out towards *his* arm and righted herself and coughed gently and was brave again and she looked up and there she was ahead of herself in the snow clasped in her lover's arms, dissolving in love.

But the picture did not fade and Mimi's hand came roughly against her arm and they stood frozen still on the snow and Mimi's sibilant intake of breath seemed like a scream but the two figures at the turn of the path did not hear.

When Emily went into the kitchen Courtney was sitting by the stove reading the paper and Connie was trying to fit together the pieces of a picture puzzle. "Where are Virginia and Mimi?" Emily asked, stepping from one world into another, from the world of love into the world of dailiness.

"They went to the village to get ice cream for dinner," Courtney said. "It seemed a reasonable enough request. But I thought if it was too cold for Connie to go skating this afternoon it was too cold for her to go get ice cream and I'd finished work for the day so I came in here to sit with her. I have a small libation made for us." He handed her a glass.

"Oh, thanks, darling. I had a Pernod at the casino with Gert, but this looks very pleasant, anyhow." She took a sip and stood leaning against the sink.

"Anything on for this evening?" Courtney asked.

Emily shook her head. "Not a thing. Bed early for a change. How about taking the three girls to the mer de glâce tomorrow? These are the holidays so couldn't you take a day off from your typewriter?"

"Why not?" Courtney said. "I think I'd rather enjoy going."

"Good. I'll tell the girls they can plan on it, then."

Connie looked up from her puzzle. "Me, too? Am I going, too?"

"Yes, Connie. You, too." The heavy front door slammed and Emily looked up, listening. "There come Virginia and Mimi now."

"May I go see them?"

"Oh—all right, Con. They had a vacation from you all afternoon." As the child ran off, Emily asked Courtney, "She didn't bother you while we were skating?"

"No. She slept till just a few minutes before you got back. And Virginia and Mimi gave her a bath before they went for the ice cream."

"Good." She looked away from him, running her finger over the scarred porcelain lip of the sink. "I was going to ask Abe and Sam for Christmas dinner but they're going on down to the South of France for Christmas."

"You've been lonely this winter," Courtney said abruptly. "You've missed our Sunday night gatherings; you've missed going out. I've realized that."

"I've managed very nicely," she said, smiling at him, reaching out to touch her finger against his lean, narrow face. As she moved her hand towards him he reached up and ran his hand across his hair, not a rebuff, exactly, but the instinctive gesture of a solitary animal disturbed and troubled by too intimate contact.

"I haven't been too lonely," Emily said lightly, withdrawing her hand. "After all, there's always Gertrude."

Courtney finished his drink and put the glass down on the bare wood of the kitchen table, polished to a silky gray from innumerable scrubbings. "Strange, unhappy creature, that Gertrude," he said absently.

"Court, what do you think of Gert and Kaarlo?" Emily asked abruptly.

His narrow blue eyes widened in surprise. "Think of them? In what way?"

"Their way of life."

"I don't imagine it can be very satisfactory."

"Do you—do you disapprove of it?"

"I don't know. I suppose they have their own reasons for not marrying." His voice was slightly impatient.

"This whole business about living outside the conventional social codes can be very confusing," Emily said.

"Why?"

"Gert's husband is dead, Kaarlo's never had a wife, neither of them has any family they need consider. So if they don't want to marry I don't see any particular reason why they should.''

"Not everybody is as unencumbered as Gertrude and Kaarlo. There's usually a husband or a child or someone around to be hurt.''

"I suppose so.''

Courtney laughed. "My dear Emily, you are as funny and sweetly naïve now as you were when I first saw you sitting in the front row at my history lectures.''

"I am not naïve!''

"Of course you are.''

"I'm a big girl now and I ought to have done some developing. It may have been funny and sweet when I was sixteen, but it would be pretty pathetic in me now.''

"All right,'' Courtney said, "you're as sophisticated as the Sphinx.''

"Do you think Gert's sophisticated?''

"Not particularly. And a fool to behave as she does to Kaarlo. Wonder how long he'll stand for it, or Gertrude herself, for that matter? Just as well they aren't married.''

"I don't think being married would stop Gert if she wanted somebody.''

"No, Emily, I know that.''

"Has she ever made a pass at you?''

"On occasion.''

"I don't think I like that,'' Emily said after a moment.

"It couldn't have been less important.''

"Would it bother you if somebody made a pass at me?''

He laughed again. "People have, haven't they?''

She laughed, too. "On occasion. And also completely unimportant. But I think I'd prefer you to be bothered.''

"All right. I'm wildly jealous. That make you feel any better? What's this all about anyhow?''

"Nothing particular. I suppose I'm just being naïve again. Would it bother you if I should—if I should ever have an affair with somebody or something?''

"I suppose it would bother me, yes.''

"Would you still want to keep me?''

"I imagine so, Emily. What nonsense you're talking. You've been seeing too much of Gertrude.''

"But wouldn't it hurt you terribly?''

"I wouldn't enjoy it, but I'd probably get over it. But you're not like Gertrude, you know, and thank God for that.''

This could hardly be construed as permission, permission even in an indirect way to sleep with Abe. But after all it wouldn't kill Courtney. After all perhaps her compunctions were simply another indication of her naïveté.

But could they do it? Could they be together a few times and then just let go? It was done, and not infrequently. It was done by any number of people. But that, she thought, was when it didn't matter, when it was purely—what was the word? Carnal. But she couldn't just say, "All right. Abe, let's go up to your room, taking care, of course, that Madame Pedroti doesn't see us and that Sam's busy elsewhere. Let's be lovers a few times and then you go on down to Bandol with Sam for the rest of the holidays and maybe I'll see you one of these years in New York or Indiana."

—But that's what I'm going to do, she thought, moving from the table and looking unseeingly into the pot of ragout still simmering gently on the stove. That's what I'm going to do because I'm weak and my desire is strong and it wouldn't kill Courtney and perhaps it will be all right, perhaps then we will be able to let this thing go and just go back to being friends again the way we were in New York. . . .

"Remember that first summer we spent in Paris?" Courtney said, "and I took you to Jacky Bowman's studio for dinner?"

She pulled herself back to the kitchen, back to Courtney. "How could I ever forget it?" she asked lightly.

"I think it was a terrible disillusionment to you," Courtney said, smiling. "I'd told you that he was living in sin with a girl from Arkansas who was in Paris supposedly studying art. They'd been living together for almost five years. So I took you there and she'd put on at least twenty pounds and there were corsets and other assorted articles of underwear hanging on lines about the room and she certainly couldn't cook and there wasn't a bottle of wine in the place."

"Evian water, I remember," Emily said. "They'd bought it especially for me."

"I'll never forget your face," Courtney said. "There was illicit love in all its squalor, and your romantic heart was almost unbearably disappointed. Let's eat now, Em. It's late and I'm hungry." He stood up and took his glass to the sink.

At dinner Virginia was so silent that Emily asked her several times if she were feeling ill; but though the child denied it, as soon as Connie was settled for the night she went upstairs, too.

After a few minutes Emily followed her up. Virginia was huddled under the covers, her eyes tightly closed, her hair rather wild-looking as though she had been pushing her fingers through it.

"Vee," Emily said.

Virginia made an almost imperceptible movement.

Emily came into the chilly room and sat down on the side of the bed, putting the back of her hand briefly against Virginia's forehead, her cheek, her neck; but the child was quite cool. "Head ache, darling?"

"No."

"Throat sore?"

"No."

"No pains anywhere?"

"No."

"Then what is it? You haven't acted like yourself all evening."

"Nothing."

Emily's hand went out and she began to stroke Virginia's forehead, gently, rhythmically, smoothing back the straggly red locks, suddenly dank and lifeless as though the child were indeed ill. After a moment Virginia moved away, burying her face in the pillow.

"Darling, what is it?" Emily asked. "Has someone hurt you?"

A shake of the head.

"You were so happy this afternoon while we were skating. What's happened to disturb you so now?"

"Nothing."

"Mimi hasn't done anything to upset you, has she?"

Another shake of the head.

"Can't you tell mother about it?"

"There isn't anything to tell."

Emily tried to make her voice light. "Any time you can't eat ice cream for dessert I know there's something wrong."—Could it be because she knows Sam prefers Mimi and she feels hurt and left out? Emily wondered.

"I think I have a slight stomach-ache," Virginia said. "Would you play the piano for me, mother? Just for a few minutes? I think maybe it would put me to sleep."

"Of course, darling." Emily bent over Virginia and kissed her tenderly, then stood up and tucked the covers in about the child's thin shoulders.

At the head of the stairs she met Courtney. "I'm coming up to read," he said. "How about putting the plumbing to bed?"

"I'll do it when I come up. Virginia wants me to play the piano for a few minutes to put her to sleep. Won't bother you, will it?"

"No, I like it. Might put me to sleep, too. Is she all right?"

"I'm not sure. She says she has a stomach-ache."

"That could be it," Courtney said. "Children always seem to get upset stomachs at Christmas-time. I know I always did. How about bringing a couple of hot-water bottles when you come up? I forgot, as usual, to fill mine."

"All right. Do you want it now?"

"No. I'll keep my socks on till you come up."

She went on downstairs. Mimi was curled up in one of the plush chairs, reading. "Virginia all right?" she asked.

"She says she has a stomach-ache," Emily said. "Do you know if anything could have happened to upset her, Mimi?"

"She's probably just in one of her moods," Mimi said, looking down at her book. "At school Virginia's famous for her moods. Just one of the problems of puberty. Don't worry about her, Mrs. Bowen."

"She asked me to play for her." Emily sat down on the rickety piano bench and held her fingers for a moment over the piano keys. Then she began a Chopin nocturne.

When she had finished Mimi said, "That was terrific, Mrs. Bowen. You ought to play more, anybody who can play like that. Your family's just too used to you to appreciate you."

Emily laughed. "Thanks, Mimi."

"Play something else now, please."

Emily started another nocturne, and then the phone rang. She ran to answer it, explaining her unwonted haste by calling back to Mimi, "It'll waken Virginia."

She fumbled for the receiver in the dark hall, banged her hand against the antiquated phone box, finally managed to tug the receiver off the hook.

But of course it wasn't Abe.

"Emily, it's Gert. I'm lonely. Come on up."

"Where's Kaarlo?"

"Oh, he's asleep. All this getting up before dawn's crack. Every once in a while he goes to bed right after dinner and I could jump up and down on him and he wouldn't notice. So do come up and keep me company."

"I can't tonight."

"Why?"

"Virginia isn't well, and I'm going to bed early myself for a change."

"Damn. Must you?"

"Yes, I must."

"What's the matter with Virginia?"

"Oh, nothing much. At least I hope not. I think it's just a slightly upset stomach."

"And you really won't come?"

"Not tonight, Gert."

"Then stay on the phone and talk to me for a few minutes, will you? I'm depressed."

"Let me get the chair from Court's study, then. No, that won't do any good, the phone's too high. Okay, but just a few minutes, hunh? I'm tired and the wall's too cold to lean against."

"Everybody in your household in bed already?"

"Everybody except Mimi and me."

"I like your Mimi," Gertrude said. "If Henri and I had had a child I like to think she'd have been something like Mimi."

"Yes," Emily said, shifting her weight from one leg to the other. "She's a nice child."

Gertrude sighed in exasperation, the sound coming sibilantly through the earpiece. "But that's exactly what she's not. She's not in the least nice. That's what I like about her."

"Do you think Virginia's 'nice'?"

"No. I pay her that compliment. I'm not—simpatico—with her as I am with Mimi. But I think Virginia's an artist. Disagreeable and terribly immature right now. But she'll grow up one day and be somebody. I don't know what. Maybe an actress or a poet. But Somebody." Then her voice changed, tightened. "I have a bone to pick with you. Might as well pick it now."

"Now what?" Emily asked, leaning for a moment against the wall that was so ice cold that she could feel it through her heavy sweater.

"Kaarlo's cousin Pierre tells me he saw you and Kaarlo going into the first hut yesterday morning."

"Yes, we did. Why?"

"What were you doing there?"

"I was out for a walk and Kaarlo was coming down from the mountain and we met just before the hut and we went in and sat and Kaarlo made coffee."

Gertrude's voice was cold as the wall. "I'll thank you to lay off Kaarlo if you please, Emily."

Emily stood up straight. "What on earth are you talking about?"

"Just what I say. Keep your hands off Kaarlo."

"You must be absolutely mad," Emily said after a moment. "Or did Pierre make up a tale? It doesn't sound like him."

"Pierre made up no tales. He simply remarked in passing that he'd seen you and Kaarlo going into the first hut. He didn't make anything out of it. I did."

"Then you can unmake it. What utter nonsense, Gert!"

"Is it?"

"You know it is."

"Well, knowing you, perhaps it is. I'm sorry."

"You'd better be."

"I said I was."

"Okay, then," Emily said, but her voice betrayed her anger.

"I wouldn't blame you, you see," Gertrude said. "So don't be mad."

"I'm not mad." She shivered. "We've been talking for hours and hours and you may have the phone by you but I'm standing up in the cold hall and it's worse than Greenland. I've got to hang up before I congeal."

"Oh, hell," Gertrude said. "All right. Going to get up to see me tomorrow?"

"Do my best."

"Make it more than your best, will you? Good night, Em."

" 'Night, Gert." Emily put the earpiece back on the hook and returned to the living room. Mimi was still there, reading, "Not ready for bed yet, Mimi?" she asked.

"Just going to finish my page," Mimi said. "But play something else first, please, Mrs. Bowen. Finish the nocturne you started and then one more thing. Please!"

Emily sat back down at the piano and held her hands out over the keys. She finished the nocturne as requested and was starting Chabrier's Suite Pastorale when Mimi asked suddenly,

"Mrs. Bowen, have you ever had an affair?"

Emily took her hands in shocked silence from the piano keys and swung around on the bench. "Good heavens, Mimi, what a question!"

"I mean since you've been married," Mimi said.

"No!" Emily's voice was still startled.

"My mother has," Mimi said, and waited.

Emily didn't say anything. She turned back to the piano and with her right hand played a few unrelated notes. Finally she said, "It's rather a strange question, Mimi. Why are you asking it?"

"Oh, I just wondered," Mimi said. She had started to say "about you and Mr. Fielding" but her courage failed her. "My mother doesn't have a great many affairs. But she does have them. I suppose Jake has them, too, but he's away on tour so much that I don't see him very often."

Still with one hand Emily played the opening measures of the Chabrier. "I suppose it's different with your parents," she said at last. "They're both very great people and they can go beyond the standards that apply to ordinary human beings."

"Is it because of morals, then?" Mimi asked.

"Is what because of morals?"

"That you've never had an affair."

"You're a most impertinent child," Emily said, though she smiled a little so that her words would not seem too cruel.

"I'm sorry," Mimi said. "I don't mean to be impertinent. It's because I've been so abominably brought up. Please let me ask just one more question. It's a matter of ethics, you see, and I'm very interested in ethics." She paused hopefully, and as Emily said nothing she continued. "You don't approve of affairs, do you?" She continued to stare as Emily's eyes turned black and the corners of her mouth drew barely perceptibly in and down.

"No," Emily said. "I don't think I do approve of affairs." There was a long silence, and then, with both hands, Emily finished the Chabrier.

While her fingers still rested on the piano keys Mimi asked her, "But do you think ethically it may be different for artists than ordinary people?"

"I don't know, Mimi," Emily said flatly. "I don't really think it should be, but perhaps it is. Perhaps artists can see beyond our confused moral code to one that is more truly ethical. On the other hand, lots of them are simply selfish and cause other people a lot of pain."

"Clare and Jake seem to have worked things out satisfactorily. I don't think they hurt people. And you're a kind of artist in your own right, aren't you?" Mimi looked at Emily's hands still resting lightly on the piano keys.

Emily took her hands and dropped them in her lap and looked

down at them. "Not much of a one," she said shortly. "Any particular reason for this conversation, Mimi?"

"Oh, no," Mimi lied quickly. "Just something in the letter I got from Clare today."

Emily stood up, relieved. "Come on, Mimi. If we're going to the mer de glâce tomorrow we might as well get a good night's sleep. . . . And don't worry about your mother," she added awkwardly.

When Mimi got into bed Virginia did not speak, but Mimi knew that she was not asleep, and after a moment she said, "Hey, Vee, I'm frozen. Mind if I come get in with you for a sec and warm up?"

For answer Virginia moved aside and pulled the covers back. Mimi got in beside her and lay there in the darkness in the narrow cot on her back, staring up at the ceiling and the faintly reflected snow light. "Been crying?" she asked after a while.

Virginia shook her head. "No."

"This is your first encounter with the rude facts of life, isn't it, Vee?" Virginia said nothing, and after a moment Mimi put a hand gently on her shoulder, saying, "Look, Vee, it isn't all that terrible."

"Isn't it?"

"Ever hear of Emile Girard, the Nobel Prize winning physicist, end quote?"

"Yes."

"He was one of Clare's."

"Clare's what?"

"I've already told you that Clare's had—that there've been other people she's cared about since she married Jake. And it hasn't been the end of the world. Or their marriage."

"You're talking too loud," Virginia said. "Whisper."

"If you don't want them to know you'd better act more normal tomorrow than you did tonight."

"I said I had a stomach-ache."

"You can't go on having a stomach-ache for the rest of the hols. Now look, dear infant, I think you're taking all this too seriously."

"Am I?"

"You're judging on circumstantial evidence only. As a matter of fact I did, too. But after all a kiss doesn't constitute an affair." Virginia was silent and after a moment Mimi continued, "People kiss for lots of reasons other than being passionately in love. After all your mother and Mr. Fielding are old friends. Hey, you're taking more than your share of the *édredon*. I'm cold.''

"If you kissed Sam that way would you consider yourselves just friends?" Virginia demanded.

"No, but I'm half in love with Sam." Mimi pulled the eiderdown about her shoulders. "Look, Vee, I think you ought to give your mother the benefit of the doubt. You've trusted her for a good many years, haven't you? And there isn't any real reason to stop now, is there? Or isn't this the first time?"

"Of course, it's the first time!" Virginia was indignant.

"Shh. Then I don't think you ought to judge without knowing the whole story."

"How am I going to know the whole story?"

"In all probability you're not, and that's exactly why you shouldn't judge. One thing I'm quite positive of and that is that your mother and Mr. Fielding haven't had an affair yet, and if they haven't had one yet maybe you're just worrying about nothing."

"Isn't a—what we saw—isn't that an affair?"

"Hush, you're the one who keeps talking louder and louder. No, it isn't. Not technically."

"What is, technically?"

"Oh, you know, Vee. The whole business. A plain kiss isn't. And I ought to know."

"Why?"

"Why do you think I got sent away to boarding school this winter?"

"I never thought about it," Virginia said. "The same reason all the rest of us were, I suppose, to get an education."

"Education my Aunt Fanny. At least half the kids are there to get them out from under their parents' feet. As for me, I already know more than half the teachers there will ever know. I was getting a far better education at the lycée than at that desiccated nursery school."

"Why, then?"

"My most unfavorite aunt found me in a compromising attitude at Claude Massein's studio." She paused for effect, but as there was no response from Virginia she continued. "I now realize that Claude Massein as well as being one of the best stage designers in Paris is also an out-and-out heel. However, at the time I was passionately in love with him, and I thought, stupid naïve idiot that I was, that he was in love with me."

"Wasn't he?"

"Tante Léonie told Clare and Clare woke up to the fact that I am a growing girl, and there was great sound and fury from Tante Léonie about just how *far* our intimacy had gone. I think in her heart she was very disappointed that I was not deflowered."

"Deflowered?"

"That I hadn't let myself be seduced. That I was—am—technically still a virgin. Well, a technicality was all I could get by on, but technicalities of that sort are very important to people like my Tante Léonie. Anyhow, Jake was away on tour, of course. He always manages to be when family emergencies arise. So Clare went to see Claude. I went along with her and I was supposed to wait downstairs, but I was so full of wild love for that louse Claude and so sure he'd explain everything to Clare and make me an honest woman as soon as I got through medical school that I went upstairs. The door of the studio was open and there he was pursuing Clare around the easel. Fortunately she's quick and she's strong and she can cope with any situation, but after a while, so that she wouldn't have to do any more coping, I made my presence known."

Beside Mimi in the bed Virginia was shivering. Mimi laid one strong hand on Virginia's thigh and sighed. She had sacrificed herself on the altar of friendship in offering Virginia the story of her humiliation, and now that it was told it seemed to have no real bearing on the issue; it had not even served to divert Virginia's attention from the picture of Emily and Abe there in the snow, locked in each other's arms; and nothing she could say would make the embrace seem casual, and no talking of technicalities make it less important. She sighed again and said, "Vee, I'd appreciate it if you didn't say anything about what I've just told you to your parents."

"Of course not," Virginia said.

"They think I'm a sweet young girl and suitable to be your companion and I don't want to disillusion them. And Vee—"

"What?"

"Don't say anything to Sam, either. I want him to—to go on thinking well of me. So if you don't mind—"

"I wouldn't say anything. You know that," Virginia said. Then, after a moment, "I'm sorry, Mimi, about—about what's his name. Claude. It must have been—I'm sorry."

"Oh, Vee," Mimi said, "love's such a funny sort of business and we go at it like bulls in china shops. At least I do. All I really wanted to say was that we don't understand as much about it as we think we do. And Clare and Jake—I know they've done things that aren't moral by lots of people's standards, but they're pretty terrific, both of them, and each one is the only person in the world for the other. They really have a *marriage,* Vee."

Virginia lay very still in the narrow bed and Mimi said briskly, "Well, night's a-wasting and we must get some sleep. I'll hie me back to my own cot." She got up and clumsily tucked the covers around Virginia before getting into her own bed. The sheets were icy cold and she pulled the covers tightly around her. For the first time Mrs. Bowen had forgotten to fill one of the copper hot-water bottles for her. She burrowed deeper under the covers, pressing her face into the pillow, whispering in a muffled voice, "Good night, Vee."

"Good night, Mimi," Virginia whispered in return.

At the hotel Abe got ready for bed. Sam was already in his pajamas, reading, and they did not talk. Sam looked up from his book once, but he saw his father's set face, the line of the jaw tight and tense, and he did not speak. He looked up again as Abe came in from the bathroom, still holding his toothbrush in his hand, saying, "Sam, I've made reservations for us in Bandol for Sunday."

Sam looked up from his book in unbelief. "Which Sunday?"

"This coming. You've never been to the South of France and I thought we might as well push off a few days before Christmas."

Sam dropped his book. "I thought the idea was we were to spend the Christmas holidays here where we could have winter sports."

"Nothing was definite," Abe said. "It's more fun to have a flexible schedule. We've had some winter sports and now I'm about ready for a little sun and warmth."

"But I like it here," Sam said flatly. "I don't want to go to the South of France. I haven't the slightest interest in spending Christmas anywhere but here."

Abe returned his toothbrush and towel to the bathroom, and came out, shutting the door behind him. "Christmas in a hotel is rather dreary. If we go to Bandol the Dunsteads will undoubtedly ask us for Christmas dinner. They have one of the show places on the Riviera and I think you'll enjoy it."

"If we stay here, I bet you anything Mrs. Bowen will ask us

for Christmas dinner," Sam said, "even if theirs isn't a show place."

"The Dunsteads have a very charming daughter," Abe said.

Sam sat up in bed. "So that's why you want to leave!" he cried furiously. "It isn't anything to do with being tired of winter sports and wanting some sun at all and you know it! Why didn't you just say what you were driving at and have done with it!"

"Now hold everything, Sam," Abe said. "Just what is this you think I'm driving at?"

"Mimi."

"Mimi?"

"If you don't approve of Mimi it would have been much better if you'd just said so, man to man."

"But I do approve of Mimi," Abe said, "though I wasn't aware that things had gone so far with the two of you that you'd accuse me of taking you off to Bandol for Christmas for that reason."

"Things haven't gone that far," Sam said. "That's one reason I don't want to go."

"I see," Abe said. "I'm sorry, Sam. Mimi doesn't have a thing to do with my decision, but I'm afraid it is a decision, and one we're going through with."

"*Why,* dad?"

"Sam, I'm afraid I can't tell you. You'll just have to trust me when I assure you that it is necessary. And that it has nothing whatsoever to do with you and Mimi."

"You do like Mimi, then?"

"Yes, what little I've seen of her, very much."

"Dad, do we really have to go? It really is that important?"

"Yes, Sam, I'm afraid it is."

"Well, could I know why, then? I'll have to tell Mimi."

"You can tell her it's business."

"Is it?"

"Not entirely."

"Dad, has anything been bothering you lately? You've seemed so sort of up and down."

"Have I, Sam? I'm sorry."

"Dad, do you mind if I kind of have a talk with you?"

"Not at all, Sam. Go ahead." Abe got into bed but he did not open the windows. He lay back on the pillows, clasping his hands behind his head.

"You know, dad, I remember some good talks we've had

about adolescence and some of the problems of growing up. They've helped me a lot.''

"Have they, Sam? I'm glad."

"You know, the facts of life and all that stuff. I'm glad I got it all from you and didn't just pick it up the way some of the other kids have had to."

"I'm glad you feel that way, Sam."

"But you know what, dad, I've read things in various magazines and books and places about men when they get in their forties. . . ."

"What about men in their forties?"

"Well, that it's a kind of dangerous period. I mean, it's sort of a time when they look around and make fools of themselves over gorgeous blondes and stuff."

Abe chuckled. "Are you worried about my taking up with a gorgeous blonde?"

"Well, no, not exactly, but this rushing off to Bandol just sort of made me think of it. I don't know whether there's anybody there you want to see or something—but if you ever should think about getting married again or anything—well, don't just rush into it. I mean you should be awfully sure it isn't just your age kicking up the way you might say it was mine if I got too serious about Mimi or something and wanted to throw my education away and everything and just go off half-cocked and get married. I mean you have a lot you could throw away, too, and so if you ever *should*—not that there *is* anybody in Bandol or anything—you should just be awfully sure."

"I promise you that if it ever happens I'll be awfully sure, Sam," Abe said.

"Well, that's about all, I guess," Sam said. "I hope you don't mind, I mean my having talked to you like this."

"Not at all."

"And I do think you're aging very well. I don't mean aging exactly. You know what I mean."

Abe laughed. "Yes, Sam. I know. I'll try to decay as gracefully as possible."

"I mean," Sam said, "none of us at school can stand parents who go around trying to be younger than we are. Mothers who look as though they wanted you to ask them for a date and stuff. We like parents who're—who're grown people. I wonder what Mimi's parents are like? I imagine they're a little bit odd but okay. And I like the Bowens. They're okay, too. I bet Mr. Bowen's a wow of a teacher in a quiet sort of way. And Mrs.

Bowen's a—I don't know, I just feel kind of good around her. Want me to open the windows a crack, dad?"

"Not yet, thanks, Sam. Think I'll take a shower first."

"Okay. Think I'll improve the shining hour and dash off a small line to my Mimi."

—My Mimi, Abe thought. Well, he's got pretty good taste. But maybe it's just as well for his sake if not for mine that we're heading for the Riviera and the Dunsteads' beautiful daughter. . . .

Night lay breathing deeply between the mountains, its pulse throbbing through the village; the house creaked and crackled against the wind and the heavy book slipped from Courtney's numb fingers and crashed to the floor, but Emily lying beside him did not waken. He leaned over the side of the bed to retrieve the book but the bed was high and suddenly the effort seemed too enormous. If it were earlier, if he weren't so bone-tired, he would like to go up to Gertrude's chalet and play a game of chess with her and the two of them get quietly drunk together. Then everything else would be lost in a fuzzy feeling of camaraderie, and if his head ached in the morning he would at least have been able to get to sleep first.

"We're two of a kind, you and I, Court," Gertrude had said once, a glass of brandy in one hand, the white knight in the other. "That either of us should be here is only an accident. And in my better moments I realize that it isn't the accident in the long run that counts; it's what you do with it or what you let it do to you. What are we letting it do to us, Court? Is it bigger than we are? Are we that small? Do we feel that God has been mean to us and we won't play any more? No wonder we have to get drunk. Not to forget our accident, but to forget ourselves. So it was a dirty deal you got shoved out of your job, but it's happened to other people before. And I'm not the only person in the world to come out of the war with TB. I knew a woman who went blind." She got up rather shakily and refilled their glasses; Kaarlo and Emily had gone to a concert that night. "A much more ghastly blow than mine. But she never lost her ability to laugh. I have, damn it. And she fought like mad, Court, but she didn't fight against being blind. That was a fact and she accepted it as such, because there was no possible way by which that fact could be changed. What she fought—or *how* she fought—was not against, but *for*—for keeping intact her integrity, her independence, her faith in herself as an individual."

Had Gertrude really said those things? he wondered now, or did he only remember them because the shoe fitted even though it pinched? Gertrude's blind woman would have denied Thomas à Kempis, have flung him across the room. But he was no longer denying Thomas à Kempis; he was denying himself.

He sat up in bed, shivering with cold, and looked at Emily. Her face was calm, its lines of care smoothed out; and in her sleep she smiled.

Why?

Usually when he looked down at Emily before turning out his reading lamp, before plunging downwards into the dark well of sleep, her face was tight, strained, as though sleep were an effort, as though staying asleep took muscle power, will power.

Why was she smiling? Why was her hand curled gently beside her cheek as relaxed as the petal of a flower? He touched one of her fingers and in the cold room it was warm.

The wind roared down the chimney; the floorboards creaked; the snow was brushed from the garden by the mad broom of wind, swept from drifts, flung wildly against the house.

This is a winter in limbo, lost in the cold, frozen in the waste, the waste frozen into space, animation suspended, validity ended, walking through my daily duties like a ghost, not feeling, not caring, not daring to care.

The only direction from here is down. To get back into the only way of life that for me makes sense I must step down.

And perhaps Emily and Gertrude and the blind woman are right and I should do it and have the courage to care, to plunge into suffering instead of pulling away from it. The only way to cross the river is to jump in and when I am on the other side maybe I can start living again. And if I don't start living again I will have lost more than myself.

In her sleep Emily laughed, actually laughed aloud, and then stretched, her body moving warmly against his. After a moment he turned off the light.

She wakened to Abe's kiss, his mouth against hers, ardent and vital. She opened her lips to him and his hand cupped her breast. In the darkness she could hear the sound of his breathing, quick and harsh, his hand moved searchingly over her thigh.

She opened her eyes in the dark, her mind awakening with her senses. It was not Abe; it was Courtney.

Why?

Why tonight after the long winter weeks of near-abstinence? Oh, Court, not tonight!

Was she like a bitch in heat?

She could not turn away from him. She had never turned away from him and tonight of all nights after that immediate instinctive response she could not pretend any of the things that it might otherwise be possible to pretend and that she had never pretended. No. Her pretense must be completely the opposite. . . .

After a moment it ceased to be pretense.

Then when it was over, when he was asleep, his face like a child's pressed against her, his breathing peaceful and relaxed, she lay awake in the dark. She could hear the slow deep notes of the church clock. Four. The night was black and unrelieved. Outdoors the trees crackled with the cold. The wind rebuked the house. There was a crack like a gun's report as an ice-bound branch snapped in the wind.

And Emily lay in bed beside her husband feeling like an adulteress.

✦ *Four* ✦

They caught glimpses of the glacier from the little train that took them to it, but their first real view was from the rocky cliff that loomed above it, hemming it in on one side as the forest hemmed it in on the other. The sight of the great, crumbled, jagged, turbulent sea of ice was like the slap of a wave of cold water against their chests, and they caught their breaths.

Kaarlo was familiar with petrified oceans like this, Emily thought; he was as at home on a glacier as a sailor at sea, more so, because many sailors cannot swim, and know the element of water only through the intermediary of their ship; but Kaarlo knew the mountains and their seas of ice directly through his body. It was an alien sight to Emily, this glacier, and an exhilarating one. She reached, unthinking, for Courtney's arm at the same moment that she was wanting Abe to be there to share the experience of the day; and perhaps at the same moment he and Kaarlo were climbing over a sea of ice, and her heart froze with fear for them. For the first time she knew how Gertrude felt each time Kaarlo went up the mountains. Kaarlo's father had been killed on Mont Blanc and this was something Gertrude could not forget each time Kaarlo went out, no matter how small a climb it might be. "I swore I'd never be an aviator's wife," she had once said angrily to Emily, "and now I'm a mountain guide's mistress. How dumb can you get?"

They clambered down the snaky path that was cut in zigzags down the cliffside, and stood side by side on the surface of the frozen sea. Then they moved away slowly, each alone, even the children separate, no longer seeking contact, because here was a sea that did not encourage human communion; it was too isolated and too huge, and too demanding in itself.

The ice was churned green and yellow and colorless, and in places it was quite brown. Not until he had clambered over great frozen waves and come to one of the crevasses did Courtney see the icy blue colors he had anticipated. The crevasse was narrow but it went down so deep that it was impossible to see to the bottom of it.

The only accident in the mountains that winter had been on a glacier: a guide was taking a small party of German tourists for a simple climb, nothing dangerous, but one of the men would not stay with the others, and fell and was killed. It happened that Courtney had gone with Emily and Connie and Gertrude that evening to the Splendide for an apéritif, and they were sitting there quietly, he stirring extra suger into Connie's lemonade, when the news came in that there had been an accident. Kaarlo was out that day with a party, and Gertrude went dead-white but did not say a word; and neither Courtney nor Emily spoke, even to say that perhaps it might not be Kaarlo, because Gertrude knew this, and it was not their fumbling words for which she was waiting. "What is it? What's the matter?" Connie asked anxiously, and Marcel, the waiter who always took care of them, placed another glass in front of each of them and a citron pressé for Connie, he also silent, and then the outer door swung open, letting in a gash of cold black air, and one of the guides came in with it and stood just inside the door beating his hands together and stamping his feet and looking around at the people at the bar and at the small tables. Then he crossed the room to them and everything seemed to stop until he said to Gertrude, "It is a German in the party with Etienne," and went out again, and then Gertrude got up and they followed her out of the café and climbed with her the slopes up behind the chalets to stand with her waiting for Kaarlo until they saw him coming and knew that she no longer needed them.

Courtney wandered slowly along the edge of the narrow and bottomless fissure, a wound that went deep into the earth, that penetrated below the extremity of ice, below the surface of the earth, that descended to the fires in the womb of the earth, a crack that was a scar in the shaping of the earth.

The cold wind hit against his face and blew back his hair, and he looked up and saw Emily, aloof and apart, wrapped in her dream, standing with her back to him, peering into a cave formed of ice. Behind her, just behind her, was a large crevasse. Courtney's heart somersaulted. One step backwards and Emily would be lost in subterranean caverns of ice.

He was afraid to call, for fear that she would step backwards in the direction of his voice. Quickly and silently he approached her. She was still peering raptly at the colors in the cave. He jumped across the crevasse, catapulted into action, pulling her roughly away from it with him. Caught in his arms she leaped in terror, such a leap as a startled mermaid caught unaware might have given.

Still holding her with one hand he leaned against a boulder of ice and realized that he was dripping with sweat.

"Court! You frightened me! What's the matter?" Emily cried.

"You frightened me! Look." He pointed to the crevasse behind them. "You were standing on the very edge of that. One step and you would have gone down."

"Oh—" she said. "I—I'm sorry. It was stupid of me to—" She looked around wildly for a moment, saw that Virginia and Mimi and Connie were safe, and that Virginia was staring at her standing there in Courtney's arms, and repeated, "I'm sorry, Court. I didn't mean to frighten you."

He released her from the close embrace in which he had been clutching her into safety. "Come on," he said, roughly. "We've had enough of this. Let's go up to the bistro and have some lunch."

In the small washroom of the restaurant Virginia and Mimi cleaned up, saw that Connie did not sit on the toilet seat, and that she washed her hands properly.

"Though Clare says the possibility of getting a venereal disease from a public bathroom is so remote as to be almost negligible," Mimi said. "It's simply a matter of personal fastidiousness."

"What's a vereal disease? Is it like measles?" Connie demanded. "What's fassigusses? Is it like chicken pox? I've had chicken pox and I was very, very sick."

"It just means ladies keep themselves clean and tidy," Mimi said. "Now dry your hands properly, Constantia Plum, they're chapped enough already." She turned to Virginia. "I say, Vee, I don't suppose it's worth mentioning, but you don't intend to say anything to anybody about, you know, what we saw yesterday?"

Virginia stopped in the middle of zipping up her ski jacket and looked at Mimi coldly. "Of course not."

Mimi looked slightly embarrassed, an unusual reaction. "I mean you do seem to tell your parents everything and I don't think it would be a very good idea. And I was thinking about Sam. He's involved in a way, too, you know, and it might bother him, and we most certainly weren't meant to see it, and it's strictly their own business—" she looked at Connie and spelled, "your m-o-t-h-e-r-s and Mr. F-i-e-l-d-i-n-g-s, not ours."

"What are you talking about?" Connie demanded, furiously frustrated at being, as usual, left on the periphery of whatever fascinating thing it was the two big girls were involved in. "What did you see?"

"Two dogs having a fight," Virginia said.

"M-o-t-h-e-r spells mother," Connie said. "Mimi spelled something about mother. I've known how to spell m-o-t-h-e-r for years and years and years. What was Mimi saying about my mother?"

"She'd have been upset if she'd seen the dogs fighting," Mimi said. "Come on, Connie, put on your mittens and let's go. I'm hungry."

"Oh, put a wrinkle in your tummy and use it for a washboard," Connie said rudely.

The restaurant had cold stone floors and innumerable draughts, but the leek soup and paté maison were delectable and the portions generous and they ate heartily. They sat and talked and looked down at the sea of ice and Courtney and Emily drank coffee, and then they played word games while they were waiting for the train to take them back to the village.

"I love my love with an A," Mimi said, "because he's aboriginal. I hate him with an A because he's avaricious. His name is Aloysius, he lives in an abattoir in Afghanistan, and I feed him on avocados."

"I love my love with a B," Virginia said, "because he's beatific. I hate him with a B because he's barbaric. . . ."

—I love my love with an A because he is ardent, Emily thought, sipping the dregs of her cold coffee. I hate him with an A because I love him only that doesn't begin with an A. I hate him because I adore him. His name is Abe and he lives in America and I feed him on adultery in thought if not in deed—

"Come on, " Courtney said, "here's the train."

It was a day of near-accidents. They ran for the train and Vir-

ginia slipped and fell head-long over a small embankment just
as a sleigh drawn by two horses came dashing up, and it seemed
as though she must be crushed under their hooves and there
were excited screams from passers-by and the driver of the
sleigh pulled the horses up so abruptly that they reared, but Virginia was not touched; no one was hurt. Emily and Courtney
stammered thanks and there were excited descriptions of the accident in French and German from various onlookers, and then
they were all on the rickety local train that had waited, puffing
enormous clouds of filthy smoke, until the excitement was
over.

While Emily was in the kitchen fixing dinner Virginia came
in and stood watching her.
"Mother—"
"What, darling?"
"Could I have a couple of aspirin?"
"Why, Vee?"
"Oh, just my time of the moon. I guess bouncing off that em-
bankment this afternoon must have brought it on a couple of
days early and it seems to have joggled me up a bit. I thought
some aspirin might help."
Emily went to the cupboard where she kept their small stock
of medicines and shook two aspirins into the palm of her hand.
"Here, Vee. Sit down and I'll have a cup of hot tea for you in a
moment. That will help, too."—And this probably explains her
depression last night, she thought in quick relief.
Virginia sat down, leaning forward a little, her arms folded
over her stomach. Looking obliquely at Emily she said, "I'm
sure Mimi's parents must be fascinating, and they lead exciting
sorts of lives, but I'd much rather have you and daddy."
"Would you, darling?" Emily asked, taking the kettle from
the back of the stove and setting it over the hot coals to boil.
"I'm glad you would because I'm afraid you're stuck with us."
"There doesn't seem to be any—any togetherness in their
family. I don't mean just Jake being away on tour a lot and
Clare staying in Paris because of the lab. I mean they don't—
they don't seem to be married the way people ought to be married."
"Oh?" Emily asked. "Why not?"
"I don't know whether Mimi says things just to shock me or
whether it's true, about her mother's lovers, oh, and she said
something once at school about what's-her-name—the dancer,

oh, Mikhailova, being one of Jake's mistresses, but I think that was just to set the girls on their ears. But it's not like a *family*, mother. Even when daddy went to Washington during the war and it was six months before he could find a place to live and send for us we were still a family. You weren't dashing around having lovers because daddy was away. I don't think I would have liked it at all if you'd gone around having lovers. I don't think I could have stood it." Still sitting in her crouched position she looked up at her mother, but Emily was pouring boiling water into a teacup and adding sugar and a slice of lemon, so rather lamely Virginia finished, "But Mimi's parents, they seem to be so busy being violently themselves they dont't have time for each other." And as Emily still stood by the stove stirring the tea, she said, "We thought we'd go see Madame de Croisenois for a few minutes. Okay?"

"Sure," Emily said. "Gert enjoys your visits. Here's your tea, darling. Drink it while it's good and hot. It'll make your tummy feel better. I'm not so terribly sure Mimi's good for you. She likes to think she's grown-up and sophisticated and so she continually feels she has to say things she thinks will shock us to prove to herself how grown-up she is. I doubt if her parents lead nearly as wild lives as she'd like us to think."

"If Mimi isn't good for me, what about Madame de Croisenois being good for you, then?" Virginia asked. "She likes to shock people, too, doesn't she?"

"True," Emily said. "But then I'm older than you are and supposed to have acquired a few more powers of discretion. Drink your tea, Vee."

Madame Pedroti, impelled by who knows what strange magnet, by what odd twinge of conscience, what unacknowledged desire for absolution, was paying one of her unwelcome visits to Gertrude. Or was it none of these things, but simply a knowledge that she could hurt and frighten Gertrude that caused her to drop in at the chalet so frequently of an afternoon?

Gertrude hated her and at the same time was fascinated by her, as one is fascinated by a fat, well-fed snake; hated her and disapproved of her and at the same time listened avidly to her juicily expectorated gossip.

She knew that at one time Madame Pedroti had scornfully called Gertrude bemused by the chasseurs alpins, that before her body became quite so ponderous she was said to have given Henri de Coisenois privileges that did not generally go with a suite of rooms at a winter sports hotel (though this Gerturde did not believe; Pedroti at her best had never been Henri's type), and heaven knew what Pedroti was saying to her little clique now after her visits to the chalet that housed this particular ménage à deux. Gertrude rebuffed her, rebuked her, made it clear by casual rudeness that she was unwelcome; but her illness of boredom was so great that she listened to the other woman, and Madame Pedroti knew that she listened.

"And they say that Thérèse Berigot is pregnant by our dear Kaarlo's cousin Pierre," Madame Pedroti was saying. "However, I really think she's simply putting on weight. One does, you know!" And she laughed gaily. "And where is our dear Kaarlo?"

"Off for a climb with Abe Fielding," Gertrude said shortly.

"Oh. I thought he might be giving Mrs. Bowen a skiing lesson."

"Mrs. Bowen has not had any lessons for some time." Gertrude tried to control her anger, saying furiously to herself—It's your own fault for listening to her vicious tongue in the first place. You're putting yourself in her power, you fool, and you know it—and so does she.

"A strangely attractive man, Monsieur Fielding. Perhaps when you're feeling yourself again he might interest you—if he is still at liberty."

"Probably won't be," Gertrude said.

"I'm not so sure. I can see that he's a man of very definite and particular tastes. Obviously anyone as well off as he is could have remarried at any time he wished. I believe his wife is dead?"

"I wouldn't know," Gertrude said indifferently. Gossip from Madame Pedroti she might receive, but she would not give the fat old slitch the satisfaction of getting any in return; the arrangement, if she was to retain a shred of pride, had to be one-sided.

Madame Pedroti, unrebuked, though she knew Gertrude was holding back on her, took a platinum cigarette case from her black bead bag, extracted a cigarette, and inserted it delicately between her lips.

"There are matches on that dish on the bookshelves."

"I have my lighter, thank you." Madame Pedroti put her pudgy hand into the bag again and drew out a lighter to match the cigarette case.

"As for Monsieur Fielding," Madame Pedroti continued,

"he may not be handsome, but he has a—" she held her fingers up as though she were holding something precious—"a certain something."

"Oh?" Gertrude said. "Kaarlo and I like him very much."

"And such a nice boy he has. A pity that big blond girl had to be here to take him right out from under the little Bowen's nose. Not a very attractive child, I'm afraid. Much too thin and that straight red hair—"

"She's at a bad age now," Gertrude said, "but she'll be coming into her own when Mimi's overblown and thick about the hips. I don't imagine her mother was much good as an adolescent."

"Ah, Madame Bowen," Madame Pedroti murmured, "so polite and so serious. And always so controlled that it makes one think she must not be happy. You know her so well, dear Madame de Croisenois. Do you think she's happy?"

Gertrude shrugged. "In a dull sort of way."

Madame Pedroti smoothed down the shiny black material of her skirt. Any material would immediately look shiny stretched over those drooping thighs, no matter how expensive. "I fear it is worse than that," she said piously.

Forgetting herself for a moment, Gertrude said, "Yes, I think Emily's miserable. I think when that kid died everything about their marriage went to pieces. Of course I don't think Courtney's too exciting, so I may be prejudiced. The only times Courtney and I are *gemütlich*—" she said the German word with a side-long glance at Madame Pedroti—"are when we've both had too much to drink. Which Emily doesn't like one bit, I might add." Then she shut her mouth abruptly.— Betraying your best friend, now, are you? she asked herself.

There was a knock on the outer door and she called, "Come in," and looked up, waiting, until Dr. Clément came in through the shed, the kitchen, into the big room.

He smiled at Gertrude, bowed formally to Madame Pedroti, saying, "I would know you anywhere by your odor, Madame Pedroti, and not your expensive perfume, but your cigarettes. Egyptian tobacco is not easy to come by."

"I have my few little connections," Madame Pedroti said modestly, running her hands again over her thighs which lapped like cushions over the side of her chair.

"And surely you must know that I prefer people not to smoke when they are visiting Madame de Croisenois?"

With a gesture that was at the same time delicate and brutal,

Madame Pedroti crushed out the glowing end of her cigarette. "I'm so sorry. I'll try to remember." She smiled coyly at Dr. Clément.

For a moment he stood looking at Gertrude, stood leaning against the bookshelves, looking tired, as though he needed the support, only his eyes alert as he looked from Gertrude back to Madame Pedroti.

Madame Pedroti rose, gave a small quiver as though to slide her bulk into its proper mold. "But I must be off! At once! With all my duties at the hotel I can ill spare the time for these visits, delightful though they are. But I do feel that dear Madame de Croisenois must not be left alone and if her old friends don't stand by her who will!"

"Old friend, my Aunt Fanny," Gertrude said as Madame Pedroti left after her usual over-long, over-fulsome farewells. "If she feels that way why does she come?"

"Why?" Clément asked, sitting by the hearth. "Does she want something from you?"

Gertrude shook her head. "No. To give her credit I think it's something more subtle than that. Clément," she demanded, "why am I sliding so swiftly towards perdition?"

"I think you only think you are. Or is it that you want to? Which, Gertrude?"

Gertrude shook her head. "I'm tired. Tired in all the nooks and crannies of my body. And in my soul, too. Pedroti always succeeds in upsetting me even when she doesn't say anything upsetting. But I've been behaving, I really have." She looked at him pleadingly. But one of a hundred patients she was to Clément, so how could be know how she listened for the sound of his footsteps almost as she listened for Kaarlo's?

As though he could see into her he said, "I'm sorry I couldn't come at my usual time."

"I suppose you had an emergency."

"It has been a day of emergencies. And I've just now finished in the operating theatre. Everything—aside from Madame Pedroti—is all right with you?"

Gertrude shrugged. "This is the best of all possible worlds. Every day in every way I'm getting better and better. Into each life some rain must fall. Oh, sure Clément, everything's just dandy."

He came over from the hearth and sat down on the couch beside her, his fingers closing firmly over her wrist. "Have you taken your temperature today?"

"What's the use? You know what it'll be."

"However I asked you—and you promised—to keep a daily record for me. We will take it now."

As he looked at the thermometer she said. "When you go take that overblown bag of fruit Pedroti left and throw it away for me, will you? She brings me the stuff that's gone too rotten to be used at the hotel."

He nodded, but did not get up to leave. Instead he continued thoughtfully to study her.

"When am I going to be allowed to live like a human being again?" she asked.

"When your body is ready." His voice was, as always, patient and quiet with her, no matter how often she asked the same questions. "And you *can* get well, Gertrude," Clément went on. "You can even do it here at the chalet, though you would do it in considerably less time if you would come into the sanatorium." ·

"Why can't you leave me alone about it!" Gertrude cried. "You know I won't! I can't!"

"Won't, perhaps, but you can."

"Shut up, Clément, shut up! Let's change the subject. Let's talk about you. Aside from your beautiful wife, of course, and in the full realization that I am *not* your type, what kind of woman is?"

He raised his eyebrows. "No particular type, my dear Gertrude. Just certain individuals."

"Well, what individuals? Name one. And don't tell me it's none of my business. I know it. Be a nice guy and satisfy my curiosity and name one anyhow."

"I can't think of anyone you might know," he said lightly, "except perhaps our friend Mrs. Bowen."

"Emily!" Gertrude said incredulously. ·

"Emily."

"The nice, quiet, monogamous, stable one, eh, who'll never kick over the traces? Not unless I know Emily a lot less well than I think I do. One thing I have discovered since I've been ill, though, is that nobody ever knows anybody, and maybe least of all the people who are closest to them. Sort of a business of not being able to see the trees for the woods. We all live in the little isolated prisons of our own bodies and there's no real contact with any other human being. That's what sex is, in a way, isn't it, a desperate striving for contact? With which cheerful Thought For Today I will bid you good afternoon."

Michel Clément laughed, the sound coming fresh and alive into the room. "You're quite a girl, Gertrude. Put your talents to getting well, will you?" He bent down, patted her hand, and left her.

One leaves Mimi and Sam alone, Virginia thought, leaves them standing, warmed by the exciting fires of discovery, in the cold corridors of the hotel, surrounded but somehow not touched by the steel cold air of midafternoon with night already seeping like black fog into corners and crevasses. And then perhaps they will move down the vestibule again with every intention of going after Virginia, but stopping there, just outside the door of the suite, standing there, their coats touching, though their hands, their lips are not yet ready, standing there with life bursting out from them, so that people leaving and entering, coming out of or going in to the hotel rooms, must surely feel it and take warmth from it, as the seed underground, trapped by the frozen winter earth and the weight of snow pressing from above, still feels the warmth of the sun, and stirs, preparing for life.

And Virginia goes down in the elevator alone, asking for the rez-de-chaussée, hemmed in by the four walls, the confining descending rectangle, terrifyingly small—And why has she always been afraid of elevators, as though when she left them the entire world could have changed, become distorted, disappeared, so that when the door with no seeming assistance from the operator (by what malignant magic?) slid slowly open as the elevator stopped, she might look out into blackness, into nothingness, with the stars receding, smaller and further, dimmer and more distant, expanding madly from the dark core which was the elevator with Virginia perched precariously on the edge. . . . It stemmed from a childhood game, played with Alice, long since forgotten and therefore doubly horrible, so that even in New York in the familiar tiny olive-green elevator with the iron-grill inner door in which she had once so badly pinched her fingers, even there she would stand, hurrying home from school and starting to tremble imperceptibly as she entered the elevator and pressed the button, and catch her breath with relief as the door opened and there was the familiar buff hall and the red door at the far end that was her door and beyond which lay safety, the family and safety.

The main floor door slid open and there, across from her, was the desk with the concierge and the mailboxes and the green-shaded light and she leaped out of the elevator, across the crack between elevator and floor, the crack which had not expanded to become the void. . . .

She left the hotel alone and started rather forlornly up the path to Gertrude's and Kaarlo's chalet, because that was where they had been going when they met Sam at the entrance to the hotel, and surely it would not be long before Mimi would join her there, and home was no longer a place to which she wanted to go. And Madame de Croisenois could never have been afraid of an elevator and a crack widening and overtaking everything with nothingness, a crack that must quickly be leaped across because, if one did not hurry, the chance for safety might be lost, and one must pursue safety by jumping off the highest diving boards in summer and skiing down the steepest slopes and being the last one in crack-the-whip in winter and jumping over the crack between elevator and floor at all seasons. . . .

She knocked gently at the chalet, opened the door, calling softly, "May I come in, Madame de Croisenois?"

There was no answer and she went on in, softly, and Gertrude was lying on the couch under the bright plaid of the steamer rug, one thin hand dangling loosely against the floor. Just as Virginia was about to beat a retreat she opened her eyes, but there was a count of fully thirty seconds before she smiled, a blankness during which she returned from wherever she had been.

"Hello, Madame de Croisenois," Virginia said hesitantly.

Now the smile was more assured. "Hello, Vee."

"Did I disturb you? Were you asleep?"

"No. Just resting. Madame Pedroti was here and then Dr. Clément, and he left just a few moments ago. Sit down, Vee. It's nice to see you. I do count on you and Mimi, you know."

"We count on you, too," Virginia said solemnly, and suddenly her eyes widened with wild speculation that here at last was someone she could ask about her mother and Mr. Fielding, because surely Madame de Croisenois would know, surely Madame de Croisenois, the heroine, had the answer and would not be grudging in giving it.

"Last night—" Virginia said slowly, not going further into the room, not sitting as Gertrude had asked her to, but standing, rigid, with her back to the partly open door—"last night Mimi and I went into the village for some ice cream for dinner, daddy said we might—"

"That was noble of Courtney," Gertrude said.

Virginia did not hear. "And we were walking back with the ice cream," she said, and began to shiver. She walked quickly to the zebra-striped chair and sat down.

"I can't see you," Gertrude said.

Virginia got up out of the zebra-striped chair and hitched a stool over to the couch.

Gertrude, not hearing the urgency behind the girl's meaningless words, rolled onto her side, saying, "Your little face is all pinched with cold. Where's Mimi?"

"At the hotel, talking with Sam," Virginia said bleakly.

"Ditching me for young love, eh?" Gertrude asked.

"Oh, she's coming right along," Virginia said. "We just happened to meet Sam on our way here. He didn't go climbing with his father today. He stayed home to take a couple of skiing lessons. So we went up to his hotel room. He wanted to show Mimi a picture of his mother. So I just thought I'd sort of leave them alone for a couple of minutes. The way things are, they don't get much chance."

"So it *is* love?" Gertrude asked.

"Um."

"So you're left out in the cold and the tip of your nose gets white and your lips blue. Or is it simply the weather and are you in love, too?"

Virginia shook her head.

"Nobody madly pursuing you, eh?"

"Oh, I'm being pursued, kind of."

"How can you be pursued, kind of?"

"Well, there's this boy," Virginia said, looking down at her feet in the clumsy ski boots with the cuffs of the heavy white socks (borrowed from Emily) turned down over them. "Snider Bean. But as Sam says his father says, Snider's snide."

"So snide Snider's pursuing you?"

"Yes. Well. Yes. Only he's called Beanie."

"So what's wrong with this snide Snider called Beanie? Is he a midget? Does he weigh four hundred pounds? Is he a moron and utterly repulsive?"

"Oh, no. He's kind of a dream boat. If I took his picture back to school the girls would all die. Only they'd all think I'd bought it somewhere. They'd never think anybody cool like that would give two looks at me."

"So where's the catch?"' Gertrude asked.

"Madame de Croisenois," Virginia blurted, deadly earnest, brows furrowed over troubled green eyes, gold of freckles deepening over white skin, fists clenched, "what do you think of anti-Semitism?"

Gertrude held back the laugh that started to rise in her throat. Gertrude, the all-wise, all-knowing, all-loving Madame de Croisenois must not laugh at such seriousness. "Is snide Snider, called Beanie, a Jew?" she asked gently.

"Oh, no. He's got a hate against Jews. And the other afternoon at the thé dansant he said awful things about Mimi and I walked out on him and now he sort of keeps after me."

"Go on," Gertrude said, the headmistress of the school interviewing the troubled student because of course all headmistresses know all the answers to all the problems.

"Well, you see," Virginia said, "I can't help feeling kind of pleased and—and flattered—but I don't think I *ought* to, but I don't know exactly how to *stop* him——and especially I don't know if I want him to stop. Even if I should."

—My God, Gertrude thought, how like Emily she sounds.

Aloud she said, "He's still pretty young, isn't he, Vee?"

"Oh, no. I think he's a couple of years older than I am."

Gertrude smiled again. "Quite grown-up, then. But I think he's still young enough to change, don't you?"

"Are people apt to?"

"You know, Virginia," Gertrude said, suddenly serious, "before the war I was quite thoughtlessly anti-Semitic in a casual way."

"You, Madame de Croisenois?"

"Yes. Of the 'some of my best friends are Jews' school. You see, I wasn't like your mother. Emily's the quiet and gentle individualist, isn't she, who goes her own way, choosing her friends for what she sees in them, not for any of their more obvious attributes of race or social position or money. Just her own private choice. And even if I think she inclines rather towards lame ducks I admire her for it."

The door was pushed open again and Mimi came in. "Hi, here I am. Have I missed anything passionately interesting?"

"Of course," Gertrude said, "but we're not going to repeat a word of it, are we, Virginia?"

"Not a single syllable."

Mimi plunked down into a chair and sighed. "I don't know why everybody is so abominable to me." She sighed again. "I never used to get into these awful adolescent moods before I got sent off to school. I'm getting as bad as Virginia. Virginia's a poet so it's normal for her to have life sad, but it's not normal for me. And Virginia's so full of fears. Whenever her mother writes that she's been skiing or gone for a climb with Kaarlo, Virginia worries retrospectively for at least a week. And now I find myself in the same category. I don't like the idea of Sam's going off skiing or climbing with that bad leg of his without my being along to make sure he's all right. So what is all this worrying? Is it my adolescence catching up with me, or is it just a reaction to the atomic age we live in?''

"Other ages have been frightening, too," Gertrude said. "There's always something to be afraid of if you want to look for it. When firearms were discovered people thought the end of the world had come if human beings used such weapons against other human beings. War would become so terrible that it would no longer be possible. But a musket doesn't seem like something to get into such an uproar over to us, does it? Every age has its own terrors.''

"Of course," Mimi said. "I should have thought that out for myself, shouldn't I? So I can't blame it on the atomic age. Just on myself. And my height.''

"Your what?''

"My height. I'm taller than Sam. And I hate it. I never minded being tall before, but now if I thought cutting my feet off would make any difference I swear I'd do it.''

"It shouldn't make that much difference," Gertrude said, smiling.

"I suppose it shouldn't, but it does. If he hadn't had polio he'd be as tall as I am, too. Maybe taller. So. This is something I have to cope with myself, isn't it? Vee, your mother said for us to stay only a minute. So I'm afraid we ought to go." She stood up and went over to Gertrude's couch. "Good-bye, Madame de Croisenois. I always feel less full of puberty and more of a reasonable human being after I've talked with you. Thank you very much.''

"Thank you, Mimi," Gertrude said. "Come talk to me whenever you feel like it. I like it. And try not to fret about being taller than Sam. We all tend to let our bodies become more important than we are. But they aren't.''

Virginia came over from the window. "She's not that much taller, anyhow. Good night, Madame de Croisenois. Olive oil.''

"Abyssinia," Gertrude said.

"Let's walk," Mimi said. "I don't want to go home yet.''

"Okay.''

—Home. I don't have a home any more. There are two people living in that house, that horrible, cold, draughty house, and I don't know either of them. And when they put on the faces of my mother and father it is as though they wore masks.

"What are you thinking?" Mimi asked.

"I'm writing a poem," Virginia lied, knowing that it was a safe lie. But then she said, "Even Connie's changing. She's not a baby any more. She's getting thinner. She's growing up."

"You wouldn't want things not to change, would you?" Mimi asked. "Think how deadly dull everything would be. And anyhow, scientifically speaking, everything would be dead in thirty seconds if things stopped changing. Life is change. Without it we'd be petrified. Frozen."

"As though we'd looked at Medusa," Virginia said, momentarily diverted by the image. And now words that might one day turn into a poem began to weave through her mind.— Where has the world been out there in the dark sea of infinity? What dread Medusa's head has chilled its life to stone, has sticken it to marble, dead, alone? What has the world seen?

They were approaching the open snow fields, and she said, "I thought you told Madame de Croisenois mother told us to stay only a minute."

"She did. But because of Madame de C. Not us. Didn't you see how tired she was beginning to look? I thought she'd had enough."

—Mimi's more observant than I. A poet is supposed to be observant.

"Oh," she said. "But let's go back now anyhow." Slowly she turned around and led the way back down to the villa.

Emily was at the piano. She had started with Bach and ended up with "Baa, Baa, Black Sheep," and Connie was sitting on her lap singing in her high, surprisingly true treble. She climbed down as the front door slammed against the wind, and ran to greet the girls.

"Vee, you had a call," Emily said.

"Oh. Who, mother?"

"Your boy friend."

"Not Beanie!" Mimi cried. "What a Thing, Vee, he's really taken a topple for you! What's he want, Mrs. Bowen?"

"He left a message for Virginia to call him as soon as she came in. I wrote his number on the pad by the phone."

"I don't want to call him."

"Oh, come on, Vee," Mimi said, "don't be so stubborn. If it's because of the cracks he made about me, forget them. I have. You can learn a lot from Beanie as long as you take him for what he is and aren't fooled by his glamor. Go on, call him."

"Come with me, then," Virginia said nervously.

"Now play 'Away in a Manger,' " Connie demanded of Emily.

Virginia went into the hall and dialed the hotel number. "I wonder what on earth he wants?"

"Only way to find out is to ask him," Mimi said.

It was several minutes before Virginia was connected with the Beans' rooms, and then Mrs. Bean answered the phone. "Oh, yes, dear," she said as Virginia identified herself. "Just a moment." Virginia heard her calling in a high, rather nasal voice. "Snider! Sni—i—der!"

Then Beanie's voice came. "Hello, Virginia, my pretty little pussycat, and how are you today?"

"Fine, thank you."

"And how's our pal Mimi?"

"Fine, thank you."

"I don't suppose you could throw her for a couple of hours this evening and come highbrowing with me, could you? There's a concert at the casino. A string quartet and a pretty good one, I'm told, and I'd be enchanted to take you."

"Oh, golly, Beanie, it sounds awfully nice, but I don't think I could."

"You mean because of Mimi being your guest?"

"Yes."

"Well, you know what, I think our pal Samuel would be very happy to entertain her. I might suggest it to him if you think that would cover the situation."

"Oh, golly—" Virginia said.

"What's he want?" Mimi demanded.

"Just a minute, please," Virginia said into the mouthpiece of the phone, and turned, flustered, to Mimi. "He wants me to go to a concert with him this evening."

Mimi put a practised palm over the mouthpiece. "Go on and go. It'll be good practice for you."

"I didn't want to go without you," Virginia said, "but Beanie said he thought maybe Sam might want to do something with you and he'd suggest it to him."

"That's the greatest idea since the invention of the wheel," Mimi said.

"Well, I'd better ask mother, then." She turned back to the phone. "Beanie, could you wait just a minute while I ask my mother? I'm sure it will be all right, but she likes me to check with her first."

"Sure," Beanie said. "Go ahead and ask."

Armed with permission Virginia returned. "She says it's all right, Beanie. Thank you very much."

"Good," Beanie said. "I'll pick you up around eight, then. And tell Mimi Sam'll call her in a moment."

Virginia went back in to her mother and stood waiting while Emily played "Bobby Shafto." "That's enough now, Con," Emily said. "I've sung myself hoarse."

Connie climbed down from her mother's lap. "I have to go talk on the telephone, but I have to wait because the lion is busy and you can *never* talk while the lion is busy."

Virginia leaned up against her mother. "I think I'm scared," she said. "I think I don't want to go."

Emily put her arm around her. "I know, Vee, and in spite of the fact that there isn't a thing in the world to be scared about you'll probably be scared until you've had a good bit more practice and gain in self-assurance. And the only way to get the practice and stop being scared is to accept every invitation like Beanie's that you get. You'll have fun when you get there and you'll enjoy the concert."

"Oh, sure," Virginia said, "but I'm not a one for chamber music the way you are."

"That's another thing that takes practice," Emily said, "so you'll be getting in lots of practice in one evening."

"Beanie has kind of pursued me, hasn't he?" Virginia asked.

"He has indeed. And Mimi's quite right. You can learn a lot from Beanie."

"In spite of what I think of him?"

"In spite of it."

"I think I like being pursued even though I am nervous about him," Virginia said. "Play something for me, mother. Something kind of gay. Maybe Mozart. No, I know. Play the Poulenc Suite."

Obediently Emily turned back to the piano. Virginia curled up in one of the chairs. From the dining room they could hear Connie's peals of laughter as Mimi played Slap Jack with her.

"Ready for dinner?" Emily asked. "I've got a good, thick stew simmering on the back of the stove, and we'd better have it, so you and Mimi'll have planty of time to change for your dates."

"Not quite yet," Virginia said. "I'm still sort of churned for some reason. Play one more thing."

"How about Granados' *Goyescas*?" Emily asked. "I feel like tackling that."

"Fine."

"And then we must eat," Emily said, reaching for the music.

After a moment of listening Virginia picked up an anthology she had left lying on the table and began turning the pages.

"You know what's one of my favorite poems?" she asked, "and I just discovered it at school this autumn. We had it in English."

Emily finished her phrase, took her hands from the keys. "What, Vee?"

" 'The Hound of Heaven.' Do you know it?"

"Yes, Vee, it's a beautiful thing."

" 'I fled him, down the nights and down the days,' " Virginia read softly.

—I suppose it's perfectly natural, Emily thought, remembering the words of the poem, that I should take all things like this as though they were directed particularly towards me, that I should twist their original meaning around to one applicable to me, *And in the midst of tears I hid from Him*, the words of the poem went. *All things betray thee, who betrayest Me*. "You haven't read me any of your poetry for a while," she said to Virginia.

"I read you the one about the woman by the guillotine," Virginia said.

"Yes, and I liked it very much. Haven't you something else?"

Virginia pulled a piece of paper out of the book of poetry. "Well, this is one daddy liked. I sort of got the idea from reading science fiction stories."

"Read it to me."

Virginia cleared her throat:

"I am fashioned as a galaxy,
Not as a solid substance but a mesh
Of atoms in their far complexity
Forming the pattern of my bone and flesh.

"I've been writing a lot of sonnets this winter," she said, looking up from the slip of paper.

"Go on," Emily said.

Small solar systems are my eyes.
Muscle and sinew are composed of air.
Like comets flashing through the evening skies
My blood runs, ordered, arrogant, and fair.

Ten lifetimes distant is the nearest star,
And yet within my body, firm as wood,
Proton and electron separate are.
Bone is more fluid than my coursing blood.
What plan had God, so strict and so empassioned
When He an island universe my body fashioned?"

"I like that, Vee," Emily said. "I like that very much. Your poetry has improved a lot this winter."

"We've been studying atoms in chemistry this year, too," Virginia said, "and they kind of fascinate me. And God. God is so tremendously exciting, mother. He's so much bigger, so much more—more enormous—than most churches let Him be. When you look at the mountains—or when you look at the stars and think how many of them probably have planets with life on them—and maybe life entirely different from ours—Mother, *why* do people all the time try to pull God down so He's small enough to be understood?"

Emily stood up and put her hands on Virginia's shoulders. "I suppose because most people are afraid of what they can't understand."

"Mother, do you suppose I'll ever be able to write poetry that will give people gooseflesh the way 'The Hound of Heaven' does me?"

"Who knows?" Emily said. "The main thing is to be as aware as you can, every single minute. Never be bored by anything. Because everything, no matter how trivial, is grist to the poet's mill. And now, my sweet, 'The time has come, the Walrus said.' We're all starved and I'm going to dish out the stew. But I did like your sonnet very much."

Out in the dark Virginia went with Beanie, into the dark and cold, warmer than the villa. This was escape, not only from the villa and from fear and anger, but escape also from childhood, for here she was walking through the night with someone beside her who was tall and handsome and assured, and surely it would not be too difficult to pretend that he was not Beanie, but that he was someone like her imaginary companions, strong and full of knowledge and (strangest of all) extraordinarily interested in her. Surely there was some way in which she could pretend safety out of Beanie.

"Why so silent, lady bug?" Beanie asked.

"I don't feel like talking." She was no longer afraid to say this because the real Beanie was not important, he did not even exist except as a stage prop, and the imaginary Beanie at her side would understand. She looked up at the sky, and although there were no stars and the mountains were obscured by clouds, words that might turn out to be poetry began to come.—*Here I am! God said. Why don't you see me! I am speaking! Why don't you hear!*

Beanie broke across the words by taking her hand. "I like the way you look tonight," he said, "angry, and sort of excited. Are you still angry with me?"

"With you. Why bother?"

He held her hand more tightly. "Stop diminishing me, Virginia. You've squelched me to a pulp already. Come on. I'll be a good boy. You be a nice girl."

She smiled at him radiantly, because tonight he wasn't Beanie. "I'll be delightful!" she said, swinging his hand. "Only I don't like your name. Either Snider or Beanie. What can I call you?"

He looked at her in surprise. "What a pussycat of moods you are! It just happens that Snider Bean *is* my name."

"Don't you have a middle name?"

"Yes."

"What is it?"

"It's creepy," he said. "It was my mother's maiden name. They had to stick it in somewhere so grandfather wouldn't forget to leave us his millions."

"Well, that is it?" she asked. "It couldn't be worse than Snider or Bean."

"There's nothing particularly wrong with either Snider or Bean. There is with Amadeus. And if you call me by it I'm taking you home right now, tickets for the concert or no."

"I shall call you Wolfgang," she said, "after Wolfgang Amadeus Mozart. Wolfgang ought to suit you just perfectly. Mimi says you like to think of yourself as a wolf."

"Call me anything you like, little Virginia, as long as you keep on being the way you are tonight. I like you this way. Not quite such an unhatched little chicken."

They were in the village now and the door to the Splendide opened, letting out a wedge of thick, stale air, and Kaarlo and Gertrude, their breaths hanging on the cold air white and like smoke, their laughter deep and happy as they brushed by without seeing Virginia or Beanie.

"We've got a while before the concert," Beanie said. "How about going in and getting a lemonade?"

She shook her head. "No lemonade."

"Coffee?"

"No coffee. I don't drink coffee at night."

"What, then?"

She grinned at him. "Champagne."

He whistled. "Expensive tastes."

"Champagne or nothing," she said.

"Okay, champagne, then." He pulled open the door and they went into the hot, heavy room. Beanie pushed his way through to a table, still holding her by the hand.

She sat down across from him and pulled off her warm gloves. Her fingers were cold and damp and a little shaky. She had never had a full glass of champagne before but tonight she was not a child, she was a woman, and Chekhov drank champagne on his deathbed and Chopin and George Sand drank champagne in a draughty palace, and surely there must have been someone with whom Wolfgang Amadeus Mozart drank champagne, because champagne was the poet's drink, the artist's drink. She smiled across the table at Beanie.

"Hi, Wolfgang."

"Hi, honey," he said. "This is more fun than I thought it was going to be."

A waiter brought the white-wrapped bottle and poured, a few drops in Beanie's glass, then a glass for Virginia, then the rest of Beanie's and smiled at them tenderly.—He thinks we're in love, Virginia thought, like Mimi and Sam, like—but that thought was like a hot coal and she dropped it, sizzling, onto the wet floor, and picked up her glass, holding it aloft. "Here's to—to life, Wolfgang."

Beanie held his glass out towards hers and they clicked. "Hey, not so fast, little one. This stuff isn't ginger ale."

She coughed and put her glass down. "A very fine vintage," she said dreamily.

Beanie poured a little more champagne into her glass. "But not too much," he said. "I like you exactly the way you are and I want you to be because of *you* and not because of champagne. Also I want you to enjoy the concert."

"Do we have to go to the concert?" She looked at him over the champagne glass.

"What a funny little thing you are tonight! Yes, we do have to go. It's a good quartet and I want to hear it. The 'cellist is particularly good and it happens that I don't play a mean 'cello myself."

She looked at him in surprise and smiled warmly. What a fine Wolfgang he was turning out to be! The top of her head felt light and airy and free and her body full of a happy warmth. "You do, Wolfgang?" she asked, and it was working, her game, it was working beautifully. "Are you going to be a musician?"

He shook his head, the lines in his face tightening. "Nope. A lawyer. I'm reading law in my spare time already."

"Do you like it?"

"No." His lips and nostrils were compressed.

"Then, why, Wolfgang?"

His thin fingers clenched. "Because I believe in making life as comfortable as possible. If I know law I can protect myself. Thanks to my middle name I'm going to come into a good deal of money when I'm twenty-one and I want to be able to know how to handle it the way I want to handle it." He shut his teeth tightly together and the corner of his mouth twitched nervously. This unhappy boy was indeed Wolfgang, and not Beanie; this was the maladjusted one, the frustrated 'cellist, the artist crying under the slick veneer.

"You don't believe in being selfish, do you?" he asked harshly. And as she didn't answer but sipped at her champagne he continued, "I do. I believe in getting exactly what I want out of life, no matter who I have to walk over to get it." Abruptly he relaxed. "Come on, little Virginia. Let's go drown our sorrows in music."

Again she grinned at him, easily, teasingly, "I'd rather drown mine in champagne," and reached for the bottle.

His fingers caught her wrist. "Oh, no you don't. I want your parents to let me take you out again. You be a good girl now and I'll give you some more champagne on our next date." He came around to her chair and helped her into her coat. To her surprise her legs felt watery and she held tightly to his arm.

When they got outside into the cold, clean, but heavy air, pressed down by clouds, she turned to him. "Everything's going to be all right soon. I feel it."

"Isn't it all right right now?"

"Right now," she said, "is the brink of hell. But soon everybody will be able to step away from it. They will have to!"

"Well, let's get away from precipices now and get to the concert," Beanie said. "We're going to be late as it is."

They struggled into their seats just as the music started. After a second of tenseness Beanie sat relaxed and listening, and Virginia could feel that the music was unwinding into him like a fine thread. But after a moment it was as though the bows of the four instruments were being pulled across the top of her head, as though the high tones of the violin were being drawn like steel wires through her eyeballs. "Wolfgang—" she whispered, but he did not hear. She clenched her fists, ducked down her head, and endured.

At last intermission. Release.

Beanie gave a long sigh and turned towards her. "Enjoy it?"

Now the steel wires of sound had been withdrawn she could breathe again without willing each breath. "I don't think champagne and music mix," she said. "Next time let's just have champagne."

He laughed at her. "Come out and let's get a breath of fresh air. Maybe you'll enjoy the next half more."

They made their way out through a side door of the casino that opened onto a dark, dank alley, stale and rank-smelling, but at least cold, at least air.

"I asked my mother to come tonight," Beanie said, "but music bores her. Know her favorite occupation?"

"What?" she asked dutifully, her head now heavy, her mind furry.

"Going to séances."

"Séances?"

"Yes. You know the kind of stuff. Dim lights and calling people back from the dead."

Her eyes widened. "You mean she really believes it?"

"Sure."

"I think maybe I'd rather go to a séance than a concert next time," she said. "Would you take me?"

"Not on your life. I wouldn't touch the stuff with a ten-foot pole."

"There's someone I'd like to call back from the dead," she said suddenly.

"Sorry as can be, honey, but it can't be done."

"Your mother thinks it can."

"Who do you want to bring back from the dead anyhow?" Beanie asked.

"Oh—someone."

"Come on, tell me."

"You wouldn't know her. She's been dead a long time. Before I was born, as a matter of fact."

"Then why do you want her?"

"I don't want her for me. I want her for somebody else."

"Who?"

She hesitated, stepped down off the step into the dirty alley. "For Sam."

"But who?"

She moved a few steps into the alley, the feel of it, the garbage and rags and snow, hideous to her feet. "His mother," she said in a low voice.

"What a nice little thing you are," Beanie said, "to worry about Sam like that. Wish you'd take it into that funny little head of yours to worry about *me* that way. I guess Sam would like her back, all right. And his father would even more. Sam has some crazy idea he's thinking about marrying again."

"Marrying who?" Virginia whispered.

"Oh, some dame in the South of France where they're going. It's nice of you to think about him. You *are* a good girl."

"I'm not a good girl," she said angrily. She moved another step away from him, then half-screamed as a dark body skidded across the alley, running right over one of her shoes.

"It's a rat," Beanie said. "Come on, let's get out of this place. It's filthy." He took Virginia's hand and drew her, shuddering, back into the steam-heated warmth of the casino, the luxurious feel of soft rugs under her feet. "I'm sorry you can't get Mrs. Fielding back for Sam and his father, little one."

"How strange it seems," Virginia said, trying to control her shivering, "to be alive when anybody else is dead. Not only people close to us, like—like my sister who died—and Beanie—Wolfgang—doesn't it seem impossible no matter how long ago they've died to think that the world can go along without them, that they haven't just moved to another city or another country the way we're living in France this year? And if we could afford a transatlantic call we could just ring them up—but *anybody*, that *anybody* is dead—it just doesn't seem to me quite possible to understand being alive while *anybody* who has ever been alive is dead." She stopped, out of breath and confused, because her head still hurt and she was still shaking with fear from the dark shadow of the rat scurrying like a lie across her feet.

"You're my very favorite idiot in the whole world," Beanie said gently. "There's the problem of over-population for one thing." He put his hand against her elbow. "We'd better go back in now."

The musicians came out onto the small stage and Beanie and Virginia joined in the applause. Beanie again disappeared into a web of sound and now Virginia felt that she was caught in the web, trapped in a mesh of music, and Sam's dead mother, Mr. Fielding's dead wife, could never return, and only the train to Bandol could save them if she could manage to pass through time safely, push them all through time safely until the train bearing Sam and Mr. Fielding left the station. Only the train speeding away from the cold and into the sun could take away the imprint of her mother and Abe Fielding standing there in the snow locked together by some private passion and her father sitting in the dark in his office typing alone and her mother lying flung across the bed. . . .

The music wound around and around her, wrapping her in a tight cocoon of pain. And all she could do was to sit there and endure, to get through time, to pretend that Beanie was Wolfgang, pushing her slowly out of today and into tomorrow.

Beanie walked her home. As they reached the turn of the road to the villa he stopped and bent down to kiss her, but she pulled away.

"What's the matter, little one?" he asked her.

"I don't think I like you well enough for that," she answered.

"Remember I'm Wolfgang," he said, "and you don't hate Wolfgang." Before she had time to turn her head he bent down and kissed her. She stood rigid, enduring it. "It's nicer if you relax," he said.

She shook her head again. "Mimi said you, being you, would probably try to kiss me."

"Mimi talks too much," he said angrily, and started to walk on to the villa. But then he paused again by the iron gate, saying softly, "Nevertheless you're my pet little carrot top and tonight's been fun and I can't stay mad at you. Not mad at me, either, are you?''

''No,'' Virginia said, and suddenly stepped closer to Beanie, shivering. ''You may kiss me now if you like,'' she said quickly. He bent down to her, gently. ''Thank you very much,'' she said. ''That was almost as nice as the champagne.'' She broke away from him and opened the door into the hall.

''Good night, little one,'' he called.

She watched for a moment as he left her, as he went up the path towards the hotel where Sam was, where Abe Fielding was. Then she closed the door and went into the house.

✧ *Five* ✧

"I never thought I could be such a sentimental fool," Mimi said, holding negligently with one hand to the T bar.

"You mean you think it's soppy?" Virginia asked.

"I wouldn't use that word. But—yes. And I think I always will be—soppy—about last night. All the idiotic Hollywood props—the sleigh and the horses and the bells jingling and the fur robe over us—and it was all as though nobody else had ever done it before." They had come to the end of the tow now, and Mimi stood there on the snow, the wind blowing at the treacle-colored hair that came out from under her cap. She seemed tall and straight as a young tree and tremendously strong.—Will I ever be strong like that? Virginia wondered.

But suddenly Mimi turned towards her with a baffled and bewildered expression. "Vee, he didn't kiss me."

Virginia looked up from adjusting the clamps on her skis and waited.

"I kept thinking he was going to," Mimi said, "but he didn't. I should have asked him to. I was a fool. I behaved like a prim prude on her first date. Just because I wanted him to so terribly. I had my first kiss when I was ten. A trombonist friend of Jake's. Jake happened to see us and he knocked him downstairs. We were spending a vacation in Majorca and the stairs in our villa were wide marble ones and he slithered down them on his back, head first, his trombone dancing down ahead of him. It was lucky it didn't kill him. . . . Did Beanie kiss you?"

"You said he would."

"But did he?"

"Yes."

"What's wrong with me?" Mimi asked tragically. "*Why* didn't Sam kiss me? I thought he liked me."

"Maybe that's why he didn't kiss you."

Mimi considered this for a moment, then shook her head roughly. "How'd you like it with Beanie?" she asked. "It *was* your first kiss, wasn't it?"

Virginia nodded.

"Well, how'd you like it?"

"I did."

"That all you have to say about it?"

"I think it could quite easily become habit-forming. Come on, Mimi, let's ski. I'm freezing."

She pushed off and it was as though she were moving over an element more subtle than anything that could cling to earth; it was as though there were no line separating the snow over which her feet moved from the sky through which her body moved, as the sea and sky seem to merge together so that one cannot tell where the one leaves off and the other begins. She passed a clump of firs, their branches laden with snow. She leaned against the air, as tangible to her body as water, and turned swiftly. She was no longer aware that she was cold.

She reached the nursery slopes ahead of Mimi and waited at the tow, watching the groups of skiers with their instructors. She and Mimi had had an hour's lesson earlier that morning and it was time to go home for lunch. She shivered, waiting for Mimi. Since they had come out that morning the sky which had been so high and blue above the white peaks had bellied down between them, deep with snow, and a whining wind was gaining force between the mountains. She wondered suddenly what her mother was doing, and she felt a terrible uncertainty as to who her mother was. Her mother had always been clear and simple and utterly dependable. Now it was as though the lens through which she had seem Emily with such clarity and detail had suddenly blurred. Or was it the lens which had changed? Was it not the subject itself?

And what was Emily doing now that Virginia and Mimi were safely off skiing? Was she doing something safe and comprehensible like playing songs at the piano for Connie? Or was she in the kitchen? Or was she talking to Courtney, which was no longer (and for many reasons) safe? Or was she with Gertrude which always seemed to unsettle her (and why, Gertrude so sure and capable and heroically stricken)? Or was she somewhere—at the casino or the Splendide or standing in the turn of the icy path—with Abe? No. That could not be. Abe and Sam were going up the mountains with their skis for the day; Sam had told Mimi this; so Emily could not be with Abe.

She was, in fact, running to answer the telphone. "I've got to get the phone before it bothers daddy," she had called to Connie, and run.

She had not seen Abe since that chance encounter at the casino two days before. Nothing had been said then about when they would meet next. She had not seen him for one whole long gaping day, and unless this were he at the phone it looked as though another would go by.

It was Gertrude.

Perhaps he was punishing her.

"What are you doing this afternoon?" Gertrude asked.

"Nothing except coming to see you."

"Good. I was hoping you would."

"I'll have to bring Connie, though. The kids are planning to go skiing again this afternoon so I won't have my baby-sitters."

"Bring her along, then. I ought to be used to her by now."

"Anything you want me to get you in the village?"

"Yes, some bread and half a pound each of brie and reblichan if it wouldn't be too much trouble."

"No, I have to go in anyhow. See you later."

She hung up and the door to Courtney's office opened and he came out, his eyes widening against the darkness in the hall. "Who was that?"

"Gert."

"Oh. I thought—" But he could not tell her what he had thought.

"What?"

"Nothing. I was a good many centuries away and the phone startled me."

"I'm sorry, darling. I tried to answer it as soon as I could."

"Yes. I heard you running." He stood leaning against the doorframe, making no move to go back to his desk.

"Work going all right this morning?" she asked him, continuing to stand by the telephone.

"Reasonably, I hope. But I think I'll stretch my mind and body for a moment. Where are the girls?"

"Virginia and Mimi are off skiing, and Connie's cutting out pictures in the dining room."

Then there was silence between them and he stood looking at her until, almost involuntarily, she moved under his gaze. "Emily," he said, stopping her before she should leave him, "I'm very glad you didn't fall down that crevasse yesterday."

She looked at him, not quite understanding the intenseness of his voice and body as though he were saying something supremely difficult. "I'd probably be down in it now if you hadn't seen me and rescued me."

"I never knew I could jump so fast," Courtney said. "Not a bad idea to find things like that out once in a while. Life seems to be a series of crevasses, doesn't it? And I'm not always very good at saving you—us—from them." Then, as though he had said more than he intended, as though to change the meaning, "I let you fight it out alone after Alice died because I was fighting alone, too. You're right, Emily. It is a weakness. I do recognize it. Try to bear with me." Then, seemingly tired physically, seemingly to make light of it, he stretched his arms above his head and yawned.

From the dining room came Connie's voice. "Mama! Where are you?"

"I'm coming, Con," Emily called back.

"Well—to work till time for lunch," Courtney said.

The telephone did not ring again. The house seemed loud with its silence. Virginia and Mimi came home and had lunch and set off again, and Emily put Connie down for her rest and did the dishes, and by the time she was done Connie, who hadn't fallen asleep, was demanding to get up.

—I'll go to Gert's now, Emily thought. He's not apt to call now, in the early afternoon. If he calls at all it would be later. He's probably off skiing with Sam or climbing with Kaarlo. That's what they came for, winter sports, and he engaged Kaarlo ahead, and if he broke any of their times together it would seem strange to Kaarlo. . . .

She helped Connie dress, got the cheese and bread, and set off for the chalet. Connie gamboled happily ahead of her, playing with the soft snow piled high at the sides of the path, though every once in a while she would turn, saying, "Mama, the wind's trying to knock me down."

"It's trying to knock me down, too, Connie, but we're almost there."

"Here, brat," Gertrude greeted Connie. "Here's your favorite book of post cards to look at, and a plate with four small cakes on it, all for you. I shall get your mother to make you some cocoa later. Meanwhile make yourself scarce.''

Connie settled herself in the zebra-striped chair, the book of cards on her lap, her fair head bent over it. Gertrude lay on the couch under the plaid steamer rug. ''One nice thing about Connie, I don't have to keep up any pretenses with her. I can be just as nasty as I like without feeling I'm shattering any illusions. Of course the illusions are for me, you understand. I don't put on my act for the people who have the illusions, but for the illusions themselves. I like people to have them.''

''Connie's very fond of you, you know,'' Emily said, coming back from hanging up Connie's snow suit and her own jacket.

''Is she? I don't know why she should be, but I suppose it pleases me. Want to make us some tea?''

''Sure.'' Emily busied herself in the kitchen and Gertrude got up slowly from the couch and leaned on the wide counter that divided living room from kitchen. ''Where's Kaarlo today?'' Emily asked.

''Off with Abe and Sam.'' Gertrude put her elbows on the counter and watched Emily readying the tea things. ''Want some of that cheese?''

''Be nice.''

Emily took the tea tray into the living room. Gertrude got down on the couch again and as Emily brought her the tea, she asked, ''Emily, do you think I'm bad for Kaarlo?''

''Bad for Kaarlo? Why, Gert?''

''Don't hedge and beat about bushes. Am I?''

Emily took a bite of bread and cheese. ''How on earth should I know?'' she asked after a moment.

''You've seen us together often enough. You certainly have an opinion.''

''Well, I don't. I never knew you without Kaarlo or Kaarlo without you. That makes a difference.''

''Why?''

''I didn't know what either of you was like before. I didn't know you as you were before you were ill or as you will be when you're better.''

Gert moved restlessly on the couch. ''I feel like hell this afternoon. You know, Kaarlo and I never meant to let romance rear its ugly head between us. It was just a question of—we'd always been friends in a careless sort of way. I'd slept with him a few times during the war when his need was great. It was more of a—a comradely gesture than anything else and I certainly owed Henri no faithfulness. Then when I came back here from Paris and I got so ill and it became obvious that I couldn't manage by myself any longer it was sort of just a business of one good turn deserves another. We'd worked together and certainly we'd been single-handedly responsible for each other's lives often enough before. . . . I swear passion couldn't have been further from our minds." She, too, reached for bread and cheese. "And then there it was. And there wasn't a thing either of us could do about it. I can't live without love, Em, I can't."

Emily glanced at her, then away again. "Who can?" she asked.

Gertrude looked at her sharply. "I would have thought you'd be quite able to."

Emily put her cup down in the saucer with a clatter. "Dear Jesus God! What kind of impression do I make!" Her voice shook with a violence Gertrude had never seen in her before.

"You've always seemed to me completely self-sufficient," she said rather hesitantly. "I've envied you for it."

Emily gave a long shudder. "Well," she said finally, "perhaps if I can seem it for long enough I'll end up by becoming it—self-sufficient, I mean." Then, changing the subject, she said, "Anyhow for heaven's sake don't worry about whether or not you're bad for Kaarlo. You're here, and aside from the sanatorium, it's the best place for you to be, and you love Kaarlo and he loves you and that should be all that matters. Surely there aren't many people who are entirely good for each other. I may not be any good at all for Courtney."

"Or vice versa," Gertrude said.

Emily shook her head. "At this point I'm inclined to feel that I'm far worse for Courtney than he could possibly be for me." She kept her voice level and casual. "I don't know what I'd have done this winter if I hadn't had Kaarlo to talk to. I always feel better after I've talked to Kaarlo even if we don't say anything at all." She began to clear up the tea things. "I saw you had a rabbit out in the kitchen. Kaarlo'll be tired when he comes down from the mountain. Want me to start it for you?"

"If you want to," Gertrude said. "It would be nice for him to have dinner waiting for a change. You see what I meant when I said I was bad for him. I suppose I could do some of the cooking."

"Clément told you not to, didn't he?"

"Sure, that's my alibi, but I don't think a little would hurt, and I don't raise a finger. I always loathed cooking. Thank God I never had to do much of it.''

Connie looked up and said in her clear, high voice, ''My mother likes to cook,'' and both women suddenly realized that they had forgotten all about her sitting there so quietly in the chair.

''Children never understand anything anyway,'' Gert muttered, and then out loud, ''Did you like looking at the post cards?''

''I always like looking at them,'' Connie said, ''particularly the ones from Kaarlo's cousins in Finland. I don't think you're bad for Kaarlo.''

''I'm relieved to hear it,'' Gertrude said, and looked helplessly at Emily.

''Come on, Emily Conrad,'' Emily said briskly. ''Help mother fix this rabbit for Gertrude and Kaarlo, and then you and I will go home and fix some tea for daddy. Its gets pretty cold in that little office of his and a nice hot cup of tea in the middle of the afternoon warms him up.''

After Emily and Connie had left, Gertrude continued to lie restlessly on the couch. She could not read and she could not relax and after a while she got up and turned on all the lights in the big room, in the bedroom, in the kitchen. Emily had the rabbit simmering on the stove and its odor, Gertrude knew, was far more delectable than if she herself had tried to prepare it. She opened the cupboard Kaarlo had built under the sink and got down on her knees to look behind the pots and pans and soaps to a dark bottle she had hidden there. She did not reach for it. She simply knelt and looked at it, then shut the cupboard door and crawled on her hands and knees out of the kitchen as though she did not have the strength to get to her feet. She crawled to the fireplace, then sat back on her heels on the hearth, looking into the fire. She wore narrow plaid trousers and a warm white woolen shirt, but she shivered as she sat there, though her cheeks were burning.

—Damn Emily, she thought, suddenly furiously angry with her for preparing the rabbit.

—And of course she did it for Kaarlo, not for me. She wouldn't give a damn for me if it weren't for Kaarlo. She's had a crush on him ever since she took those skiing lessons from him. Why did he have to bring her here to see me? I wish to hell he'd just let the relationship stay professional. Then it would have been over long ago. He wouldn't have brought her here to meet me if he hadn't liked her especially.

She stared into the fire incredulously.—Am I jealous of Emily? she asked herself. I don't honestly think there's anything between her and Kaarlo, that there ever has been or ever will be. If she seems different lately it's not Kaarlo. It's the kids being home for the holidays that makes her seem happy.

She got up and walked back to the couch, but she did not sit down.

—We've had boredom and a dull sort of unhappiness as a bond holding us together and now all of a sudden it's not there any more. That's what's been bothering me. She's not bored and she's not unhappy. Not in the same way. What the hell's happened?

—I can't stand it, she thought. When will Kaarlo be home?

She walked back to the kitchen, her mind carefully blank, as though if she did not know what she was doing it would be better.

—I've been being so damned good! she said out loud, and got down on her knees before the cupboard again. This time she reached in and pulled out the bottle.

Virginia and Mimi headed home after their long day's skiing. They moved slowly over the snow, their desire for speed satiated, their cheeks windburned, their eyes stinging. As they neared Kaarlo's chalet, lights blazed out onto the snow and suddenly there was Gertrude, in her white parka, standing out in the snow shaking a dust mop, the motes of dust caught in the light coming from the kitchen window, dust and dirt falling, drifting through the shaft of light onto the clear snow.

"Hi, kids, come on in for a moment," Gertrude said, as though there were nothing strange about her standing there in the dark shaking the mop.

They followed her into the shed, stood waiting while she took off her parka (and the white of the parka was soiled like the snow on which she had shaken the mop), tossed it at a hook, which it missed, bent clumsily to pick it up, missed the hook again, finally got the parka hung by the collar on the third try, left the dust mop lying where she had dropped it on the floor, so that anyone entering or leaving would trip over it.

She went into the living room where the fire was going and a Mozart concerto playing and a half-empty glass of dark liquid stood on the bookshelves, firelight flickering against it, gold, amber, alive. She picked it up and drank, then turned around to look at the two girls who had come in after her and now stood, Virginia awkward, embarrassed, Mimi leaning against the desk, casual, waiting.

Gertrude moved to Virginia, the liquid moving in her glass, catching and holding again the firelight. "Virginia," she said, "why are you so skinny? Why are your eyes so big and green?"

"She's a poet," Mimi said quickly. "All poets are skinny. Can you imagine a fat poet?"

"Who asked you?" Gertrude turned up the volume on the phonograph, deliberately rude, Mozart suddenly loud and distorted to drown Mimi out. "People are skinny because they aren't loved. *I* know."

"Would you like us to make you some coffee?" Mimi asked.

"And what the hell exactly are you implying?" Gertrude took a step backwards, lost her balance, and down her elbow went on the record and the Mozart let out an agonized shriek and the record broke in two. "Look what you made me do!" Gertrude whimpered. "That was one of Kaarlo's favorites."

"You can tell him Virginia broke it over my head in a fit of temper," Mimi suggested, at which Gertrude unexpectedly broke into a spasm of laughter.

"We have to go home now," Virginia said timidly. "Mother's expecting us."

"Do you have to do whatever your mother says?" Gertrude asked. "Or your father? I should think you'd want to do the opposite, so under no circumstances would you grow up to be like them."

Virginia raised her head. "I'd like to be *exactly* like them."

"And why, miss? Your father was fired for incompetence, wasn't he?"

"He was not!"

"So he comes here and sits on his ass like a sick fish all winter writing stuff so dry nobody's ever going to read it, and your mother's scared to play the piano in case anybody should hear her, in case anybody should catch on to the fact that she's so goddamned unhappy even I look happy in comparison—"

Suddenly in the firelight Virginia's freckles seemed to leap out as her color receded. "You lie!" she cried. "You're jealous!"

"I am not jealous!" Gertrude shouted back, bringing her face down close to Virginia's, so that the two of them stood panting at each other like two angry children. "What the hell have I to be jealous of?"

"Because they have each other!" Virginia shrieked. "Because my mother has my father and my father has my mother and they love each other and you don't even know what love is about and all you've said is lies, foul, slimy, filthy, contemptible, abominable, stinking lies!" Her arm went back and her hand hit, sharp and loud against Gertrude's face, and Gertrude's skin turned white where the hand had slapped.

"Well, thank you very much for the visit, Madame de Croisenois," Mimi said. "I really do think Virginia and I should be going now. Come, Virginia." There was a lightly mocking irony in her voice, but her eyes were deeply troubled. She pushed Virginia ahead of her, leaving Gertrude with her cheek slowly turning red, out of the living room, through the kitchen, into the shed, where Virginia fell over the dust mop. Mimi picked her up, leaned the mop against the wall.

"So our precious images are as easily smashed as that Mozart record. Come on, Vee, let's get out of here."

"She lied!" Virginia cried, her voice high and shrill.

"Of course," Mimi said. "She was drunk. She didn't know what she was talking about. Haven't you ever seen anybody drunk before?"

"Sure," Virginia's voice dropped bitterly. "Plenty of times." Then, "I shall never touch a drink again in my life! Never!"

"That's nonsense," Mimi said. "You can't just generalize about anything. It's like saying you'll never take a drink of water because you might fall in a river and drown."

"I'm tired of people being tolerant!" Virginia shouted. "If I don't want to drink I won't drink and nobody can make me!"

"So who said anybody wanted to?"

"I hate you when you're tolerant and sophisticated! I hate Gertrude! I hate Kaarlo! I hate sin! I hate Mr. Fielding! I hate Tommy O'Hara! Daddy *wasn't* fired!" She began running down the path, slipping, sliding into snowdrifts, sobbing, slithering, falling, Mimi after her, not quite able to catch up, just reaching the yard as Virginia banged on the door of the villa, fumbling with the knob, at last pushing it open, rushing into the dark hall, through the empty living room, the dining room, into the kitchen where Connie sat in the hip tub singing to her rubber fish, and Emily and Courtney, each holding a glass, stood by the stove. With one furious gesture Virginia snatched the glass out of her father's hand and flung it against the far wall where it shattered, glass and liquor splattering about wall and floor.

"Virginia!" Emily cried, looking at her daughter's mottled, distorted face.

Connie began to shriek.

Mimi came blundering in. "We were at Madame de Croisenois," she said. "She was quite drunk." Her throat was so dry she could scarcely get the words out.

Throughout the house there came a wild gust of cold wind.

"Oh, the door," Mimi cried, and disappeared again.

Emily put her glass down. She caught Virginia in her arms and it took all her strength to control the shaking body, the flailing arms. She could do nothing but hold her tightly and wait until the spasms of sobbing had subsided.

Mimi came back in and clumsily began to sweep up the shattered glass.

Connie, abandoned, forgotten in the tub, redoubled her shrieks until Courtney picked her up, stood her naked, dripping body on the table so that bath water splashed down into the bowl of salad Emily had set aside. Taking the warm towel from the chair by the stove he wrapped it around her, dried, and dressed her in her nightclothes.

As suddenly as Virginia's hysteria had started it stopped. "I beg your pardon," she said, formally, coldly. "I will go to my room."

"Just a moment, Virginia." Courtney raised his hand to halt her. "Don't you think you owe us an explanation?"

"I guess I was feeling like Carry Nation," Virginia said. "Down on the drink."

"And why, all of a sudden and so violently?"

Virginia sat down, hiccoughing, exhausted. "Because of Madame de Croisenois, I suppose."

"What about Madame de Croisenois?"

"Oh, daddy," she wailed. "I can't explain! She was drunk and she was awful and she made me angry."

"What were you doing at Gertrude's?" Emily asked.

"We were on the way home," Mimi said, shaking the pieces of glass out of the dust pan into the bin. "She was standing outside the chalet and she saw us and asked us to come in."

"I'm sorry," Virginia said. "I've told you I was sorry. Please couldn't I go to my room now?"

"It's time for dinner," Emily said.

"I'm not hungry."

"If you sit still for a moment and calm down you will be."

"Virginia," Courtney said. "You haven't had a tantrum like this for years. What happened?"

"I'm an adolescent," Virginia said. "I'm supposed to be unstable. I write poetry. Poets are supposed to be difficult. I fell under two horses and almost got killed. It also happens to be my time of the moon. I'm emotionally shaken."

"You have a facile and excellent gift with words," Courtney said. "I'm sorry I don't quite believe you."

She raised her swollen, unhappy face to him. "Oh, daddy, I'm grown up now, I've left home and gone away to school and been on my own. There're some things I can't tell you and mother, particularly when I don't understand them."

"Don't you think we could help you understand them?" Courtney asked gently.

She shook her head. "If you want another drink, daddy," she said, "I won't throw this one on the floor."

Emily sat across the table from Courtney in the small and hideous dining room that night and her heart ached with a flood of love for him and she wanted to get up from the table and rush to him and fall on her knees before him and bury her face in his lap and cry, "Oh, Court, Court, I do love you. I do love you, nothing that happens can ever make my love for you stop!"

And what a sound and fury if she did that! Almost as much as if she burst into a torrent of tears or tore into a tantrum like Virginia's.

So she sat there and Virginia said, "Mother, I realize that after my behavior this evening I am in no position to ask favors, but do you think we could go up on the télépherique tomorrow? I mean would you go with us? It's something we want quite frightfully to do."

Emily looked at her child, the freckles still unusually dark against the dead-white skin, the green eyes huge and pleading. "I don't see why not," she answered lightly. "But I think you'd better go to bed early tonight."

"May I go tomorrow?" Connie asked. "Am I secluded?"

"Yes, Connie, very," Virginia said, "and you may go. And I *am* going early to bed."

"I'm going early to bed, too," Connie said. "Will you tell me a story, Vee?"

"Sure, Con."

"A made-up story or 'Little Black Sambo'?"

"Whichever you like."

"A made-up one, then. Like the one where if you could understand the trees talking you'd know *everything.*"

It was, Emily thought, a fine example of a quiet domestic scene. Only in a movie might the background music remind the audience of violence, that a glass had for no reason been thrown, that a young girl had been hysterical, and only Mimi with her candid violet eyes knew the answer. And Emily herself, the mother sitting at the table, enfolding all with the gift of her love, did not belong in her place at the head of the happy family group, handing Mimi a plate of cakes, giving Courtney a second dish of compote. For her, too, the background music would be dissonant, off key, schizophrenic to indicate her double life, her life here, which was real, and her life with Abe which was the dream, the life on a different level, almost a different dimension, as a dream can seem a separate dimension, so that when she was away from him her belief in him seemed to dwindle in precisely the same way that on waking one loses the shocking reality of a dream. Her happiness in his presence and her faith in his love for her seemed to fade like gaily colored material under the too-bright light of reality, like music when doors and windows have been slammed against it; that was it most of all: when she was away from him it was impossible for her to believe that he loved her.

She looked at Connie and the child was still eating dessert and she took the spoon and began to feed her, and while she was doing this familiar duty, her mouth automatically opening and closing as she raised the spoon to the child's mouth, took it away and dipped it again in the saucer, she began to feel almost peaceful, as though the background music too had changed, as though nothing had happened.

Immediately after dinner Virginia and Connie went up to bed. Mimi sat alone in the living room playing solitaire, forgetting, in the sadness that was as deep about her as the clouds about the village, to offer to help Emily with the dishes. Sam had not kissed her; she was upset by Madame de Croisenois' behavior; she was somehow a failure. She slapped the cards down on the small table half-heartedly. Once she tiptoed upstairs, but Virginia had already fallen into an exhausted sleep so she came back down to her cards. When the phone rang she leaped to answer it like a bullet out of a gun.

In the kitchen Emily, too, dropped what she was doing and started to run until she realized that Mimi was ahead of her. She stopped, then, in the cold hall, waiting until she could tell the call was for Mimi, Abe's son, not Abe, and returned to the kitchen.

"A giant has fallen," Mimi told Sam. "A marble figure has toppled off her pedestal and disclosed feet of clay."

"Mimi, dear," Sam said, "I haven't the faintest idea what you're talking about."

"My heart is dry as a bone with disillusionment. Here I thought she was a little tin god and now I discover she isn't any different from half of Clare's friends."

"But who?" Sam asked. "Not Mrs. Bowen!"

"Good heavens no" Mimi cried. "Madame de Croisenois. It really isn't important, Sam. It's not that she's in any way changed. It's just that I never saw her before as she really is. I'm sorry to have gone on so about it. Did you call about anything in particular?"

"No. Just to talk. Dad's gone over to Kaarlo and Gert's place, as a matter of fact, and he said I might give you a buzz."

"Good. I'm glad you did." Her voice softened. "Thanks again for the sleigh ride, Sam."

Sam's voice in his turn cracked with shyness. "It was nice, wasn't it? The way the snow blew up in clouds in front of us, and the way behind us it sprayed out like the wake from a boat. . . . Wish we could do it again. Might keep us both from feeling blue."

"Are you feeling blue?" Mimi asked. She stood with the small of her back pressed against the cold damp of wall, her legs stretched across the narrow passage so that her feet pushed up against the opposite wall.

"Kind of. Dad seemed upset this evening and that always bothers me."

"Why?"

"Well, wouldn't you be bothered if your father was upset?"

"No, but Jake's always getting upset. It's his temperament. What I meant was, why was your father upset?"

"That's just it. I don't know. We had a wonderful day on the mountain with Kaarlo, but then all through dinner instead of relaxing the way he usually do after a day like that he was— well, tense and sort of—I can't describe it. I hate him to be upset and not know why and not be able to help. Maybe I wish dad would fall in love and get married again after all, but somebody like—like Mrs. Bowen, not Betty."

—Like Mrs. Bowen, Mimi thought dryly.

Her cheek against the wood of the phone box, she stood there silently. She felt so sad that she was almost tempted to drop the earpiece and sob out loud there in the dark hall, to return, as Tante Léonie had wished her to, to childhood, where everything, as in fairy tales, was obliged to turn out all right in the end, and adults on their Olympian heights were never hurt, or betrayed by passion, or confused, or sad.

"Hey, Mimi, you still there?" Sam asked at last.

"Yes, here I am, Sam," she said.

By the time Emily had finished the dishes Mimi was through her phone conversation and was back at her game of solitaire; Virginia and Connie were deeply asleep; and Courtney was settled at the kitchen table with a silk handkerchief about his throat and a pile of books before him. Emily turned to the piano, withdrew her hands as they stretched out over the keyboard. Connie would not stir, but it might bother Courtney at his books and it might waken Virginia and Virginia had had more than enough disturbance for one day.

"I think I'd better go up and see if I can find out what happened at Gert's to upset Virginia so," she told Courtney, and set out. At the top of the first steep rise beyond the hotel she stopped, standing there in the dark and cold, raising her eyes, lifting them unto the hills for help. The Alps like guardian angels, she thought, were the first things to waken in the morning and the last to darken in the evening. Before night had given any indication of leaving the valley, the white peaks would flush a faint, pearly pink; then, as wisps of mist began to be visible ribboning about the trees and houses, the mountains would turn deep rose, and, as the mist began to disperse, crimson. When the mountains finally shone in blinding silver light, day would have come to the village. At night, long, it seemed, after dark had fallen, there would remain a faint flush on the mountain peaks. It was too late now for even the faintest lingering glow, but later the mountains would turn to silver as the old moon slowly rose above them. She stood there in the shadow of the sanatorium gates looking up at the sky and after a moment she shivered and started walking again.

As she passed the church she heard someone at the organ and she pushed open the door and went in. Several other people were there, but there was no service going on. They sat apart, one or two praying, each alone, wrapped in his individual problems. Emily sat down in the back and the music from the organ poured over her and it was healing, as music almost always was healing to her; and the dim lights and the small glow from the scattered votive candles gave her a quick hope that perhaps here she might find the answer, for if she had set out for Gertrude's and Kaarlo's hoping on the conscious level to find out what had so disturbed Virginia, there was also the hope that she might find Abe there, and she could not keep from acknowledging it.

She sat there in the church for several minutes, leaning forward, her head bowed over her hands, unable either to pray or to think. When she heard the outer door creak she looked up and back and saw a woman coming into the church, a dark, tall, handsome woman, with the traces of tears still wet and incongruous on her cheeks.

—I am not alone, Emily thought, as the woman half fell onto her knees in front of the rank of candles beneath a statue of St. Jude. Everyone here tonight is seeking for an answer and if I cannot pray to St. Jude it is perhaps my loss and not so very clever of me after all. . . .

She knelt then on the wooden bench and pressed her face against her hands and she had no answers. She was confronted with problems and varieties of love and she had no knowledge with which to solve them, or even any understanding of the people she loved. She did not know why Virginia threw Courtney's drink against the wall. She did not know why Courtney was less real to her than Abe and yet it was Abe who was in the dream. The more she tried to reach Courtney with her love the further he withdrew, until it was as though she were looking at him through the wrong end of a telescope. She did not know Courtney: she did not know anyone. She did not know a mountain or a tree or a flake of snow. We are, as Plato says, like prisoners in a cave, and all that we see of things as they are is the shadow on the wall. And this cave, she thought, this prison, is the limitations of our own bodies. When she looked at a tree she was not seeing a tree. She was only receiving impressions on her five senses. She saw the tree, its dark branches laden with snow, through the sense of sight. She could hear the wind in its branches and the wind in pine trees sounded to her like the rushing of water or the beating of wings. She could feel the bark of the tree with her fingers, could feel the long, resinous needles. She could break off a handful of the needles and smell them. She could even, if she was so minded, taste them. She could receive these impressions. But is this a tree? Did she, Emily, know the tree? Or was it just the shadow on the wall?

—So how can I expect to know a human being?

—How can I hope to know Virginia?

—Or Courtney?

—Or Abe?

Shuddering, she thought consciously the dark thing that had lain, an unacknowledged and heavy shadow on her mind:

—I would like to have a child by Abe.

—That is a terrible thing.

—How can one love two people at the same time? Is it some sick and fearful flaw in my nature?

She was shivering as one shivers with the onset of fever, her face burning hot, her hands and feet icy. She rose from her knees and stumbled from the church.

She went then, not quite knowing why she had hesitated so long, to Kaarlo's chalet. Abe was there, as she had known he must be, and when he greeted her she thought she saw in his eyes that he had known she would come. Gertrude was drunk, not badly drunk, as she must have been when Virginia and Mimi were there, but talkative. Kaarlo offered Emily a cup of coffee and she realized that if there was any liquor left he had put it away. He handed Gertrude coffee, too, and for a moment Emily thought she was going to knock the cup out of his hands, but then she took it and drank down half the steaming cup, black.

"Did you ever have gas at the dentist?" Gertrude asked, but she expected no answer. "When I had my wisdom teeth pulled I had gas, and I played a kind of game with myself as I went under."

"A game?" Kaarlo asked.

"Yes. The point was to see how long I cared whether or not I was me, how long it was important to me to be Gertrude de Croisenois."

"How long?" Kaarlo asked.

"I don't know," Gertrude said. "It doesn't really matter. What matters is that while I was under the gas I discovered the secret of the universe. Lots of people discover the secret of the universe under gas, but I don't know of anyone who's ever remembered it. Except me. Or is it I? You can't possibly say except I. Anyhow I remembered the secret of the universe when I came to, struggling, unwilling to resume consciousness, to accept again the burden of individuality.''

"What is the secret?"

"It doesn't matter."

"What?"

"It doesn't matter. That's the secret. Nothing matters. Whether or not I'm Gertrude de Croisenois, whether or not I'm conscious, whether or not *anything*—simply doesn't matter."

"You know that's not true," Abe said.

"I know," Gertrude said. "The trouble with the secret of the universe is that once let the mind grab its hold on individuality again—and, my God, how we do grab—and everything *does* matter. Everything matters terribly. You may remember the secret of the universe that was vouchsafed you during the four days you had your four wisdom teeth pulled, but it no longer means anything. That's the trouble. We'd all be much happier if things didn't matter."

"How could we possibly be happy if things didn't matter?" Abe asked. "If nothing mattered being happy wouldn't matter either."

"Oh, Abe, you're so literal," Gertrude said. "You'll never marry again if you're so literal. Do you want to marry again, Abe?"

Before Abe had to answer Kaarlo said. "We were going to have some music," and went to the phonograph.

Emily sat on the couch near Abe, not quite touching him, and she wanted terribly to reach out and take his hand for comfort and assurance. Normally she was unable to offer or receive any overt demonstrations of affection except within the close circle of her own family, stiffening up with prudish obviousness at the casual kiss, turning aside her face so that lips glanced off her ear, removing her hand from the lingering hand-clasp, trying to cover her inhibitions with too eager a flow of conversation; but now to put her hand in Abe's, to press her cheek against his, would have been the completely natural thing for her to do, and she had to will her muscles away from him.

Kaarlo played a Bach record and then Gertrude said, her voice over-casual, "Oh, I meant to tell you, Emily, Oscar Troyat's getting up a little concert to be held at the casino the day after Christmas, and I said I'd ask you if you'd play a couple of things."

Emily looked up, appalled, but she spoke quietly enough.

"That was rather pointless, wasn't it, Gert? You know I don't play in public."

"Oh, I knew you'd squawk in horror and say no," Gertrude said, "but I told Oscar I'd try. What *is* this about not letting anybody hear you?"

"I'm not good enough." Emily looked down at her hands. "I get into a panic. You know that."

"These damn perfectionists," Gertrude said. "Kaarlo's one, too. That's why he won't play the violin. Because he can't be Isaac Stern. So he won't play. Why can't you be satisfied with just being damn good, Emily? No, you have to be Rubinstein. And you're like that as a person, too, always trying to be more than you are."

"What do you mean?" Emily asked in a stifled voice.

"Nobody's as perfect as you'd like to be," Gertrude said. "Stop trying to be so damn good. Go on and say you hate it here. Go on and say you're bored stiff with everything about your life."

"But I'm not," Emily protested, knowing that she sounded pompous.

"Then if you're not, you ought to be. And don't try to kid me. You know you've been ready to yap all winter you've been so miserable. And why the hell won't you play a couple of things for Oscar at the casino? You play well enough for that. Afraid he'll make a pass or two at you? So. He probably would. He does at me any time I'm there alone and I don't think it's because of my life of sin, it's just the nature of the beast. I bet you've never kissed anyone besides Courtney in your life."

"I'm not sure I want to start with Oscar," Emily said, trying to keep her voice light. "He's not exactly my type."

"Who is?" Gertrude demanded. "Why don't you make a pass at her, Abe? Somebody ought to thaw her out."

"I might try it at that," Abe said. "But I didn't realize she needed thawing so terribly."

"Then you don't know her very well. Mid-Victorian inhibitions. You name 'em. She has 'em."

"What about me?" Abe suggested. "Do I need thawing, too?"

"Oh, no," Gertrude said in her definite way. "I have a feeling you're capable of being quite predatory." She stopped suddenly and said, "Oh, hell, I'm going out to the kitchen and make some sandwiches. We never got around to dinner." At the door she turned, her voice suddenly thin and child-like in its intensity. "Kaarlo, come with me! I don't want to go alone!"

Kaarlo followed her, and through the passway into the kitchen Emily could see him put his arms around her. Abe stood up and stretched and then put another log on the fire. "Getting cold in here," he said. He moved about the room aimlessly, like an animal. Then he crossed to Emily and stood looking down at her, smiling. "And so we see ourselves as others see us. I really don't think I'm the wolf Gert thinks I am. I don't know why she does. I look more like a skidding prize-fighter than Valentino."

"But you're a football hero." Emily smiled up at him.

"And you, my darling," he said, "are not inhibited and you don't need thawing. Wouldn't Gert be furious if she knew how wrong her diagnosis of you really is?"

—Tonight it will be all right, Emily thought. Tonight we will start down the hill together and then I will go with him wherever he says.

"I like your earrings," Abe said.

She put her fingers up to touch them, silver and amethyst ones Gertrude had given her for her birthday. "A present from Gert," she said. "I don't—I don't like to wear things from Courtney when I'm with you." (So she was admitting that she had expected he would be at Gert's and Kaarlo's that evening.)

"I know," Abe said. He reached his hand out for her. "And I can't give you anything."

"But I don't want anything from you—" she started to protest stupidly, lying; and stopped because both of them knew that she was lying.

"You know the little shop right by the casino?" Abe said. "I saw a necklace there I wanted for you. And a dress. Silver-blue like a Renaissance princess'. And I can't even get you a little thing. I can't get you a box of scented bath powder. I want to get you small intimate things that can be shared only by lovers."

She bowed her head. "I want that, too."

"I want to take care of you," Abe said. "I want you to be able to play the piano wherever you want to, whenever you want to. And for me whenever I want you to. I don't want you to get tired and cold and over-worked."

"I'm not over-worked," she started to protest, when Gertrude called out, "Hey, Abe, put on a record, will you?" sticking her head through the passway and looking in at them, a bread knife brandished in her hand.

"Okay," Abe said. "Hold your horses while I look for something." He squatted before the record cabinet Kaarlo had made to house his precious collection. "Still more seventy-eight rpms than thirty-three-and-a-thirds," he said, "which has its advantages. In the first place technically the thirty-threes are never going to beat some of the seventy-eights, and in the second place it's a lot easier to play just a single movement or part of a movement when that's what you want, and that's what I happen to want right now." He pulled out an album.

Emily stood close to him, looking down at the records. "What is it?"

"The third movement, the adagio, from Rachmaninoff's Second Symphony." He looked up at Emily as though asking a question; then, as she did not speak, he held the record carefully over the turntable, saying, "My second wife, who could not tell one note from another, considered Rachmaninoff the nadir in low-browedness."

"Did she?" Emily asked. "I like him. Physical music, but I love it."

Squatting before the turntable Abe looked up at her. "That's exactly the word. Physical. This particular movement of this particular symphony in particular." Then he added in a low voice, "So I'm probably a fool to be playing it now." He lowered the needle carefully onto the record and the music began to wind out into the room, aiming not at their minds but at their bodies, not through their ears alone, but through every pore and sinew and nerve. For a moment Emily felt weak and she sat down on the floor near the phonograph.

"It's too cold there," Abe said. "Come nearer the fire." He held out his hand to her. She took it and moved closer to him.

"Just this one side of the record," Abe said in a low voice. "That's all I can—"

"Nice schmaltzy music," Gertrude said, coming in with a plate of sandwiches, followed by Kaarlo with coffee. "Let's eat, kids."

Abe took the record off and returned it carefully to the album. "Now what?" he asked. "Any requests?"

"Oh, something gay," Gertrude said. "That thing always makes me want to weep."

Abe turned on a waltz and turned to Emily. "Come on, let's have a whirl. Up you get."

Obediently she stood up and moved to him and they started to dance. When the record was over Gertrude said, "Why the hell didn't we think of doing this before? Come on, Abe, my turn. You're quite a dancer on top of everything else, aren't you? You and Emily looked quite professional there. More hidden talents, Em. Didn't know you could dance like that." She went to Abe and put her hands on his shoulders. "Come on, Abe, dance with me. I'm not too heavy on the toes, either."

Kaarlo put the needle back to the beginning of the record. "Emily?" He held her more closely than Abe had done, but she was hardly conscious of his nearness. "This is good for Gertrude," he said once while they danced. "We should do this sort of thing more often."

When the record was over, Abe took a sandwich and poured himself a cup of coffee. "Sam tells me you and the girls are planning to go on the télépherique tomorrow, Emily," he said. "Mind if we hitch a ride?"

"We'd be delighted to have you."

"Fine. Frankly, I think Sam and Mimi cooked this plan up. We're just invited along as chaperones. As a matter of fact I wasn't really invited at all, but I think I'd rather enjoy the télépherique myself." He finished his sandwich and rose. "Wonderful evening. Gert, but I think I'd better go. I don't like to leave Sam too long in the hotel alone."

Emily turned towards him, to go with him, to go with him wherever he wanted, she would speak to Gertrude about Virginia the next day, it would wait, but Gertrude caught hold of her hand and said with desperation, "Please, Emily, please don't go yet. And you stay, too, Abe, please. Sam's all right."

"Yes," Abe said. "I know. But I'm tired myself so I think I'll get along. It was a good evening, Gert. Thanks and good night. Good night, Emily." And without looking back he walked out of the room.

For a moment it was as though he had slapped Emily across the face, as though she had offered herself, saying,—Here I am; take me, and he had turned on his heel, spurning her. But she had not in words offered herself to him and how was he to know that she had resolved to trample on her scruples? How was he to know that Courtney had said, albeit indirectly, that it would not kill him, so that instead of killing Courtney she was planning to kill her conscience?

And would she have been able to? If Abe had not left, if they had been able to walk away from Gertrude and Kaarlo under the high starry sky, would she have been able to go with him?

—Oh God, I don't know, she thought rather wildly. It wouldn't be from fear of Abe if I hadn't. It's not that of which I am afraid. I know that it would be beautiful with him and my loins tremble with wanting him. . . .

—Oh, damn senses of sin, damn senses of responsibility, damn sex anyhow!

—He should not have played that music and then left me!

She looked very carefully around the familiar room as though she had never seen it before, at the books on the shelves that Kaarlo had built, Gertrude's tall art books and the Tauchnitz and Albatross and Penguin editions, at Kaarlo's ski trophies on top, at the high wide window, black and cold against the night, at the Braque silk screen, at Kaarlo sitting on the couch where Abe had sat, at Gertrude's silky hair falling across her face; at the fire crumbling again to embers—staring deliberately from one thing to another in order to keep the tears from her eyes. She couldn't quite manage not to blow her nose.

"Catching the village cold?" Gertrude asked.

"I hope not. I may have picked it up from Courtney, though his seems pretty well licked."

It was all right. No tears. She could go from Mrs. Jekyll to Mrs. Hyde again and not have hysterics at the transition. But which was Mrs. Jekyll and which was Mrs. Hyde?

Gertrude handed her the plate of sandwiches and she shook her head. "Got something on your mind tonight, Em?"

"No. I'm just tired. Or maybe it is a cold."

"Go to bed and take four aspirin and four ounces of whiskey," Gertrude said. "That'll cut it for me sometimes."

Kaarlo stirred lazily on the couch. "Gertrude believes in kill or cure."

"What's this Sam of Abe's like?" Gertrude asked, jumping as usual from subject to subject.

"A nice kid. You know as much as I do. He and Mimi seem quite smitten with each other."

"Oh? Not Virginia? I thought you thought he might be a

beau for Virginia.'' She let just a trace of maliciousness slip into her voice.

"That was your idea. A friend of Sam's has been rather hotly pursuing Virginia.'' Emily stuck up for her child, quickly, instinctively.

"Yes, I know,'' Gertrude said. "Snide Snider. Sam's better looking than his father. Note on national characteristics: why are professional American athletes always ugly, like Abe; English ones stringy; and European ones beautiful, like Kaarlo? Now don't tell me I'm generalizing. I know it. I like to generalize. By the way, Kaarlo says Abe could be a good climber if he did enough of it. Didn't you, Kaarlo? I say, Kaarlo!''

"Hush,'' Emily said. "He's asleep. I'd better go.''

"Wait a minute,'' Gertrude said. "I know you have something on your mind. You have had for days. I can always tell. So you might as well get it off.''

"Nothing's been on my mind for days,'' Emily said, "but you're right tonight. There is something I want to ask you.''

"Fire ahead.''

"What was Virginia so upset about when she and Mimi left here this evening?''

"Was she upset?'' Gertrude asked innocently.

"You know perfectly well she was.''

"I'm sorry if she was, then,'' Gertrude said, "but it was nothing but typical adolescent hysteria. And none of your business.''

"It's very much my business.''

"If Virginia or the little Oppenheimer want to tell you they probably will. Now let's get back on the subject. I want to talk about *my* problems, and if you don't think they're problems you're batty.''

"I know they're problems, Gert.''

"I adore Kaarlo, you know,'' Gertrude said.

"I know you do.''

"I divorced my first husband to marry Henri. Did I ever tell you?''

"No.''

"Dear Bob. A typical Rotarian. Prosperous, and paunchy by now, I'm sure. Last I heard he was president of the Junior Chamber of Commerce and had spawned four children.'' She shook her head roughly to fling back her silky mane of hair. "You know, in a way I suppose Bob acted very decently about

Henri. What do you think Courtney would have done in Bob's place, Emily? Would he have quietly gone home to the family business like Bob and found himself another dame? Or would he have gone all self-righteous and the heavy husband and started a nice sizzling adultery suit?''

"I can't imagine Court acting self-righteous," Emily said.

"Can't you? I can. And what do you think he'd have done? Would he have taken the children away from your pernicious clutches? Would he have started divorce procedures? Or what?''

"I don't know. . . ." Emily said.

"When I went back home after the war I had a vague idea of getting back with Bob again," Gertrude said. "The wife—a *dull* girl—and the kids were rather a shock. I used to agonize on the hour every hour about how horribly I'd hurt Bob, and all the time he was happily consoling himself with another dame. What a waste of conscience. Love's a funny thing, Emily. . . . I had a bitch of a mother. In a manner of speaking, that is. Probably what I really mean is the opposite of bitch. Cold and domineering with bosoms corseted till they were hard as the Rock of Gibraltar. But she did give me some good sound advice about loving. Don't do too much of it. Don't let it get too big a thing. People don't like it. They want you to love them, but moderately. They're afraid of you if you show them you love them too much. It's too big a responsibility for them. It smothers them. Good advice, Emily. But I haven't followed it with Kaarlo and I don't give a damn. I may treat him like hell but I don't think he can have any doubt in his mind that I love him and if he ends up throwing me out—well, that'll be that. That's one of the reasons I wouldn't stay in the sanatorium, you know. If Kaarlo wants to kick me out, okay, but just to let him drift away from me because I'm shut off from him is—oh hell, I don't suppose any of this makes any sense to you anyhow.''

"Of course it does," Emily said. "What kind of cold fish do you think I am?''—I'm not following Gert's mother's advice, she thought. I'm letting Abe see. . . .

"I don't know," Gertrude said. "Have I misjudged you? I almost always misjudge people when I resent them. And I only resent people when I think they're better than I am so it's really a back-handed compliment. Did you ever love anybody wildly, madly? I haven't any right to ask. I'm just curious. You don't need to answer.''

"I don't mind answering," Emily said. "Yes."

"In other words I'm not so damned unique? Somehow I can't imagine getting violently passionate over Courtney."

"I did," Emily said.

"Did? There. You're putting it in the past tense."

"Do, then."

"Do you?"

"Yes, in a funny sort of way."

"Funny? How funny?"

"You know I'm no good at talking about myself, Gert," Emily said. "I don't enjoy all this analysis."

"Now you're cross. Okay, I'll stop trying to pry into your purple past. Maybe I ought to marry Kaarlo after all, maybe I'd feel safer. I suppose he could remarry and have kids and stuff after I'm dead. Funny thing, the marriage ceremony. It seems so damned serious at the time. Do you suppose it would make any difference if all married couples had to go to church and repeat the business of being married once a year on their anniversary? Not all the fanfare, just going to church and standing in front of the altar and saying those things. Be a fine way of making some extra money for the churches anyhow. I wonder if I'd still be married to Bob and going to country club dances on Saturday nights and beefing about baby-sitters like his present spouse?" She knelt in front of the bookshelves and ran her fingers over the volumes until she came to the Book of Common Prayer— something Emily had not expected to see there. Still kneeling, Gertrude pulled it out and riffled through the pages. Then she began to read aloud:

"Dearly beloved, we are gathered together here in the sight of God, and in the face of this company, to join together this Man and this Woman in holy Matrimony, which is commended of St. Paul to be honourable among all men: and therefore is not by any to be entered into unadvisedly or lightly; but reverently, discreetly, advisedly, soberly, and in the fear of God."

She looked over to the couch where Kaarlo was sprawled. He had fallen asleep as he lay there, his face pillowed childishly on one hand, his mouth fallen slightly open so that his even, white teeth showed.

She looked down at the Prayer Book and read aloud again:

"Wilt thou have this Man to thy wedded husband, to live together after God's ordinance in thy holy estate of Matrimony? Wilt thou obey him, and serve him, love, honour, and keep him in sickness and in health; and forsaking all others, keep thee only unto him, so long as ye both shall live?"

Emily got up and walked jerkily to the fireplace, picked up some sticks and put them into the fire, keeping her back turned to Gertrude.

" 'I take thee to my wedded Husband,' " Gertrude read, " 'to have and to hold from this day forward, for better for worse, for richer for poorer, in sickness and in health, to love, cherish—' "

"Stop!" Emily cried.

"Am I being blasphemous?" Gertrude asked. "Sorry. I didn't realize it would bother you." She put the Prayer Book back on the shelf and stood up.

"No," Emily said. "It's not that—"

But Gertrude was still wound up in the cocoon of her own problems and did not notice Emily's trembling fingers.

"When I married Bob I thought it was going to last forever," she said. "What is it, Emily? Is the human being incapable of sustaining the heights of love? And we don't want to be satisfied with less? Is that why so many marriages go to pot? We start off with a bang and end up with a whimper. Or something like that. I'm quoting somebody, I think. You know, there's something most of us miss about marriage, some sort of development, some sort of step we can't quite manage to take. Seems to me you and Courtney've taken it. I envy you, Emily. All secure in a nice, quiet love. Do you think Kaarlo and I'll ever simmer down to being nice and quiet? I don't even know if I want to."

"I have to go," Emily said. "It's late."

"You're upset about something," Gertrude said curiously. "What is it?"

Emily shook her head. "I'm just tired. I probably am coming down with grippe or something."

"I'll wake Kaarlo to walk you down."

"No," Emily protested quickly. "Please don't, Gert. He's tired. Don't make him come out in the cold. I'm perfectly okay. I could find my way home from your place blindfolded in a blizzard, and it's a clear night. Goodnight, Gert. Be seeing you."

* * *

When Emily got back to the villa from Gertrude's she was surprised to find Courtney still up. He was still sitting in the kitchen by the stove, reading.

"Not in bed yet, darling?" she asked. "Are you all right?"

He had a half-empty glass on the kitchen table. "Trying to drown my sorrows in drink," he said. "Yes, I'm all right. After you'd left I wished I'd gone with you. As a matter of fact I almost went after you. Told Virginia and Mimi I might, but in the end I didn't quite feel up to Gert. How about going somewhere for a night cap now? Or are you too cold?"

She looked at him in surprise. If there was anything Courtney had balked at all winter it was going out in the evening. "No, I'm not too cold. What about the children?"

"Told them we might go out for a few minutes. Mimi went up about an hour ago. And Vee and Connie haven't stirred since you left."

"Okay," Emily said, "get your things on and let's go." She felt suddenly tired and not in the least like going out in the cold again, but it was an odd suggestion on Courtney's part and she knew he must have a particular reason for it.

"Where shall we go?" he asked as they went out the door.

"Wherever you say."

"Let's just go up to the hotel, then. Much as I hate to give Madame Pedroti a single other sou after all she sinks us for this rathole it's the closest place and it has the added advantage of being downhill on the way home."

It would not make sense to Courtney if she were to say she did not want to go to the hotel for fear they might meet Abe there, so she said nothing. They could hear the music and Courtney walked quickly towards it. They did not speak until they reached the hotel. Courtney was breathing heavily from the exertion of climbing, and Emily, panting too, her breath coming in white gusts against the dark, was willing that Abe be gone to bed, that they not bump into him. She followed Courtney across the lounge, grateful not to see Abe among the people there. When they were safely seated and had ordered, she breathed a small sigh of relief, and Courtney said,

"I had a letter from Tom Russell today."

For a moment she went completely blank; she had no idea who Tom Russell was or why a letter from him should be so important that it take Courtney up to the Grand Hôtel late on a cold night. Then her brain cleared and she asked, "What did he say?" trying now to give all of herself, all of her attention to Courtney.

"He wants me to give him a definite decision about next year. Which, of course, is only fair. Well, how about it, Emily? Shall we go to Indiana? Shall I accept the position? Or not? What shall I do?"

When they left the villa it had not seemed as though Courtney had had too much to drink, but now, with only a sip from the glass that had been brought him, he was no longer quite Courtney.

"Darling, it's your own decision," Emily said gently. "I can't make it for you. You wouldn't want me to."

"But it isn't just my decision," Courtney said. "I'm not going to Indiana alone. It's you and the children, too. Would you be happy there?"

Emily looked at him in surprise, sensing his effort. Then she said steadily. "We will be happy wherever you are."

"Emily, I want to go to Richwood," he said, almost desperately. "I'm not a writer. I'm a teacher."

"Then you must go."

"And you won't miss New York?"

"I probably will," Emily said, "and you will, too. It's been our home for a good many years. Yours even longer than mine. But that's not the point. If we go to Richwood we'd probably feel the same way if we were leaving there to go to New York."

Courtney looked around for the waiter and beckoned him to bring another drink.

Madame Pedroti, poured into black lace over pink satin, waddled over to them. "Monsieur and madame are enjoying the holidays?" she asked.

"Yes, thank you," Emily answered.

"Our festivities are simple but enjoyable," Madame Pedroti said, assured that her festivities were not simple at all, and highly lucrative. "Now if there's anything in any way special I can do for you—"

"Nothing, thank you. Everything's fine," Emily said, willing her to go away and leave them.

But Courtney was saying, "Yes, if you would have the orchestra play *Chanson des Rues*—they know it, don't they?"

"But of course, monsieur. They will be enchanted." She waddled majestically across the floor.

"Why that particularly?" Emily asked.

"Oh, it reminds me vaguely of you," Courtney said.

"And at least a dozen other girls." She smiled across the table at him. "I remember my last two years at college we were all playing Jean Sablon records like mad and I guess that was our favorite. You must have heard it every time you were asked to the dormitory for dinner."

He picked up his glass and gently swirled around the small amount of liquid left in it. "Tom says we'll be able to find a nice house near the campus. He says it's a nice little town and a pleasant community and that he's sure we'll like it."

"Good," Emily said.

"Believe it or not, I'll be teaching some actual Greek as well as everything else. Haven't done that in a long time and it ought to be fun."

"Yes," Emily said.

"Emily, where are you? You're so far away."

"I'm right here, Court," Emily said.

Across the room the orchestra began playing the *Chanson des Rues*.

"Nice sentimental music," Courtney said. "Hey, there's somebody waving at us."

Emily's heart went cold with fear (and why was she so afraid now of seeing Abe when she had run so eagerly after him earlier that evening?), but it was not Abe, it was Michel Clément, sitting with the beautiful and expensive woman who was his wife. Emily waved back.

"Let's have another drink, Emily," Courtney said.

"Oh—" she reached across the table for his hand and smiled and then yawned—"let's go home, Court. I'm half asleep."

"Home? Where is home? Is that villa with the spiders home? I hope Tom's right about the house. I want a nice conventional little white cottage with green shutters and a hundred feet of bookshelves, floor to ceiling."

Emily started to push her chair back. "Come on, darling."

"No. Got to listen to the music. Playing it expressly for us. Got to give them a pourboire for playing it expressly for us. Pretty sentimental ditty. Let's have another drink."

—Well, at this point why not? Emily thought. Getting all rigid about drinking never stopped anybody from having another. More apt to make them take three more. "All right, darling," she said, and signalled to the waiter.

Courtney listened to the music for a moment, then: "Isn't much alternative, Em."

"Alternative to what?"

"Richwood College. Indiana. I don't like writing in a vacuum. I like fitting it in between a dozen other things and swearing because I don't have enough time to do it. If I'm a writer I'm a teaching writer. So we have to go to Indiana. There isn't any place else."

"There are other universities," she said, denying now the words she had spoken to Abe.

"No place I want to go. Every place I've offered myself the responses have been full of enthusiasm and cordiality—and negative. I've written a few letters this winter. I haven't shown you the answers."

"There's nothing wrong with Tom's college," Emily said.

"Except we like living in New York."

"Maybe we'll like the Middle West."

"Not much like New England, I don't think," Courtney said. As he put down his glass he slopped some of the contents onto the table and Emily wondered how she was going to get him down the icy path to the villa. "As for me," he said, "I was born and brought up in New York and the only time I've lived out of it was my first teaching years and the stint in Washington during the war. I like the filthy lying slut of a beautiful city. Let's have another drink and a toast to New York and to the great primordial womb that spawned among other things Courtney Bowen."

It got later and later and still he did not want to leave and she realized with a feeling of panic that he would never be able to make the icy path back down to the villa without falling. He had chosen the hotel because they would be walking downhill on the way home, but it looked as though he would do more sliding and tumbling than walking; and it was too cold a night to think of struggling along with him, pulling him up out of snowdrifts, trying to keep his feet steady on the ice, with anything but a sinking heart.

Now he began to recite poetry, his voice a little too loud so that people at neighboring tables turned to look at him.

* * *

"Lars Porsena of Clusium"

Courtney intoned,

> *"By the nine gods he swore*
> *That the great house of Tarquin*
> *Should suffer wrong no more."*

"Please, Court," she said softly. "Please stop." She could see Dr. Clément dancing with his wife, and once he looked over at her and smiled and she was afraid that he might come ask her to dance.

Courtney continued, his voice still loud and clear:

> *"But when the days of golden dreams had perished*
> *And even despair was powerless to destroy,*
> *Then did I learn how existence could be cherished,*
> *Strengthened and fed without the aid of joy."*

"*Please,* Court," she said again.

He smiled and put down his glass. "Perhaps Virginia will be able to write that way some day. Though I hope she'll never feel that way. Please God."

Suddenly the lights in the room went down and they were plunged into complete darkness for a moment before a spotlight splashed onto the center of the dance floor. Vincent, Madame Pedroti's sleek and suave master of ceremonies, introduced a singer. She came slinking through the tables in a long chartreuse dress, undulating her hips suggestively until she reached the spotlight and the microphone. As though it were her lover she held the microphone to her, and started singing throatily into it.

"She's trying to be a combination of both Piaf and Dietrich," Emily whispered to Courtney, "and succeeding at neither."

In the corners of the room the tables were in almost complete darkness so that people had to guess at where their mouths were if they were eating. Little red points lit up the blackness from cigarettes, and when a match flared it was as though a tiny spotlight were thrown for a moment on a particular table. There was a kind of soothing magic about the darkness in spite of the spotlight on the center of the floor and the deliberately hoarse voice of the singer.

There was considerable applause as the song was finished, the spotlight went off and the lights went on, making everyone blink a little, and the singer swayed over to a table where an obese man in evening clothes, with an expensive cigar, waited, and sat down next to him, passing her hand caressingly over the rolls of fat on the back of his neck. Now the spots showed on the tablecloths, the cigarette butts in the ashtrays, lipstick stains on napkins, signs of strain and dissipation on faces.

Clément and his wife left. They looked over at Emily's and Courtney's table; Madame Clément inclined her head slightly, coldly; Dr. Clément smiled warmly.

"Let's have some coffee," Emily said.

"Rather have your coffee when we get home. Don't feel like paying old octopus Pedroti for her filthy coffee. Rather have Emily's coffee. Much better coffee any old how."

Finally then he sent for the bill which he had to sign. He walked fairly steadily as they left the hotel, but rather as though he were on ice, and it was when they actually got on ice, she knew, that the trouble would begin. And indeed, as they stepped out into the cold, Courtney turned to her, saying, "Emily I'm very wobbly on my feet."

She put her arm around him. "We'll manage," she said. "Just don't try to take it too fast."

The hotel driveway itself was not so bad. Courtney leaned on her and put one foot gingerly in front of the other, then slipped and almost fell, finally finding his balance by putting both arms around her neck and nearly throwing her. "This leaving New York and going to Richwood," he said, "This is not a step up. No one could possibly construe it as a step up."

"The important thing is that you'll be doing what you want to do and what you should be doing," she said. "Only snobs will be thinking about whether or not it's a step in either direction, and they don't matter."

"Emily, don't you see," he said, desperation in his voice. "You want me to share and I've been trying to share, I tried tonight, but right now you're asking too much of me. It's as though I were ill, as though I were mentally ill. I know I'm isolated from you, from the children, from life. It's as though there's a great sheet of glass between me and the rest of the world. I can see people, I can talk to them, but there's no actual contact with anyone. It's even between us, between you and me, this strange, cold barrier. And if, by isolating myself, I've also isolated you from me, if I should—if I should have driven you from me, I—But I'm going to break it, Emily, I promise you one of these days I'm going to be able to break it. Physical effort has been almost impossible for me this winter, but I did save you from the crevasse on the glacier, didn't I?''

"Yes, darling, you saved me," she said.

They turned out of the hotel driveway now, crossed the main road, and started down the narrow lane to the villa. Almost immediately Courtney's feet went out from under him and, this time, clutching at Emily did not save him; he fell full force into a drift at the path's edge, fortunately not hitting the hard-packed ice of the path itself. For a moment she thought he was going to disappear completely into the snow, but then he flung himself free, waving arms and legs, and shouting with laughter. "Come on," he cried. "Pull! Pull!"

She took hold of his hands and she began to laugh, too, as she stood there, tugging.

"Court!" she gasped. "Come on, try to help yourself. I can't budge you."

He continued to laugh. "I'm freezing to death! Come on, Emily, pull!"

"How about a helping hand?" a voice behind her said, and she whirled around.

"Dr. Clément!" she cried. "Hello!"

He took Courtney's hands and with one quick, strong jerk had him on his feet. "Now," he said, "I'll go the rest of the way with you." He took one of Courtney's arms and indicated to Emily that she take the other.

"Isn't it rather late for a doctor to be out gallivanting?" Courtney asked, still weak with laughter.

"I'm not on call. Come on, Bowen, let's step it up a bit."

Now that he was firmly supported on either side Courtney could walk along quite steadily, and he started to sing *La Marseillaise,* for some reason obscure to Emily. "Come on, you two," he shouted. "Sing!"

Quite unconcerned Clément lifted his voice to the night also and their voices were clear and strong across the snow:

"Allons, enfants de la patrie,
Le jour de gloire est arrivé!"

"Come on, Emily, sing!" Courtney insisted, and she joined in, and they reached the villa, still singing. Clément went in with them, helping Courtney up the stairs.

"Get him to bed with a couple of hot-water bottles," he said to Emily. "I'll wait for you downstairs."

"Thank you," Emily said, "you've been terribly kind, and you really don't need to wait. Everything's fine now." She went back into the bedroom where Courtney was sitting on the side of the bed pulling off his shoes and socks. "Darling, please get undressed. I'm going downstairs and fill the hot-water bottle and fix a glass of warm milk for you."

"You're nice, Emily," Courtney said, "you're very sweet, very kind." He dropped one of his shoes on the floor with a thump.

"Try to be quiet so you won't waken the children." She bent over and kissed the top of his head, gently, as she might have kissed Connie.

Clément was waiting for her at the foot of the stairs and he followed her out to the kitchen, watching her as she built up the fire in the stove and pulled forward the kettle.

"Thank you again for rescuing us," she said, pouring milk into a saucepan. "Everything's really all right now, so please don't feel you need stay."

"I don't," he said. "Aren't you going to offer me a cup of coffee?"

"I'd love to." She looked up at him in some surprise. "It won't take a moment for the water to boil for the hot-water bottles and the milk to heat for Courtney."

Clément sat down. "I gather this kind of thing doesn't happen very often?"

"No. And every man's entitled to it once in a while."

"It doesn't upset you?"

She laughed. "Yes, it does. But that's quite stupid of me. I exaggerate its importance." She picked the kettle up from the stove, filled two copper bottles, and wrapped them carefully in towels. "I had an uncle I adored who was an alcoholic," she said, pouring the hot milk in the big cup Courtney used in the morning. "I suppose that has something to do with it. I'll be right back down."

When she returned Dr. Clément had the coffee pot on and the fragrant smell was beginning to pervade the kitchen. "Oh—

thanks," she said. "You're really very handy to have around, aren't you?"

"Sit down," he ordered in his peremptory doctor's manner. "You look tired."

"I am, a bit." She pulled up one of the kitchen chairs and dropped into it. "I'm afraid it's a sad commentary on my advancing age. I never used to get tired as easily as I've seemed to this winter."

"But you've been well?"

"Oh, yes," she said carelessly. "I'm strong as a horse. Just old age. Or maybe it's premature senility. I haven't felt very alive most of this winter. And I've resented it."

"And now, at this moment?"

"What about this moment?"

"Are you alive?"

She turned from him to get down coffee cups. "Yes, I'm alive." She poured the coffee and handed him a cup.

He settled himself more comfortably, and stirred his coffee as though deep in thought, saying after a moment, "Do you know you are a very attractive woman, Mrs. Bowen?"

"I?" She pushed the milk pitcher and sugar towards him.

He looked at her over his coffee cup, his eyes serious, his lips smiling. "Did it occur to you to wonder why I came along just at the moment I did tonight?"

"I was too grateful to wonder."

"I saw that you were having difficulties in getting your husband home, and all winter I have thought, here is a woman I would like to know better; so after I had taken my wife home I turned around and headed back for the hotel."

She sat silent, drinking her coffee. The night noises were suddenly loud around them, the creaking of the house, the baying of the dogs, the ticking of an old tin alarm clock on the kitchen shelf. Upstairs one of the children coughed in her sleep. Finally Emily said, "I'm very grateful that you did come when you did. It was a most propitious moment. Thank you."

"May I take that as a double entendre?"

"No," she said. "It was quite straightforward."

He held out his coffee cup to be refilled. "How did you meet your husband?"

"He was one of my professors at college. I got to know him while I was doing some graduate work."

He reached out and touched one of her hands. "You really are very charming, Mrs. Bowen. When I ask you questions you answer me just like a good little girl. Sometimes I wish my wife weren't quite so sophisticated. Let us talk about each other, shall we?"

It took an effort for her not to look at the clock on the shelf. "All right. You talk about yourself."

"I am very simple," he said. "I am a doctor fortunate enough to be connected with an excellent hospital. I have a wife who is far too beautiful for her own good and who would not stay with me for a minute were I not reasonably successful; and I, who have for some time known this, therefore have no compunction in pulling the rather inebriated husbands of attractive women out of snowdrifts and insinuating myself into their homes. I suppose you would be very upset if I were to kiss you?"

"I would prefer you not to."

"I was afraid that would be your reaction. A pity. But in any case tell me about yourself."

"You already seem to have found out almost everything," she said.

"Gertrude de Croisenois says you play the piano superbly."

She stood up angrily. "This is getting very exaggerated. I play the piano reasonably well. I get a great deal of personal pleasure from it. And that's as far as it goes."

"Sit down," he ordered. "There is nothing to be upset about. You never wanted to be a professional?"

"Sure, when I was fifteen I had the usual romantic dreams of being a great concert pianist and playing in a gorgeous evening gown, the ugly duckling turned into a swan, to all the greatest and most distinguished audiences in America and Europe. Fortunately I gained enough musical knowledge to know that I could never be anything but second class. My music is one thing I've managed to be realistic about."

"Will you play for me some day?"

She sighed. "This is becoming a Thing, too. Yes, if you like."

"Now tell me more about yourself," he said.

She finished her coffee without speaking. Then, "You know all about me. But perhaps you could help a friend of mine solve a problem."

"Go ahead," he said. "I enjoy personal problems when I have no responsibility as a physician to solve them."

"She told me," Emily said, "because sometimes it clari-

fies issues to tell them to someone else, to put them into
words.''

"Go on."

"This woman—she's about my age—has a husband she
loves deeply. And a while ago she fell madly in love with another man.'' The drinks she had had with Courtney, which
were giving her the courage to make this confession to
Clément, had also befuddled her mind and she knew that she
was doing it stupidly. And perhaps it wasn't courage at all
but the utmost in cowardice which was causing her to spill
over now, a weak inability to contain her problems within
herself.

"And?" Clément asked.

"And—and now she doesn't know what to do.''

"She is this other man's mistress?''

"No. She—she was brought up in New England in a climate
of opinion where something like that is considered a terrible
sin, and it's deeply embedded in her. And I told you that she
loved her husband. Oh—'' she said, "this is the old classic
gambit, isn't it? You know perfectly well I'm talking about myself.''

"Go on,'' he said gently. "Perhaps it *will* help you to clarify
it if you can talk about it. But what I don't see is, if you love this
man— You do love him?''

Her voice shook. "Quite terribly.''

"Then I don't see why you don't sleep with him. He loves
you, too?''

"He says he does.''

"Why, then?''

"It is no virtue of mine that I haven't,'' she said despairingly. "I think it's more of a sin this way than if I had. Having
done it in intention I've already sinned as much as though I had
done it in actuality.''

"This sin business,'' Clément said. "I am sorry, but I do not
understand it.''

She tried to unclench her hands. "Maybe I'm a prude,''
she said. "But there's more to it than that. A being utterly
confused. Oh, Clément, there don't seem to be any valid
values left anywhere. . . . But sometimes I'm really con-
vinced that it's simply a question of standing up for what you
believe in.''

"What do you believe in?'' Clément asked.

"I don't believe in affairs. I don't believe in betrayals.''

"And whom are you going to betray?"

"That's just it. I've betrayed myself to the point that now whatever I do I'll be betraying someone, I'll be hurting someone. I never should have let this get started in the first place. There was where I did the wrong. Having started it I should have had the courage to go through with it. To go ahead and hurt someone I love. You see the whole thing's impossible now whichever direction I look. But I was dead and now I am alive. So I can't wish it not to have happened. I can't wish to be dead again."

"But—"

"But I have no right to play around with people's lives and that's what I've been—what I am—doing."

"Let me ask you something," he said. "Was Courtney the first man you loved?"

She shook her head. "No. But only one other who counted at all."

"Tell me about him."

"My father was a country doctor. He was his assistant for a while."

"And?"

She put her cold hands up to her hot cheeks. "I loved him like a—like a fool. And I thought for quite a long time that he cared about me, too. Then I found out that he was simply using me as a sort of bait to get another girl."

"I see. And there has been no one since your husband?"

She shook her head. "No. Except that I know that the seed of this thing between Abe and me has been there for a long time. It could have happened any time. I've been in love with him for years in a half-acknowledged way. I suppose it's an indication of my—my essential depravity."

Dr. Clément leaned across the table and took both her hands in his, holding them so tightly that she gasped from pain, but he did not release his grip. "These words you use," he said, "sin, depravity, I'm sorry, but they are quite distasteful to me."

She nodded, shame-faced. "I know. They really just help to confuse the issue, don't they? But what it comes down to is this: before I was married what I did was my own affair—that wasn't meant to be a pun—and as long as the only person I hurt was myself it was my own business. But when I married and when I had children I assumed responsibilities and those responsibilities I have no right to cast aside just for—for my own emotional and physical needs. Isn't that it?''

Now he released her hands. ''Would it hurt your children so very much?''

She spread her fingers apart. ''The odd thing is that it isn't my children I've been thinking of all through this. It's my husband.'' She stirred carefully with her spoon in the empty cup. ''Anyone who has known Courtney only this winter really hasn't known him,'' she said after a moment. ''To-night when he was—when he'd had too much to drink and he was laughing when he was stuck in the snowdrift, and then singing on the way home, he was more like himself than he's been all winter. I don't mean the drinking; I mean the ability to enjoy things, to have gaiety and excitement. That's what I mean about this winter. He hasn't been able to enjoy anything. And he's—he's stifled himself so that he hasn't even allowed himself to suffer.'' She stood up abruptly and her chair scraped across the floor with a harsh sound. ''You don't understand why I haven't slept with Abe,'' she said. ''Neither do I. But you can put part of it down to gratitude.''

''Gratitude?'' he asked, raising his eyebrows.

''Yes. Gratitude to Courtney. If I've become the kind of woman Abe can love—or that you can offer to kiss—if I've become a person in my own right it's because of Courtney.''

''And how is it because of Courtney?'' Clément asked, leaning back in his chair, his legs crossed, his expression alert, compassionate, but above all quiet; and it was the quiet that made it possible for her to go on talking.

''Because before I was married to Courtney I wasn't anybody. At school—at home at high school—most of the kids didn't didn't even know I was there. I went to classes and did my homework but that was all and the rest of the time I stayed home and read and played the piano and daydreamed. Sometimes my cousins fixed up dates for me but they were always flops.''

''What about your parents?'' Clément asked.

''My father was as busy as most country doctors are, and though he was a man of great—great probity, my younger brother was always his favorite and he never tried to hide it. Our mother died when we were quite young and father's sister kept house and as long as we kept our rooms tidy and were prompt for meals that was all she cared about. She wasn't a—a loving sort of person. Then I went away to college and nothing much changed. I went to classes and did my work and spent the rest of the time in one of the practice studios and nobody knew I was there."

"Go on."

"Then I took Courtney's senior seminar and the whole world changed for me," she said. "I went back to do graduate work in music but I took another of Courtney's courses, too, and . . ." She was silent, then, for a long time. Clément did not speak either, but sat there quietly, smoking, dropping his ashes into his saucer, and at last Emily said, "I don't know why he ever asked me to marry him, what he saw in me. Just a gauche, unattractive stick. But I married him and I—it was as though I had become a completely new human being. I discovered I had a personality of my own and I began to enjoy being myself. I stopped freezing up whenever I had to meet anybody and I actually began to enjoy parties. We had the students over a lot and they liked to come and that meant a lot to me, too."

"Why do you suppose it happened, this great change?" Clément asked her.

"I suppose it was because I was loved," she said, looking across the table at him. "I was loved, for the first time in my life, and so anything became possible. We had Virginia, and she was an enchanting baby, fat as a butterball, believe it or not. Then came Alice, and with the children an added kind of security, a cementing of my feeling that I was of some value as a human being."

"Alice?" he asked gently.

"She died when she was eight," Emily said, "While we were in Washington."

Again his hand touched hers. "And that was something else to bring you and your husband closer."

She shook her head. "No. While she was—while she was dying he was magnificent. But afterwards—he retreated, as far as Alice was concerned. He took his grief and hid it somewhere so deep inside him that no one could even see that it was there. We met Abe shortly after that and it was Abe who came close to me then. Not the way he is now. Just as a friend. We had—we had death bringing us together. He helped me with Alice and I could listen to him while he talked to me about Kristina—his first wife who died when Sam was born."

"And your youngest little girl?" Clément asked.

"She was—unexpected," Emily said. "We had Virginia and

Alice right away and we wanted more but nothing happened. I
went to a couple of doctors and there wasn't any reason we
didn't have more children, it was just that—" she shrugged—
"nothing happened. I'd given up even thinking about more
children and right after Alice died it was the last thing that was
in my mind. When I found out that Connie was on the way I
was horrified. I didn't want her. It seemed like—the ultimate
betrayal of Alice. I had horrible morning sickness which I
hadn't had with either Virginia or Alice and it was like a kind of
psychological rejection. Of course now I can't imagine life
without her." She realized that she was trembling and she sat
down again. "I didn't mean to go into all this," she said shakily. "Only to say that anything I am I owe to Courtney. If I'm
a—a fulfilled woman who can thereby be attractive to—to
someone like Abe, it's due to Courtney. Out of most
unpromising material he made Emily Conrad Bowen."

"Or Emily Conrad Bowen made herself," Clément contra-
dicted her gently.

"But I couldn't have done it without Courtney." She stood
up again then and took the coffee cups to the sink. "I should
never have bothered you with all this. I had too much to drink,
too—though I'm not going to blame it on that. It's terribly late
and you've already been more than kind and it was most
thoughtless of me to keep you up pouring out my problems like
this."

He stood up, too, but he did not make any move to leave. Instead he asked her, "Does Courtney know about the young
doctor you mentioned?"

"Of course."

"Does he have any idea of what is going on now?"

Her hand flew to her throat as though in panic. "No. And he
mustn't. Ever."

"You have beautiful eyes," Dr. Clément said. "I hope
you're told that frequently."

"I'm not." She put the cups and saucers on the drainboard
and dried her hands.

"You know, of course, that there is nothing I can say that
will help you? I can say, 'Go to your lover,' or, 'Stay with your
husband,' and neither answer will satisfy you. It is something
you have to work out for yourself." Again he took her hands in
his.

"Oh, I know that," she said. "And I'm not fool enough to
think that things can ever be the same with Courtney and me

again. But I've got to belive that out of something different I can make something good. Or—'' She stopped. ''Well, it's up to me, isn't it?'' she asked. ''Thank you for listening. I somehow had a terrible need to say it out loud. I wanted to tell someone that I am in love. I wanted to stop hiding it.''

''Whenever you want to talk about it,'' he said, ''please come to me.'' Then he bent down and kissed her gently and firmly on the lips and walked out of the kitchen and after a moment she heard the front door shutting behind him.

✧ *Six* ✧

At the breakfast table Virginia sat next to her father and discoursed on history, trying to make up with casual prattle her violence of the night before. "I'm not too fond of history," she announced, "except to write poetry about, and then you don't have to stick too closely to the facts. Could I have the milk, please, mother? Thank you. You know what I mean about history, don't you, now really, daddy? It's full of trends and it talks about nations as though they were individuals and individuals as though they were nations and just people get lost in the shuffle."

"Virginia's on a talking jag," Mimi said to Emily. "She gets this way once in a while."

"Maybe you learn something about individuals like Caesar and Napoleon and Hitler," Virginia was saying earnestly, "but history never seems to bother about how completely different the same world is for different people. I mean, I know my world, but I don't know a bit what the world would be like if I were a—a Puerto Rican kid growing up in New York—just a few blocks from our apartment, even, and having to live with ten or fifteen people in a couple of dingy rooms and not enough to eat and dope-pushers after me—and never having heard of—of El Greco or Ernest Hemingway."

Connie hitched her chair closer to Emily's. "Tell me all about Goldilocks and the three bears," she suggested.

"Or if I were a Korean kid," Virginia went on, "or in Red China. Or India. I don't know anything about that kind of world. Or if I were growing up in Israel, fighting the Arabs and hating the English and Egyptians—or an Arab kid hating the

Jews. Historians don't ever think about things like that. They just generalize.''

"Aren't you generalizing a little about historians, too?'' Courtney asked.

At that moment the front doorbell rang. At first Emily thought it was the telephone and leaped to answer it; then she realized that it must be the doorbell and therefore Madame Pedroti; everyone else knocked, the doorbell looked so rusted and unfunctional. "It's Pedroti,'' she said. "We don't owe her any money, do we, Court?''

He looked startled. "Good heavens, I don't think so. Last night, I suppose. But she can hardly have come to collect that yet. You made out her check at the beginning of the month, didn't you?''

"Yes, of course.''

Virginia, who had gone to open the door, returned, saying, "Madame Pedroti would like to see you, mother.''

Emily stood up. "Okay, thanks, Vee. I'll go in to her.''

"Your breakfast will get cold.'' Courtney did not lower his voice.

"It doesn't matter. I'd almost finished.'' Emily put her napkin down on the dining table and went into the living room.

Madame Pedroti heaved her bulk out of one of the puce chairs; it was a tight fit. "Ah, good morning, Madame Bowen. I hope I am not disturbing you.''

"Not at all, Madame Pedroti.''—Polite and a lie.

"Madame and monsieur enjoyed themselves yesterday evening?''

"Yes, thank you, very much.''—You old witch.

"And Mademoiselle Virginia? She is enjoying the holidays?''

"Yes, thank you.''

"Such an attractive child! It must be a joy to madame to have her home.''

"It is, thank you.''

"I trust madame will always let me know if there is anything she desires?''

"Yes, Madame Pedroti.''

"I was just passing by this morning so I thought I would drop in to tell madame that Etienne has procured the boards for the bridge for the door to the alley and any time it would be convenient for you to pay for them—''

"Pay for them?"

"Etienne got a very good price. Boards are usually very expensive but Etienne was able to get enough for the whole affair for only nine thousand francs."

"I'm sorry," Emily said, "I don't quite understand. What are the boards for?"

Madame Pedroti gave her a how-can-you-be-so-stupid? sort of look. "Why, for the spring thaws, madame. The garden will be flooded but Etienne thinks so highly of you that he himself will build the bridge from the house to the alley."

"Madame Pedroti!" Emily said. "I think you can hardly expect us to pay for these boards."

"But who is to pay for them, Madame Bowen?"

"When you rent a small villa you don't expect to find that you are surrounded by a moat when the spring thaws come and are supposed to buy a drawbridge."

"Madame Bowen is always so witty. I am not, but, nevertheless, madame, you can hardly say that I am responsible for the melting of the snow."

Emily tried to smile, to make her voice reasonable, to sound pleasant as she said unpleasant words. "You are responsible for building a house in a hollow and for renting it without telling your tenants that their garden, and, I presume, cellar as well, will be completely flooded during the spring months."

"Of course, madame, if you don't want the boards I shall be only too happy to—"

"To what?"

"To forget the whole matter."

At that point Emily saw a mental image that made her burst into laughter. Madame Pedroti raised her brows and Emily said, "I'm so sorry, I was just visualizing your coming to get your monthly check in a rowboat." She laughed again. Then she said, "Madame Pedroti, it isn't even quite Christmas yet. March and the deluge are still three months off. Suppose we forget the subject—or rather, suppose you go home and think about it and we'll discuss it later."

"Very well, madame. As you wish." Then she lifted her upper lip into what must have been meant for a smile. "It has been pleasant for madame to have her friend here, has it not?"

"You mean Virginia's friend, Mimi? Yes, she's a delightful child and we're enjoying very much having her."

The upper lip was raised again. "I did not mean the little Oppenheimer."

—What is she driving at? Emily wondered.

"The American gentleman who is staying at the hotel."

"Oh. Mr. Fielding. Yes, it has been very pleasant for my husband and me to have him here."

"Mr. Fielding thinks most highly of you. I can see that."

"We have been friends for a number of years," Emily said. Madame Pedroti pulled on her gloves, pushing her pudgy fingers down carefully into each finger.

—How I detest the woman, Emily thought. I'm sure I see her through a distorted lens. She cannot be as repulsive as she seems to me.

"Such an attractive man, Mr. Fielding," Madame Pedroti said. "Attractive in the American way, of course. It would not mean a great deal to me. But I can see that in the American manner he has a great deal of charm." Again the smile, showing her discolored teeth. "And yes, I'm quite sure your charming husband must enjoy having him here, too. But I must not keep madame any longer. And I assure madame that I will think about the matter of the boards."

Emily stood quite still in the center of the room and did not even see her to the door.

—Blackmail?

—I am such a fool, she thought, that I don't know. Perhaps it was entirely innocent. Perhaps it was just her way of making conversation, of turning an unpleasant business discussion into a social chat. Perhaps it is only my own guilty conscience that makes me read anything sinister into her mentioning Abe. How could she possibly be suspicious? I had dinner at the casino with him. And went to his room. Perhaps she saw me then. I walked home from Kaarlo's and Gertrude's with him but that was late at night and she couldn't have seen us. I went skating with him but the children were along. We walked home from the casino together.

And all the things she had done with Abe could have been exactly the same done without love and she would have no sense of guilt about them and Madame Pedroti could have said the same things, cast the same aspersions, and she wouldn't even have suspected blackmail.

So she had gone to his room. It would have looked neither more nor less guilty if she had gone simply to talk to him, if she had gone with no thought of love as in New York she had gone

on occasion to his apartment for dinner or he to hers when
Courtney happened to be away. Undoubtedly to Madame
Pedroti that would have been full of implications, too.

Virginia came in then, saying, "The old ghoul gone?"

"Yes."

"What'd she want? Anything important? You do look distraught, mother. Good word, that, isn't it? Distraught. Rhymes
with all kinds of things. Taught. Brought. Ought. Wrought.
Caught." She felt the almost giddy light-headedness that always followed her violences.

"Yes, it's a fine word," Emily said.

"But what are you distraught about?"

Emily laughed. "Oh, it seems that come spring the front
yard will be a flood and we'll have to build a sort of bridge from
the door to the alley. It's a long way till spring, though, and a
lot of things can happen between now and then, so let's forget
it. Confidentially, I don't believe the snow is ever going to
melt."

"If winter comes, etcetera," Virginia said. "Query: Where
are the snows of yesteryear? Answer: In my mother's garden."
Suddenly she flung her arms about Emily. "Oh, mother, I do
love you so terribly much."

A little surprised (for Virginia had for some time felt that
she was too old for the overt demonstrations of love), Emily
drew the thin body to her. "I love you terribly much, too,
darling."

"Please don't ever change," Virginia begged. "Please don't
ever be any different."

Emily looked down at the girl's imploring face. "But, darling, people are always changing and developing. Even grownups. I don't think I'm apt to change in any important essentials,
though."

"I want you and daddy to stay just the way you are, always."

"We'll do our best." Emily made her voice light, and kissed
Virginia.

"What I really came in to ask you about," Virginia said, "is
it okay if Mimi and Connie and I walk up to the hotel to pick up
Sam and Mr. Fielding? Mimi wanted me to ask you if it's all
right if they go with us."

"But, Vee, it's been snowing off and on all morning. You
don't want to go on the télépherique today. You won't be able
to see a thing."

"But we do want to go. We want to go awfully. It will be exciting. And your promised."

"You may go if you want to, Vee. I just don't think it'll be very much fun."

"Then may we go up to the hotel now?"

"Yes, if you like."

"We'll come by for you and yodel when we get within a hundred yards of the villa. Mind you're ready and waiting."

"I'll be ready," Emily promised.

She was waiting for them by the gate as they came down the narrow path. Mimi and Sam were walking ahead; Abe came behind, Virginia and Connie one on each side. Emily opened the gate and stepped out to join them.

"Not a very good day for it," Abe said conversationally. "Sky clouded over right after sunrise."

"The children want to go anyhow, but it seems foolish in a way when we won't be able to see much."

"Yes," Abe said. "It's a gorgeous view, but we'll take them again."

—He's forgetting that they're leaving, she thought. He's talking as though things were going to go on, as though there were a future.

Virginia and Connie ran on ahead and caught up with Mimi and Sam, and Emily fell into step beside Abe. "Hello, darling," he said in a low voice.

"Hello."

Ahead of them Virginia's voice rose cheerfully. "There are all kinds of things I want to do when I'm dead. I'd like to have all my life go before me like a play, only I'd be in it and I'd be watching it at the same time. And I'd have it repeated and repeated so I really saw all of it, so I could be really aware of every minute. We miss an awful lot of our lives while we're living them. And I'd like to hear everything everyone ever said or thought about me. All the bad things and all the good things. A complete evaluation. The height of egotism—or is it egoism—?"

"Same difference, I think," Sam said.

"Anyhow I know it's the height of it, but you must admit it's a fascinating idea and would take care of quite a few centuries out of eternity."

"Very entertaining thinking, old girl," Mimi said, "but it

doesn't gibe with what I imagine you've been taught about God.''

"Oh, okay, Mimi Opp, I know how you feel about God and you're just trying to get me into an argument, but for once I'm not going to bite. As for you and God, people didn't believe in the possibility of airplanes or radios, either, or, to put it more in your pet terminology, in anaesthesia or vaccination, but those things were there waiting to be discovered all the time. Maybe God's waiting to be discovered, too.''

"Pretty profound, your daughter," Abe said.

"And quite right about being an egoist or -tist, I'm afraid.''

"No," Abe said. "Just a good healthy awareness of a developing personality. I like your children, Emily.''

"And I like Sam. I think we're really pretty lucky, both of us. On the whole we've produced rather nice specimens.''

"I would have liked a lot of kids," Abe said, his face suddenly darkening. He looked at Emily and opened his mouth to say something and closed it again.

"What?" she asked.

"Something better left unsaid. Come on, the kids are ahead of us. Let's catch up.'' He took her hand and they ran, laughing and gasping for breath, the cold air tearing their dry throats. They caught up with the children at the télépherique station. The place lay deserted in the damp cold, without the usual group of tourists milling about, and only the engineer and Pierre Balbec, Kaarlo's cousin, in attendance.

"You mean you want to ride?" Pierre asked incredulously.

"Sure we want to ride," Sam said. "Six of us.''

Pierre shook his head, his hair dark and sleek in contrast to Kaarlo's sun-bleached straw. "Nobody in his right mind wants to ride the télépherique on a day like this. Jules Pépain's mother is sick and he's gone to Lyons taking his wife with him and there's nobody to take their place till tomorrow; at this time of year everyone is already working. You won't be able to get anything to eat or drink. No chocolate bars. No hot soup.'' He explained expansively with his hands.

"That's all right," Sam said. "We just want to go for the ride. We're not looking for views.''

Pierre grinned at Abe and Emily. "It's a good thing you're not looking for a view because you won't get one. You'll be lost in the clouds. It's going to start snowing again any minute, too. However—'' He shrugged.

"That's okay," Sam said. "When do we start?''

"Kids," Pierre said. "I wish I still liked to do crazy things the way I used to when I was a kid. But ever since I had that bad fall on the mountain and broke my leg I've preferred staying at home. Well, get on in. I'll take you myself. Philippe is in bed with an inflammation. Everything is out of order today and you have to come demand a ride." But he said it with perfect good nature and led the way up the steps to the wooden platform beside which the small red car was suspended from the heavy cable. As it hung surrounded by the gray day and the lowering mountains it looked like an incredibly rickety antique from an amusement park.

"You first, Madame Bowen," Pierre said, and as he moved they could see that he still limped from the accident on the mountains. "Now the children. And Monsieur Fielding."

"Should we all ride together?" Abe asked. "Aren't there too many of us?"

"Couldn't we go alone, dad?" Sam begged quickly. "Please let us."

"Oh, yes, please, mother," Virginia said.

"We'll take good care of Connie," Mimi promised. "And you and Mr. Fielding could go in the next car, Mrs. Bowen."

"Well they don't have to go if they don't want to," Virginia said.

Abe looked at Pierre. "Would it be all right for them?"

Pierre lifted his hands and shrugged. "Why not?" They're good kids. I'll look after them. But if you want to ride you'll have to wait for me; there's no man for the other car with Philippe out."

"Please, dad," Sam said.

Abe put his hand on his shoulder. "All right, Sam. I trust you to take care of the three girls. And all of you do exactly as Pierre tells you. Right?"

"Right," Sam said.

Emily got out and stepped back onto the platform; Pierre closed the door and pulled the lever that started the car up the mountain.

Abe and Emily stood looking after the car, watching it dim and then disappear entirely as it climbed into cloud. Emily took a step closer to Abe and her coat touched his, and the very contact of their clothes was a caress.

"It's cold out here, dearest, and we can't see them any

more,'' Abe said. He put his arm around Emily and led her into the small empty station. There was a wood fire burning in the stove and the windows were streaming with steam. The engineer was in the room beyond but the door was closed and they could not see him or he them. Abe drew Emily to him and kissed her. For a moment she relaxed in his arms. Then she moved away and he turned and walked to one of the small windows and stood there as though he were looking out. ''Sometimes I think I can't stand it,'' he said. ''Here is something simple and lovely, and the way the world is has conspired to make it complicated and difficult so that last night I had to run away from you. I couldn't bear being with you but not being with you a moment longer.''

Emily sat down on one of the wooden benches against the wall. After a moment Abe came and sat down beside her. He took one of her hands and very carefully pulled it out of the glove. He handed the glove to her and then held her hand in his. ''This is our last day, Emily,'' he said. ''Tomorrow Sam and I are going for a climb with Kaarlo, and the next day we leave. Could you come out to dinner with me tonight? Could we dance again?''

''No,'' Emily said.

''Why not?''

''What about Courtney?''

''Ask him to come along.''

''Are you crazy?''

''Yes.''

''Oh, Abe,'' she said, ''you know I want to, more than anything. You know it would be lovely. And you know that I can't.''

''Of course I know it. And we're having this time together and we're wasting it agonizing. Kiss me and don't pull away.''

They kissed. They sat there side by side on the wooden bench in the small station and they kissed each other and for the moment there was nothing between them but love and joy; and, as always when they kissed, lost in the moment, suspended in time with nothing behind and nothing before, they were so happy that they would pull apart laughing for sheer joy; and then they would kiss again.

''Look,'' Abe said, breaking away at last. ''Can you come to me tonight?'' He did not look at her as he said it. He pulled her to him again and pressed his face against her.

No.

There was no answer but no.

In the cold light of day coming so palely in the small soiled windows there was nothing to say to him but no.

She had made up her mind the night before that she was going to sleep with Abe, that she was going to "get him out of her system." She had Courtney's permission, albeit in a back-handed sort of way, and she had thought that she could do it, and she couldn't. In spite of the pain of wanting it, she could not do it. (If Abe had not run away from her the night before at Gertrude's would she have been able then in the freshness of her resolution to break through every barrier with which her upbringing and beliefs had surrounded her and go with him?)

"I can't," she whispered.

"Why not?"

"I can't," she repeated. She got up and walked over to the stove and held her hands out to it, saying lamely, "Pedroti made a phony excuse to come see me this morning just so she could make some insinuating remarks about us. If she saw me come to your room tonight it'd be all over the village by morning."

"There are other hotels," he said. "There are hotels where we aren't known."

"I can't," she said.

"Why?"

She turned from the stove, took a step towards him, stopped, and beat her hands together as though to warm them. "Abe, I'm married to Courtney. I can't do it to him."

"What about me?"

"Oh, Abe, don't."

"Is it asking too much for you to divorce Courtney and marry me?"

"Yes!" she shouted, because her reaction was almost a physical one. This was the one question that he must not ask, the one question that she could not answer, because it was the one question that demanded an answer. An irrevocable answer.

For a moment it seemed as though she had actually given him a shove. He asked again, shouting back, "Why?"

Then it was that the door burst open and the children tumbled in. They had not heard them. Abe moved over to the window again, his face gray against the glass.

"Golly, peoples, it was terrific!" Sam said.

"Oh, Mrs. Bowen, you and Mr. Fielding have to go," Mimi said. "It couldn't have been more beautiful with a view."

"I was a small amount scared," Virginia said. "Sometimes infinity can be a little too awe-inspiring. But it was worth it."

"Pierre doesn't speak English," Connie said. "He speaks French and German and Italian and he says he's prob'bly the only man in the village who doesn't speak English and he says I speak very good French."

"You do, you little villain," Mimi said.

Sam gave Abe an affectionate shove. "Pierre's waiting. Go on, dad."

"You don't have to go if you don't want to," Virginia said to Emily in a small voice. "Or I could go with you or something—"

But Abe had opened the station door. "Come on, Emily." His voice was brusque.

They went out to the car and Pierre turned to Abe. "You're going to have to ride this toy or the kids will be down on you."

"We're going," Abe said.

Pierre was beating his mittened hands together, and kept the car steady only with one foot as Emily stepped in. It swung out from the platform a little and she reached instinctively for Abe's hand.

"It may sway a little because the wind is rising and we are so few," Pierre said, as Abe secured the door with the heavy leather strap and rusty buckle. "But don't worry, madame, it's perfectly safe." He raised one hand to signal the engineer, then moved the heavy lever across the floor. With a grunt and a groan the car started moving; a few jerks and they were beyond the platform, hanging ten feet above the snowy ground.

That was all they could see. Snow on the ground below them, snow in the sky above them and wind moving like a great bird between. Occasionally they drew past a tree, its branches blackened with ice, with patches of white drawn here and there by snow. In the hanging car their breaths came out in white gusts. As they reached the halfway mark up the mountain they passed the car coming down, empty and swaying.

All this time not a word between them. Occasionally Pierre would point out something to them; once he remarked on the unusually long cold spell and the sickness it seemed to have brought. They replied to him but there was a chasm between them far greater than the one over which they hung. "A lot of 'flu this year," Pierre said, "and all at once and of course at the busiest season."

They reached the top of the ascent, the car still swinging lightly on the cable. Pierre unstrapped the door and they clambered out onto the platform, Emily following Abe and Pierre into a gaunt stone building that had the austere beauty of a monastery. The restaurant, café, and restrooms were barren and locked, and the stone ceiling made a hollow echo as they strode across the engine room with the great oil-smeared machines that operated the cables. Pierre spoke briefly to the old man who tended them; then he led them out of the engine room through another exit. They stepped out onto the platform and the wind brushed by Emily with the insistence of a man.

Pierre opened the door to a red car similar to the one in which they had come up the mountain, holding it steady. They got in and he pulled the lever that operated the car and it jerked and swung away from the peak of mountain by which it had been resting. Now they were lost in clouds. They could see only the briefest length of cable above them before it was lost on either side in whiteness. It seemed incredible that the cable reached from mountain peak to mountain peak. The car was moving slowly along in space, swinging a little, and though there was no end to the space it seemed to Emily that there must be an end to the cable.

She knew that the valley was miles below them, that they were suspended over a great drop. But she found it difficult to believe that the valley was below them at all. The entire world seemed to have dissolved in the whiteness of cloud.

Abe turned to her. "Why?" he demanded in English as though he had never been interrupted.

She looked quickly over at Pierre but his back was to her and he was gazing out into space. She knew that though he claimed (with an odd sort of pride) to speak no English he probably understood a good deal and she kept her voice low, almost inaudible. "I love Courtney. I can't do it to him."

"Do you love me?" he demanded.

She said the words as though in anger or pain. "You know I do!"

Then they were silent again. "On a clear day," Pierre said,

still staring out into cloud, "the visibility is well over a hundred miles."

"We will have to come again," Abe said politely in his precise, schoolboy French, "on a better day."

"Monsieur is staying for long?" Pierre asked.

"No, but I hope to come back."

Silence again, and drifting through white blankness: compulsively Emily turned to look at Abe and he said, "Emily, *how* do you love Courtney?"

"What do you mean?"

"Do you love him as you love Virginia and Connie, for instance, or do you love him as a man?"

Great drifts of silence kept moving between their words, but finally she managed to say, "I'm told there's no love like that of a mother for her children, a lioness for her cubs."

"But it's not enough for you, is it?" Abe persisted. "Or this would never have happened."

"I don't know," she said. "I don't know."

"Emily, I've been like a lost soul, and now I'm found. You can't push me into outer darkness again."

She took a step towards him and the car began to sway. She stood still but reached out her hand until it touched the sleeve of his coat. "Oh, Abe," she said, "It's not as easy as all that."

"We love each other," Abe said. "Doesn't that help any?"

"Oh, Abe, if it—The trouble is that you're—"

"I'm what?"

"Of the two of you, you and Courtney, you're the strong one."

His voice was bitter, a little angry. "Am I?"

"You know you are." Silence again filling the car, as tangible as the cloud through which they were drifting. "I can't do it to him," she said despairingly. "Not while he's down and unhappy."

"Has he told you he's unhappy?"

"Courtney doesn't tell people things like that."

"Suppose the situation changed so that he was no longer unhappy? Could that make a difference to you?"

She continued to hold on to the stuff of his sleeve, unthinking of Pierre standing near them. She whispered, "I don't know. . . ."

Suddenly a shape loomed up at them out of the whiteness, a dark shadow that appeared to be bearing down on them. So this was it: death swinging at them from the void through which they were travelling. She gasped. But it was only the opposite car, passing emptily by them at the halfway point. She drew a breath only half of relief and watched as it swayed by them and was lost almost at once in the clouds.

"My wife," Pierre said, speaking to them, but still turned away from them, staring out the window into nothing, "would not ride the télépherique on a day like this when there is no visibility if you offered her a diamond necklace. It is as safe as any other day, but she has an enlarged sense of danger, and she would be crying and moving about in her fear so that the car would swing and then she would be even more afraid, even though there is nothing to fear."

Now at last the shape of mountain began to appear out of the clouds, emerging like an island out of the glacial sea of sky, foreign and cold, as though they were moving slowly to another planet. Pierre stopped the car at the platform, asking them, "Would you like to get out?"

Abe shook his head. "No. We had better go back. I don't want to keep the children waiting too long."

Pierre reversed the lever, then turned carefully away from them again, and the car started back across the void, out into cloud as alien and cold as outer space.

Moving very carefully so as not to set the car in motion, Abe moved close to Emily, reached down and raised her face and looked into her eyes. "Darling, I don't mean to do this to you, to make you look like a little, desperate, sticken animal. But I'm desperate, too. I'm pleading with you."

She looked back into his face and it was no longer a young athlete's face, ugly and vital. It was tired and it was hurt and yet suddenly it was so beautiful to her that she could hardly bear it. She reached up with one finger and touched the tired lines at either side of his eyes, the strong crooked nose, the lips—

He caught her hand and pressed her fingers to his mouth and kissed them and then she said dully, "We haven't even discussed the children."

"I love your children," he said. "I want your children, too, for myself and for Sam."

"I can't do that to Courtney, either," she said. "You know I can't."

Abe reached for a cigarette. This time he did not offer Emily one (and smoking together had been a kind of intimacy with them, an unacknowledged caress). His match flared, the flame almost invisible in the pervading whiteness. He cupped his hand about it and lit his cigarette. He stood there smoking it, and they did not speak. After a while Pierre, still with his back to them, lit a cigarette, too.

Then it began to snow, first a few isolated flakes, then more and more, till they were surrounded by the white falling, large, and soft and beautiful as flowers.

"I am not a person who begs, Emily," Abe said in a low voice, "but I am begging now. I am pleading for my life. I think you know—don't you?—that if what is between us were not desperately serious we wouldn't have been either as happy as we have been this past week—or as reticent." She did not answer, and after a moment he went on. "If I had been just casually interested in you—as I must admit to you I have been in some women—I would have been better at seducing you. I'm quite sure I *would* have seduced you. But I'm not casual about you, Emily. I want you as part of my life always. Perhaps that first evening I may have thought fleetingly of a brief vacation affair that we could look back at with intimate nostalgia on my rare visits to you and Courtney. But it outgrew that phase almost before it had started, and that is exactly why it has *not* been an affair. You must have realized this."

"I've tried not to—not to realize anything about it," she whispered.

"But now you must, Emily. The time has come when a decision has to be made, and you're the one who has to make it."

She nodded mutely.

"I don't want you to give me your answer now," Abe said, "even if you feel you can."

But she shook her head again.

"Tomorrow night," Abe said, "after I come back from the mountain, we must meet. That will—that will have to be enough time, Emily. I will go to the casino at six o'clock. I've gone there with Kaarlo, and you've been there often with Gert, haven't you?"

"Yes."

"So it will be all right for us to be there together. All right?"

"All right," she said. She waited a moment and then she said, very low, her voice seeming to be hushed by the snow, to disappear into it, "All right, darling."

"That's the first time you've said it," Abe said.

"Yes."

"Say it again."

"Darling."

Then they were silent, moving through whiteness. They were silent as they changed cars, moved back down the mountain. As the station began to loom at them out of the mist Emily took Abe's hand and whispered, "Darling, I love you." Then she stepped away from him, almost holding her breath as they drew up to the platform and Pierre unstrapped the door.

Seven

After a restless night Gertrude wakened early. She would not have known morning was approaching in the dark of Kaarlo's small bedroom if she had not heard him moving about in the big room and the kitchen; and the smell of fresh coffee came through the closed door to her.

She got up and put on her heavy woolen coachman's robe. It had, she knew, great simplicity and style, and it was the warmest thing she owned, but it was so heavy that it dragged her down and she never wore it except on the rare mornings that she got up so early that the stoves and fireplace had not taken the damp chill from the chalet.

She went into the kitchen to Kaarlo, holding her face up to him to be kissed. He looked down at her gravely, raised one hand and pushed her rumpled, sleep-roughened hair back from her face.

—Dear God, she thought, I would rather have died than let Henri see me looking like this, no make-up or perfume and my hair a mess. . . .

"Did you have a bad night?" Kaarlo asked.

She nodded.

"Then we will have a cup of coffee together to warm you up, and then when I go to meet Abe and Sam you will go back to bed and try to get some more sleep."

They sat together in front of the fire. "It's going to snow tomorrow," Kaarlo said.

Gertrude shuddered. "Hell, oh, hell. Another of those filthy closed-in days when you can't see the hand in front of your face? I hate it when the mountains disappear. There's no point living with mountains if you can't see them. When you can't see them the whole weight of them sits on your chest." And then, with scarcely a change in inflection, "You don't eat enough breakfast."

"I eat as much as I always have."

"But for a full day on the mountain—"

"I climb better if I haven't eaten too much." He put his strong, browned hand for a moment over her fragile, pale one. "You should have wakened me to walk Emily home."

Gertrude looked at him sharply, then shrugged. "You were sleeping so peacefully and she said not to. Anyhow she's perfectly capable of getting home by herself."

"I know," Kaarlo said. "But if she should slip and fall on the ice—this is perfectly possible. And during the season when there are so many strangers in the village I'm sure Courtney would prefer not to have a woman as attractive as his wife out alone late at night."

"Do you think Emily's attractive?" Gertrude asked.

"Yes. Don't you?"

"Not particularly. But I'm not a man. Hadn't you better hurry now, Kaarlo?"

"I suppose so. Why do you sound cross all of a sudden?"

"I'm not cross. Just tired."

"I'll take you back to bed."

"No. It's too cold in there. I'll lie down on the couch."

As easily and as gently as though she had been a lamb lost in the snow, Kaarlo picked Gertrude up and laid her down on the couch, covered her with the plaid steamer rug. "Now I must go," he said. "I won't be late today. I should be back before six." He bent down and kissed her forehead and left her.

After he had gone she actually did fall into a fitful sleep, but when she wakened she felt unrefreshed. She lay there for a while staring at the firelight flickering on the ceiling, the cold gray morning light coming in the windows above the couch and bathing her in a pale wash. Finally she heaved herself up and washed and dressed, brushed her hair with slow, dragging strokes as though the brush were intolerably heavy. She put on lipstick, viciously, so that her mouth stood out from her face startlingly red. She looked without interest at the books, at the records, ended up by going back to the couch and sitting there, her elbows on her knees, her chin on her fists, simply sitting there while the minutes slowly moved by her.

When Madame Pedroti came she was actually glad to see her, although her first reaction was usually a smoldering anger, more at herself for allowing Madame Pedroti to come than at Madame Pedroti for coming.

Madame Pedroti settled herself comfortably, the bulk of her enormous thighs spreading amorphously over the zebra-striped chair, the inevitable bag of over-ripe fruit sagging on the table in front of the fire.

"I had such a charming visit with dear Madame Bowen yesterday morning," Madame Pedroti cooed. "It's such a pleasure to see her spirits so much improved."

"Oh, did they need improving?" Gertrude asked.

"And how is Madame de Croisenois today?" Solicitude dripped out of Madame Pedroti's voice like her flesh out of the chair.

"Madame de Croisenois is very well, thank you," Gertrude said crisply.

"And is the marvellous Dr. Clément pleased with your progress?"

"Pleased enough."

"Such a charming man. And, I am told, with a reputation that covers all Europe as well."

"Yes, indeed," Gertrude said, wondering,—Now what the hell is she driving at? Is she trying to shove me in bed with him, too?

But Madame Pedroti asked, "A friend of Mrs. Bowen's, is he not?"

"Of Emily's? No, I don't think so. Not particularly."

Madame Pedroti sighed heavily, gestured with her stubby fingers at the browned sagging flesh under her eyes. "I have suffered sadly from insomnia for the past two years."

"Oh?" Gertrude said, shutting her mouth tightly to keep from adding—Caused by a guilty conscience, no doubt.

"And so it was," Madame Pedroti said blandly, her voice soft as the whipped cream she served with her coffee, "that I happened to see Dr. Clément leaving Madame Bowen's quite late—or rather, quite early. It must have been around four yesterday morning."

For a moment the anger flashed uncontrolled into Gertrude's eyes; she lay there on the couch fighting it back, anger at Madame Pedroti, an even greater anger at Emily if this unwarranted reversal of the usual condition of things should possibly have taken place, and she lying on the bed listening always for the sound of Clément's feet coming through the shed.

"And so," Madame Pedroti was saying blandly, "I simply assumed that they must be great friends. American women seem to have so many friends."

"Far more likely that he was there in a professional capacity," Gertrude said. "Perhaps Connie, the little girl, wasn't well."

Madame Pedroti smiled and lowered her heavy, bruised-looking lids. "Perhaps."

—Is that what she came for? Gertrude wondered. The dirty bitch. I don't believe it anyhow. Emily wouldn't have the guts and anyhow she's not his type.

But then she remembered that according to Michel Clément himself Emily *was* his type.

"Your friend does seem to enjoy visitors late at night," Madame Pedroti said. "So often I've seen our dear Kaarlo coming or going from her place. And Mr. Fielding, too," Madame Pedroti leaned back in the zebra-striped chair, stretching her puffy legs bound in by elastic stockings towards the fire. "I believe they have been seen everywhere together, even dancing at the casino."

With a tremendous effort Gertrude kept her voice lazy. "The day we start paying attention to malicious gossip will really be a dull one, won't it? If most of your tales have no more foundation in fact than these about Emily I wonder you find them worth repeating. The Bowens have known Abe Fielding for years in New York; he's one of their closest friends, and the night Emily and Abe went to the casino Courtney was home with a bad throat."

Madame Pedroti held out her pudgy hands, then dropped them heavily to her side. "You know how it is, Madame de Croisenois. The nicer someone is the more eager people are to talk. I myself feel there is nothing in this talk about Monsieur Fielding. Nevertheless I have often been amused to notice that it is sometimes the quiet ones who are really not quiet at all. In any case I should think it would put your mind at ease to have our dear Kaarlo kept happy and certainly in the long run you could not choose anybody safer than Madame Bowen since she is nicely tied down to her husband and children. A most satisfactory arrangement all round, is it not?"

The color ebbed from Gertrude's face. She sat up on the couch, shaking. "You—you pismire!" she whispered. "Why do you come here when you know you're not welcome? You filthy vulgar collaborating neurasthenic pathological liar! Get out!''

''Why Madame de Croisenois! What is the matter!''

Gertrude continued to whisper, rage depriving her of voice. ''Every time you come here I have degraded myself by letting you cross the threshold. By listening to you I have sunk right into the slimy pit you wallow in, you—you female hippopotamus bathing in putrefaction, you dunghill, you cesspool, get out and stay out and never darken my door again. . . .''

With a show of dignity Madame Pedroti rose. ''Madame de Croisenois, you are unwell. I shall go now as you suggest and I assure you that I shall remember none of the things you have said in your excited condition, for I am sure you have meant none of them.''

''I meant every word,'' Gertrude croaked. ''If you come here again I shall throw something at you, you low traitor.''

Now in her turn the color ebbed from Madame Pedroti's face. ''I am not a traitor, Madame de Croisenois. I betrayed no one. Everybody knows that. The Germans had to live somewhere and what would have happened to me if I had refused to allow them in my hotel? But they learned no secrets from me.''

''Do you think you would be alive now if they had?'' Gertrude asked contemptuously. ''Do you think we didn't know every move you made while you were getting fat and rich fawning on the Nazi bastards? Is it perhaps because you are ashamed of the way you spent your nights—until you became so fat and repulsive even the Nazis wouldn't have you—that you feel you have to make up lies now about Emily? Go on. Get out. The only thing I have ever done in my life that I am completely ashamed of is having allowed you to come here.'' Madame Pedroti opened her mouth to speak, but Gertrude cut her off. ''Get out. At once. And never come back. Get out. Go.'' She stood up and took a few tottering steps towards Madame Pedroti.

''You are not well today,'' Madame Pedroti said again, nevertheless beating a hasty retreat. ''I shall send Dr. Clément to you.''

As Madame Pedroti left Gertrude fell back on the couch, face down on the plaid blanket. She was seized by a violent chill which shook her limbs in uncontrollable spasms. When she finally stopped trembling she fell into a black pit of exhausted sleep, waking only when she felt a strong hand on her shoulder.

"Gertrude."

She opened her eyes, shuddering. Clément stood by the couch looking down at her, his eyes grave, concerned.

"Gertrude," he said again, "Madame Pedroti called me in some excitement, saying she feared you were gravely ill."

Gertrude closed her eyes again. "So she got scared, did she?"

"Scared about what?" He sat down on the couch by her.

"I finally did what I should have done the first time she waddled up here to see me. I threw her out."

"And got over-excited doing it?"

Pushing aside his hand Gertrude sat up. "Were you at Emily Bowen's house in the middle of the night last night?" she demanded.

He looked at her in surprise. "No. Last night I was in the hospital all night. As a matter of fact, I *was* at Emily's the night before. Why? Did she tell you about it? What is all this about, Gertrude?"

"No," Gertrude said, "Emily didn't mention it. But Madame Pedroti did."

"Oh? So?"

"It seems she has insomnia these days—or rather, nights—and she couldn't wait to tell me she'd seen you leaving around four in the morning."

"And you let the malicious tongue of a vicious village gossip upset you? I'm surprised at you, Gertrude."

"Why were you there at four o'clock in the morning?" Gertrude asked.

"If Emily wanted you to know I imagine she'd have told you."

"Emily—" Gertrude said. "You call me Gertrude as though I were a child, an idiot, but you call Emily Emily as though she were a human being, as though she were really there. Are you honestly not going to tell me why you were at the villa?"

"Is it that important?"

"I don't think Courtney would like the idea of Emily's receiving nocturnal visitors. Neither do I." And did he know that she was skirting around the story, talking about him only in order not to mention, not to think of Kaarlo?

"Courtney knew I was there."

"Was Connie sick or something?"

"No."

"Were you there in a professional capacity?"

"No."

"What then?"

He got up from the chair and came to the bed. "Gertrude, Gertrude, what is this to get so excited about? Emily and Courtney were at the hotel having a drink. I happened to be there, too. I walked home with them. Emily gave me a cup of coffee and I left and came home. That is all."

"Oh, so Courtney was drunk and you helped Emily get him home."

"This is your day for jumping to conclusions, isn't it? First because of a congenital busybody you decide Emily and I are having a rendezvous, and then, when you realize that that is hardly likely to be true, you decide Courtney has to be drunk. Why can't you just accept my simple explanation?"

"Because I know Courtney and he'd never have been out that late in the first place if he hadn't been stewed to the gills. He goes on a bat occasionally, not a real one, he's no alcoholic, but he doesn't always know when he's had enough. I know, because Court and I have staggered home under the influence more than once, much to Emily's horror. Anyhow it's very nice of you to try to protect her feelings. She'd be much happier if she thought I didn't know Courtney'd ever touched anything stronger than tea, but since, as I've said, several of Courtney's bats have been with me, that's hardly possible. Okay, I won't let her know Pedroti's vile insinuations."

"That sounds a little better," Clément said, "Are you somewhat calmer now?"

She did not answer that question. Instead, she said, "You weren't the only one Pedroti was trying to put Emily to bed with."

"Oh?"

"Kaarlo and Abe Fielding, too. What do you think of that?"

"What should I think of it? Typical malicious, vicious gossip made up to provide titillation when there isn't anything happening to keep wagging tongues busy. You certainly wouldn't have me take it seriously, would you?"

Gertrude shrugged. "I suppose not."—But did a faint ambiguous flicker come to his eyes at Kaarlo's mention?

"Is this what has upset you to the point of actually making you ill?" Clément asked sternly.

Gertrude sighed heavily. "I don't really know, Clément. I don't know what's upset me."

"Gertrude—" his face was serious, his tone severe— "something is happening to you that I expected never to have to worry about with you."

"What?"

"You've always lived such a full personal life of your own that I thought it would stand you in good stead during your time of enforced withdrawal from your usual activities. Some of my patients develop a morbid curiosity about other people's affairs and a tendency to meddle that can be dangerous. I don't expect you to fall into that category, but I can see that we are going to have to watch it."

"Is it morbid curiosity about other people's affairs that I'm upset when Pedroti tells me my best friend is having affairs with three different men, including my doctor and my—and Kaarlo?"

"Of course you are upset and angry at vicious gossip told you solely with intent to hurt. But, knowing Emily as you do, it is not sensible of you to take it seriously, and I am disappointed in you. Now I would like you to rest very quietly this morning and not have any more visitors until this afternoon. You don't want to give Madame Pedroti the satisfaction of having caused you a setback. . . . Now I am going to do something I do not often do; I am going to give you something to help you get quiet and then I am going to leave you to rest. I will look in on you again later on and I want you to have forgotten everything Madame Pedroti said to you. And you may rest assured that the next time I see her I will give her what you Americans call a piece of my mind. And I will see to it that these disturbing visits cease."

She lay quietly while he prepared the hypodermic. She knew that her cheeks were flushed, that the physical manifestations of her anger still showed, the dilated eyes, the too rapid pulse. She lay quietly, but she was still angry, angry with Madame Pedroti, angry with Emily, angry with Clément.

For a while Gertrude slept, the effects of Clément's injection soothing her; but soon her slumber became fitful, and her mind, tossed halfway between sleep and waking, churned restlessly.

—All those pretty little fillies learning how to ski had better keep their hands off Kaarlo, and their eyes, too. I don't mind so much when he goes off in the mountains; I don't even mind when he takes a party up Mont Blanc though I can't eat till he gets home and I waste every centime I have looking for him through those lousy telescopes and imagining he's buried in an avalanche or fallen into a crevasse. That I can take. It's the nice safe jobs with the little slitches learning how to ski that really scare me. My God, I was one of them once myself. . . .

She dozed. She was skiing with Kaarlo through a world of snow. No houses. No trees. Nothing but snow. White. Blinding. And they themselves in white ski clothes fading into the snow, only the dark ash of their skis marking dark lines on the snow to prove that they existed at all. . . .

She wakened again, stirring restlessly on the couch, her skin dry and burning.

—I couldn't tell Clément about Kaarlo and Emily, not the way things really are. He'd have been angry with me. He'd have said it wasn't true. He'd have said it was all Pedroti.

—But is it?

—How do I know? How do I know?

She crawled into the kitchen, reaching with trembling fingers into her hiding place under the sink. She drew out the bottle, poured herself a tumblerful and dragged herself back to the big room. She knew that she had worked herself up to a fever and perhaps the brandy would help calm her down. She sat by the fire because, although her skin was raging hot, inside her body she was freezing, and stared fiercely into the flames so that she was half-hypnotized by their flickering. When she seemed a little warmer in her shivering core she set the brandy on the hearth and went to the phonograph to put on a record, any record, to bring herself closer to Kaarlo. The first thing she touched was the Rachmaninoff Second Symphony and the music poured warm and sensual into the cold, ascetic room. She poured herself more brandy and started walking around the room.

—I'm in a mood. Old Gert de C.'s in a lousy, filthy, dirty mood. Abe and the kid are leaving tomorrow. We can discount Abe. That leaves Kaarlo and Clément.

—You're crazy, Gert. If there'd been anything you'd have noticed it.

—Would I?

—Sure you would. You're not in the habit of *not* noticing things like that.

—But I did notice it. About Emily and Kaarlo.

—Yes, but you didn't take it seriously. Why are you taking it seriously now? Don't give Pedroti the satisfaction. And anyhow wouldn't you find out something like that before Pedroti?

—How the hell would I find out anything stuck up here in this chalet?

—You live with Kaarlo, don't you? And Emily's *your* friend, isn't she? She comes to see you every day.

—If Emily were having an affair with Kaarlo do you think she'd be likely to tell me? Gert dear, I've just become Kaarlo's mistress. I'm keeping him happy for you like Pedroti said. Isn't that nice?

—Turn the record, Gert you old fool. How many times has Kaarlo told you it's bad for the needle to let it go round and round?

She turned the record, carefully, had some more brandy, pulled up the heavy, white cable-stitched socks she was wearing. Then she spoke to herself severely again.

—Gertrude de Croisenois, this is the craziest thing I've ever heard.

—Why's it so crazy?

—But Emily!

—Sure, I thought Pedroti was making it up when she first told me. But why would anybody, even Pedroti, make up a story like that about Emily? If it weren't true?

—But you said Pedroti had her cavorting with half the town.

—Oh, you know Pedroti. That was just her way of leading into it. She always has to make a good story better. Clément and Abe are hardly likely.

—And Emily herself is hardly likely.

—What did Pedroti say about the quiet ones? You heard her. I'm not at all sure that she wasn't right. And Courtney can't be very exciting to live with day in, day out.

—Is Emily looking for excitement?

—Maybe she's not looking for it, but maybe she wouldn't turn it down if it were offered to her.

—Why would it be offered to her?

—I don't make it any too easy for Kaarlo, let's face that. I've always known he'd throw me over some day. Though I didn't think it would be for Emily.

—Exactly. Why Emily, when every day he sees so many women who're—who're—much more his type?

—Who knows what anybody's type is? Maybe he's tired of

the obvious ones. And he's seen a lot of Emily this winter. Always making excuses to have talks with her or ask her here to listen to records. I thought it was for me. Now I'm not so sure.

—Oh, Gert, Gert, Pedroti's a bitch with ruffles, but don't give her the satisfaction of letting her do this to you.

—But she has, damn her, she has. Oh, lord, I've just had a ghastly idea. Do you suppose Pedroti's gone to Courtney with her pretty tales?

—That's a happy thought. I don't think Courtney'd take kindly to Emily's two-timing him. Courtney's one of those people who doesn't get angry easily but when he does he does a good thorough job of it.

—Now look here, Gert. None of that.

—Well! I hardly think it's my place to tell him in any event. It just seems to me he shouldn't hear it from Pedroti.

—Or from you. Okay, forget it. Change the record, Gert. You're letting it just go round and round again.

She went to the phonograph, took the record off carefully, put it in the album, took the next record out and put it on the turntable. Accidentally she brushed against the volume control and the rich music roared out into the room. She flung up her arm against it, then rushed out, leaving the record to continue its circling unheeded on the turntable, the music crashing through the loudspeaker, grabbed her white parka from its hook in the shed, and started as fast as she could down to the Bowens' villa.

When Gertrude had left, the door to the villa slipped out of her feeble grip and slammed violently in the wind. Courtney could not go on with his work. She had said nothing, but she had depressed and disturbed him and he did not know why she had come.

She had appeared, rather wild-eyed, in the doorway to his office, and her speech was just perceptibly thickened from brandy. She had demanded without preamble if he were all right, if he were happy, and then she had said, quite loudly and clearly, "Oh, no you don't, Gert de C. This you do not do. This kind of a bitch you are not going to be."

"What's the matter, Gert?" he had asked her.

And she had responded vaguely, swaying a little. "A gesture. That's it. I must make a gesture," and without a word of farewell she had left.

He thought now that perhaps it was not only that she had had too much to drink. Her cheeks had been hectically flushed and her eyes had the bright glitter of fever. He should have kept her there. He should not have allowed her to go off into the cold dank air alone and ill.

He put his head down on the desk.

—I have failed again, he thought. Even in the littlest things I am a failure.

—Where is Emily?

—She had gone out again and she has not told me where.

—Why?

—What am I going to do about Emily? Oh, God, what am I going to do?

He raised his head from the desk and shook it like a swimmer coming out of water, but he could not clear it of the evil buzzing that was congesting it so that it felt huge, and too heavy to support.

—The glacier, he thought, and the crevasse, and I cannot jump across and save her before she steps backwards into it. I have neither the courage nor the strength.

—But I did it once!

No, it was not Emily, it was he who had fallen into the crevasse, down into the ice blue depths, the walls of ice closing in on him, pressing the life out of him, crushing him deep into the center of the earth where the ice would turn to flame and he would be lost forever in the molten fires, absorbed into the inferno. . . .

Suddenly he was aware that there had been a tapping at the door and a voice saying something and there in the shadow of the partly open door stood a darker shadow (was it Gertrude come back to tell him whatever dreadful thing it was she had not had the courage to say?) and he shouted something at the shadow and his words blurred in his mind like ink on blotting paper and the shadow disappeared and he put his head down on the desk again.

He should have gone after Gertrude. How could he save Emily from the crevasse if he let Gertrude go off into the snow when it was obvious that she was so drunk—or so ill—or both— that she could scarcely stand?

He got up from the desk, moving heavily, as though he were old and tired. He went into the hall and pulled on his boots and without telling the girls that he was going out he left the villa and went to look for Gertrude. When he had found Gertrude he would look for Emily. What he would do or say when he found her he did not know.

He climbed slowly up to Kaarlo's chalet. He knocked but there was no answer so he pushed open the door and went in, calling out, "Gertrude? Hi, Gert?"

There was a light on in the kitchen, and in the living room the fire was just beginning to fade. He heard a low, humming noise and noticed the record still going round and round on the phonograph with the needle scratching on it, and he moved the needle arm gently and turned the machine off. He looked all around and realized that the chalet was empty.

He saw the three-quarters empty bottle of brandy by the fireplace and picked it up and stood looking at it, thinking—She shouldn't have any more of that when she comes back.

He picked the cork up off the floor where it had rolled and rammed it into the bottle, and again held the bottle out to the firelight so that it shone like amber, holding it and thinking. Finally he pushed it into the big pocket of his overcoat where it made an unwieldy bulge and the neck of the bottle stuck out through the flap.

He went back outdoors, looking about. Below him lay the sanatorium and the hotel, both bright wtih lights at this time of day, almost all the windows illuminated. Above him the snow stretched up to the pines, up to the snow fields beyond, and to the peaks towering above all.

—Now what? he demanded. Where do we go from here?

Once Gertrude had passed Kaarlo's chalet, her own chalet, the climbing became easier. It was as though her burning flesh had dissolved and now it was the phoenix risen from the ashes climbing up towards the pines. No, not the phoenix after all, for it seemed as though she had no body; these were not legs pushing her forwards and higher with each thrust; she had no physical sensation except for an enormous airiness as though the damp night air were flowing through her as well as around her.

—A gesture, she thought again. A gesture for Kaarlo, for Emily, for Clément, for them all.

She moved through the trees and she thought that if she wanted to, she could do this literally, move her disembodied self right through one of the dark pines.

When she came out into the snow fields and when she sighted

the first hut she veered to the left because she must not meet Kaarlo and Abe and Sam coming down the mountain.

Coming hungrily down the mountain towards warmth and light and dinner.

Perhaps hunger was part of the disembodied feeling. She had had nothing to eat since the coffee with Kaarlo early that morning and the brandy in the afternoon. Yet she did not feel hungry.

She kept on climbing. Or rather one foot continued to move in front of the other and her body followed her footsteps. Upwards and to the left. She felt that she was listing like an unseaworthy ship, but she kept going. Now her mind was becoming as numb as her body and it seemed to float above her like a pale moon, beckoning her on. The landscape, too, was like the surface of the moon, snow and shadows and snow-filled sky joining the snow-covered earth and no atmosphere between, for there is no atmosphere on the moon; one does not have to breathe for there is nothing to breathe. And if her mind was pale and cold like the moon, then it was her mind she was walking on; tread softly on the snows of the mind for who knows what is underneath the snow?

When the snow shifted under her feet and she felt herself falling there was hardly any sensation to her descent until her leg doubled under her and she lay on it on a ledge of rock and her body came back to her again in a sudden violent shock of pain.

The extraordinary thing about time, Emily thought, walking at last towards the Splendide, is that it does pass; one does eventually move through it. In her ski clothes she walked through the village and it was as though she were pushing through time, as though with each step time opened and then closed in behind her. It was still too early to meet Abe, so she would stop at Madame Berigot's to pick up a paper, and then she would have dislodged another chunk of time. There had been walking and then some blank, gaping minutes at the church, and again no help was given her, no sign to indicate her way, the whole question was thrust back at her, and she had walked again, up through the pines, up looking for help from the hills, and then back to the church again, to say, kneeling there in the candlelight—No, I was wrong to be angry with You, of course it is my own problem. And then at last there was no place to go but the village, the Spendide, nothing else to do with time but to take it with her into the Splendide and spin it out there.

Madame Berigot smiled at her as she always did; no matter how depressing the day, no matter how many things had gone wrong, she could always count on warmth and friendliness from Madame Berigot.

"Madame looks well," the older woman said to Emily.

Emily fished in her pocket for change and put it on the counter. "Thank you."

"All of a sudden," Madame Berigot said, "so much younger. Before this I have not realized that Madame is beautiful."

Emily blushed. "Why, thank you!"

Madame Berigot looked across the counter and laughed. "Is it all because of Mademoiselle Virginia and her friend being home for the holidays?"

"We have a lot of fun together," Emily said, grateful that she was already blushing.

"They are splendid children," Madame Berigot told her. The bell on the door tinkled and a customer came in.

"Good night," Emily said, and hurried out.

It was just a joke with Madame Berigot, meant to make her laugh. The feeling of deceit was her own entirely.

She walked slowly along the street towards the Splendide, waiting for her flushed cheeks to cool off, looking in the shop windows at the holiday cakes and at jewelry and skiing equipment and post cards. In the shop next to the casino was the dress Abe had said he wanted to buy for her, the Renaissance princess' dress, and she stood looking at it. From the skating rink came the music of the loudspeaker, blown through the night air of the streets faint and clear, *C'est l'eternel et doux songe qui sonne aux heures d'amour.* . . .

It was almost time to go meet Abe and simply by going to him, walking blindly through the snow without an answer, she was by indirection giving him an answer. Either she ended it or she didn't, and indefiniteness was not ending it. It was saying at least maybe, and this time there could be no such thing as a maybe. If she went to the Splendide, to Abe, it meant the end of her life with Courtney.

She stood there in the middle of the icy street, not moving, not seeing the people who walked by her, hurrying to keep warm, going in and out of the shops, several turning to stare at her as she stood there, sightless, motionless.

This was the time. The answer must be made now. The two

worlds had to meet and she was free to stay in Courtney's or to move forward into Abe's. But if she moved into Abe's world it must now be a world of reality; she had to step out of the dream world in which she had lived with Abe and into the waking world in which the future must be spent.

A large woman, coming out of the boulangerie, her arms full, bumped into Emily, and this jolting started her walking slowly down the street, but still she did not see where she was moving. She was shivering violently, and automatically her step quickened, but she did not realize that she was cold. She wanted most horribly to cry, she who had cried more in the last few days than in the rest of her life put together.

For suddenly she realized that there was no decision to be made. Once the dream was over, once the eyes opened to the daylight, there was no choice except to leave the world of the dream. In the dream it was possible to imagine a life with Abe and without Courtney, but once she was awake she had to accept the fact that it was a dream. It did not mean that her love for Abe had not been—was not—real; it was simply that the world in which this love could continue to flower was not real, and the world of Courtney and the children was, and that was the world where she must stay.

Now she saw the street around her again and she realized that she had walked past the casino. She turned around and stood looking at the door for a moment, at a man walking out, at two women smiling over-brightly at him as they went in. She was still shivering but her cheeks were burning hot and she felt that she had reached the turning point in an acute illness.

Plunging her gloved hands deeper into her pockets she continued to walk away from the casino.

There was something terribly wrong with the day and Virginia did not know what it was, a precariousness, a darkness to the approaching night that had nothing to do with the absence of light. It was going to storm tomorrow, everybody said so, and it must be this, the tension presaging the storm, that made her move restlessly through the villa, up the stairs, up into the cold of the bedrooms, into her parents' room, to turn around slowly as though looking for them, though she knew that they were not there, her mother out, her father in his study, then to stand, her elbows on the marred surface of the wood (for it was undoubtedly something become too shabby to use at the hotel), her chin on her fists, staring at the pictures there. The picture of her mother, first, with Virginia, sullen, scowling, her hair stringing to her shoulders, standing leaning against her mother's knee, and Alice, golden-curled like Connie, sitting on her mother's lap, a smiling, enchanting baby, reaching up to stroke her mother's cheek, while Virginia continued to glare at the photographer. No comfort in that picture, although Emily's hand rested lovingly on Virginia's shoulder and her tender smile was equally for both children.

One of Virginia's elbows slipped off the edge of the chest, jolting her. Looking around quickly as though she expected to see someone standing in the doorway, a witness to her humiliation, she replaced her elbow gingerly, and focused now on the double frame from which her father stared. On the right-hand side was Courtney sitting in his office in the library building at the university, the desk and floor and bookshelves piled with books, and papers characteristically spilling out of the wastebasket and a cigarette held loosely in his long stained fingers and a half-quirk of a smile on his lips and in the close-set blue eyes; this was the father who was safety and stability and she stood there staring until her eyes refused to focus and the image shifted and doubled and retreated and returned. Then she looked to the left-hand picture, her father because she had been told it was her father, a grinning freckled boy, in white flannel slacks and a sweater, holding a tennis racquet and a silver cup under one arm and an enormous book under the other, and only the book seemed familiar and imaginable.

Next to the double frame, to Courtney known and unknown, was propped a snapshot of Connie in her high chair in the kitchen in New York with a corner of the stove showing and a saucepan of something cooking on it and beside it some open music with the salt cellar plunked down on one of its pages. No separate picture of Emily, and—What does she look like? Virginia thought, suddenly, wildly—What does my mother look like?

And she did not know.

—It's because I love her. You never know what the people you love look like because you love beyond their looks and you see a different image, more than a camera can catch, more even than a portrait painter, and maybe that's why some painters paint such awful messes, because they're trying to paint the insides as well as the outsides, because the outside is such a small part of a thing, and if I could see my mother in my mind's eye as she is in the picture with Alice and me I wouldn't be seeing her at all.

—Oh, mother, oh, daddy, oh, people, oh, world, does anybody ever see anybody whole?

She fled the room and the pictures with a sense of guilt as though she had been eavesdropping, and around her, still, the air was full of tension, the barometer dropping; she thought—It always does this to people, like something heavy and yet fragile falling from tremendous heights and shattering upon you into thousands of fragments.

About the villa the wind slapped. Take that. And that. And that.

Where were the stars?

She ran to the dark window in her bedroom and peered out into nothingness, the sky clamped down relentlessly, the lights of the hotel somehow pushed further up the mountain.

She ran around then, turning on lights, thrusting away the darkness, giving warmth—See, I can pull this cord and there is light, *it comes!*

She ran downstairs. In the living room all the lights were on and the windows were blind with steam. Mimi and Connie were shrieking with laughter, Mimi on all fours on the floor and Connie riding her.

"Mimi Opp's a camel!" Connie shouted, seeing Virginia. "And I'm a wise man riding to the stable with presents for baby Jesus, presents and presents and giddyap and presents and presents and presents and . . ."

Virginia moved away from the light and warmth, through the dark narrow hall to her father's study, past the telephone, a dark shadow hanging on the wall, to the study door, closed and blank.

There was no line of light coming from under it.

But where was he? He had not gone out with Emily. That she knew because Madame de Croisenois had come in to see him and then had hurried out without stopping to call goodbye.

She knocked gently.

"Daddy."

No answer.

She knocked again.

"Daddy."

She pushed the door open.

The room was dark and he was sitting at the desk, his head down on his arms. Was he asleep?

"Daddy.

"Daddy."

He looked up. He looked at her for a moment without seeing her.

"Get out of here, damn you."

He shouted at her. He shouted that.

She fled.

Never. Never before. Never like that. It was not just the storm, the barometer falling, the wind flailing, the stars lost, that made the terror in the air.

She fled to the kitchen.

She took the back of one of her mother's marketing lists and tried with trembling fingers to write.—Poetry. Help me. Save me. Poetry. She could not write poetry. Poetry had to write her, she had to open herself to it, and she was closed, closed tighter than a sea animal clamping tight its shell, not a chink open for the poetry to come through.

She heard the front door slam.

And no footsteps coming in. She ran to the door and opened it and her father was walking, running, up the path.

—*Why? What has happened?*

Where could she go? What could she do? Where could she run?

—*Get out of here, damn you.*

As though he were shouting those words at her now she shut the front door and ran as though pursued back to the kitchen.

In the living room Connie shrieked with laughter. Connie. She could give Connie a bath.

She dragged out the tub, clattering it against the chairs, against the stove. Crash. She splashed in water from the kettle. Put on more water. Stalked into the living room.

"Connie. Come take your bath."

Connie, all blue eyes and golden curls and laughter, still playing with Mimi, "Not yet, Vee. Mimi and I are having fun."

"It's time for your bath." Virginia's voice was harsh.

And Mimi, lazy, casual: "Oh, there's no rush, Vee."

"I'm still taking my presents to the baby Jesus. Now I'm a shepherd and Mimi's a sheep."

"That's blasphemous. Stop it at once," Virginia said.

"Virginia!" Mimi's voice was sharp.

"What?"

"It's not blasphemous and you know it. What's the matter with you?"

"Nothing," Virginia said, her voice starting to gallop, her lip to tremble. "It's time for Connie's bath and I wish her to take it. Emily Conrad Bowen, come here at once. Mimi, will you kindly bring her nightclothes." Now the tears began spilling out of her eyes and she fled back to the kitchen.

"Yes, matron, right this minute," Mimi called after her, but her face was troubled. She turned to Connie. "Run along, Con, we can play some more after your bath."

"What's the matter with Vee? Is Vee cross with me? Was I naughty?"

"No, daffodil, you weren't a bit naughty. Something else must be bothering Vee and she's taking it out on us. You run along to the kitchen, and I'll get your nightclothes and come protect you from Villainous Virginia in nothing flat."

Slowly Connie trailed into the kitchen, where Virginia stood, wiping the back of her hand harshly against her eyes.

"Get undressed, Connie," she said. "I'm sorry if I shouted at you. Come on, I'll take your shoes off. Come on, sit in my lap."

"I can get undressed myself," Connie said.

"Okay, then *get* undressed."

Mimi came down bearing nightclothes and Virginia poured more water into the tub. "Okay, get in."

Connie stepped into the tub and immediately jumped out, starting to scream. "It's too hot!"

"All right," Virginia said. "I'll put in some more cold water, don't make such a fuss!" Tears sprang to her eyes again.

Mimi put her hand in the water. "It's not so hot, Constantia. Your feet are cold and it just feels hotter than it is."

"I'm not Constantia, I'm Emily Conrad," Connie said, getting in more gingerly as Virginia poured in a pitcher of cold water and then turned to the stove and pretended to be shaking down the coals.

Mimi went to her and put an arm about her shoulders. "What's the matter, Vee?" she asked gently.

"Oh, don't be nice to me!" Virginia cried, her face contorting with the effort not to cry.

"Take it easy," Mimi said. "Something happen?"

Virginia nodded.

"Want to talk about it?"

"Oh, I can't—I don't know—I don't want to cry—"

"Where's your mother?"

"Out somewhere. I don't know where she is."

Mimi looked at the clock. It was after six and nothing had been done about dinner.

Virginia looked at the clock, too. "Sam hasn't called you yet. Didn't he say he was going to call you as soon as he got back from the mountain?"

"He will."

"I'm a seal in Central Park Zoo," Connie said, and rolled over in the tub with a splash.

"Connie, please don't get water all over the floor. And wash yourself."

"I want Mimi to wash me. I'm a seal and Mimi's the zoo-keeper and I want her to wash me and feed me fish."

Mimi picked up the soap and cloth and began to scrub Connie. "If we go out with Sam and Beanie tonight I suppose we'll wear those dratted dinner uniforms again. I'd just as soon wear ski clothes. But you look most passable in the good old black velvet, Vee. Let me help you with your make-up and your hair and borrow your mother's amber beads again and Beanie'll be wowed all over again. Clothes oddly enough look well on you. You wear them with a cachet that's going to stand you in good stead when I'm blousy and middle-aged. I'm the kind who's going to look reasonably beautiful or like an old witch, but you have a kind of chic that's far more valuable than beauty. Why do you keep looking at the clock? Haven't you heard a thing I've said?"

-"Yes, Mimi, thank you. Connie, you're clean enough. Get out of the bath now. Mother apparently has forgotten dinner. So I'll cook you some eggs."

"But I want mama," Connie said. "I want daddy."

"They're out," Virginia said, her eyes filling again, "and something seems to have held them up, so we'd better go on and eat."

"Your father out, too?" Mimi asked.

"Yes."

"Where?"

"I don't know. He just went out." She dried Connie roughly.

"You hurt," Connie said.

"I've got to get you dry or you'll catch cold."

"Don't take it out on Connie, Vee," Mimi said softly.

"Will you please let *me* handle it!" Virginia cried.

"I want mama," Connie said.

"She's not here, Con. She'll be back soon. Come on, get your pajamas on."

"When?"

"Right now."

"I mean when will mama be back?"

"I don't know, Con, but I imagine soon."

"How soon?"

"I don't know, Con. Put your slippers on."

Mimi took eggs from the bowl on the window sill. "Might as well eat, don't you think, so you'll have plenty of time to get ready?"

"It doesn't take me long to get ready," Virginia said. "Anyhow they haven't called."

"They will. And if you want to be a succès fou in the social world, my girl, you'll have to learn to take longer," Mimi said. "I'll just make a quick omelette. Hand me the plates, Vee."

"I want awfuls," Connie demanded.

"You can't have awfuls," Virginia said sharply. "You know perfectly well there isn't a waffle iron here. Please *behave*, Con!"

They did not go into the dining room but sat around the kitchen table, because suddenly even to Mimi the dining room seemed cold and empty without Emily and Courtney.

"Whatever it is—" Mimi started, but Virginia cut in.

"Can't you leave it alone, Mimi! Can't you ever stop prying into people! You always want to know everything!"

Mimi stopped abruptly and a strange look came into her face and Virginia saw that she had hurt her.

"Come on, Constantinople, eat that good dinner," Mimi said, holding out a forkful to the child. "Have another bite."

They heard the front door slam then and Virginia ran wildly out into the hall. Her father stood there and she rushed at him in relief, flinging her arms about him.

He disentangled her. "Where's your mother, Virginia?"

"Mother?" she asked blankly. "Isn't she with you?"

He shook his head.

Her eyes widened again with fear. "You don't know where she is, daddy?"

"Would I be asking you if I knew?"

"She didn't even start dinner before she went out and it's late, daddy!" Virginia cried in a high, quivering voice.

Mimi had come, carrying Connie, out into the hall; shifting Connie easily to one hip, she put a restraining hand on Virginia's arm.

"What time did she go out?" Courtney asked.

"I don't know. Sometime in the middle of the afternoon. She was at the piano and then she just got up without finishing what she was playing and she said she was going for a walk and went out."

"I see," Courtney said thoughtfully, and stood there in silence.

"What's happened, daddy?" Virginia asked shrilly. "Do you think something's happened to mother?"

"No, I don't, Vee. Now, let's go into the living room where it's warmer. It's too cold for Connie out here. Mother isn't expected to account to us for every minute of her time, you know. She's probably just been detained somewhere."

As they went into the living room the phone began to ring. Mimi turned to dump Connie into one of the plush chairs and run to answer it, but Courtney stopped her with a sharp, "Please stay where you are, Mimi. *I* will be the one to run to the phone for a change."

In the small, closed-in living room with the spider chandelier hovering above their heads, they stood listening, scarcely breathing in order not to lose Courtney's low words.

"No, she's not here. . . . No, I don't know where she is. She went out this afternoon and she hasn't come back. . . . No, she didn't say. . . . I don't know where she is either. She was here this afternoon and she didn't seem well. She'd had too much to drink but she was ill, too, I thought. . . . I don't think she was looking for Emily. She seemed to have something she wanted to tell me but whatever it was she didn't tell me. . . . I got worried about her later on and went up to the chalet to look for her. . . . There wasn't anybody there but she'd left the phonograph running. . . . I checked at the casino and the Splendide but she wasn't at either of them. She might be now, of course. . . . Have you tried Dr. Clément?. . . Okay, I'll try the casino and the Splendide again. . . . Right, Abe, I'll do that."

When he came back into the living room Mimi asked, "Were you talking about Madame de Croisenois?"

"Yes, Mimi. Now I am sorry but I must leave you two girls

in charge of Connie. Madame de Croisenois seems to have disappeared and I told Abe Fielding I'd join the search team by looking in the village. He and Kaarlo and some of the guides are going up the mountain. If by any chance she should come here please do your best simply to keep her, and one of you go up to the first ski tow where Pierre Balbec will be waiting and tell him. Understand?"

"Yes, daddy."

"Yes, Mr. Bowen."

As he left he touched Virginia's head gently and for a moment from the security of the gesture the terror stopped throbbing in her throat. Mimi looked compassionately at her dilated eyes, but she herself could not keep back a pleasurable thrill of excitement.

"I wish I could go up the mountain with Monsieur Balbec and Mr. Fielding to help look."

"Do you think she's gone up the mountain?" Virginia asked.

"I don't want mama to be up the mountain," Connie said.

"Not *mother*, Con," Virginia said quickly. "Madame de Croisenois."

"But where's mama? I want mama!"

"Yes," Virginia said bitterly. "In all the excitement over Madame de Croisenois everyone seems to have forgotten mother. She's lost, too."

"Your mother can take care of herself," Mimi said. "In any case I don't think your father's forgotten her."

There was a knock at the door and with a wild glance at each other they ran pelting to answer it. But it was not Gertrude, or even Emily, it was Sam and Beanie, in ski clothes, their faces wet and raw from the damp wind.

"Come in, oh, come in," Mimi said, pulling them in and shutting the door against the cold. "Have they found her?"

"Not yet," Sam said, stamping snow off his boots. "Dad and Kaarlo and a group of guides have gone up the mountain, and Pierre and Dr. Clément are waiting by the ski tow. Where're Mr. and Mrs. Bowen?"

"We don't know where mother is," Virginia said starkly, "and daddy's gone into the village again to look for Madame de Croisenois."

Her arms about Connie, Mimi said. "Take off your things. Come on in the other room."

"We thought we'd go have a look in the village for her ourselves," Beanie said. "You girls want to come along?"

Virginia looked quickly at Mimi. "Daddy left us in charge of Connie."—Please, you mustn't go with them and leave me here alone with Connie, her mind signalled wildly.

"Can't you bring her along?" Sam said. "We'll hold her hands and take good care of her."

"Okay," Virginia said after a moment. "Come on, Con. Let sister put your snow suit on." If they went into the village they might run into Emily—coming from where?—and it would give her at least a feeling of doing something which would be better than the blank waiting in this hated house that was at the same time stifling and icy. In action, particularly in group action, there was a kind of comfort and safety.

Staying close together they went out into the dark. Virginia and Beanie each took Connie by a hand and her short, still-babyish legs slowed them on the icy path. Mimi and Sam went on ahead, occasionally pausing to wait until the other three came in sight, then going on again. Lights from the outlying houses threw warm golden rectangles against the snow, outlined the delicate branches here of a tree, there of a small stone lion sitting on a gatepost, snow drifted up to the pale paws that seemed curled up against it. Walking along with Sam, holding his hand, Mimi forgot for a moment why they were there, though she still kept her sense of excitement. But now the excitement was transferred to Sam, to his nearness, to his departure the next morning, and she said, turning towards him, "Sam, you've never kissed me."

"I know I haven't, Mimi," Sam said.

"Why?"

For a moment Sam didn't answer. Then he said quietly, "Because I don't want to."

It was to Mimi as though there were suddenly a change in temperature, in air pressure. After a moment she said, carefully keeping her voice light. "That's a nice, crushing thing to say to a girl. Is it because I'm not attractive to you?"

"You know it isn't," Sam said. "As a matter of fact I thought of kissing you that night on the sleigh ride but I decided against it." With no further explanation he lapsed into silence again.

"Well, that effectively kills *that* conversation," Mimi remarked. "At the risk of being slapped down again, am I wrong in thinking that you may have engineered Beanie's date with Virginia so that we could have the sleigh ride together?''

"Not entirely wrong," Sam said, "in that I did think about it very seriously. But after some of the things Beanie said, and the way Virginia, and all of us, feel about them, it hardly seemed fair to Virginia. But I must admit that when Beanie said he wanted to take Virginia out and asked me if I could take you off her hands for a few hours I jumped at the chance.''

"He has better taste than I credited him with," Mimi said. "Good for little Vee.''

"And I do think he's changing his way of thinking. Honestly I do. I've talked to him and I had dad talk to him. He's still a first-class louse for my money, but maybe he has a chance of crawling out of it into something more resembling a human being.''

"Oh, sure," Mimi said. "Anyhow I suppose one can learn to cohabit with rats as well as Russians.''

Sam grinned. "I think the word is coexist, but I get what you mean. It's a funny thing, Mimi Opp. Here we all are, but tomorrow dad and I leave—whether they find Madame de Croisenois or not—and next year Virginia'll be in Indiana and Beanie'll be going back to Detroit and you'll probably be in Paris and none of us will ever see each other again.''

"I know," Mimi said, stopping. They were on the last dark stretch of path before turning in to the main street of the village. She looked back, but Virginia, Connie, and Beanie were not in sight. "That's one reason why I—Sam, I want you to kiss me. Please. I've never had to ask before.''

"That's just it," Sam said, looking at the pale oval of her face against the darkness of the evening. "Please don't get me wrong, Mimi. If you were little, untouched Virginia I felt this way about, I probably would kiss you.''

"But what's wrong with me?''

He took her hands in his. "I'm trying to explain. It's because I want to keep what we have together, special. It's because kissing has become something that's too easy for you. When I kiss you I don't want it to be just because you're a girl who's accustomed to kissing. I want it to be important. Do you see what I mean?''

Standing there in front of him she could not keep a hot tear from slipping out and trickling down her cheek. She bit her lip to control herself but suddenly she let out a loud, child-like sob which startled her as much as it did Sam. "I'm sorry,'' she said as Sam looked at her in appalled silence. ''I'm sorry,'' she aplogized again, ''but oh, Sam, everything's so sad!''

''No, it isn't,'' he said, pulling her towards him and putting his arms about her protectingly, though it was he who could have rested his head on her shoulder. ''Oh, no, it isn't, Mimi. It's the most tremendously exciting thing in the world, no matter what happens. Do you know what I believe? I'm going to kiss you someday. I don't know where or when but it's going to happen. We're going to write each other but even if we stop, even if a lot of years go by and we forget each other, someday we're going to meet again and we're going to kiss each other. I believe it! Stop crying, Mimi, please stop. It's not sad, I promise you it's not!''

They were still standing holding each other when Virginia and Beanie, half-carrying Connie, caught up with them.—I'm tired of seeing people kissing in the snow, Virginia thought petulantly, too emotionally drained for anything but crossness, and not noticing that Sam and Mimi were, in fact, not kissing. They all started walking on again.

''Let's look through one of the telescopes,'' Beanie said. ''If they have lights we might see something. Have you any change, Sam? I have a couple of francs at least to stick in the gadget.'' As they drew up in front of the brasserie where the first of the telescopes stood he drew out a franc. ''You can go first, Virginia.''

''No, go ahead,'' Virginia said. ''I'm no good at finding anything with them.''

''I want to look! I want a turn!'' Connie cried.

''Let Beanie look,'' Virginia said.

He put in the franc and squinted into the telescope. ''I can't see a thing. Nothing but snow.'' He moved the telescope around on its stand, adjusting it. ''Hey, I think I see a light! Look, Vee, right there to the left.''

Virginia put her eye to the telescope. ''Where? Oh, there! I think I see it, too!'' Then there was a click and she said, ''Oh, what a gyp. It's shut off. They don't give you much time for a franc, do they?''

''Let me try,'' Sam said. ''Come on, Mimi,'' but neither he nor Mimi could find the light Virginia and Beanie thought they had seen. Connie in her turn saw dozens of lights and was highly insulted because the others did not believe her.

''I'm Thursday,'' she wailed. ''I want some hot cocoa.''

They started walking again, Sam carrying Connie on his strong shoulders. Virginia said in a low voice to Mimi, "What are we doing out here? It's just like a bad dream and we're all running around in circles pretending things make sense when they really don't."

"We're looking for Madame de Croisenois," Mimi said. "That makes sense enough to me."

"Why is everybody all upset about Madame de Croisenois and paying no attention to mother?"

"We all trust your mother," Mimi said.

"And not Madame de Croisenois?"

Mimi hesitated. Then she said, "Not when she's drunk."

"Do you think that's it, then?"

"Must be."

"But why would she get lost? Why would she go up the mountain?"

"Why did you throw your father's drink at the wall?"

"But that—"

"Why does anybody do anything?" Mimi asked impatiently. "Most of the time we don't know—any of us."

"Our philosopher," Beanie said.

Mimi gave him a quick look, but his words were perfectly casual and friendly, and indeed he seemed to be trying in every way except directly apologizing to make up for the incident at the thé dansant.

They looked cursorily into Madame Berigot's shop on the off chance that Gertrude might have gone in to buy cigarettes or a paper. As they came out a blast of wind beat at them, and Connie, atop Sam's shoulders, began to whimper with the cold.

"This is awful weather for Madame de Croisenois to be out in. It'd be even worse on the mountain," Mimi said. "Let's just take a quick look in the Splendide and the casino and then we'd better take Connie home."

They looked in the Splendide, in the boulangerie; they continued on down the street peering through steaming windows, through doors that let out quick rushes of warmth. Connie leaned heavily on Sam, drooping with sleep.

Then Virginia let out a cry, for there were Emily and Courtney coming around the bend of the street, caught by the wind and hurled towards the children.

* * *

"But we can't just go back to the villa and wait!" Mimi protested.

"You can and you will," Courtney said sternly. "All five of you. Virginia, you will please put Connie to bed and see that she goes to sleep."

"But what are you going to do, daddy?"

"We're going to the ski tow to see if Pierre has heard anything. The moment there is any news we will get word to you, I promise you."

"Meanwhile," Emily said, "Why don't you make some cocoa? It might help Connie get to sleep. And then it would be a good idea if you'd make a good big pot of coffee and just have it ready."

They left the reluctant children at the villa and went on up the path, climbing side by side. "If anything's happened to Gertrude, and it very well may have, it's best if the children don't see her," Courtney said. "Are you dressed warmly enough?"

"Yes, Are you?"

"Yes. Though this wind tonight would penetrate anything."—Abe is up the mountain with the guides helping in the search. Pierre with his injured leg has to wait by the ski tow. And I—I was sent to tour the bars.

They walked in silence till they had passed the hotel gates. Then Courtney said, his voice rough, "Where were you going?"

Emily looked down at her feet in heavy ski boots pushing her forwards and upwards on the icy path. "Nowhere. I was just walking. How did you know where to find me?"

"I didn't," Courtney said. "I was looking for you."

"To tell me about Gert?"

"Partly." He shut his mouth closely and did not explain himself any further.

"Does Kaarlo really think she went up the mountain?"

"He seems to."

"But why? Why?"

"Something must have upset her quite terribly," Courtney said. "As I told you."

"But on a night like this," Emily said, "she could never—" and then stopped.

They were silent until they reached the nursery slopes where a small group was waiting by the ski tow. As they joined the fringes of the group Pierre Balbec looked at them and shook his head to indicate that there was no news as yet. No one was talking very much and all the faces were grave. The group consisted mostly of men from the village who knew Kaarlo and Gertrude and were waiting to see if they could be of any help, but there was also a smattering of tourists from the hotel or who had heard at the Splendide or the casino that a woman was lost on the mountain and were there out of thrill-seeking curiosity. Emily and Courtney stayed slightly apart, silent, waiting.

"Half the time on these rescue parties it's someone else who gets hurt," Courtney said once. "Damn Gertrude anyhow. Look what she's caused by her selfishness." His voice was low but quite violent, and Emily looked at him in surprise, but in the darkness his face was only a shadow.

"How many men are out?" she asked.—Abe doesn't know the mountains as well as the others, he's not as skilled as they are, it's terribly dangerous for him, Kaarlo shouldn't have let him. Courtney's right, it's always someone else who gets hurt—

"About a dozen, counting Kaarlo and Abe, I should think. I should have realized this afternoon that she was in a desperate mood."

"No, how could you?" she asked. "It's Gert's nature to seem desperate. When she's upset she precipitates herself at life instead of retreating from it."

He grabbed her then by both arms, his hands rough through her ski jacket. "And which is worse?" he demanded.

"What do you mean?"

"Damn you, Emily," he said, "damn you," half-dragging her away from the waiting group. He shook her furiously, his breath coming in short angry pants, crying again, "Damn you!" Then with equal violence he flung her from him so that she almost fell, and reached into his pocket (not the pocket that still held Gertrude's brandy bottle), and pulled out his crampons and bent down to put them on.

"What are you doing?" Emily asked in a stifled voice.

"I'm going up the mountain after Gertrude."

"No, Court, I shouldn't have said—I didn't mean—"

"You didn't say anything." He pushed off her restraining hand. "You didn't put my crampons in my pocket, did you? I got them right after Abe called, before I went out. I'm going to Pierre to see what signals they've arranged."

She did not follow him but stood there away from the cluster of people, watching Pierre gesticulating, Courtney simply shaking his head in a stubborn manner, and finally Pierre waving his arms wildly and then dropping them to his side, and Courtney moving off and upwards, not looking back towards her, crampons on his boots but his overcoat cumbersome and completely unsuited for climbing.

He moved quickly at first, climbing briskly across the frozen surface of the snow until he was out of sight of Emily, of Pierre, of the group of people waiting for news of Gertrude. There were no stars and the sky was heavy about him and the wind that moved harshly against his body seemed to be part of the sky. When he reached the pines he was in complete darkness and he had to move slowly, one arm held blindly ahead of him to fend off the trees that seemed to be moving towards him, converging upon him. A handful of cold needles brushed against his face, stinging him, making his eyes water.

—If I can just do this one thing, he thought, not necessarily finding her, but being part of the men who are in the search party, if I can just be one man among others so that I can know that I am a man again. . . .

—For if I am a man again, ultimately there is hope.

At last the trees thinned, parted, and he was out in the snow fields. He moved, as Pierre had suggested he do, slightly to the left, climbing upwards and to the left, upwards and to the left, going around great turrets and castles of snow that were only darker shadows in the snow-filled dark. Every once in a while he paused to listen, calling softly, "Gertrude."

Once he slipped and fell and it was a moment before he could pick himself up, weighted down by the cumbersome overcoat and the bottle of Gertrude's brandy in the right-hand pocket and the climbing things he had stuffed hastily in the left-hand pocket, pitons and hammer and rope and light as well as the crampons. He stood there, catching his breath, thinking,—No, no, it is Gertrude we are hunting for, not Courtney. You will spoil everything if you are inefficient enough to hurt yourself now.

—Typical, wouldn't it be? Join the hunting party in a grand gesture and fall and break a leg and have to be rescued yourself. What a laugh. What a laugh they'd all get out of it, Kaarlo and Abe.

And then he realized that no, they wouldn't laugh, Kaarlo and Abe; Abe and Kaarlo would not laugh at him, but their casual compassion would be far more cruel than Tommy O'Hara's hilarity. Damn you, Courtney, no. It's in the shadows of your mind that you're only part of a man and when you aren't whole it's because you don't want to be whole, it's too damn difficult to be whole. But if you retreat again this time there's no coming back to life again.

He fell. This time it was more difficult to get up and it seemed that the ultimate in happiness would be to lie there in the enveloping snow and become one with its shadowy nothingness. But he struggled to his knees and crawled across the snow, calling, ''Gertrude! Gertrude! and then he was on his feet again, struggling on, up and to the left, up and to the left.

—It is not Gertrude I am hoping to find, he thought, it is Emily.

The mountain seemed to loom directly above him, to become one with the snow-filled sky that enclosed him, containing him in a small shell of solitude, isolating him so entirely that he was not one with the other searchers, but entirely alone with the edges of the shell clamped down tightly about him. He stood still for a moment, listening, but he could hear nothing but the wind, no call from anyone in the search party, no signal light, nothing. Below him the lights of the village were blotted out by the shell of clouds and only a faint sickly mauve tinge in the sky showed him where it lay, showed him that indeed it still existed. He paused again to catch his breath, then he struggled upwards, up and to the left.

''Gertrude!'' he called softly, urgently. ''Gertrude!''

At last it seemed to him that he heard an answering cry, below him, still further to the left, and he moved towards it, calling again, ''Gertrude!'' with a sudden burst of joy through him so that he moved easily, as though the wind had ceased beating against him, flapping his coat like the wings of an enormous bird, beating against his legs in an effort to drive him back down the mountain. Again he heard the faint cry and he moved towards it and then he was kneeling on the edge of a ridge off which he had almost fallen, and peering down at the shelf below on which was the twisted shadow that was Gertrude.

He flashed his signal to the others and got an answering light from far to the right above him. So they had been there after all, he had been one of them, he had not been alone on an alien mountain, he and Gertrude, the two lost souls never to be found.

On his hands and knees, moving cautiously so that he too should not dislodge the snow and topple with it over the ridge, he looked down the ten or twelve feet to where Gertrude lay.

"Gertrude," he called urgently.

"Here," she whispered.

He brushed away loose snow until he came to ice into which he could hammer a piton. In spite of his caution more snow fell away and tumbled down onto the ledge. Moving slowly, carefully, he tied his rope to the piton and climbed down beside her. The shelf, he realized with gratitude, was solid rock under the snow, and large enough for both of them. He knelt beside her. In the beam of his flashlight her eyes held a glazed look of pain and her lips were blue. He did not brush the snow off her legs because for the moment it afforded her some protection from the cold, and the ledge on which she lay, he realized immediately and with relief, was mercifully protected by the overhanging ridge from the wind. He took out the bottle of brandy, raised her head very gently, and let a little of it trickle between her lips. After a moment she was able to swallow.

"I botched it," she whispered. "I didn't mean it to be this way."

"Don't talk, Gertrude," he said. "Kaarlo and Clément will be here with the stretcher almost immediately and everything will be all right."

"Let me have some more brandy," she whispered. He gave her more and she said, "I think I've broken my leg."

"Yes," he said. "Don't worry. It's going to be all right. I promise you." He spoke with the gentle conviction he used with his children and almost imperceptibly she relaxed. He gave her some more brandy and although her eyes were still glazed a little of the blue left her lips.

"I didn't mean to cause all this trouble," she said. "it was for Kaarlo and Emily." Then she shut her eyes tightly so that the lids were wrinkled with pain and whispered. "Oh, no! I shouldn't have said that!"

"Shouldn't have said what?" he asked, though he knew he should discourage her from talking.

"About Kaarlo and Emily. Or did you know anyhow? I was going to walk until I was really ill, until there was no choice. And then I was going to Clément and the sanatorium and then they would have been free of me hanging like a millstone about their necks."

"Don't talk, Gertrude," he said automatically, but then he asked, "Who would have been free?"

"Kaarlo and Emily."

"Free for what?"

"Free for each other . . . to love each other. . . ."

"Kaarlo and Emily—" he repeated.

"They love each other . . . I'm so sorry, Court . . . I'm so damnably sorry. . . ." she said with an effort of strength.

"No, Gertrude," he said. "No! You're entirely wrong! How could you ever think such fantastic nonsense?"

"Is it—so fantastic?" she gasped.

"Of course it is. I know Emily. And Kaarlo. Don't you know Kaarlo any better than that?" He gave her more brandy, looking down in appalled silence at her pinched white face, still not quite able to credit what she had told him. He remembered, as he knelt there looking at her in the beam of his flashlight and letting the brandy trickle into her mouth, how he had once picked up a sparrow from one of the paths in the park. He had held it in his strong, living hands, trying to warm life back into its chill body; he had taken it home and tried giving it brandy from an eye dropper; for a moment it had pecked feebly against the tensile skin of his palm; for a moment it had turned its small bright head and looked up at him with Gertrude's stark pleading. Then its eyes had glazed over and its gentle body had turned stiff in his hands.

He looked down at Gertrude and he knew he could bear no longer the pain in her eyes, the pain that had nothing to do with her broken leg.

So this must be the ultimate humiliation, must it?—the utmost plunge into the chasm of despair, the descent to the final depth of degradation, before he could climb up and stand on his feet again, a man among men. And was it for Gertrude that he must do this, Gertrude who might not even be trustworthy? Finding Gertrude had been nothing, a fluke, a lucky accident. Saying what he now had to say was the act of courage which he had been dreading but which he knew to be necessary, and he knew that it must take place here in the

shelter of the overhanding cliff of snow on Gertrude's small
ledge of safety.

"Gertrude," he said. "Emily doesn't love Kaarlo. I know."

"How do you know?" she demanded. "Are you as sure of
her as all that?"

He shook his head. "I'm not sure of her at all. But as far as
Emily and Kaarlo are concerned I *know*. I *know* Emily doesn't
love Kaarlo. Not in that way."

"But *how* . . . how can you know?"

God, why was it to Gertrude that it had to be said? Of all people, to Gertrude?

He knelt there by her on the ledge and gave her more brandy
and then he said, "Because Emily is in love with Abe Fielding."

A frantic look flickered across her face. "Abe?" she whispered.

"Abe." The lights approached; the others were coming; but
it had been said.

"But how do you—how do you know?"

His voice was as dry as his mouth and lips. "Believe me,
Gertrude. I know."

"Abe—" she whispered again.

"Abe," he repeated, the word each time like a sword. "Not
Kaarlo. Never Kaarlo, Kaarlo loves only you."

"Oh, Jesus," she whispered. "Oh, Jesus God. Then this
was—" She moved one hand feebly. "No," she whispered.
"It still had to be done."

At the first hut Clément, looking with his flashlight at Gertrude, had them carry her in and put the stretcher down on one
of the bunks.

"Clément, I—" she started to whisper.

But he said sternly, "You are not to say a word, Gertrude.
Not a word until I give you permission." To Kaarlo he said,
softly, turned away from her so that she would not hear, "I
must massage her heart. If I can do this and not start a
hemorrhage—if we can get her down to the sanatorium—
then she will perhaps have a chance. The leg is nothing." To
Abe he said. "Go down to the sanatorium and tell them to
make ready for us. Speak to Sister Mercanton personally."
Then he knelt on the floor beside the bunk on which Gertrude lay.

"Emily—" she whispered.

"You will see Emily as soon as you get safely to bed at the hospital," he promised, "but if you are to get to the hospital at all you must try not to talk now." His fingers massaged with strength and caution, firmness and gentleness, and under their touch her heartbeats gradually gained in strength and rhythm.

"We'll take her on down now," he said, and gave a brief, reassuring nod to Kaarlo. "All right for the moment." Then to Gertrude, "I shall have to set your leg without an anaesthetic. I will give you a hypodermic that will help the pain a little, but there will be pain. However it will not last long and I know that you are not afraid of that kind of pain. What you must remember is to keep absolutely still." She answered him with her eyes, not even nodding. "Good girl," he said.

They carried the stretcher slowly, keeping an even rhythm, taking infinite care not to jolt Gertrude. Clément walked beside her so that when she opened her eyes she saw him by her side, and she knew that Kaarlo was at the head of the stretcher. She still felt incredibly light, disembodied, but no longer as though she were skating over a thin film of ice. The ice had broken and she had fallen through but she had not drowned.

When they reached the hospital, Emily, Courtney, and Abe were waiting, not speaking, not sitting in the comfortable chairs, the three of them simply standing here.

"Please wait if it's at all possible," Clément said to Emily before disappearing with Kaarlo into the hospital with Gertrude. "She has been asking for you."

They continued to stand there until Abe said, "That was pretty terrific work, Court. If Gertrude comes through this it'll be thanks to you."

Courtney shook his head. "Any one of us could have found her or not have found her. It was looking for a needle in a haystack. Simply a matter of luck."

"Pretty good work anyhow," Abe said. "I didn't realize you were in the search party."

"I went in late." Courtney turned away from Abe, towards Emily. "I'm going home now. The children shouldn't be left alone any longer, and we promised to let them know right away. I'll wait for you to eat, Emily. I believe your son's at our place, Fielding. Shall I send him up to the hotel?"

"Please," Abe said. "Tell him I'll be there right away."

"Right." Without saying good-bye, without looking at either of them again, he left.

"Emily," Abe started, and then shook his head. "No. Not here. Not now . . . Did you go to the Splendide?"

"No."

A nurse pushed through the glass doors then, saying, "Mrs. Bowen?"

"Yes."

"Good, you're still here. Will you wait?"

"Yes," Emily said again.

"Perhaps you'd like to come upstairs. The floor sitting rooms are a little less formal."

"Thank you," Emily said. Yes, I would." She followed the nurse out of the lounge, away from Abe.

Gertrude lay flat on the high bed, her hair pushed damply from her face, staring at the ceiling, the ceiling pure and white and undefiled, a ceiling that could not disturb feverish patients with phantom pictures imagined in the cracks or stains, as Gertrude had been disturbed by faces in the dark beams of the ceiling at the chalet, or as Courtney at the villa was obsessed by the spider dangling at the light fixtures. Her eyes were still dark with pain and fever but some of the glazed look had left them. Kaarlo stood by the bed and smiled at Emily and his eyes had the same look of pain as Gertrude's, as though he had somehow managed to take some of her pain upon himself.

Gertrude managed half a grin, then whispered, "Emily . . . alone for a minute, Kaarlo, please."

"Clément says you are not to talk, Gertrude," he said gently.

"No. . . . Just a brief word . . . promise."

Kaarlo went out into the hall and Emily stood by the bed, putting one hand lightly over Gertrude's.

"Clément says . . . if I'm good . . . I might live. Think I'll try to be good . . . for a change," Gertrude whispered.

"That's right, and you mustn't talk now, Gertrude," Emily said.

"I'll stay now . . . here . . . sanatorium . . . till I get well."

"Good for you."

"Did it for Kaarlo," Gertrude said, "for Kaarlo and you. But messed it up. Thought you and Kaarlo loved each other."

"Kaarlo and I!" Emily cried in horror, forgetting to be cautious. "But why!"

"Little things . . . my own lousiness . . . driving him to it . . . and you've been different. . . ."

"Oh, no, Gert!" Emily cried. "I love Kaarlo, but not that way! Nor he me!"

"I know," Gertrude said. "I know now."

"But Gert, you mean that was why you—to let Kaarlo and me—?" But then this was all my fault, too, the whole thing—"

"No," Gertrude whispered. "Could have just gone to Clément and said I'd come to the sanatorium—but no, not Gert de C. Had to do it with a big gesture, make a production of it . . . . Didn't mean to come quite so close to ending myself . . . . Kaarlo . . ."

"Kaarlo," Emily called, and he was back in the room immediately.

"I'd better go now," she said. "Will you call me later tonight, after you've talked to Clément again? Or any time if you need me." Then she bent down and kissed Gertrude's forehead. "I'll see you tomorrow, old Gert de C," she said gently. "Take care."

When the children were finally quieted down and in bed Emily said, "I'm going out for a little while."

"Isn't it rather late?" Courtney asked.

"I won't be long."

He did not ask where she was going. She went into the hall and pulled on her ski boots.

—I should have known before this afternoon, she thought—before I couldn't go into the casino. Thank God, it was then I knew, so that it was not what Courtney did, an outside thing, making up my mind for me instead of the other way round.

—So we reached our decisions simultaneously, and apart, and if I knew that Court was fighting a battle, did he, too, sense mine? Did it have anything to do with his coming back into life again? For he is here, I am no longer living with a marble image. And I will never know why. Court being Court I can never ask him why; we wrestled with our problems alone and we must live alone with the answers. And is it part of a marriage. part of being a human being, that we must always reach our decisions alone?

She groped for her ski jacket in the always dim light of the hall and pushed her arms into the sleeves and then stood there again, not zipping up the jacket, not moving.—I'm part of Courtney, she thought. I can't shed him as the snakes used to shed their skins in the spring down by the orchard wall. I'm part of him and he of me forever, all the countless days we have shared, and the nights, the hours and minutes joining us inextricably together. We have had three children together. And if we managed to live again after Alice's death we can surely survive Tommy O'Hara and Indiana and we can survive this. And if Abe takes a part of me away with him on the train to Bandol I have learned that one can live with a mutilation. I know that I will be happy again. Perhaps that is the most terrible and frightening thing of all, that I know that some day I will be happy again.

She went into the living room and put her hand on Courtney's arm. ''I think we're going to be happy in Indiana,'' she said. ''I have a feeling. . . .''

He looked up at her and smiled, but said nothing.

''I won't be long,'' she said.

She climbed the familiar path to the hotel. Here were the doors she had gone through with Abe, the lobby where she had stood with him, the palms in the glazed pottery pots, the odor of heat and wax and expensive furs. . . .

''My *dear* Madame Bowen!'' And she was borne down on by Madame Pedroti. ''And it was Monsieur Bowen who found our dear, dear Gertrude! How proud you must be of him''

''Yes. Thank you.'' Emily said.

''And Kaarlo, too,'' Madame Pedroti said. ''He must be overwhelmed with gratitude to your noble husband.''

''It's not a question of gratitude,'' Emily said rather sharply. ''Court was one of a number of men and he was simply the one who happened to find her. It could just as easily have been one of the others.''

''Monsieur Fielding, for instance?''

Emily looked at her levelly, contemptuously. ''Or Kaarlo himself. The important thing is that she *was* found. And, we hope, in time.''

''Yes, indeed! And of course now she is having the best of care! Our dear Dr. Clément is said to have effected miracles! But don't let me detain you, Madame Bowen!'' With another smile as over-ripe as the bags of fruit she brought Gertrude, Madame Pedroti rolled off.

She went up in the elevator and it seemed that in this small iron cage she had run the gamut of emotions for had she not gone up in it with Abe that night after dinner at the casino, and had he not come down in it with her, their bodies pressed intimately together, although at that time they had been the only passengers? Now a man in evening clothes stood against her and there was a group of students, in ski clothes, laughing loudly.

She got off at Abe's floor and went to his rooms.

"Abe, I had to come say good-bye." she said.

Without speaking his arms were about her and his lips against hers and then his cheek pressed against her and she felt a tremor against her body and her cheek was wet with his tears.

"Oh, Abe," she whispered, holding him, soothing him. "Oh, my darling, no, no, darlingest one, no."

When he spoke his voice was quite controlled. "I'm sorry, Emily."

"Oh, darling, darling," she said, and she did not realize that the tears were streaming down her own cheeks. "You've known all along, haven't you? We've both known. I've tried to pretend that I didn't. I even started out to the Splendide to meet you this afternoon, I wanted so desperately to have it be possible. But it isn't possible, Abe. And I've been a complete moral coward. I've hurt Courtney. I've hurt you."

"And what about yourself?" he asked harshly.

"For myself," she said slowly, "all I feel when I think of you is great glory. It's all I shall ever feel."

"Emily—"

"No," she said. Please don't, darling. Please don't try to weaken me. I'm so very weak, but on this one thing I—Abe, I love you so very terribly and I always will. You'll always be an enormous part of my life. But if I tried to come to you now, if I left Courtney and the children, or if I tried to take the children away from him—"

She stopped and after a while he said, "You wouldn't be the person I fell in love with."

She moved into his arms, holding up her face, whispering, "This is good-bye now, darling."

His kiss was gentle but it was long and searching and when he finally released her he did not speak and she turned from him and left the room without looking back.

Abe
Abe Fielding
Abraham K. Fielding

She had never found out what the K stood for.

She left the hotel and walked down the drive and stood for a moment alone in the cold and the dark and the snow heaped in drifts by the great iron gates before she started down the path to the villa and Courtney.